PRAISE FOR S___

"For a fun, sexy, unputdownable r___ l."
—#1 *New* ___ Carr

"Lively and fun!"
—*New York Times* bestselling author Susan Elizabeth Phillips

"Bright, smart, sexy, thoroughly entertaining."
—*New York Times* bestselling author Jayne Ann Krentz

"Sassy, snappy, and sizzling hot!"
—#1 *New York Times* bestselling author Janet Evanovich

"Sexy, suspenseful, funny . . . a fabulous story."
—*New York Times* bestselling author Stella Cameron

"Sizzling, snappy, sexy fun."
—*New York Times* bestselling author Jennifer Crusie

"Guaranteed snap, sizzle, and sass!"
—*New York Times* bestselling author Carly Phillips

"Andersen again injects magic into a story that would be clichéd in another's hands, delivering warm, vulnerable characters in a touching yet suspenseful read."
—*Publishers Weekly* (starred review)

"A smart, arousing, spirited escapade that is graced with a gentle mystery, a vulnerabl___ hero and served up with em___
—*Library Journal*

Books by Susan Andersen

Historical Novels
The Ballad of Hattie Taylor

Stand-Alone Novels

Shadow Dance

Present Danger

Obsessed

On Thin Ice

Exposure

Baby, I'm Yours

Be My Baby

Baby, Don't Go

All Shook Up

Burning Up

Notorious

It Had to Be You

The Marine Novels

Head Over Heels

Getting Lucky

Hot & Bothered

Coming Undone

The Showgirls Duo
Skintight
Just for Kicks

The Sisterhood Diaries Novels

Cutting Loose

Bending the Rules

Playing Dirty

Running Wild

The Razor Bay/Bradshaw Brothers Novels
That Thing Called Love
Some Like It Hot
No Strings Attached

The BALLAD *of* HATTIE TAYLOR

Susan Andersen

Jove
New York

A JOVE BOOK
Published by Berkley
An imprint of Penguin Random House LLC
penguinrandomhouse.com

Library of Congress Cataloging-in-Publication Data

Names: Andersen, Susan, 1950– author.
Title: The ballad of Hattie Taylor / Susan Andersen.
Description: First edition. | New York: Jove, 2021.
Identifiers: LCCN 2020021008 (print) | LCCN 2020021009 (ebook) |
ISBN 9780593197868 (trade paperback) | ISBN 9780593197875 (ebook)
Subjects: GSAFD: Love stories. | Western stories.
Classification: LCC PS3551.N34555 B35 2021 (print) | LCC PS3551.N34555 (ebook) |
DDC 813/.54—dc23
LC record available at https://lccn.loc.gov/2020021008
LC ebook record available at https://lccn.loc.gov/2020021009

First Edition: January 2021

Printed in the United States of America
1 3 5 7 9 10 8 6 4 2

Cover design and photo composition by Rita Frangie
Book design by Alison Cnockaert

They say it takes a village.
This is dedicated, with love, appreciation, and gratitude, to my various tribes
and villages for all the fabulous help I received on Hattie's book.

To

The women of Port Orchard: Lois Faye Dyer (with particular thanks
for coming up with the fabulous title), Rose Marie Harris, Krysteen Seelen, Kate Breslin,
Darlene Panzera, and Ramona Nelson. You helped make this a better book—
and are just plain good company.

To

My hooligan-writer-friends crew: Stephanie Laurens, Victoria Alexander,
Linda Needham, Suzanne Enoch, and Karen Hawkins. Y'all have been my support group
from the mid- to late nineties right on through to today, with our retreat each year and
all the little trips in between. I value our friendship beyond measure.

And last, but by no means least,

To

My agent, Meg Ruley, and my editors Cindy Hwang and Sarah Blumenstock. Meg,
you rock, and have since we worked on our first book together (also in the mid-nineties).
Cindy and Sarah, you two are my absolute dream team. I love the way you truly
got Hattie's story and how much your suggestions improved it.

So, the ubiquitous "they" say it takes a village.
I wholeheartedly agree but will just add this: women friends and colleagues are the best!

PART

1

1

Mattawa, Oregon
TUESDAY, MAY 9, 1899

JACOB MURDOCK SQUINTED into the sun, his gaze following the empty railroad track to its vanishing point between tree-topped rocky outcrops. Yanking his timepiece from his vest's watch pocket, Jake clicked its cover open to check the time. With a muttered curse, he closed the watch and stuffed it back in its pocket. And glared down the length of the track with uncharacteristic exasperation, willing the train into the station.

He rolled his shoulders, trying to shake his guilt over his impatience. Generally, he was pretty damn easygoing and accommodating.

Still, when he'd agreed to pick up Augusta's little orphan and deliver her back to his mother's house, he hadn't counted on the train being late. That was shortsighted of him but, dammit, he was raring to discharge his duty. He'd had a spot of courting in mind today. Quite firmly he'd had it in mind to see a certain someone.

Reluctantly, he conceded a visit to Jane-Ellen Fielding might have to wait. He'd just have to hope she would still be receiving callers when he finished his errand. Provided he ever did. Jake searched the tracks again, knowing damn well the sound of the train's whistle carried on the hot, dusty wind and would reach the station before the train itself came into view.

Trying to pin his attention on anything *other* than this never-ending wait, he once again mulled over his mother's decision to take in a young girl none of them had even met. Hattie Taylor's relationship to their branch of the Murdock clan was slim at best.

Not that, other than a singular time, he'd bothered debating the wisdom of Augusta's decision with her. His mother was an incredibly strongwilled woman. Some might say a stubborn one—although not to her face. Not if they were smart. Jake grinned, trying to name a soul brave enough to accuse Augusta Witherspoon Murdock of an uncompromising nature. That was a conversation he'd pay to hear.

Yet, "stubborn" could be Augusta's middle name. Jake had a mental image of the imperious tilt to her silvering head as he'd seen it just the other day when he'd had the effrontery to question her decision. He shook his head, remembering.

Jake had heard out his mother's plans in silence over breakfast, mentally filing the pertinent information. When Augusta had finished her list of arguments, he'd merely stared at her for a couple of heartbeats before quietly remarking that he wondered if she had considered the ramifications.

"You're a smart woman, Mom, so I trust you realize what you're proposing has a sizable risk factor attached." Raising a silver lid from the warming dish on the sideboard, he pinched a fluffy bit of scrambled egg with his fingers and popped it into his mouth. Laughing out loud, he adroitly dodged the swat aimed at him by Mirabel, his mother's housekeeper. The older woman was Augusta's confidante and friend as well—and damn near a second mother to Jake. Swallowing, he turned back to Augusta. "What do you know about this kid, after all, besides the fact that from the age of six or seven, she lived in virtual isolation with a couple of crusty old miners?"

"I know she is a Witherspoon, Jacob," Augusta replied repressively. "What else need I?"

"Her mother was a Witherspoon," Jake corrected. "No one knows her father's antecedents. From what you've said, the man was nothing but a grubby prospector."

He sounded like a snobbish little shit. Still, the girl's story was a strange one and her unique upbringing was bound to produce problems. Jake had a feeling his mother didn't fully comprehend what she was letting herself in for by agreeing to raise the child.

Elmira Witherspoon, Augusta's fourth—or maybe even fifth—cousin, had been a quiet, unassuming spinster who'd never given her family a moment's concern. Until the day she was literally swept off her feet on a busy San Francisco street by a miner named Jeremy Taylor.

According to family scuttlebutt, Elmira had been shopping with her maid on the day in question, when she'd carelessly stepped into the street without first determining if it was safe to do so. Family lore had it a milk dray, emptied of its day's wares, was racing down the street at a respectable clip when Elmira stepped directly in its path. Frozen at the sight of the huge draft horse bearing down on her, she had been in the midst of saying her final prayers—one could only assume—when, out of nowhere, an arm suddenly encircled her waist and swept her out of harm's way and back onto the safety of the wooden sidewalk.

Her rescuer, of course, had been Taylor. And the rest of the story was, if not history of national import, then at least grist for the family gossip mill.

Because Elmira Witherspoon had raised her timorous eyes to her rescuer and succumbed to that often-touted-but-rarely-believed-in Love at First Sight. And the phenomenon wrought monumental changes in her heretofore overprotected, uneventful life.

"I must admit I was rather amazed at the girl's fortitude," Augusta confessed when recounting the story. "I had always found Elmira to be quite timid. So, for her to suddenly stand firm against the combined condemnation of her entire family and insist on marrying her miner . . . ? Well, it must have taken a good deal of courage. Quite frankly, I'd never have believed she had it in her."

She suddenly smiled at Jake, and it was a huge, wholehearted beam. "Yet Elmira did precisely that. She stood firm—even when they disinherited her for her temerity." Her smile fading, Augusta sighed and shook her head. "I hate to admit it, Jacob, but some of the Witherspoons can be quite unyielding."

"Which probably explains why they refuse to take the kid in now both her parents are dead," Jake inserted. "At least I hope that's the reason. It doesn't say a great deal about their sense of charity, but it's better than the alternative."

Augusta regarded her son with exasperation. "Really, dear, must you persist in calling her 'kid'? It makes her sound like some dreadfully scruffy animal rather than the young girl she is. And what, pray tell, might the alternative be?"

"That they took the trouble to meet her and found her entirely incorrigible after her sojourn in the wilds of wherever she was." Jake shrugged. "It's been, what—four years since her mother died? And in that time, she's lived in the back of beyond, attended only by her old man and some other old coot whose antecedents are likely equally questionable."

"Jacob, honestly," his mother remonstrated. "'Old man'? 'Coot'? Where do you pick up these vulgarities?"

"Mamie Parker's place, I suppose," he promptly replied and hid a smile as he watched his mother and Mirabel pretend outrage.

It was not done for a man to mention the local cathouse in the presence of the gentler sex. Jake, however, was convinced Augusta and Mirabel secretly delighted in being shocked by him. Regardless of the belief that ladies didn't appreciate being subjected to daring, ribald conversation, it had been his observation that his outrageousness often brought a twinkle to their eyes. They would go to their graves rather than admit it, of course. But diligently as they tried to suppress it, the sparkle was there . . . even as his mother lamented his unforgivable penchant for vulgarity and Mirabel sternly informed him he wasn't too old to have his ears soundly boxed.

Unlike past transgressions when he'd skated scandalously beyond the boundaries of good taste, however, this particular episode didn't elicit

Augusta's customary long and imaginative lecture regarding his lack of manners. She immediately returned to the subject of her new ward. "I don't want to hear another word against my decision, Jacob," she said with a regal arrogance he rarely heard from her. "The child's mother was a gentle, well-bred woman—a Witherspoon, my dear—and breeding will tell. Hattie Witherspoon Taylor is coming to live with us, and I expect you to treat her as part of the family."

She gave him her "I mean business" stare. "The subject is closed."

Hell, Jake thought now as he paced the station platform, that was fine with him. It wasn't as if he'd had a serious objection in the first place. His only concern was for his mother. She was hardly old, but neither was she a young woman. He feared rearing a rambunctious youngster would wear her out.

But perhaps it was precisely what Augusta needed. He often suspected his mother was bored—particularly since she'd been emotionally blackmailed into moving to town. He knew damn well she'd been lonely since his father's death. She undoubtedly looked forward to the prospect of a new challenge. There was, after all, nothing Augusta Murdock liked better than managing other people's lives. Perhaps she looked upon the advent of a youngster in her life as a God-given opportunity to bend a fresh personality to her formidable will.

The train's whistle blew a low and mournful note in the distance, and Jake walked to the end of the platform to await its arrival. The sight of smoke and cinders, glimpsed above the trees as they blew from its smokestack, preceded it into view.

Then suddenly it roared around the bend, its vibration and noise increasing from a rumble to clattering thunder as it hurtled toward the station.

The whistle wailed and the brakes screeched in a high-pitched shriek of metal on metal while the brakeman plied his trade. The wooden station house shook with a teeth-jarring rattle as the train thundered in. Brakes still screeching, the great black engine rumbled past, slowing to a

Susan Andersen

shuddering halt at the platform's far end. An immense gust of steam belched forth with a sound that made Jake think humorously of a fat woman releasing her stays.

Moments later, a door on one of the passenger cars slammed open and the conductor stepped out, placing a metal step box on the platform, bridging it to the train's stairwell.

Portly and red-faced, wearing a blue uniform with polished brass buttons, the railroad employee stepped to one side. He mopped his brow with a wilted handkerchief as a salesman stepped down, banging a large sample case through the opening. Once he was clear, the porter leaned into the car, extending his hand. He stood that way for a moment; then he made an impatient grab at something out of Jake's sight in the doorway's shadow.

"Keep your sonovabitchin' hands to yourself, mister," a young and irate voice instructed him. The man lunged again, his upper torso momentarily disappearing into the car's doorway. He reappeared with a wild-haired, wild-eyed, spitting, struggling moppet in his grasp.

With resigned premonition, Jake started forward. "Hattie Witherspoon Taylor, I presume," he said dryly upon reaching the pair.

2

HATTIE WRENCHED HER upper arm from the porter's grasp and glared up at him for a moment before directing her attention to the immaculately dressed young man standing before her. He returned her regard with a half smile. Impatiently hitching up a sliding strap on the boys' overalls she wore, she shook her heavy hair out of her eyes. "Who wants to know, mister?"

"Jacob Murdock, at your service, miss." He doffed his hat, replacing it at a cocky angle on the back of his head. "You can call me Jake. I'm Augusta Murdock's son."

"Yeah?" She studied him suspiciously for several long moments. Finally, her mouth twisted derisively. "Skinny little sonovabitch, aren'tcha?"

"Mind your mouth!" the porter snapped and made a grab for her. Hattie knew from experience he was prepared to shake some manners into her.

But the Jake fella merely grinned and deflected the porter's movement by reaching out to grasp the man's hand. Shaking it, he thanked the man for keeping an eye out for his young relative, and surreptitiously slipped him a bill. Hattie would bet big cash, if she had any, that the money was more to get rid of the railroad man than any doubtful assistance he might have given her.

Mumbling dire predictions, the porter moved away.

And Hattie, who had already hopped nimbly beyond his reach, turned back to the new person in charge of her.

As they eyed one another, Jake reflected wryly that the kid wasn't the first person to mistake his build for skinniness. He was on the lean side and looked slimmer still in his lawyering duds. It didn't bother him. More than one man had discovered to his cost that lean didn't equate to weak. Because Jake's body beneath the deceptive camouflage of tailored clothing was roped with long, flat sinew and muscle, honed to a strapping toughness by an active life. Anyhow, he knew he'd probably gain more bulk as he grew older, because his father had been a muscular man who had often remarked that Jake's build was like his own as a young man. And Jake, at twenty-two, had begun noticing a bit of additional bulk to his physique.

With a dull thump, a carpetbag suddenly landed on the platform next to Jake's feet, kicking up a puff of dust. He looked up in time to see the porter withdrawing into the railroad car once again, but lost interest in the man when Hattie dashed forward to snatch up the bag and hug it to her chest. She turned her head and glared at him, all big eyes and defiance.

Jake felt something shift inside him at the vulnerability briefly flashing across her face, abruptly belying her fierce display of independence. *Well, I'll be damned,* he thought. The rowdy little faker wasn't nearly as tough as she'd like him to believe. He took a good, hard look at her.

She was a funny-looking little creature: all lips, eyes, and hair. Her wide, mobile mouth was a feature she'd probably grow into one day, but right now it was too large for her round little face. And, good God. That hair. She possessed the wildest hair he'd ever seen. Thick and corkscrew-curly, it was the color of a copper penny that had been kicking around in a farmer kid's pocket. God knew she was grimy. But her hair's untamed mass seemed to possess a life of its own, and he would stake his life on it glowing like a bed of coals once the dust was washed out.

Her eyes were huge and round and the amber hue of a good whiskey, ringed in a deeper shade of brown and fringed with thick reddish-gold lashes. They were framed by even thicker golden-red eyebrows, which resembled commas rocked onto their sides. He wasn't certain how, but those eyes managed to convey defiant fearlessness and a frightened vulnerability at one and the same time. It was the eyes, in the end, that really got to him.

"Whatchu starin' at, mister?" Hattie demanded belligerently, drawing herself up. Normally, her skin was what her mama used to call alabaster pale beneath scattered dustings of freckles. But Hattie felt heated color burn along her cheeks, and her shoulders twitched in annoyance. Horace had once described sideshow attractions to her—and she didn't enjoy being gaped at as if she were one.

Ever since leaving Nevada on this trip north to Oregon, she'd been stared at as though she were a freak of nature. It had been a long, arduous journey, first by mule, then by rail. She would never admit this, but it'd been sort of scary to go so far all by herself. And for some dang reason, all along the way people had gawked at her, whispering behind their hands and pointing.

Well. She tossed her hair. She had not suffered their regard in silence.

"Not a thing." Jake smiled. He reached out a hand to touch her hair, biting back a laugh when Hattie jerked her head out of reach and swatted at his fingers. "I was just admiring the color of your hair. It's very pretty." The brief touch confirmed his suspicions: the texture had felt aggressively alive beneath his fingertips. He watched hesitant pleasure shine in Hattie's eyes.

"Yeah? You think so?" she asked. "Sonovabitchin' lady on the train said it's heathen hair, sign of the devil's handmaiden. Horace always said it was the hair of angels, though." She pinched a strand, studying its color uncertainly.

"I'd believe Horace if I were you," Jake advised, wondering if Horace was also the person responsible for teaching her to swear with such conviction. "Whoever he may be."

"Horace was my friend," Hattie snapped defensively, afraid there had been a criticism somewhere in that sentence. "He lived with me 'n' Papa in Nevada." And her brief pleasure in Jake's compliment was abruptly buried beneath the renewed misery of her enforced separation from Horace. She had begged him not to send her away, but he'd been adamant.

"Ain't right for a young lady to grow up in these here hills with no female for guidance," he'd said. " 'Twere different when yer pa was alive, but he's gone now. Yer ma was a gen-u-wine lady, and it's only 'cause of her you can read and write so good."

"She told me it would give me a rare freedom." Hattie had never forgotten those words.

Horace had nodded. "You're already way past what I can show ya. It's time you go to her people. I already writ 'em, Hat, so it's no use tryin' to change my mind."

Hattie hadn't missed Papa all that much when he died a few months back. Since Mama's death he hadn't shown much interest in anything, anyhow, 'cept prospecting and whiskey. But Hattie sure did miss Horace. And she knew he was missing her, too. She'd seen the tears in his faded blue eyes when he'd put her on the train in Silver City—and she'd seen him slip money to that sonovabitchin' porter to watch over her. Big waste of his hard-earned money that had been!

Jake watched the sudden, dejected slump of her shoulders, the fire in those big, lawless eyes suddenly quenched, and experienced another uneasy sensation, as though his stomach suddenly dropped out of place. For all Hattie's bravado and tough talk, she was only a child.

A child who'd clearly had a fair share of upheavals in her young life. "Come on," he said gruffly and wrapped an arm around her shoulders, surprised when she allowed it. He'd half expected her to shrug it off. "Let's go home. Mother and Mirabel are anxious to meet you." He guided her through the station house and out to the open buggy.

She was quiet on the ride through town, staring down at her scuffed boots, and on impulse Jake pulled up before Bigger's Saloon. "Be back in a jiff, kid. Stay put."

He was in and out in minutes. After pulling himself up into the open buggy, he handed Hattie a bottle with a straw bobbing in its opening, then unhooked the reins.

"What's this?" she asked, sniffing the neck of the bottle suspiciously.

"Sarsaparilla."

"Sass-prilla? Never heard of it."

Jake nudged the bottle toward her mouth. "Try it. I think you'll like it."

Picking up the reins, he watched from the corner of his eye as Hattie took a cautious sip through the straw. A look of wonder crossed her features and she drew on the straw eagerly. As she savored the drink, her natural curiosity seemed to reassert itself, and she sat up straighter.

Looking from side to side, she took in the sights of the busy town. By the time they stopped in front of Jake's home, she was almost what he assumed was her normal, pugnacious self again. It had been all he could do not to laugh out loud as he'd listened to her return a rude remark to two boys on the walkway who had yelled insolent commentary on her attire.

She wilted a little, however, as she stared up at the large, ornate house. Even as her chin jutted out stubbornly, she shifted a little closer to Jake on the leather seat. "So, who is this Mirabel?" she asked.

"She's my mother's friend and housekeeper." Jake looked down at her, thinking of the likely reaction she was going to get from the women. "Let me give you a little friendly advice, Hattie, gained through my personal experience. Don't even think about swearing in front of Mirabel. She'll wash your mouth out with soap quicker 'n you can shake a stick. She's done it to me and, believe me, it is not an experience you wanna court." He swung out of the buggy.

Hattie didn't reply but her chin jutted up farther yet. Clutching her carpetbag, she disdained Jake's extended hand and jumped to the ground unaided.

He opened the front door and ushered Hattie into the foyer. "Son of a bitch," she whispered in awe, turning in a slow circle as she stared up at the high ceiling with its crystal chandelier, at the open staircase with its curving, carved-wood banister and faded tapestry runner. She peered through the open French doors on either side of the foyer, gaping at the ornately furnished dining room on one side and the parlor on the other.

"Jacob? Is that you, dear?" His mother's voice came from within the parlor, and Jake turned Hattie in that direction.

For just a moment she balked, staring up at him with wide, frightened eyes. Then her mouth set, her chin jutted even more, and she swaggered ahead of him into the room.

Augusta rose gracefully from a horsehair settee and crossed to meet them. Mirabel tucked the feather duster she'd been unnecessarily dusting the piecrust table with into the pocket of her voluminous white starched apron. She stood ramrod straight, her hands crossed at her waist.

Augusta stopped in front of the young girl. "You must be Hattie," she said warmly.

"Yes, ma'am, guess I must," Hattie replied, clutching her carpetbag and the empty soda bottle. She stayed close to Jake's side.

"I'm your aunt Augusta." When Hattie just stared at her without speaking, Augusta elaborated. "Well, perhaps I'm not an actual aunt; the relationship is a bit convoluted. But I would like it very much if you would honor me with the title."

Hattie continued to stare at the older lady, hiding her awe. She'd never met anyone so clean. Well, perhaps Mama had been, for Hattie's memories were of someone sweet-smelling and soft-spoken. But her recollections had grown hazier with each of the four years that had gone by since her mother passed. She hated that she couldn't always remember Mama's face.

Augusta turned slightly to indicate the woman behind her. "This is Mirabel."

Taking one look at the severe features of the woman in the starched white apron, Hattie's chin, which had relaxed beneath Augusta Murdock's kind-eyed regard, shot up once again. At the same time, she took a cautionary step backwards. "I know about you!" she said in alarm. "You're the one who washed Jake's mouth out with a sonovabitchin' bar of soap!"

With Jake's warning still ringing in her ears, her reaction to the stern-faced lady was instinctive and involuntary. But she was thrown into a state of confusion by the three disparate responses it elicited as they aired simultaneously, tumbling and overlapping one another.

"Young lady!" Mirabel snapped repressively. "Oh, my dear child," Augusta murmured faintly. Jake roared with laughter. Fortunately for Hattie, it was Jake who reached her first, for Mirabel was advancing with a gleam of battle in her eyes, which Jake knew from experience meant being led by the ear to the nearest water closet for the aforementioned mouth washing. He wrapped his arm around Hattie's shoulders and whisked her out of reach.

"Now, now, Mirabel," he coaxed, unable to erase the bit of laughter still lurking in his tone. "It's her first day. Let the kid shake some of the dust from her trip before you start rearranging her manners."

Hattie craned her head back to peer into his face, her amber eyes filled with genuine bafflement as they met his. "What'd I say, Jake?" she whispered. "How come everyone's got their tails in a twist?"

It was the utter lack of comprehension over her words' effect that ultimately lightened the atmosphere in the parlor. Mirabel's face softened slightly; Augusta suggested temperately that Hattie must be hungry after her long trip and proposed she accompany Mirabel to the kitchen.

When it grew clear that Hattie thought going with Mirabel was a plot to trap her alone with the woman, giving Mirabel a chance to carry out her nefarious deed, Jake gave her shoulder a gentle nudge. "There will be no mouth washing with soap today," he promised solemnly.

Hattie studied him for a moment, then nodded and left with Mirabel. Jake watched her go, smiling at the way she appeared to be on the alert but apparently cautiously prepared to give them the benefit of the doubt.

The parlor grew quiet as Jake and Augusta were left facing each other. A moment passed before Augusta turned away and resumed her seat on the settee. She watched Jake cross over to the mahogany sideboard and pick up a decanter. "Really, Jacob," she said faintly. "Must you grin like a ninny? I'm sure I do not comprehend what you find so amusing."

Jake looked at her over his shoulder. "Yes, you do, Mother."

Augusta was silent for a moment. She accepted a small goblet of sherry from her son, took a tiny sip, and sighed. "Yes, all right. I am getting precisely what I deserve, I daresay. I don't know what I expected—"

She correctly interpreted the meaning of Jake's raised eyebrow and smiled wryly. "Oh, very well. I guess I expected a sweet little girl to dress up in flounces and ribbons. I also suppose it's fair to say I willfully disregarded the possible complications, even when you persisted in trying to present them to me. Of course Hattie's a bit uncouth: she's lived out of touch with the world as we know it since she was seven years old. In the company, moreover, of two men who obviously didn't see fit to guard their language in her presence. Goodness gracious, Jacob, they dressed her like a boy!"

"The kid has guts, Mother."

"Honestly, dear, can't you say 'intestinal fortitude'? 'Guts' is such a repulsive word." She looked down into her wine and then back up at her son. "Yet, I daresay she does, doesn't she? Those eyes . . ." Augusta took a sip of her sherry. "Jacob, when she walked into the room her eyes were so scared, and yet she faced everyone so bravely."

"Yeah. She's a pistol. I know I argued against her coming here, Mother. But I've changed my mind. You'll both be fine."

Augusta smiled and finished her sherry. "Yes, I'm sure we shall," she agreed. "The girl is a firebrand; there's not much doubt about that. But I believe she is also quite sweet. Mirabel and I will teach her what she needs to know."

A short while later Mirabel joined them. "I declare," she said in amazement. "That child doesn't even realize what she's saying when she curses. Every other word out of her mouth was . . . well, it was—"

"Sonovabitch," Jake supplied helpfully, hiding a smile at Mirabel's repressive glare.

"Precisely," she agreed crisply. "Praise the Lord it appears to be the only swear word she knows. And her table manners are simply deplorable." Her expression softened. "She's a bright one, though. And willing. When I explained the rudiments of proper table behavior, you could practically see the wheels turning in her head as she concentrated on doing it exactly right."

"Where's Hattie now, Mirabel?"

"I left her taking a bath. Judging by her griminess, I thought she'd go screaming and kicking into the tub. But she was tickled pink at the prospect, particularly when she discovered the water would be hot. It seems a Saturday night bath was her biggest entertainment up in those hills." Mirabel smiled softly. "You should have seen her reaction when I threw in a handful of my heliotrope-scented Epsom salts and swished some soap around to make bubbles. You would have thought I was Santy Claus himself. That young'un hasn't had an overabundance of treats in her life, I'll be bound."

Jake glanced at his mother. "How do you plan to dress her once she's done bathing?"

"Oh my." Augusta set her wineglass on the nearby table. "I don't imagine she has anything suitable in that satchel she was carrying." She gave the matter a moment's thought, then with brisk decisiveness began issuing orders. "Jacob, ride down to the modiste on Commercial Street. Tell her what needs to be done and do your best to persuade her to accompany you back here. Have her bring anything ready-made in Hattie's approximate size." She was already turning to Mirabel with further instructions as Jake left to do her bidding.

On the short trip into town, Jake realized he hadn't felt so entertained since returning to Mattawa three months ago. Although glad to be home, he'd had a difficult time readjusting to the slower pace and more restrictive social conventions of his hometown after four years in Eugene.

It wasn't that he particularly missed studying at the University of Oregon or the apprenticeship he'd served with a Eugene lawyer. By accepting a limited partnership with Roger Lord, the Murdock family lawyer, he'd begun the process of launching his career in Mattawa. And in truth, that was a challenge he much preferred to the role of student or of newest hire in a city firm. He had plans for his career, plans he figured he would one day realize.

No, the difficult part was adapting to the lack of privacy. In a town this size, everyone knew everyone else's business, and he often felt he was conducting his social life in a brandy snifter.

Mattawa was small; if he paid a call on a pretty girl, everyone in town knew about it before the morning paper was delivered.

He'd grown accustomed to Eugene. You could flirt with a debutante at a charity ball, or pay your two dollars at a bawdy house and take your pick of any girl in the establishment.

At least your affairs, be they innocent or sordid, weren't bruited about town by the time you emerged for breakfast.

Of course, Jake admitted with a certain wryness to himself, it was entirely possible that Eugene might not have impressed him as being so much freer and less hypocritical had he spent more time there courting the city's nice girls and less time visiting the women in the various bawdy houses. It likely boiled down to a matter of perspective.

In any event, the arrival of Hattie Witherspoon Taylor was a welcome one . . . if for no other reason than she didn't monitor every damn word she spoke before it left her mouth. He imagined, for her own survival, that would change. But for now, at least, she harbored no fear of appearing less than morally upright in the public's eye. That little girl said exactly what was on her mind. It was a quality Jake admired. Even if it was one he seldom saw in this small town.

Not that he in any way regretted his return to Mattawa.

Sure, he missed some of the pleasures and the anonymity to be found in a larger town. But this was his home. It was where his mother lived, and she was his only remaining close relative. It was where he was building his career and would someday raise his own family. And as an unequivocal plus, Mattawa boasted Jane-Ellen Fielding.

The town had acquired a new doctor while Jake was in Eugene. According to the letter Augusta wrote him at the time, Doc Fielding's arrival was heralded with only a little less fanfare than she expected the Second Coming to garner. That wasn't the blasphemy a stranger might believe it to be, for there had been only one other doctor in town at the time, and anyone with a lick of sense knew better than to rely on Doc Baker's help after four in the afternoon.

Old Doc Baker was a notorious tippler and the tremors in his hands became more pronounced as the evening progressed. The need for emergency medical treatment was a ghastly occurrence to be avoided at all costs, as anyone who'd ever had the misfortune to require stitches after dusk could attest. Small wonder the new doctor had been welcomed so warmly.

Augusta had also written about Doc Fielding's lovely daughter, Jane-Ellen. At the time, Jake was caught up in his life away from home and hadn't paid much attention. More fool he.

Shortly after returning to Mattawa, Jake was introduced to Jane-Ellen. His captivation had been immediate and total. She was perfection personified. Were a textbook written on the budding flower of womanhood, Jane-Ellen Fielding would be its model. She was sweet natured, blond, and beautiful. The ideal woman. And suddenly, years before he ever contemplated he would, Jake Murdock was entertaining the notion of matrimony.

"Entertain" being the operative word at this point. He pulled up to the hitching post in front of the dressmaker's establishment.

It wasn't difficult to convince the modiste to accompany him back to the house. Augusta Murdock was a valued customer, and the prospect of supplying an entire wardrobe for her young ward was clearly an enticing one. The woman gathered her pattern books, fabric samples, and such ready-made apparel in Hattie's general size as she had on hand. After locking up her shop, she allowed Jake to assist her into the buggy.

THE PANDEMONIUM COMING from an upstairs bedroom assaulted their ears the moment Jake opened the front door. Hattie's voice, strident with anger, overrode the faint murmurs of the two older women. The actual words were indistinguishable, but the tone was unmistakable. Ushering the dressmaker into the parlor, Jake ignored her avid curiosity and excused himself. He loped up the stairs two at a time.

Following the noise down the hall, he reached the room Augusta had prepared for Hattie and tapped on the door. His knock apparently went unheard over the commotion inside, so he turned the knob and pushed the door open. "What the *hell* is going on here?" he demanded. "Hattie, hush up."

To his surprise, Hattie hushed. She stood with her back to the wall, swathed in Augusta's dressing gown, which was four times too large for her. The blue fabric pooled around Hattie's feet and gaped in the front, exposing her sturdy flat-planed chest. Droplets of moisture still dappled her pale skin and her drenched, copper-bright hair clung to her skull, sleek as a seal's and darkened by the water plastering it in a fan across her shoulders and down her back. The robe's arms had been rolled several times, yet still hung to her fingertips.

Cutting herself off in mid-tirade, she picked up the skirts of the dressing gown and ran to Jake. Gripping his hand, she stared up at him with big, demanding eyes.

"Make them give me back my bag!"

"Oh, for . . . Mother, give her the bag. Mirabel, go down and offer the modiste refreshment."

Mirabel handed the carpetbag to Hattie and left the room. Hattie immediately dropped to her knees on the floor and opened it up.

"I was only trying to prevent her from donning another pair of those dreadful boys' overalls," Augusta murmured.

He patted her hand. "I understand, Mother. But the satchel appears to be the only thing she can call her own." Glancing across the room, he swore beneath his breath.

"Hattie!" he roared. "Put that wrapper back on this instant!"

3

J AKE'S LOUD VOICE made Hattie jump. Having just located a clean pair of overalls in her bag, she'd shucked out of the oversized wrapper Mirabel had given her without a thought for modesty. It never occurred to her that just because a man was in the room she shouldn't disrobe.

Horace and Papa had never minded.

Hattie blinked at Jake in confusion as he crossed the room in two giant strides and manhandled her back into the wrapper. He pulled the two sides together and yanked the tie at her waist so tight she could barely breathe. Ripping the overalls from her hands, he tossed them across the room. "Hey!" she protested.

He stared down at her with unsmiling sternness. "You won't be needing those. Mother has arranged for a fitting with a dressmaker."

Narrowing her eyes, she stared up at him. "I don't want no sonovabitchin' dresses!"

"Well, that's a crying shame, kid, because new dresses are exactly what you're going to get! How many other girls have you seen running around in boys' pants?"

She thrust her chin at a mutinous angle, and he growled, "The girls in Mattawa wear skirts, Hattie Taylor, and I'll be damned if you'll embarrass your aunt by strutting around in those sorry pants. And don't even think about throwing another fit in front of the dressmaker, or I'll blister your butt so hard, you'll be eating your dinner off the sideboard for a week!"

"Jacob, please," Augusta protested weakly. Really, this was too much. It was one thing for him to pepper his conversation with outrageous language when there was no one to hear except her and Mirabel. She derived a sneaking enjoyment out of it—reminding her as it did of her darling Luke. It was something else entirely, however, to mention . . . well, the unmentionable in front of an impressionable young girl. One did not speak of the anatomy in mixed company. And most certainly not with such vulgarity.

Hattie didn't share Augusta's qualms. Threats of a thrashing were things she understood. Plus, her mama had said to look for silver linings when life gave you black clouds. Jake was her silver lining. In just a few hours, she'd already become accustomed to his flashing grin and teasing ways. This hard-eyed man laying down the law just wasn't the same, and she'd do almost anything to bring back her new friend. "Okay," she agreed ungraciously. "I'll wear the stinkin' dresses." She just wanted him to smile at her again.

He did. "That's my girl," he said and grinned. He bent to clamp his hands under Hattie's arms. Jake lifted her high in the air, planted a swift kiss on her lips, and set her down again. He ran his hand down her wet hair. "I'll send the dressmaker up," he said. And left the room.

Since her mama's death, kisses were rare occurrences in Hattie's life. She pressed the unaccustomed warmth of Jake's into her lips with her fingertips in hopes of making it last a little longer. Out of the corner of her eye, she saw Augusta watching her and immediately knuckle-scrubbed her mouth. "He better not kiss me again," she muttered gruffly.

"Oh, I'm sure he shan't," Augusta replied, hiding a smile when her words elicited a flash of disappointment across Hattie's face. She studied the little girl. "How old are you, child?"

"Eleven." Hattie looked around the room and, as she took it in, her jaw sagged. Concerned about her carpetbag, she hadn't given the room her attention earlier. Now she stared in awe.

It was large and airy, illuminated by two tall windows with tops curved like spread fans of leaded glass. Ruffled muslin curtains, tied back with green bows, fluttered in the breeze. Sunlight cast dappled shadows through the tree outside, painting patterns across the hardwood floor. Hattie wondered if it was the fresh air blowing in or the bottles of hartshorn and camphor on the dressing table that made the room smell so good. Almost as good as Aunt Augusta.

In addition to the scents, the dressing table contained an ornate set of silver-backed hair accessories. She studied all the beautiful items atop the dresser, then drifted about the large room, staring at everything, touching nothing. Each item seemed prettier than what caught her eye before, but Hattie's perusal was merely a stopgap to keep her from grabbing the one thing she really wanted to touch more than anything in the world. The doll. The bed had a high mattress, four posters, and a pale gold satin comforter, piled with tiny pillows of satin and lace. Perched on the top was the doll. Hattie gazed at it hungrily.

Augusta, watching her, felt a pang for the child's obvious longing. At the same time, she experienced a little thrill of vindication. Hattie's language might be coarse, and she'd arrived looking as dusty and unkempt as a vagrant ragamuffin. But her mother's early training had clearly stayed with her. Hadn't Augusta told Jacob breeding would tell? Hattie's awe of the room and her hunger for the doll shone like a beacon from her freshly scrubbed face. Yet she hadn't so much as touched one item, let alone grabbed indiscriminately as might be expected from a child allowed to run wild and unsupervised the past few years.

Augusta swooped across the room and swept the doll off its pile of pillows. She extended it to Hattie. "Her name is Lillian."

Hattie reached out a cautious hand for the doll, eyeing Augusta warily, as if afraid it would be snatched back if she reached for it. Augusta relinquished it the instant Hattie's hand closed around the doll's middle and watched as the little girl promptly bowed her head to give the gift her undivided attention.

Lillian's head, hands, and feet were made of China bisque, her painted features delicate. Hattie inspected the way the china portions attached to the sawdust-filled cloth body and the detailed clothing the doll wore. Tipping up its skirts, she examined the fine lawn drawers and full petticoats from an earlier era, then turned the doll upright and patted its clothes back into place, carefully arranging its tiny, high-buttoned boots. She ran her fingers over the doll's fine blond hair, then reluctantly tried to hand it back to Augusta. "Dolls're dumb," she muttered gruffly. Then with innate honesty, she added, "Lillian's real pretty, though."

"I'm so glad you think so," Augusta replied smoothly, pretending she didn't see the doll being offered her. "She very much needs someone to take care of her, and I'm afraid I am simply too old. She's been very lonely on this big old bed all by herself and has quite anxiously awaited your arrival."

Hattie promptly clutched Lillian fiercely to her chest, and, hiding a smile, Augusta gently touched the girl's still-damp hair. Attention absorbed by the doll in her arms, Hattie didn't notice.

Mirabel arrived with the dressmaker in tow, and the fitting went much more smoothly than Augusta had dared hope. She wasn't sure if it was Jacob's threat of a spanking or Hattie's enthrallment with Lillian that made the difference, but the little girl kept her squirming to a minimum, and she only uttered her infamous swear word once, when the dressmaker accidentally stuck her with a pin.

Augusta quelled the dressmaker's shocked curiosity with a stern look. She wasn't above a spot of genteel blackmail. Clearly, they needed to work with Hattie before her introduction into society. The era they lived in demanded high moral standards of its young ladies, and Augusta was determined that Hattie take her rightful place in society. Damned if she'd tolerate anything hampering the child before she even had a chance to begin.

Tomorrow they'd retire to the ranch. For now, Augusta let it be tacitly understood she'd know precisely where to place the blame should tales of Hattie's verbal indiscretion make the rounds of Mattawa. The retaliation was clear: her patronage would be withdrawn. She only hoped her value as a customer was enough, for she knew well the dressmaker's love of gossip.

By the time Augusta noticed Hattie starting to wilt, the child's thick hair had mostly dried into heavy waves and tight, flyaway ringlets. A fiery nimbus outlined its thick mass when the lowering sun poured through the window. Hattie's shoulders had developed a droop, her arms hung limp at her sides, and for the first time since Augusta gave her the doll, Lillian wasn't carefully cradled in Hattie's arms or clasped to her chest. Instead, the doll dangled from the girl's hand, swinging gently with the slight sway of Hattie's body.

Even as Augusta watched, the child's eyes slid shut, then blinked open, her head nodding wearily. Clad only in her new ready-made white chemise and drawers, she looked like a vulnerable little soldier as she struggled to stay awake on the slipper chair where they'd bid her stand for her fitting.

Augusta promptly concluded the arrangements. Hattie had been measured to within an inch of her life, and the adults had pored over the pattern books, discussing fabrics and trim as they went. She saw no need to prolong the session when the child was so obviously exhausted. Helping Hattie down from the chair, she urged her to sit as Mirabel showed the dressmaker out.

Picking up the silver-backed brush, Augusta pulled it through Hattie's thick hair. She spent several minutes enjoying the unaccustomed chore, before braiding the girl's hair into a thick plait that fell to Hattie's waist. Next, she tucked Hattie into a new batiste nightgown. She offered tooth powder and a brush, and when Hattie returned from performing her ablutions, Augusta had turned back the covers on the bed. She patted the mattress. "Come to bed, child."

Yawning, Hattie stumbled across the room. "Am I going to sleep in here?" she asked, then tumbled onto the high mattress without awaiting an answer.

"Yes, dear. This is your room." Augusta pulled the covers over Hattie's shoulders and smoothed an errant tendril of bright hair back into the braid.

"It's real pretty." Hattie yawned again and her eyes drifted closed. Then her eyes flew open and she jerked up onto one elbow. "Where's Lillian?" As quickly as the question was posed, the child subsided. "Oh. She's here." She pulled the doll from under the covers and tucked it into the crook of her arm. "Thanks, Aunt Augusta." Her fan of lowered lashes flickered against her pale cheeks, and she sleepily raised a hand to rub at her nose. "For the room," she murmured around a yawn, "'n' for Lillian."

Augusta smiled down at the young girl in the bed. She had a feeling she was very much going to enjoy having Hattie Taylor live with her. Very much indeed. "You're welcome, dear. Good night."

There was no answer. Hattie was already sound asleep.

4

Doc Fielding's house
WEDNESDAY, JULY 5, 1899

JAKE SAT IN the Fielding parlor and wondered how much longer Jane-Ellen would make him wait. He shifted in restless irritation. His dad had taught him to work hard from the time Jake was knee-high to a grasshopper, so idleness wasn't his long suit.

Up until moments ago, he'd at least had Jane-Ellen's father to keep him company. Doc was a blunt-spoken, down-to-earth man, and Jake liked him. They'd enjoyed a comfortable conversation before the Fieldings' housekeeper stuck her head in the room to inform the doctor his services were needed on a ranch outside of town. Doc had poured Jake a stiff shot of whiskey, given him a conspiratorial wink, assured him Jane-Ellen wouldn't be very much longer, and excused himself.

Gazing into his whiskey, Jake absently noted it was the same color as Hattie's eyes. The thought made him smile. For pure entertainment value, thinking about the newest member of the Murdock household beat hell out of checking his timepiece every two minutes, impatiently awaiting Jane-Ellen's appearance. In the eight weeks since her arrival, Hattie had made her presence felt in every corner of the house. Not a small accomplishment, considering children were supposed to be seen but not heard.

It was quickly evident no one had bothered to inform Hattie that silence was golden. She talked all the time. Her curiosity was boundless and she had questions about every aspect of the new life she'd been thrust into. Jake had overheard Mirabel just the other day, discussing Hattie with his mother.

"I have never," Mirabel grumbled, "heard a body use the word 'why' so often! Why is it so green here, when it wasn't in Nevada? Why do I do something that way—why not do it this way instead? Heavens, she even wanted to know why the crocheted pieces on chairs' headrests and arms are called tidies. Who but her would think to ask?"

"I know," Augusta had agreed wearily. "The gardener threatened to quit if she doesn't stop badgering him for details about every plant in the yard. I also found her trailing Ethel around while the poor girl was trying to finish dusting so she could leave for the day. Hattie wanted to know everything about Ethel's nine brothers and sisters."

Jake grinned into his whiskey glass. You never knew when or where Hattie would pop up, Lillian in hand. But you could be sure she'd be found engaging her latest quarry in conversation, endlessly interrogating the poor sod or espousing opinions of her own. He, too, had come under her conversational guns. But unlike a good many adults, he enjoyed it.

Since Augusta removed the womenfolk to the ranch the day after Hattie arrived in Mattawa, he hadn't spent as much time with her as his mother and Mirabel. With his schedule, there wasn't time to make the trip from town to ranch and back during the workweek—not without getting up before the crack of dawn to get to the office, then coming back home late in the evening. But during his weekend exposure to Hattie, he found her extremely interesting.

The girl was one of a kind, her personality no doubt a result of the unique circumstances that allowed her to run wild before arriving in Mattawa. Or perhaps her outspokenness stemmed from the fact that she didn't harbor a shy bone in her sturdy little body. Whatever the reason, she was pretty damned adaptable; you had to admire that. Her life to date couldn't have been easy.

All the myriad rules governing proper behavior were obviously new to Hattie and, clearly, to her way of thinking, often incomprehensible. He didn't doubt for a moment that she could be a trial for his mother, for she was a volatile little package. He'd heard her shouting with rage one minute and laughing uproariously the next. It was exactly that behavior, truth to tell, he found so fascinating. The things that set off other girls, reducing them to tears, seemed to elicit a different response entirely from Hattie.

Jake had never seen her cry. He'd heard her respond with anger or laugh something off with an unexpectedly timed sense of humor. But he'd never seen her blubber or lament. Even the day when her cursing finally caused Mirabel to follow through on the threatened mouth washing, Hattie hadn't shed a tear. She had come up spitting out soap and screaming at the top of her lungs. And if her eyes had glittered, it sure as hell hadn't been with tears. She was a stubborn little cuss, but he'd noticed she didn't let it carry her to the point of idiocy. Since the mouth-washing episode, Jake hadn't heard the infamous swear word pass her lips. He'd heard her whisper, "Hell's bells," a couple times, but Mirabel must not feel as strongly about that combination. Well, either that or Hattie had yet to use it anywhere near her.

A tutor had been engaged for her when they discovered how sorely her education had been neglected. Now Hattie had John Fiske to hound with her endless questions, and she appeared to take full advantage of his services. She was already on book five of the six-volume series of McGuffey's Readers, which pleased everyone. Hattie's mother had given her a good start in reading and writing, but it had been *only* a start at Elvira Witherspoon Taylor's death. Hattie had had limited access to books after that. Luckily, she was a quick learner with an inquiring mind.

Last night he'd brought the females back to Augusta's house so Hattie could watch the town's Fourth of July fireworks from Augusta's bedroom window. He, his mom, and Mirabel had gotten a huge kick out of watching the kid's enthrallment with the display. Less thrilling were the piano lessons Augusta insisted Hattie have. She hated being confined indoors doing repetitive scales and wasn't shy about sharing her opinion. They had all come to dread those moments when her frustration got the best of her and she took it out on the piano keys, pounding up and down the scales, filling the house with discordant, earsplitting noise.

A rustle in the doorway and subtle drift of attar of roses alerted Jake that he was no longer alone. Looking up from the contemplation of his whiskey glass, he saw Jane-Ellen standing just inside the room. Thoughts of Hattie fled, along with his irritation at having been kept waiting. He set his glass on the nearest table and rose to his feet.

Jane-Ellen moved into the room. "I'm sorry I took so long," she murmured.

"It was worth the delay," Jake replied and smiled widely, eyeing her in appreciation.

Jane-Ellen blushed beneath his frank regard and decided it was worth having deliberately delayed coming downstairs in order to fuss with her hair and change her dress three different times. She peered up at him from under partially lowered lashes. Her friends simply swooned over Jake Murdock. He was fun, he was *very* nice to look at, and he had prospects beyond the already established wealth of his family. He was considered one of Mattawa's finest catches, and Jane-Ellen loved being the envy of her friends. It made up in part for the fact that his virility sometimes frightened her to death. "Um, may I offer you some refreshments?"

"No, thanks," Jake replied. "Actually, I hoped you'd ride out to the ranch with me."

Jane-Ellen accepted immediately, excited at the invitation. She'd heard of the Murdock Ranch; everyone knew it was where their wealth originated. But she had never been there.

It was exhilarating to bowl along the country roads in the summer sunshine. Autumn's approach was still in the future and it was beautifully warm but not yet ungodly hot. Jake raced the buggy along a straight stretch of road, and clamping her hat to her head with one hand, Jane-Ellen turned to study him. "I don't believe I've ever known anyone who owns two residences," she confessed, raising her voice a little to be heard over the pounding of the horse's hoofs.

Jake laughed, enjoying the weather, the speed, the girl at his side. He turned his head to look at her. "We moved permanently into our town house just before my father died."

At Jane-Ellen's quizzical look, he said, "Dad knew he didn't have long to live and he wanted Mom settled in town. Before he became ill, we rarely used the town house."

"I've heard Luke Murdock was a wonderful man." Jane-Ellen smiled at him.

"Yeah, he was." Jake was surprised by the strength of the grief that could still sneak up and wrap him in its grip. It had been several years now since the funeral. "I still miss him."

Jane-Ellen noted the veil of sadness flitting across his hazel eyes and felt a surge of tenderness for this usually easygoing man. "He was sweet to see your mother situated in town."

Her remark made him laugh, dispelling his sadness. "Mom didn't think so. She loved the ranch. My parents built it together from scratch and it was her home for all but the end of their married life." He grinned. "But she loved Dad more and he wasn't above fighting dirty, using his illness to make her promise to stay in town. He thought she needed people around her, and it bothered him to think of her way out here without his protection."

Jake slowed the mare's pace with a tug of the reins, then turned his attention back to Jane-Ellen. "Mother still comes here for extended periods. She and Mirabel brought Hattie here the day after she arrived to begin the civilizing process away from the town's prying eyes. They went home last night so Hattie could see the fireworks from the house, but they'll be back tomorrow."

Jane-Ellen's curiosity was piqued by Jake's mention of Hattie's name. Few people had yet to meet the Murdocks' ward, but already there were whispers about the girl's outspokenness, rumors she'd been allowed to run wild before her arrival in Mattawa and had arrived wearing boys' clothing.

Firmly, Jane-Ellen suppressed her avid interest. Jake wouldn't have said as much as he had if he didn't believe she could be trusted not to carry tales. Instead, she asked, "What about you, Jake? Do you miss the ranch as well?"

"I do." He slowed the rig to turn onto a private road. Clucking at the horse and dragging on the reins, he halted the buggy at a wrought iron gate.

Jake swung down from the buggy and walked the gate open. He guided the horse and buggy through, then closed and fastened the gate behind him. Slinging an arm over the mare's rump, he thumbed back his hat to stare up at Jane-Ellen.

"I love this ranch, but Dad considered me too young to take over for him when he fell ill," he said regretfully. "As long as I can remember, he wanted me to be a lawyer. Or at least to receive the education he never had. And I like being an attorney. But, it's an odd thing, Jane-Ellen. I miss ranching more than I thought possible. Particularly working with the horses."

Jake slapped the horse's rump and swung back up into the buggy. "Maybe someday, when my practice is well established, I'll move out here and have the best of both worlds. Part-time rancher and part-time lawyer." Grinning at her, he shrugged. "Who knows?"

Jane-Ellen didn't know what to think about that. She had only ever lived in towns and cities; she knew nothing of ranch life. Still, she found the afternoon exhilarating, enchanting. Jake left her in the ranch house, which was unexpectedly grand, while he attended to business on the spread. She was given tea and a brief tour of the house by the cook.

As the afternoon waned, she was served dinner. For just a while, as she ate in solitary splendor in the plush dining room, she pretended she was Mrs. Jake Murdock, mistress of all she surveyed. It was a daydream, but a harmless one. And it was exciting to pretend.

The sun was lowering in the western sky before Jake reappeared, noisily entering the parlor where Jane-Ellen sat. She glanced up at his arrival and gaped in surprised dismay. She had only seen him immaculately attired. Certainly, she'd never seen him all . . . sweaty.

He wore a pair of those heavy work pants by Levi Strauss, tight and slightly faded, and a cotton shirt with a western yoke. Wet rings spread between his shoulder blades and under his arms, and he was covered in dust. His usually well-groomed hair was plastered to his forehead, bent oddly by the hatband of the disreputable Stetson in his hand.

Her nose wrinkled with distaste. He smelled strongly of horse. Her smile stiffened as he advanced into the room. Somehow, she had expected his inspection of the ranch to be more . . . gentlemanly. Poring over accounts in a tidy office or something of that nature. This was a side to him she'd never seen before, yet had always instinctively feared to see. A raw, earthy, and—oh dear, dare she even think it? A lusty side.

"I apologize for appearing before you in this state," he said properly enough, but it was obvious he was in high spirits. "I just wanted to let you know we'll be leaving as soon as I clean up. That should allow us enough time to reach town before the sun sets. I'm sure your father wouldn't want you traveling these country roads after dark." He ran his fingers through his disheveled hair. "Is your wrap still in the buggy? It's getting cooler."

Jane-Ellen assured him she would be ready, and he grinned as he excused himself and took the stairs two at a time. When he returned surprisingly quickly, looking once again like the Jake she knew, she'd donned her redingote and gloves and was in the process of anchoring a pearl-headed hatpin through her hat. She thanked the cook for her courtesy and allowed Jake to usher her out to the buggy.

Jake was in a marvelous mood, and all the way back to town he regaled Jane-Ellen with progress reports of the ranch, unstintingly praising the foreman's custodianship. When Jake was away from it, he tended to forget how much he loved the place, with its clean country air and particularly its stables, redolent of horses and hay. He caught himself just as he was about to launch into an enthusiastic accounting of Thunder's mating with Buttercup. *Lord, man,* he reminded himself in the nick of time, *you can't tell a gently raised female that!*

But he grinned in the gathering dusk. There was nothing quite so elemental as witnessing a stallion cover a mare. It was nature at its finest, basic and honest and inherently erotic, with the stallion's advance, the mare's retreat—until both were quivering with expectation. He'd watched Buttercup reject Thunder again and again. It wasn't until she was damn good and ready that the stallion had finally cornered her and climbed over her back, teeth sunk into her neck to hold her in place. Then, with thrusting haunches, Thunder had completed his mission.

Jake had envied that damn horse. And he'd sympathized with the amount of effort needed before the beast finally achieved its goal.

When Jake walked into the parlor and saw Jane-Ellen sitting there, cool and pristine on the velvet settee, he'd wished for a moment they were married. Wished he had the right to stride across the room, roll Jane-Ellen onto the floor, throw up her skirts, and take her right there on Augusta's antique carpet. He longed for the right to muss her up a little. There was something a bit unearthly about Jane-Ellen, which he figured originated in her perpetual tidiness. As a result, he was endlessly careful with her. But, Lord love him, in his imagination—?

Jake harbored too many pent-up emotions right this moment to be satisfied with chaste kisses, so in his mind he kissed her with every bit of passion in him.

They arrived at Jane-Ellen's house just as the mauve streaks of twilight faded into night's darkness. Jake escorted her to her front door.

"Thank you for taking me with you," she said and smiled at him. "I had a lovely time." She stood on tiptoe to deliver a chaste kiss. She'd learned from past experience that there was a high level of pleasure to be derived from kissing Jake Murdock.

But then he slipped his hands into her hair and twisted his mouth over hers, breaking the closed seal of her lips. And with a small groan, he slid his tongue into her mouth.

Slapping her hands to his chest, Jane-Ellen shoved him away. "Jake Murdock!" she exclaimed, experiencing the small surge of distaste she'd felt when he'd invaded the ranch parlor reeking of man, horse, and work. She pinned a reproachful stare on him as she patted her mussed strands of hair back into her coiffure.

Jake blinked down at her. It only took him an instant to note her patent disapproval, and it flicked him on the raw. In the cool silence, broken only by the nightly chorus of frogs and crickets, he acknowledged her inexperience and mustered a smile. But he couldn't block the trace of coolness in his tone when he said, "You needn't look as though you kissed a toad."

"You put your tongue in my mouth!"

"It's a lover's kiss, and the way men and women show affection . . . desire. Don't expect me to apologize for it."

Jane-Ellen blushed to the roots of her hair and Jake sighed. Running a hand around the back of his neck, he looked down at her. "Jane-Ellen, do you like me?"

"Yes, you know I do."

"I like you too. Very much. I think perhaps I even love you, girl. But I need to show my feelings with more than the virtuous little kisses we've exchanged up until now." Annnnd . . . shit, she looked scared to death. So, he smiled gently as he brushed his fingertips over her cheek. "Nothing improper, Jane-Ellen. But I need to kiss you like a man kisses a woman."

"With your tongue?"

"With my tongue."

She shivered a bit, but then she tilted her head up. "Very well."

She acceded to his wish with all the enthusiasm of Saint Joan offering her executioners a match, but Jake smiled and leaned over to kiss her the way he'd wanted to for so long. He kept it brief and gentle, but even so she stood stiffly in his embrace.

He raised his head, disappointed in her response. But he reminded himself she was a virgin and that this was all very new to her. He pressed a final, closed-mouth peck on her lips, and she seemed to perk up. Stepping back, he whispered, "Good night."

"Good night, Jake." Jane-Ellen gazed up at him. That kind of kiss wasn't quite so terrible when you were braced for it. She supposed, if she had to, she could grow accustomed to it. "Thank you again for taking me to the ranch."

Jake sat in the buggy for a moment after Jane-Ellen went inside. Finally, he picked up the reins. And eschewing Mamie Parker's sporting establishment, where he'd really like to go, he headed home.

5

Augusta's house
SATURDAY, JULY 22, 1899

HATTIE RIPPED THE big bow from her hair. "I look ridiculous!"

She had been unnaturally subdued the past few days, but it wasn't until this moment that Augusta realized why. In all honesty, Augusta hadn't questioned the reasons at first. She had simply given thanks for the respite.

Hattie was imbued with excessive energy that at times plumb wore Augusta out. It reminded her of Jacob as a boy, only somehow worse, for she supposed she'd never questioned the bromide decreeing it acceptable, even expected, for a boy to be rambunctious. Girls were supposed to be quieter and easier to raise.

Not to mention Luke was alive when Jacob was a young, energetic scamp hell-bent on driving her crazy. Her husband had possessed an uncanny knack for sensing when she'd reached her limit. He'd take Jacob with him to some far-flung corner of the ranch so she could catch her breath. And of course, she'd been a decade-plus younger then.

So instead of looking for reasons why Hattie was uncharacteristically subdued the past few days, Augusta had merely said, "Thank you, Lord," and put her feet up for a spell.

But it was a funny thing. Once she'd had a day's rest, it began worrying her when Hattie remained quiet and withdrawn. Augusta was sometimes wearied by the child's antics, but more often they amused her. In the handful of weeks since Hattie had come to live with them, Augusta had grown extremely fond of her. It disturbed her to realize that Hattie wasn't comfortable enough in return to share her troubles. And now, like a thunderbolt, as she watched the girl in the cheval glass fussing unhappily with her attire, comprehension struck.

Today was Hattie's official coming out, her introduction to society. A dinner party had been planned for weeks, and as parties went, it would be a small affair. Only Jacob, Hattie, and herself, plus Dr. Fielding and Jane-Ellen, Hattie's tutor, John Fiske, and the family lawyer, Roger Lord. And, clearly, Hattie feared the impression she'd make.

Augusta chastised herself for not realizing sooner. But Hattie always appeared so fearless it simply hadn't occurred to her. Augusta crossed to stand behind Hattie at the mirror. She straightened the skirt of the eleven-year-old's dress and fluffed the sleeves. Then she picked up the brush and restored order to the riotous mass of copper curls. As she retied the bow holding Hattie's hair back, their eyes met in the mirror. "I think you look perfectly sweet," she whispered. "Our guests are going to be very impressed."

Hattie studied her own reflection in the mirror, then raised her gaze to meet Augusta's. "I don't see how," she said in a surprisingly adult tone. "*You* tell me you like me just the way I am. But you're always instructing me on ways to change." She turned to face Augusta, her expression uncertain. "What will strangers who don't know me at all think?"

"Oh, my dear." Augusta bridged the distance between them, reaching out to hug her ward. As always, when a glimmer of vulnerability broke through Hattie's tough little exterior, Augusta's heart melted. Leading her to the bed, where they both sat, she picked up and held one of Hattie's hands in both of hers. "Sometimes your perception is frighteningly mature. It's not always easy to remember you're not even twelve years old yet."

"I will be in January."

"Yes, I know." Augusta took a deep breath. "Hattie, I truly do like you just the way you are, and I'm certain others will, too. But there are a great many rules that govern the behavior of young ladies in our society, dear, and females of good family are expected to adhere to them faithfully. Some are fairly basic: such as good table manners. Others are subtler, and I suspect you'll have to learn a few of those by trial and error. But I wanted to instruct you on as many as I possibly could before you went out into society. You're expected to observe the proprieties, but unfortunately you don't even know what many of them are." She freed a hand to gently brush an unruly curl away from Hattie's eyes. "That's why I've been stuffing you full of rules and regulations. Folks can be mighty quick to judge, darling. I don't want them judging you so quickly by your mistakes that they don't give themselves a chance to become acquainted with the real Hattie Taylor. Do you understand what I'm trying to say?"

"I think so. Mirabel says I'm barely housebroken."

"Oh dear. Did that hurt your feelings?"

Hattie flashed a smile. "Nah. Mirabel likes me, so I expect she's sorta saying what you just said. Like, if I were a puppy and I piddled on the parlor floor, people might be so shocked at my behavior they'd never realize I was actually a right fine house pet."

"Exactly." Augusta hid a smile. What an apt analogy.

Hattie studied the room for a moment. Then she looked up at her guardian. "Aunt Augusta? Did you know my mama?"

"Not very well, dear. That branch of the Witherspoons lived in California. I've spent the majority of the past twenty-four years here in Oregon. But I did meet her on a few occasions, and I remember her as a warm and gentle woman."

"I can't recollect what she looked like anymore. But I remember I loved her. And she was a lady, wasn't she? A real lady, I mean, like you?"

"She was, dear. In every sense of the word."

"Then, I 'spect I'll try to be a lady, too. Like she was, and you are."

Augusta squeezed Hattie's hand. "I can't think of a nicer way to keep your mama's memory alive," she said and rose from the bed, pulling Hattie up with her. "Come, dear. It's time to go downstairs. Our guests will be arriving any moment."

Hattie had been dreading this day far longer than anyone knew. For the first hour, she sat stiffly on the edge of her seat, ankles primly crossed and hands tightly clasped in her lap, her stomach fluttering uncomfortably as she willed herself not to say or do anything stupid. She even declined the hot spiced cider, which she dearly loved, for fear she would slurp, spill, or otherwise embarrass herself or Aunt Augusta.

That earned her sharp scrutiny from Mirabel, who was passing the tray around, and a surreptitious laying-on of cool, bony fingers to her forehead. Hattie grinned and accepted a cup after all. Listening to the conversations around her, she gradually relaxed and conceded that perhaps this wouldn't be as difficult as she'd feared. Covertly, she studied their guests.

Her tutor, John Fiske, she already knew, of course. He was a mild man who wore steel-bowed spectacles and was so quiet and self-effacing it was easy to overlook him. She did so now in favor of more interesting viewing.

She had been curious about Jane-Ellen Fielding for some time, wondering about the woman Jake was so besotted with. Jake was Hattie's favorite person in the whole world. She'd already decided she was going to marry him when she grew up. A tiny bit jealous his affectionate attention was not exclusively hers, she had been prepared to dislike Jane-Ellen Fielding on sight.

She could not. Jane-Ellen was pretty and soft-spoken and sweet. She smiled at Hattie and engaged her in conversation, listening to Hattie with patently genuine interest.

Roger Lord, on the other hand, disregarded her utterly. Oh, upon being introduced, he spent a moment exchanging polite pleasantries; then he turned away and ignored her. He was the handsomest man she'd ever laid eyes on. Hattie was awed by his golden hair and pale blue eyes and the romantic cleft in his chin. But pretty is as pretty does, Mirabel said, and Hattie found it kinda difficult to like a person for whom she clearly didn't exist. Scrutinizing him unobtrusively, she noted that even with the adults he didn't appear particularly warm.

Doc Fielding was warm. A short, stocky man with thinning hair of indeterminate color, he laughed, talked, and cussed a blue streak, suffixing his swearing with a "Pardon me, ladies."

It made Hattie uncomfortable. She kept glancing at Mirabel, as the housekeeper moved about the room with trays of refreshments, expecting at any moment she'd grab the doctor by his ear and drag him off to wash his mouth out with soap. She liked Doc Fielding, and she wanted to spare him from what she knew was a heinous ordeal. Finally, on pins and needles each time he opened his mouth, she placed a hand upon his sleeve to detain him as the group was called to dinner. When he turned to her, she raised on tiptoe and whispered in his ear.

Fielding's laughter drew unwelcome attention. Hattie turned her back on the speculative glances and scowled up at him. "What's so funny?"

"Nothing. Sorry." Doc stifled his amusement. He reached out to touch Hattie's cheek. "Thank you for the warning. It was da . . . uh, right neighborly of you." He escorted her to dinner.

During the meal, Doc struggled to curb his cussing. At one point Hattie caught Jake regarding her speculatively and she grinned at him, proud of her accomplishment. Although she'd heard Jake swear many times, she noticed he didn't around company. His manners and speech were very correct and she suddenly understood what Augusta had told her earlier about observing the proprieties. Hattie decided to follow his example.

Half an hour later she nearly forgot her new resolution. When they repaired to the parlor after dinner, Augusta requested she play a piece on the piano for their company. Hattie hated the piano. She liked to be proficient at things she tried, yet she hated the practice necessary to attain that proficiency. Playing the piano wasn't like learning to ride a horse, where the learning was almost as much fun as mastering the skill.

Piano was *boring*, and she hadn't progressed very far. Still. Augusta asked very little of her. So, as much as she dreaded displaying her lack of ability, she decided to give it her best effort. With as much grace as she could muster, she launched into "Long, Long Ago."

Midway through the piece, she hit a sour note. She resisted the temptation to pound the keyboard in frustration, but she did automatically mutter, "Oh sonova—"

Immediately tasting the bitter flavor of soap, she bit off the expletive, whispering, "Hell's bells," instead. Gritting her teeth, she silently chanted, *Observe the proprieties, observe the proprieties.* She managed to finish the piece without exploding, although she felt red-faced with the effort. The polite smattering of applause only served to deepen her flush. Obviously, their guests had also heard the lesson about observing the proprieties. She slammed her method book closed, sketched a brief curtsy to her audience, and stalked over to glare out the window.

Jake nearly exploded himself, trying not to laugh. God, she tickled him. All that red hair practically crackled with the force of her emotions. He decided to help her by shifting the spotlight away from her. Squeezing Jane-Ellen's hand, he rose. Picking up a teaspoon from the service on the table, he tapped the side of his brandy snifter. "If I could have your attention?"

Hattie turned from the window, grateful the focus of interest had shifted. Jake was assisting Jane-Ellen to her feet, smiling into her eyes. Hattie suppressed a frown as she watched him lift Jane-Ellen's hand and kiss her fingertips. She was embarrassed for him when he did things like that. It made him look like such a dolt.

While Jane-Ellen blushed, Jake turned to the gathering. "I would like to take this opportunity, while all of us are gathered here, to inform you Jane-Ellen consented to be my wife last night."

"Oh, my dears . . ."

"Married! Well, son of a bi—uh, gun!"

"Congratulations, Miss Fielding, Mr. Murdock . . ."

"No!" In the multivoiced pandemonium, Hattie's instinctive denial rang loudest. The felicitations died a sudden death, and in the ensuing

silence, all eyes turned to her. She stared at Jacob as if he'd suddenly grown a second head. Married?

He couldn't. She was barely growing accustomed to having to share his affections at all. He was her special person; he couldn't get *married*. Not only was he supposed to wait for her, but Jane-Ellen wouldn't let him tease her anymore and make her laugh, or bestow those light kisses that made her feel so special. Jane-Ellen would take him away. Oh, her insides felt simply *awful*.

She became aware that everyone was staring at her. Expected behavior. *This*, then, was what Aunt Augusta had *really* been talking about. This was what a young girl aspiring to be a lady had to do even though her stomach roiled with rebellion and she wanted to scream and kick and say, *"Sonovabitch!"* Even though she wanted to declare, *"You can't* do *this!"*

Hattie licked her lips nervously and pasted on a weak smile. Knowing her first social lie was expected of her, she opened her mouth twice before the words came. Finally, hoping her voice wouldn't crack, she said, "I mean"—she swallowed hard—"isn't that nice?"

6

First Presbyterian Church
SATURDAY, SEPTEMBER 30, 1899

THE CHURCH WAS filled to capacity. It had been autumn a full week, but the soft rain drizzling down the stained-glass windows, along with the filled-to-capacity interior, made the chapel warm and steamy. Clothing rustled beneath the organ music as necks craned to catch a first glimpse of the bride, poised on her father's arm, in the doorway at the base of the aisle.

At the altar, Jake had eyes only for the bride. He stared at Jane-Ellen in wonder, thinking, *Tonight. Tonight* would be the culmination of all his erotic longings. Finally, to learn the feel of her without the constrictive presence of whalebone between them. Finally, to have the right to teach her the physical aspect of love. The service couldn't be performed fast enough to suit him.

The bride, on the other hand, looked at her groom up at the altar staring at her with hot eyes and was seriously tempted to call the whole thing off. He was so dark! When had that happened? When she first met Jake, less than six months after his return home from Seattle, he'd been fashionably pale. Apparently, his time spent at the ranch this past year had weathered him, and he no longer looked tame and easygoing. No, he looked dark and dangerous.

Gracious sakes, but she wished her mother were still alive! She needed someone to talk to, for no one had prepared her; no one had told her what to expect. Well, Aunt Clara, who had come to help with the wedding arrangements, had spent a few moments with her while she was dressing this afternoon. But all she'd said about consummating a marriage was a wife must endure.

Endure what exactly? An act necessitating endurance didn't sound promising. Aunt Clara also said the wedding night might be painful the first time, but to recite scriptures to herself and the things her new husband did to her would soon be over. No amount of cajoling, however, would elicit the information Jane-Ellen most needed to know: what exactly *did* a man and woman do once they were married?

Her father surreptitiously squeezed her hand on his arm, and they began their stately march down the aisle. The palpable admiration of the wedding guests turning to watch her procession helped dissolve some of Jane-Ellen's tension. It also served to remind her she wanted to be Mrs. Jacob Murdock. Nobody was forcing her into this marriage. She was indulging in a case of the vapors; that was all. Fashionably pale or dangerously dark, she knew Jake's basic personality wouldn't change. She didn't believe for a moment this perpetually laughing man would ever deliberately harm her. But she still wished someone had told her what to expect.

In the front row of the assembled guests, Hattie sat ramrod straight on the hard pew, her chin at its most imperious angle. In the ten measly weeks since Jake had announced his nuptials, she'd more or less resigned herself. She supposed it was unrealistic to think he would ever marry her. He was a grown-up man and she was just a kid. During the past two months, he'd gone out of his way to tell her—and attempted to show her—he would still be there for her, married or not. She guessed she would simply have to be content with that.

Which was all well and good, but it didn't address the fact that she was left sitting in church surrounded by people who disapproved of her. Today even more old busybodies were in attendance than the usual assortment she saw at regular Sunday services. She hadn't missed Miss Eunice Peabody's comment to Miss Martha Smits earlier when she and

Aunt Augusta passed their pew. Even when speaking sneakily, Miss Peabody's voice carried. "There's that Taylor hellion," she'd hissed in her strident whisper. "Looks like butter wouldn't melt in her mouth, don't she? Well, mark my words, Martha, that red hair of hers signifies a wild nature."

Hattie had thought her whispered, "Pruney-faced old harpy," was said under her breath, but Aunt Augusta had squeezed her hand warningly. Augusta had also stopped and greeted the two old biddies with regally flawless manners, relentlessly holding their gazes until they were flushed and squirming. Once they'd been properly subdued, Augusta calmly ushered Hattie up the aisle to their front-row pew.

Hattie didn't understand why people said mean stuff about her. She wasn't so wild. Well, okay, there had been that one incident at school with Moses Marks. But, heck, even he had agreed he'd brought it on himself.

Just before the beginning of the school year, Augusta had decided Hattie was ready to attend the local school. John Fiske had been dismissed with glowing references, and Hattie had joined her peers in class.

On the Friday of her first week in attendance, Moses Marks, who sat directly behind her, had surreptitiously dipped her braid in his inkwell during lessons. When Hattie rose for lunch with the rest of her schoolmates, her hair, slapping against her back, had splattered the ink all over. Her dress had been ruined.

Naturally she'd tried to knock his block off; who wouldn't have? And it wasn't as if she'd broken his nose or anything—it had simply bled a lot. But the way people acted, you woulda thought he hadn't had it coming.

Moses himself hadn't held it against her. They had hissed insults at each other as they'd stood with their noses pressed in the middle of the two circles the teacher had chalked on the blackboard. But his face had crumpled with genuine distress when she'd arrived at school the following day with her hair a noticeable three inches shorter. He swore he hadn't realized the ink wouldn't wash out and gave her a cookie come lunchtime by way of apology. And that was that.

So why couldn't everyone else forget about it?

Hattie swallowed a lump in her throat as she watched Jake and Jane-Ellen exchange vows. What was it that caused a person to like another above all others, the way she liked Jake? Was it because he was so affectionate, always tussling with her or hugging her or kissing her nose? Was it because he was always laughing? He alone in the whole town, it seemed, had found her problem with Moses amusing—and applauded the way they'd worked out their differences.

She experienced such a surge of pleasure every time she caught sight of Jake. And something inside ached as she watched him pledge his troth to Jane-Ellen Fielding, even though Jane-Ellen had always been nice to her and Hattie actually liked her a great deal.

Not until the ceremony ended did Hattie breathe easier. Now all she had to get through was the party at the Buchannan.

No one appeared to enjoy the wedding reception quite as much as Jake Murdock. He drank champagne, danced with all the ladies, joked with the men, and through it all, he never stopped laughing. His happiness and high spirits affected everyone, including Jane-Ellen, despite her growing nerves over the upcoming wedding night.

At one point in the festivities, Jake found himself standing momentarily alone. He watched his mother waltz by with Doc Fielding, her face politely blank when Doc trod on her toes. Over in the corner stood Roger Lord, stiff and aloof as usual. A strange man, Roger—arrogant and difficult to warm up to. He'd been their family lawyer for several years now, and Jake had worked with him for almost a year—yet he felt as if he barely knew the man. As soon as Jake and Jane-Ellen returned from their honeymoon, Jake planned to set up his own practice, and he looked forward to creating a work atmosphere more congenial than Roger's offices.

A flash of red caught his eye, and his mouth curved in a smile against his champagne glass as he observed Hattie. She was trapped in conversation with Aurelia Donaldson, one of Mattawa society's guiding lights. A favorite affectation of Aurelia's was an old-fashioned lorgnette, which she wielded to great effect. As he watched, she alternated between peering fiercely through the lenses at the bristling little redhead standing before her and tapping the frame against Hattie's arm to underscore a point in her conversation. Hattie was clearly struggling to remain polite, but she looked seconds away from snatching the mounted glasses and snapping them in two.

Before Jake could push away from the wall to go to her rescue, Jane-Ellen swept up, exchanged a few remarks with Aurelia, and deftly whisked Hattie away.

Hattie's flaming mop reminded Jake of his going-away party at Mamie Parker's establishment the evening before announcing their engagement. Not that Mamie's hennaed hair compared with the natural brilliance of Hattie's, but it was dyed in a close enough approximation to elicit a small synapse of remembrance. Mamie had lamented Jake's upcoming marriage, swearing over the tinny piano music that her girls threatened to don black to mourn their favorite customer's passage from bachelor to husband. She'd grinned around the black cheroot clenched between her teeth and told him his next visit was on the house.

"Thank you kindly," he'd replied. "But as of tomorrow, my heart belongs to Jane-Ellen."

"Honey, she can have your heart," Mamie had replied with a dirty laugh. "What I want is a whole lot farther south."

Jake had grinned and left it at that. But he had every intention of being a faithful husband. He had a whole lot of love to give, and he'd merely been whiling away the hours with Mamie's girls until Jane-Ellen was his. He wouldn't have gone to them at all if Jane-Ellen had allowed him to express his love with a little more freedom than a few openmouthed kisses.

He'd rather hoped that once engaged, Jane-Ellen wouldn't find it quite as necessary to adhere so rigidly to the rules. But she was highly moral, his Jane-Ellen. And the few times he'd tried to touch her breasts, she'd frozen in shock and indignation.

Well, hallelujah, they were legally married. In a few short hours, his very own wife would supply everything he'd formerly obtained from Mamie's girls. *More*, because he loved Jane-Ellen.

Jake grinned broadly and straightened from his indolent slouch against the wall. Slipping his empty champagne glass onto a passing waiter's tray, he spied his wife in the crowd. He swooped down on her, laughing, and swept her onto the dance floor for a waltz around the ballroom.

7

It was Jake Murdock's wedding night. Roger Lord turned away from the rain-streaked window and crossed the room to take a chair in front of the unlit fireplace. For several long moments, he stared broodingly at the prearranged kindling and logs; then he rose to tug the bell pull. The logs required only a match to set them ablaze, but Roger saw no reason to do a chore himself when there were servants to do it for him. He poured a brandy and resumed his seat.

The maid entering the room was young and nervous. She shot an apprehensive glance at Roger and scurried to do his bidding. As she was leaving moments later, his voice stopped her. "When I looked in on her, my wife was asleep."

The girl nodded jerkily. "Yes, sir. She wanted to stay awake to hear all about the wedding, but she fell asleep quite early this evening."

He nodded as well. Gertrude had been quite animated when she'd asked him to make note of all the details so he could relate them to her. She was a good woman. But she'd been an invalid for years now and was frail. "Wait for me in my room," he commanded the maid, enjoying the fear that entered her eyes. He watched her hurry out of the library and thought about Jane-Ellen Murdock, Jake's new bride.

It was obvious she was a virgin. One, moreover, who was clearly terrified of the night ahead—and no doubt damn near everything else the least bit earthy. The mere thought of tearing into that tender, unused body, of looking into her eyes and seeing her pain, her fear and revulsion, aroused him tremendously. She was perfect, just ripe for the teaching.

And utterly wasted on the likes of Jake Murdock.

He'd heard the talk at Mamie Parker's place. They said that even with the whores Jake took his time and tried to ensure their enjoyment. Their enjoyment, for Christ's sake! The man was a fool. Worse than that, after working with him Roger knew Jake possessed an even more damning weakness: he was a damn bleeding heart.

Roger didn't understand. Murdock was a superior personage by right of birth. He was a member of the higher classes, he was *male*, and he had a standing to uphold in the community. Yet more than once he'd accepted pro bono cases over Roger's objections.

It was ludicrous, a man of such obvious breeding wasting his very real legal talents, working gratis to solve the problems of people of the lowest echelon!

Watching Jake misuse his rightful powers filled Roger with contempt.

He detested weakness but exploited it where he could. There were times, however, when a situation could not be turned to one's advantage no matter how much research one put into it. Tonight was one of those. Jake had an opportunity for which Roger would give much—that of breaking in a well-born virgin. And the fool was going to mishandle that, too.

A woman should be dominated from the onset, trained to know her place. Not looking at it that way was Murdock's weakness. A man who tried to give whores pleasure with his God-given sword hardly displayed the necessary intelligence to indoctrinate his new bride to her proper place. Oh, what Roger would give—

He was bored with debauching servants. It was too damn easy; all he really had to do was ensure the women entering his employ lacked a family to look after them. Where was the challenge in that for a man of his superior intellect? His deepest desire was a chance at someone like Jane-Ellen, a complete innocent whose descent into pain and fear would be all the sweeter for having been sheltered all her life.

Gertrude had begun fading away these past few years, and he didn't believe she was long for this world. He supposed he could always remarry—the mamas of Mattawa loved parading their fragile flowers under his nose, even with his invalid wife still alive. But ultimately fear left a woman's eyes and resignation took its place. And who wanted to be saddled with a whining female once the thrill was gone? Not when it was a simple matter to write an excellent reference for his current toy, then put the maid on a train to Eugene or Portland and move on to the next.

It galled Roger that a fool like Jake should be awarded a prize like Jane-Ellen when there were men eminently worthier to show her her place. Cursing softly, he finished his drink.

Then he retired to his room to wreak vengeance upon the hapless body of the latest in a succession of orphaned, friendless servant girls.

IT WAS JAKE and Jane-Ellen's wedding night. Hattie sat on the edge of her bed to tug off her shoes, wiggling her toes the instant she liberated them. She'd overheard two men at the reception laughing and exchanging low-voiced jests about wedding nights and fornication. Was that what Jake and Jane-Ellen were doing?

Hattie had a vague knowledge of fornication, gleaned from overheard snatches of conversation and by once sneaking into the stud barn at the ranch to watch a stallion cover a mare. The stallion had possessed this huge, glistening thing between his rear legs, which he'd plunged into the mare. He had then worked it in and out with powerful thrusts of his haunches, and it had made Hattie feel very peculiar. Repelled for the most part. Yet a bit drawn by the act as well. She remembered feeling flushed and sort of weak, and to her embarrassment she especially remembered the strange lightning-like darts of sensation streaking through the not-to-be-mentioned private place between her legs.

Was that how Jane-Ellen felt right now? Did Jake possess one of those things like the stallion, and if so, where did he hide an extremity of such size during the day?

Wearing only her white silk stockings, rolled, then twisted around a penny to secure them above her knees, Hattie glanced guiltily around the room as if Mirabel or Aunt Augusta might appear at any moment to deliver a lecture on the virtues of maidenly modesty. When no one materialized, she crossed to stand in front of the cheval glass. She stared at herself in the mirror.

Her body had been undergoing a great many changes recently, and criminy was it confusing. She was growing bosoms. At first, they'd merely been two barely there swellings on her chest. Then the little flat disks in the center of them had puffed up. That had kind of shaken her, so she'd asked Aunt Augusta about it.

Augusta, usually so unflappable, had grown all flustered and turned red. But not one to shirk her duty, she'd finally informed Hattie the disks were called nipples and what Hattie was experiencing was natural for a girl nearly twelve years old.

Feeling ever so much better, Hattie had tried to work the new word into a couple conversations, but that had only landed her in all sorts of trouble. Like "sonovabitch," "nipples" was a word apparently best discarded if you didn't want your mouth washed out with soap.

Looking at herself in the mirror, Hattie had to admit her bosoms were beginning to assume a womanly shape, having grown beyond that first immature swelling. They weren't as fully developed as a grown-up lady's, but already their new shape had attracted some unsolicited attention. The least amount of activity seemed to make them bounce beneath her thin chemise, and just last week she'd completed her turn at the jump rope and looked up to find Moses Marks turning four shades of red as he stared at her chest.

Imagine what his face would look like if he saw what was happening to her private place.

If "nipples" wasn't a word to be bandied about, she didn't have to be told her secret place was not a topic for polite conversation. It was growing *hair* and she needed to talk to someone about it. But imagine asking about that at the dinner table! Lord, she wished Aunt Augusta hadn't been so uncomfortable over the nipples inquiry. Why on earth was this happening to her?

She studied the sparse ginger-colored wisps in the mirror and worried what people said about her might be true. Maybe she *was* wild. True, the hoity-toity girls at school had taken Hattie accidentally flashing her knickers climbing the schoolyard tree and blown it *way* out of proportion. They'd even blabbed to their parents, which Hattie learned when it got back to Aunt Augusta. So, was this new development on her secret place a brand testifying to her wildness?

But if that were so, wouldn't it be placed in a more conspicuous spot for all to see? Pastor Stone loved to thunder about the wages of sin, but Hattie didn't see how that applied to her. Biggest sin she'd ever committed was helping Moses put that little garter snake in Miss Cooper's desk, and that wasn't even a real sin, was it?

She had never killed, stole, coveted, or lied. Well, okay, she'd told a number of half-truths this past year, but according to Aunt Augusta that was deemed acceptable behavior. Like remarking on the pretty color of Miss Martha Smits' gown when asked how she liked it, instead of pointing out the style made her look like a pumpkin.

Hattie donned her nightgown. The hoity-toity girls didn't like her much. They either ridiculed her or ignored her, and she knew from comments they made they didn't consider her as properly civilized as she should be.

So, clearly, she couldn't ask one of them if they experienced anything the likes of which she was undergoing. The farm girls were nicer, but they kind of stuck together and left the minute school was over to lend a hand on their ranches or farms. The boys liked her better, but she was pretty sure this was one of those things where it was best not to solicit a boy's opinion.

Hattie climbed into bed and picked up Lillian, who spent more time on the pillows these days. She hugged the doll to her chest, trying to alleviate the feeling of emptiness there. She hated to cry, hated the loss of control, but hot tears leaked from the corners of her eyes despite her efforts to stop them.

There was only one person she felt she could ask about the strange things happening to her without embarrassment. Only one person who would not be horrified, talk about her behind her back, or ridicule her. But he was on his wedding night.

JAKE HAD RESERVED a suite at the Buchannan, where their reception was held. Tomorrow he and Jane-Ellen were leaving for a two-week honeymoon up in Seattle. Tonight, he opened the door to their room and swept Jane-Ellen up in a billow of lace and satin. Stepping over the threshold, he kicked the door closed behind them. Still holding her against his chest, he whirled in a circle and laughed down at her. "Welcome to your honeymoon suite, Mrs. Murdock."

Jane-Ellen smiled up at him with radiant joy. It momentarily eclipsed the fear, which had steadily increased as the evening shadows grew longer across the ballroom floor. She tightened her arms around his neck. "Mrs. Murdock! Oh, Jake, that sounds so wonderful." She raised her mouth to bestow a warm, chaste kiss on his lips.

Jake was swamped by a nearly overwhelming emotion. He had an urgent desire to devour her, like a wolf tossed a scrap of raw meat after being tethered just beyond reach of a meal. Starved for her affection, he wanted to sink his teeth in, slake this awful hunger, and take without regard to fine manners, finesse, or gentleness.

Shaken by his impulses, he very carefully returned Jane-Ellen's virginal kiss and set her on her feet. Running a finger beneath his stiff celluloid collar, he glanced around the suite, grateful to spy the service trolley in the sitting room. "Good, they sent up the tray I ordered. Sit down and let me serve you. You barely touched a bite downstairs." He seated his new bride on the silk-covered settee and pulled up a small table in front of her. He dished up portions of oysters, prime rib, steamed carrots, and flaky oven-fresh rolls. He poured her a glass of champagne, watched her take a few sips, then hand-fed her bites from his own plate.

And all the while his need grew, simmering and percolating below his surface attentiveness.

After their meal, Jake drew a bath for Jane-Ellen and left the bathroom to give her privacy. Then he spent what seemed an eternity pacing and trying to gain control over the emotions rampaging through him like spooked cattle. God, he'd waited a long time for this! But he needed to cool down. He already knew she was apprehensive. She'd die of fright if he went at her like a mad dog.

Jake eyed the opened champagne bottle longingly but saved it for Jane-Ellen. She'd need it to relax her. He, on the other hand, could make it easier for her by keeping his wits about him.

He crossed to his portmanteau and extracted the case holding his straight-edge razor and badger-hair shaving brush. After setting them atop the dresser, he removed his collar and cuffs and added them to the growing clutter. With nothing left to do, he examined the room's furnishings and stared out the window at Commercial Street two stories below. Finally, he pulled out his timepiece, snapped it open, and checked the time. Was she *ever* coming out of there?

FOR THE TENTH time, Jane-Ellen rearranged the fit of her fine lawn night rail. She studied her reflection in the wavy mirror, looked around the room, and knew she'd delayed as long as she could. Heart beating heavily, she opened the door a crack and slipped through.

Jake crossed the room, stopping to pour her more champagne before coming to stand in front of her. He extended the flute to her. "You look beautiful," he murmured in the deepest voice she'd ever heard.

"Thank you," she whispered and sipped her champagne. Her heart pounded as her new husband ushered her over to the bed. "Wait here," he instructed in a gentle voice. "Have more champagne if you like. I'll only be moments." Gathering his grooming supplies off the bureau, he went into the bathroom and closed the door.

He must have raced through his toilet, for he was back in record time, wearing only a towel around his midsection. Jane-Ellen's eyes flared wide in panic. Wasn't he going to put on a nightshirt?

The mattress dipped as Jake sat on the side of the bed and reached for her. She tried to relax but couldn't shake the stiffness in her spine as she allowed Jake's embrace. When he would have kissed her, however, she whispered, "Jake, the lights."

"I want to look at you."

Dear God. "Please."

He got up and doused the lights. Then, in a darkness only slightly relieved by the dim glow of a streetlamp down on the corner of Commercial and Main, Jake crossed back to the bed. Dropping his towel on the floor, he climbed under the covers. He rolled over and pulled her into his arms. "God," he said hoarsely. "I thought this day would never come." He kissed her.

Jane-Ellen had never truly grown accustomed to Jake's openmouthed kisses, but she tried desperately to relax and respond. Her arms around his neck held him limply as she lay waiting for what would happen to happen. Time seemed to stretch endlessly before Jake's mouth left hers and he trailed his lips down her throat, pressing kisses into her skin. He slipped the tiny buttons of her night rail from their loops and she couldn't stop herself from going rigid as her nightgown parted down the front.

"Shh," he whispered with the same softness he'd use to soothe a fractious mare. His fingertips gently brushed over her collarbones. "Easy, sweetheart. I'll be gentle. It can be so beautiful, Jane-Ellen. You'll see." His mouth moved lower, pressing soft kisses across her chest. Slowly, one of his hands lowered to carefully cup her breast.

"Noo," she moaned and hunched her shoulders.

"It's okay, sweetheart. Easy, now. It's okay." He kissed her nipple lightly, as if not to cause her the least discomfort. "God, I love you. You are so beautiful."

His words were a balm, but they didn't compensate for the embarrassment of having all her private places exposed and touched. Jane-Ellen squeezed her eyes shut, praying he would just get it over with. But when his hand smoothed down over her belly, moving lower, her eyes flew open. He wouldn't dare!

He dared. His fingers moved between her thighs and she wanted to die of mortification. Not even she touched herself there except when absolutely necessary for hygienic purposes. It was unthinkable, and, oh dear Lord, his fingers were separating her.

When Jake slid his fingers between Jane-Ellen's legs, he found her completely dry. Bringing his fingers to his mouth, he gathered some moisture off his tongue and returned them to lubricate the arid folds. Something curdled deep inside him when his actions made her shudder with revulsion. Jesus, being scared was one thing. But didn't she desire him at all? He pushed up on one elbow and looked down at her. "Jane-Ellen, did anyone tell you what to expect?"

"N-no."

"Shit," he breathed and raked a hand through his hair. Lifting her right hand, he brought it, resisting, to his chest. In easy stages, he smoothed it across his pectorals and down the ridged muscles of his stomach, before descending to his lower abdomen until her fingertips touched the thick tangle of hair surrounding his phallus. He raised her palm to brush his erection.

She struggled to extricate her hand, but carefully Jake wrapped it around the throbbing thickness and whispered, "It's okay, Jane-Ellen. This is a cock." He released her hand and she snatched it away.

Tenderly, he ran a finger down the cleft between her legs and pushed his middle fingertip against the portal of her vagina. "It goes in here."

"No!" she protested. "It's too big; that can*not* be right."

His finger circled the small muscular ring guarding her entrance, attempting to stretch it out a little to ease her coming discomfort. "It is right, sweetheart. This is the way we make love . . . and how babies are made. I know you don't think so at the moment, but it can feel good, Jane-Ellen. Let me show you."

He returned his mouth to her breast and his newly redampened fingers between her legs. Jane-Ellen went rigid with obvious distaste. She rejected every overture he made, clearly neither knowing nor caring about the discipline he exerted over his own emotions. He could practically hear her thinking, *Please, let him stop touching me and just do what he has to do.*

Finally, Jake rolled on top of her and gently spread her resisting legs. Her obvious repugnance had killed his joyous anticipation, and the most he could hope for was that once he breached her maidenhead, she'd relax enough to begin feeling the pleasure that could be hers. Very carefully, he aligned himself with her virginal opening.

As he gently pushed forward, Jane-Ellen's eyes opened wide. She tried to close her legs, which was impossible with Jake's hips firmly entrenched between them. He thrust in a tiny bit farther, a feat made difficult by the dryness of her passage.

"Jake, stop!" his new bride said. "Please, don't do this. It hurts."

"I'm sorry, sweetheart." He held himself very still. "Try to relax. It'll be so much easier for you."

Relax? Jane-Ellen stared at him in disbelief. He could *not* be serious. Her most private place was being torn apart by an object a simpleton could tell was much too large to fit inside it, and he was telling her to *relax*? Why didn't he just stop? This was horrible! She inhaled with relief as she felt him begin to withdraw. Then suddenly he lunged forward. She felt something tear, and pain she never knew existed exploded inside her. Jane-Ellen opened her mouth to scream, but Jake's hand was there to muffle the sound.

"Shh, shh, now. It's done." He removed the hand gagging her and brushed away her tears. He kissed her tenderly. "You're no longer a virgin, Jane-Ellen, and it will never hurt like that again. Easy, sweetheart. Give yourself a minute and the pain will go away."

He was correct; the pain did fade. But still that large intrusive part of him was inside her, and it made her feel dirty and vile. When he suddenly began to move, at first slowly and then with gathering speed, she whimpered and tightened all her muscles in protest. The pain returned, all the worse for having been momentarily eased.

Peeking up at him through narrowed eyes, she was horrified to see Jake's face that of a stranger: teeth bared, eyes blindly staring—and the low sounds he made frightened and disgusted her. She remembered Aunt Clara's advice and, knowing now what it was she must endure, she began to recite scriptures in her head. Quite suddenly, Jake's head reared back, his hips thrust forward, and a longer, louder groan rattled in his throat. A second later he collapsed. Oh, thank goodness; was it finally over?

Jake pushed up on his arms, relieving her of his weight, and tenderly brushed wisps of hair away from her face. "Are you all right?"

"Y-yes. I think so." He rolled off her and Jane-Ellen grimaced at the rush of hot liquid streaming between her thighs. Burning with embarrassment, she stammered, "Uh, Jake?" Oh goodness, how could she tell him she had wet herself? She would just die.

But Jake, discerning her problem, threw back the blankets. He scooped a bit of white fluid from her thigh, visibly winced at the amount of blood mixed with it, then determinedly brought it up to show her. "This is my seed. I transfer it to you when I'm inside you, and when it meets your eggs, it makes babies."

For God's sake. Jane-Ellen closed her eyes. She had always found Jake to be delicate in his dealings with her, but tonight she was seeing a different side of his personality. One she didn't appreciate one bit. Men simply did not discuss bodily functions with women—of *course* she was appalled at his lack of decorum. She pulled her night rail together and began buttoning it with trembling hands. When Jake reached out to gather her in his arms, she shrugged him away and rolled to the edge of the bed. "I'm going to the necessary."

Jake dropped back onto the pillows and watched his new wife hobble to the bathroom like a woman decades beyond her age. How had things gotten so out of hand? This was supposed to be the happiest day of his life.

Give her a chance, Murdock, a voice whispered in his brain. *The poor thing lost her virginity tonight. It was obviously a traumatic experience for a gently reared girl. Especially one no one bothered to tell what to expect, so she would be prepared. But things will get better.*

Unfortunately, even when Jane-Ellen returned to bed and allowed him to hold her in his arms, Jake could sense her censorious regard. And long after she slept, he lay awake.

Filled with an awful, hollow feeling in the pit of his stomach.

8

Murdock Ranch
SUNDAY, AUGUST 4, 1900

SOMETHING SHARP STUNG Hattie's neck and she slapped her hand against the spot. She thought she'd been stung by a bee. But the skin of her palm encountered a small, soggy lump of paper. Oh, for pity's sake, it was a spit wad. Peeling it off her neck, she looked over her shoulder into the grinning face of the culprit. "Clever, Moses. Very mature."

Moses shrugged unrepentantly and dropped to sit cross-legged beside her. His white-blond hair glinted in the brilliant sunlight. "We're twelve. Ain't s'posed to be mature." He helped himself to a piece of her watermelon. "This is good. Wanna have a seed-spitting contest?"

Ordinarily she'd love to, but she felt less than chipper all of a sudden. She had no idea why. Until now, she'd been having a grand time. It was a hot summer day, and the Murdocks had opened their ranch for a church social. Hattie had eaten her share of sweets this afternoon. But she'd never suffered from overindulgence in the past, and it hadn't slowed her down during the sack races or the penny hunt through the hay pile. She'd simply enjoyed running and laughing with the boys, relishing the heat beating down on her hatless head.

Then out of nowhere a band of pain had gripped her stomach and lower back, her head felt achy, and stranger still, her bosoms hurt. Suddenly the noise and laughter grated on her nerves, and most mysterious of all, she felt like crying.

So, she refused his offer. "I'm not feeling so good," she said by way of explanation when he showed signs of persisting. "I think I'm gonna walk down by the creek."

"You want company?"

Unaccountably, Hattie's temper rose, tempting her to snap at him. "No, thanks," she retorted with strained patience. "I just wanna be by myself for a little while." Offering him the rest of her plate, she stood and walked away.

Once she had distanced herself from the festivities, her mood lightened. She followed the creek through a patch of woods and out the other side to a spot where the banks widened and the creek formed a shallow pool. This was one of her favorite spots in all of Mattawa. She'd discovered it last summer, shortly after coming to live with Aunt Augusta.

Hattie sat on the grassy bank and struggled with her shoes. They weren't easy to unfasten without her buttonhook, but finally she freed her feet and quickly rolled down her stockings, grabbing their toes to pull them off. After carefully placing the thin stockings in her shoes, she gathered up her skirts and petticoat and stepped into the water.

Glacier fed somewhere in the Cascades, it was ice-cold even on the hottest days, and Hattie hissed in a breath at the shock of it. Its temporarily numbing chill, however, didn't prevent her from edging across the pebbled creek bed until she was immersed to her knees.

Then, growing accustomed to the chill, she sighed with pleasure. She was tempted to strip down to her chemise and drawers so she could plunge into the depths of the pool where it deepened in the lee of a jutting outcrop of boulders. If the ranch wasn't swarming with people, she'd have already done so. Thinking about the privacy she'd lost, she experienced a flash of resentment toward the church congregation for overrunning the ranch.

And promptly felt ashamed of herself. Criminy, the ranch wasn't even hers; she didn't understand her sudden possessiveness and grumpy mood at all. Climbing out of the creek, she collapsed on the grassy bank and sat with her legs thrust out in front of her, skirts cocked around her thighs to allow the sun access to her damp skin.

It wasn't like her to give in to such mean-spirited moodiness. If she was happy, she generally smiled and laughed. If she was angry, she yelled. If she was sad, she cried—but in private, if possible, because she hated the defenseless, out-of-control feeling crying created. It was bad enough to find herself a helpless victim of tears. The last thing she needed was to have another person witness them.

So, her disposition was ordinarily straightforward. It wasn't like her to be having a grand time at a church picnic one minute, then resenting the people who helped organize it the next.

Heavy cramping in her lower back and stomach struck suddenly, and Hattie's knees pulled into her chest in an instinctive attempt to lessen the pain. Wrapping her arms around her shins, she hugged her legs tightly to her body and rolled into a fetal position on her side.

What in mercy's name was the matter with her? She was getting scared and for the first time realized perhaps wandering away from the crowd hadn't been in her best interests. When the pain lessened a little, she pushed to a sitting position and reached for her stockings.

She was just working her toes into the first one when she felt a warm, liquid rush between her legs. Skirts canted up around her hips, she stared in horror at the blood slowly spreading a darkening red stain across the pristine white crotch of her drawers.

"Hello, Moses."

"Hiya, Mr. Murdock. This is some swell picnic."

"It turned out pretty nice, didn't it? Have you seen Hattie around?"

Moses swallowed the too-large bite of apple pie he'd just forked into his mouth. Knuckling the crumbs off his mouth, he replied, "She said she didn't feel so hot. Last I saw of her, she was heading for the creek. Said she wanted to be alone when I offered t'go with her."

"Okay, I'll track her down from here. Thanks."

"Sure thing, Mr. Murdock." Moses scraped the last of the pie into his mouth and headed back to the dessert-laden table.

Jake struck out for the woods, glad to leave the festivities. In the ten months since his marriage, he'd had less and less reason to laugh, and it was exhausting pretending to be happy when he wasn't. It didn't help knowing he had no one to blame for his predicament but himself.

The signs had all been there, but he'd refused to read them. Jane-Ellen hadn't changed overnight; she was still the sweet girl she'd always been. He couldn't even fool himself into thinking she'd tricked him by pretending to be enamored of his physical advances before their marriage. The truth was, he'd been so eager to believe she was anticipating the intimacies of marriage as much as he was, he had willfully ignored every indication to the contrary.

If he hadn't allowed himself to be so ruled by lust every time she was near, he might have noticed she disdained his tongue when they were kissing, that she knocked his hand away whenever it trespassed in the vicinity of her breasts.

He blew out a frustrated breath. He might have noticed they actually had very little in common. But, no. He had let his cock do his thinking and now he was reaping what he'd sown.

Yet . . . what twenty-three-year-old man didn't? Jake bent to scoop up a few stones and furiously flung one at a felled tree. What the hell had he ever done to deserve being shackled for life to a woman who found his touch repulsive? He winged another rock, watching it hit the exact same spot. *Repulsive*, for Christ's sake! He hammered the spot again with his last stone.

A caustic, humorless smile twisted Jake's mouth. Well, how the mighty had fallen. The uncontested prince of the pleasure palaces not only couldn't arouse his own wife; she found his touch repugnant. What a bitter joke. Too damn bad he'd forgotten how to laugh.

Impatient with his self-pity, Jake wondered what ailed Hattie. She'd looked the height of health when he'd noticed her earlier skipping rope, skirts flying, fat braid bouncing, its ribbon trailing untidily as usual into the explosion of curls beneath its constricting knot. If she'd been stuffing herself at the same rate as her friend Moses, she probably had a stomachache, although according to Mirabel she possessed a cast-iron constitution that was decidedly undeserved.

Stepping from dim woods to sunshine was momentarily blinding, but not to the extent that he couldn't recognize Hattie down by the creek pool, naked as the day she was born, except for her chemise. A smile tugged the corner of his mouth. Hell, she'd just snuck off for a swim.

Then her frantic movements made a frown furrow his brow. Why was she splashing water up her legs like a dog spraying dirt digging up a bone? As Jake drew closer he was shocked to see tears pouring down her cheeks and realized her actions were tainted by hysteria.

He broke into a run. "Hattie?"

Hattie's head snapped up. "Jake?" She scrambled out of the creek and threw herself into his arms. She was never so relieved to see anyone in her life. She'd torn off her dress, petticoat, and bloomers before wading kneedeep into the stream in a frantic attempt to rinse the blood away. But it kept trickling out of her despite her efforts to staunch it.

"Oh, Jake, there's something the matter with me. My stomach and back hurt so bad and I'm bleeding and it won't quit . . . uhh, jeez!" She bent double with a new cramp, her arms wrapped around her middle.

Jake scooped her up and carried her to a level spot on the grassy slope. Placing her on a patch, he sat beside her and whispered, "Shh, baby, it's okay. Show me where you're bleeding and I'll fix you up. Did you crack yourself on something?"

She clutched his pastel suspender in a frantic fist. "No, you don't understand. It just started for no reason at all, and it's coming out of my private place and won't stop. Please, we've got to stop it before I bleed to death. Please, Jake."

"Your private . . . ?" Jake froze. His one brief, involuntary glance down showed him budding breasts beneath Hattie's thin chemise—and wispy curls gracing her mound, lighter in color than the brilliant copper on her head. A bit of blood smeared her thighs. Oh.

Oh shit. He whipped his head in the other direction, staring determinedly through the trees as he kicked himself for being so wrapped up in his own life these past long months, he'd neglected to notice the changes she was undergoing. At the same time, he sagged with the relief of knowing she wasn't seriously hurt. "Hattie, honey, I think you're getting your first menses."

Jesus, the poor kid must have had a million and one questions and no one to answer them. He was filled with a quiet fury. Neither his mother, nor Mirabel, nor his wife, apparently, had seen fit to prepare her, and consequently she'd been unnecessarily terrified. His fury raged hotter at the damned hypocritical system deliberately fostering ignorance in its young women in the name of purity and morality.

He wanted to hit something for the fright Hattie had received and for Jane-Ellen's unnatural fear of sexual intimacy. Instead, he removed his handkerchief from his pocket, folded it into a pad, and, keeping his eyes averted, instructed her to press it between her legs. He gathered Hattie's clothes together, rinsed her soiled drawers, and spread them in the sun to dry. He instructed her to dress and watched the leaves of a nearby aspen flutter gently in the breeze. Finally, he resumed his seat next to her. After a brief hesitation, Jake pulled her onto his lap.

And began to talk.

Hattie listened with growing relief as Jake explained about menstruation and all the other bodily changes she'd been experiencing. He stressed it was a natural element of growing up, explained the reasons for the changes, and briefly described how babies were made.

Hattie had been in a state before his arrival. When Jake finished furnishing her with information covering every single thing worrying her, she was almost giddy with relief. Her stomach still hurt dreadfully, but she could cope with the pain now she knew it wouldn't kill her. Jake said there was medicine at the house to help ease her discomfort, collected her mostly dry knickers, and, back turned, handed them to her to pull on over the pad he'd made.

The medicine turned out to be a cordial glass filled nearly to the brim with straight whiskey, which burned her throat and made her cough. But it exploded warmly in her stomach and eased the awful pain gripping her innards. He assisted her slightly tipsy progress to her room and left her there, promising to send his mother.

A chastened Augusta entered Hattie's room a short while later. Jacob had lit into her furiously, and quite deservedly, she admitted. She couldn't help feeling, however, there was something else behind his unexpected tirade.

She hoped he wasn't changing his mind about him and Jane-Ellen living with her for the next year while he established his practice. True, no one had to twist his arm to gain his acceptance to Augusta's proposal, and his manner toward the family females was as it had always been.

Yet she couldn't help but sense a new tension in him since his marriage. All newlyweds underwent a period of adjustment, of course, but Jake and Jane-Ellen had been married nearly a year. All Augusta knew for sure was that Jacob didn't laugh as frequently as he used to, so perhaps his sudden dip in humor was because he was chafing beneath the lack of privacy.

She mentally shrugged as she gazed at the young girl she'd let down. She'd address Jacob's mood swings later. A more immediate apology needed to be made.

ONE WOULD NEVER guess Augusta was in the throes of a dilemma the next day if they saw her sitting serenely in her parlor, her face tranquil as she sipped her tea. But what in heaven's name was she going to do about Hattie's friendship with Moses? It was quite improper, now Hattie was officially a young woman.

Augusta knew she should put an immediate stop to it before the child's reputation was further damaged. As things stood, in the year Hattie had been here, she had yet to be fully accepted. A continuing friendship with the Marks boy now that Hattie was budding so rapidly into womanhood would only serve to alienate her further. Past a certain age, it was unheard of for a young man and woman to associate beyond a rigorously structured social setting. A setting that was carefully approved and chaperoned by responsible adults.

Quite rightly so, Augusta had always believed. And yet . . .

Moses was Hattie's only friend. The other young women in their social circle avoided her assiduously and, worse, carried tales home to their parents. Just envisioning her young ward's loneliness should Augusta insist on terminating Hattie's one and only friendship made her heart ache. Upon reflection, it also made her angry. No, it wasn't proper that a boy was Hattie's only friend. But neither, in Augusta's opinion, was total isolation. Hattie was gregarious and sweet, given half a chance. Unfortunately, that was something she *hadn't* been given in this town, except by Moses and the ranching community. And unfortunately, the latter didn't signify, if Hattie was to find a place in the society they moved in.

If Augusta did the proper thing, she knew perfectly well what Hattie's reaction would ultimately be. She was a headstrong girl who could only practice piano so many hours, only take so many solitary horseback rides. Sooner or later she'd rebel.

Plus, Moses Marks was a likable, presentable young pup, far more agreeable than a good many young women in this town. Yes, better by far if Augusta allowed their friendship to continue in the open where she could maintain supervision. Better than risking driving it underground where ideas thus far not even considered had an opportunity to flourish.

But, *Lord*, it was easier raising a boy! How unfair that males could get away with worlds more than girls. God knew, it wouldn't be Moses Marks the town whispered about if Augusta failed as a diligent overseer of the boy's friendship with her ward. No, indeed. It was Hattie's reputation that would tatter beyond repair. Yet Augusta felt she had to take that chance. She was quite sure having no one at all to call friend would destroy something vital in Hattie.

Please, God, help me guide that sweet child past the pitfalls of the next few years.

Then let her fondest wish be realized. Let Hattie someday find someone who would love her the way Augusta's Luke had once loved her. The way Jacob loved his Jane-Ellen.

THE WAY JACOB loved Jane-Ellen changed during the next several years. He had known the newly-in-love feeling couldn't last forever. But he'd expected it to gradually grow into something deeper, like the relationship he'd witnessed between his parents.

When Jane-Ellen repudiated an entire aspect of him, his love for her changed in directions he'd never envisioned. He pitied her for harboring such fear. He also resented it. And it wasn't always possible to rationalize away the pain her rejection caused or to take the sympathetic view. He was a man, dammit, a healthy, virile man. He hungered for a night with a woman who actually *enjoyed* that aspect, instead of fearing it. The best he could manage was accepting the fact he and Jane-Ellen had created false ideals of each other. Ideal mates who never existed outside their imaginations.

But Jake's love, once given, wasn't easily abandoned. He was hurt. He was sorry for Jane-Ellen's terror of intimacy. And he was angry. None of his needs were being met, but how could they be when his wife had no concept of desire? But he was bullheaded—a fighter who refused to relinquish his feelings without first giving their marriage his all.

Most of his life he'd been spoiled by women. He genuinely appreciated them and learned early how easily they were pleased by simple kindnesses and honest praise, traits that fostered their appreciation in return. So, since his first full day as a husband, he'd attempted to make what had worked for him in the past work for him now. He courted Jane-Ellen as assiduously after the wedding as he had before it. She was affectionate, sweet, and appreciative of his efforts. But it didn't change the fact that as each evening edged toward bedtime, her conversation grew forced, and she tensed up and suffered an inordinate number of headaches.

Jake thought buying their own home might make a difference, but his wife panicked at the mere suggestion. Jane-Ellen didn't want to leave Augusta's. With newfound cynicism, he decided she probably enjoyed the relative security of knowing he couldn't bother her during the day there. He began to spend less time at home, putting long hours into first establishing, then growing his law practice or going out to the ranch to exhaust himself with hard physical activity.

For more than four years he remained faithful. But the day arrived when he relinquished his last hope of making his wife desire him in any physical sense. In the last two years, it had become increasingly apparent that sexual matters between them were never going to change. He'd nonetheless hoped that, as was the case of the new century—bombastically coined an era of peace, prosperity, and progress—his personal life would also miraculously flourish. But he finally grew tired of waiting for changes that were never going to happen. Hell, he was tired of it all. Tired of catering to Jane-Ellen's fears; tired of denying his own needs; tired of feeling like a monster in his own bed. Until one night he finally said the hell with it and began frequenting Mamie Parker's establishment again.

Shortly after that, he realized he was happiest at the ranch. For as long as he could remember, he'd prepared to be an attorney. It was what his father had wanted for him, and as the child of a rancher, Jake, too, had dreamed of a sophisticated career in town.

But the boyhood fancy held little satisfaction for the man he'd become. There were moments he still loved practicing the law. More often, however, he felt stifled by the confines of his office. Ultimately, the day came when he walked into his suite of offices, sat down in his leather chair, and, seeing the spring day beckoning outside the window, knew he didn't want to do this for the next thirty years. He made arrangements to turn all except a few select clients over to the partner he'd taken on the previous year. He'd retain his license and practice in a limited capacity. But he'd do so from the ranch. He was going back to what he loved best.

He informed Jane-Ellen of his decision that evening and told her to pack her bags.

"Just like that?" she demanded. "No discussion?"

"Just like that," he agreed coolly. Frequenting whores had satisfied his body for a brief time but left him feeling hollow to the core. His law practice still provided an occasional thrill, yet mostly left him feeling like a caged wild animal.

This, at least, was something he could arrange to suit his needs—and nothing was going to stop him. "If you don't want to go with me, then stay here. If you're ready to let go of Augusta's apron strings, pack up. Either way, I'm moving out to the ranch tomorrow."

He started to leave the room but paused in the doorway. "If you're worried I'll suddenly begin demanding my rights as a husband five times a day, rest easy. I'm not planning to approach you any more frequently than I do at this time. I'd happily leave you alone entirely, Jane-Ellen, except I'd like to have a kid someday."

She flushed scarlet, manifestly mortified, humiliated, and relieved all at once. But gathering her dignity around her, she drew herself up proudly. "I am your wife," she said primly, ignoring his cynical smile. "Of course, I go where you go. Now, if you'll excuse me, I'll see to the arrangements."

Jake and Jane-Ellen Murdock, married four years, five months, two weeks, and six days, left Augusta's house the next day to establish their own home on the Murdock Ranch outside of town.

9

HATTIE SAT IN the tree outside her bedroom window, her hips wedged into the angle where sturdy branch met trunk, her feet braced against a lower limb. She wasn't invisible if one knew where to look. But for the moment at least she was hidden from view, which was her primary objective. She wanted to be alone.

Last night should have been a highlight in her life. She'd graduated high school, second in her class, in the Buchannan hotel ballroom. She'd worn a new white gown with pale yellow ribbons, and Augusta had arranged Hattie's hair in a Gibson Girl that had actually stayed up for the entire evening, a feat she never accomplished on her own.

Next week while Aunt Augusta and Mirabel embarked on a two-month trip to San Francisco, Hattie was moving out to the ranch, her favorite place in the world, to stay with Jake, her favorite person in the world, and Jane-Ellen, who was seven months pregnant.

Originally, she'd been scheduled to accompany her aunt on the trip, but on April 18 an earthquake leveled a large part of the California city and Augusta canceled Hattie's ticket. Augusta had family there and felt she might be of assistance. She didn't feel the need, however, to possibly endanger her ward.

Hattie much preferred staying at the ranch anyway. This would probably be her last unencumbered summer. In the fall, she was leaving for

Seattle Normal School to learn to be a teacher. All year she had been looking forward to the opportunity to experience life in a big city.

Everything should be bully, as President Roosevelt was fond of saying.

Well, it was easier to be bully when you were the youngest president in American history, popular, and loved for your rough-and-tumble crusade. Less easy was living in a small town that labeled you the resident bad-girl trouble maker. Hattie drummed her heels on the branch supporting them, sending a shower of bark filtering through the leaves to sprinkle the lawn below. She didn't understand how she'd come to acquire her reputation; it just seemed to start dogging her footsteps the instant she'd set foot in town.

Fine, sometimes she wasn't as tactful as she should be, but she was constantly working to correct the fault. And she did have a tendency to argue, occasionally quite loudly, and to point out some of the inequities in this town. And, yes, her hair was red. But, for goodness' sake, she had no control over that. The way people talked about it, however, one would think she'd intentionally chosen it for the sole purpose of irritating them. Nobody in their right mind would ever choose to be a redhead. If God had offered her the choice, she would have said, *Make me blond and refined like Jane-Ellen. Or brunette like Alice Roosevelt, who is my absolute idol. But, please, God, whatever You do, please please* please *don't give me red hair.*

God had clearly not consulted her, so therefore she had no control over the color. Sure didn't stop the town from talking about it as if it were the major contributor to her character, however, and there wasn't a blessed thing she could do except hold her head high.

But now they were saying she was *loose*? How on earth had they come to that conclusion? True, her ex–best friend was a boy. But she was half a year from turning nineteen—an age in this town equated with spinsterhood for unwed young women—and she had never even been properly kissed!

Tiny pebbles flew past her and rattled against her bedroom window. Peering down through the branches, she watched through narrowed eyes as Moses scooped up another handful and tossed them at the second story. Carefully, she drew as far into the sheltering screen of leaves as she could go.

"Hattie!" Moses hissed in a stage whisper. "I know you're up there. C'mon out and talk to me."

She kept quiet, hoping he'd give up and go away. But after waiting a few moments for a reply, he tossed another handful of pebbles, which bounced off her windowpane. "Hattie!"

"Oh, for . . ." She leaned down. "Go away!"

Moses tipped his head back and peered up at her. "There you are! Still mad at me, huh?"

"Yes! Git."

"Nah, I don't think so." Agilely, he climbed the tree until he was perched on an adjacent limb. Brawny arm looped around the trunk, feet braced on the branches below, he gazed down at her solemnly. Moses had grown considerably over the past few years and was both taller and more strapping than most full-grown men in Mattawa, so he occupied a sizable area. "I came to apologize and I'm gonna do it. I'm sorry about last night, Hattie. I let you down badly."

She eyed him coldly. "Do tell."

"C'mon, Hat. I said I was sorry."

"Oh, and that's supposed to make me feel better?" If eyes could flash lightning bolts, Hattie knew hers would be doing so. "By all means, then, I forgive you. After all, I realize you were quite bowled over by Florence-May Jordan's big blue eyes. Heavens, why should I have expected you to stick up for me when she and Barbara Norton were tearing my reputation to shreds in front of you? It's not as though you and I are *friends* or any-thing."

Moses flushed painfully from collarbone to hairline. "Oh shit," he whispered, and peered at her hopefully, waiting for her to exclaim, *Why, Moses Marks, I'm gonna tell your mama.*

But she remained silent, regarding him levelly with hurt and angry eyes. It was the hurt that really killed him, and he cleared his throat. "I don't have a good excuse, Hattie. Hell, I don't even have a weak one. I was flattered by Florence-May's attentions. And when she said those things about you, it made me mad, but I opted not to defend you because I was afraid it would ruin my chances of walking her home from the Commencement Ball. I've been dreamin' of stealing a kiss from that girl for the past six months."

"That's another thing!" Hattie snapped. "Florence-May Jordan has lived in this town for less than a year, and everybody just loves her to death. I've lived here for seven years, yet all of a sudden everybody's saying Hattie Taylor's 'no better than she should be.'"

"Well, maybe if you wore your damn corset once in a while—"

"What?!" Hattie snapped erect on her tree limb.

"Your corset, girl." Moses knew he was all red-faced again, this time with embarrassment, but he refused to look away. "Your figure is, it's . . . well, hell, it's lush. And the men in this town are noticing."

"Corsets," Hattie said with restrained vehemence, "are nothing more than—"

"Yeah, yeah; heard it before," Moses interrupted, "'one more instance of man perpetuating the myth of female subservience.' Well, in this case, girl, your failure to strap down what is a truly spectacular figure is giving every man in town ideas about you!"

Hattie looked genuinely baffled by the idea. "But I'm not pretty like Florence-May or—"

"What you are," he interrupted her, "is something a helluva lot more . . . exciting. You aren't pretty in the way currently popular, no. But men notice you. And women notice their men noticing. Your coloring is flamboyant, your posture is excellent, some say your mouth is downright wicked, and you're bold, Hattie, in both appearance and speech. If you're smart, you'll start lacing up your whalebone like every other decent woman in town. 'Cause, girl, men are getting an eyeful, watching you bouncin' and swayin', and they like the experience of feeling real flesh beneath your dress when they dance with you. They're starting to entertain notions."

"What sort of notions?"

"They're wondering what it would be like to help you warm up a cool set of sheets. I've heard them in my father's barbershop, talking about you."

"How dare they!" she screeched, shifting her weight on the branch with such agitation, she nearly fell out of the tree. Clinging to the trunk, she bristled with righteous indignation.

"Settle down, Hat. They're just wondering. No one's ever actually claimed to know you." She realized from the uncomfortable way he failed to meet her eyes that Moses was speaking in the biblical sense. A heat wave of rage and humiliation pulsed in her chest, her cheeks, her forehead.

"How truly magnanimous of them," she said through clenched teeth.

"Partly, I suppose," Moses said, "that's due to the realization if word ever got back to Jake, he'd kill them."

"How about the fact it simply isn't true?"

"Come on, Hattie, when has that ever stopped this town from talking?" Moses scratched his head and looked as if he wished he'd never started this conversation. "You know how Mattawa loves its gossip. You can't take it personally."

"Can't take it per— Oh no, I mustn't do that. It's only my reputation being ripped to shreds by a pack of lies, after all." She stared at him incredulously. "Moses, you cannot *get* more personal than that!"

"Well, the way you flirt with everything in pants," he roared in response, "sure as hell isn't helping your cause any!"

"What in tarnation is all this shouting going on?" Mirabel poked her head out Hattie's bedroom window. "Hattie Taylor, you get out of that tree this instant! And you, Moses Marks, present yourself at the front door like a civilized young man." She leveled him with a steely gaze. "And that best not have been a curse I heard you yelling, sonny. You may have grown into a giant, but you're not too big for me to wash your mouth out with soap. Hattie, come in here at once!" She disappeared back into the bedroom.

"Meet me at the door," Moses whispered, beginning to climb down the tree.

"I think you've said enough," Hattie replied stiffly. His comment about her flirtatiousness wasn't untrue, but it hurt all the same to hear him say it. She had begun flirting outrageously this year, for it was the one area in which she'd found acceptance. The girls in their social circle had taken a dislike to her from her first day in school. The boys hadn't, however, so naturally she'd found it easier to talk to them. As she'd matured, it had seemed a natural progression to take it a step further into harmless flirtations. But once again, it appeared her actions had backfired, embroiling her up to her lily-white, lightly freckled neck in trouble.

"C'mon, Hattie, meet me at the door," Moses implored from the ground, craning his neck to look upward. "I smuggled us a copy of the *Police Gazette* from Dad's shop." Pulling the tail of his shirt out of his pants, he flashed the paper tucked into his waistband.

When her long, narrow nose remained up, he became indignant. "Fine, then. Be that way. It's not me spreading stories about you. Heck, except for last night, I've stuck up for you plenty, and it isn't fair to punish me for what others are saying." But unable to sustain his anger, he cajoled, "Hat?"

Moses watched her edge over to the house and angle headfirst through the window. "C'mon," he called. "I'll rent us a tandem bike from Armstrong's Livery and we can ride out to the country for a while. What-aya say?"

He glimpsed a flash of ankle when her round hips and long legs slithered over the windowsill as she disappeared into her room, and he exhaled gustily. Jeez, she was stubborn!

But a moment later her head poked back out the window. Bracing her hands on the windowsill, she leaned out. "Five minutes," she said and pulled back inside.

"I know what I should do," Hattie said a short while later as the two of them approached the livery stable. "I should make an appointment with Doc Fielding and then take out a full-page ad in the *Clarion*." She tugged on the stable doors. "I'll have them run a document with his signature on it and an official seal prominently displayed, kind of like our diplomas. It'll say, 'This is to verify Dr. Fielding has examined Miss Hattie Witherspoon Taylor and found her to be an intact maiden of sterling virtue.' That would put a damper on all the talk."

As they stepped from daylight into the dim interior of the livery, Hattie bumped into someone. "Excuse me," she apologized. Then, recognizing Aunt Augusta's lawyer as her eyes adjusted, she added politely, "Oh, good afternoon, Mr. Lord."

His hands, which had reached out to steady her, tightened momentarily as Roger Lord coolly eyed her from head to toe. Then he released her and tipped his hat. "Miss Taylor." He stepped out of the livery into the sunshine flooding the stable courtyard and strode away.

"That man is the handsomest specimen I have ever seen," Hattie murmured as she watched his departure. "But for some reason he forever makes my blood run cold." Moses didn't reply, and she turned to look at him.

He was staring at her in horror. "Jeez, Hattie, are you plumb crazy?"

"I can't help it, Moses, he gives me the shivers."

"Forget Lord. I'm talking about this ad business! Jake would probably take a buggy whip to your backside, and Mattawa? Shit, girl, the townspeople would run you out of town on a rail." He glared at her. "Tarred and feathered."

"Why, Moses Marks, I'm gonna tell your—"

"Shut up, Hattie!" he roared and grabbed her arm none too gently, dragging her out of Armstrong the blacksmith's earshot. Moses shook her impatiently. "Jesus, girl, you don't have the sense you were born with!"

"I disagree. The examination would prove conclusively . . ."

"Arrgh!" Clutching handfuls of his pale hair, he tugged viciously. With exaggerated patience, he said through clenched teeth, "Nice . . . girls . . . do *not* . . . discuss . . . Unmentionable Subjects . . . with *any* man. And . . . they . . . never . . . *ever* . . . take . . . out . . . *full-page ads in the MAT-*

TAWA CLARION!" He shouted the paper's name into her face, his nose a scant inch from hers.

"All right, all right," she replied sulkily, stepping back and putting some distance between herself and his anger. "Don't get your tail in a twist. It was merely a thought."

"I have never heard such horse-pucky in my life." He stalked away, still muttering, and Hattie went out into the livery yard.

Criminy. If he was going to act all unreasonable and huffy, he could just handle the bicycle transaction by himself. She found a spot in a circle of sunlight, sat down, and, turning her face up to the sun, closed her eyes.

10

⁂

ACROSS THE ROAD, kitty-corner from the livery, Roger Lord stood inside the swinging doors of Bigger's Saloon, watching Hattie. Her lazy-cat posture infuriated him. That young lady was in serious need of instruction. She all but begged to be taught her place.

Roger believed in man's supremacy over woman and the upper classes' right to rule the masses as they saw fit. He'd considered himself a member of the ruling class for so long now, his actual, lesser origins were but a dim memory. No one in this town knew his standing came courtesy of his marriage to Gertrude. And why would they? It would be clear to a blind man he ought to have been born into the social status he enjoyed. Marrying into it had merely been a formality correcting that which should have been his due from the day he was born.

Self-righteous in his convictions, he was outraged at the remarks he'd overheard. The outspoken little bitch—place an ad declaring her virginity, indeed! Her arrogance galled him. Haughty chits failing to realize their proper status fairly begged to be given a dose of reality.

Roger knew from experience that the most effective way of teaching proper respect in a recalcitrant was through pain and humiliation. Arousal beat in his loins as he visualized training Hattie to subservience. He'd thought the pinnacle of satisfaction would be in defiling a well-born young lady of timid nature. Watching her quiver in terror, viewing her helplessness.

He'd been wrong. The ultimate hedonism, he now knew, would be breaking a well-bred lady of proud nature. Indoctrinating fear into one who'd harbored no fear before. Watching *her* terror, *her* revulsion, for an act he'd bet money she expected to reward her. After all, wasn't that why virtuous girls sold their virginity? For a ring on their finger and all it implied? But damn few of them enjoyed the marital bed. He'd bet the farm, had he possessed one, that Hattie Taylor wasn't among their numbers. Unfortunately, the same obstacles preventing him from debauching a timid, well-born virgin applied to Miss Taylor as well. Fate was damned unkind.

Roger scowled as he watched her tow-headed, muscle-bound friend roll a tandem bike out of the big double doors of the livery across the way. The two teenagers mounted the bicycle, and Roger stayed to one side of the saloon's swinging doors, staring after them until they pedaled beyond his range of vision. Then he slowly turned away and walked to the bar.

Someday, somehow, an opportunity at his ultimate fantasy would come along. And when it did, he'd be ready. Until then he would simply dream of giving Hattie Taylor her just deserts.

WITH NO DESTINATION in mind, Hattie and Moses headed out of town. Pedaling as fast as they could one moment, then lazily coasting the next, they meandered aimlessly. Hattie found it difficult pinpointing their exact location with Moses' wide shoulders blocking everything in front of her. But when she said as much and demanded he exchange seats with her, he refused, claiming her steering was too erratic. So, the next time he began to pump furiously, grunting at her to pick up speed as they approached an incline, she instead raised her feet off her pedals and braced them on the cross section of her handlebars. Sweeping the back of her dress skirt up, she tucked its voluminous fabric between her knees to prevent it from tangling in the spokes.

Hattie grinned as she watched perspiration rapidly spread across the cotton shirt stretched between Moses' shoulder blades. He stood to attain maximum leverage from his efforts, and by the time he glanced over his shoulder at her at the top of the hill, his breath was uneven from the exertion. "Christ Almighty," he gasped, steering them off the road into a meadow.

By mutual consent, they hopped off the bike and watched it roll upright for a couple of feet before toppling into the high grass. "No wonder that was so much work. I shoulda known you'd taken a holiday."

They strode through tall grass to the creek bisecting the field. It was still too cool for wading, but they lay on their backs in the grass and absorbed the warmth of the late spring sun. Eventually, Moses pulled the *Police Gazette* out of his waistband and smoothed the wrinkles out of the paper. Rolling onto their stomachs, they pored over lurid tales of murder and mayhem.

Hattie was still reading an article when Moses began tickling her neck with a blade of grass. She brushed the stalk aside, but he kept whisking its tip from her ear to the neckline of her gown. "What's this?" he asked, brushing the grass blade back and forth over a gold chain showing at her nape.

Hattie sat up, the article forgotten. Hooking the chain, she pulled it from her bodice. The fine, delicate gold supported a small gold locket. "Aunt Augusta gave it to me for graduation. Look at this." Smiling with pleasure, she popped the locket open and extended it as far as possible for his inspection. Inside was a miniature daguerreotype of a woman with soft dark hair. "My mother." Smiling, she gazed at the image. "Mirabel told me that since I arrived in Mattawa, Aunt Augusta has written to my mother's people in San Francisco at least once a year to request a likeness of my mother for me. For reasons known only to them, the Witherspoons consistently ignored her entreaties."

Hattie beamed. "So, this year Aunt Augusta sent a letter demanding they either send a miniature of my mother, or Jake would begin proceedings on my behalf for a portion of the Witherspoon estates. Mirabel said the picture arrived quite speedily after that. Isn't she the *best*? And I never heard a word of this from Aunt Augusta herself. She only said she was sorry she couldn't locate one of my father as well."

"She is one fine lady, all right," Moses agreed. He pointed his fore-finger at the small timepiece pinned above her left breast. "This is new, too, isn't it?"

The dainty watch on her chest was attached to a retracting chain, enabling her to check the time without unpinning the artfully crafted bow-shaped clasp securing it to her bodice. "It's from Jake and Jane-Ellen. Since her confinement kept her from everything last night, Jake gave it to me." Her eyes gleamed with hero worship. "Hand to God, Moses—his timing couldn't have been better. When you let Florence-May say nasty things about me, I felt lower than a snake's belly. I'd just walked away from overhearing that when Jake asked me to waltz. It was a relief to dance with someone who didn't expect clever conversation. I was in no mood to be witty."

Hattie pulled out the dainty watch to admire it, smiling with dreamy satisfaction. "After the waltz, he escorted me to the veranda for some air and gave me this." Closing her eyes, Hattie lay back in the tall grass. "Jake Murdock," she vowed solemnly, "is the most wonderful, honorable man in the entire world."

Moses looked away. He had worked in his father's barbershop after school and Saturday mornings since he was twelve. Customers took him for granted as he swept up, straightened magazines and newspapers, and ran errands for the clientele. Given his size, he didn't blend into the woodwork. But he'd started his first growth spurt when he was fourteen, and men didn't bother monitoring their conversations around boys the way they did around females.

Moses admired Jake Murdock nearly as much as Hattie did. But he'd heard the talk. Hell, he'd probably known within two days when Jake once again began frequenting Mamie Parker's place. Moses didn't judge. But he knew perfectly well that Hattie, who tended to view situations as either black or white, would be destroyed if she knew. Not that there was the remotest possibility it would be brought to her attention. Gossip of this nature did *not* circulate in Mattawa parlors. The men in town all adhered to a code of silence when it came to protecting their own.

In a way, Moses almost wished it wasn't so. Much as he admired and respected Jake, there were moments he fiercely resented him. Hattie thought Murdock walked on water, and who could compete with that? Jake was just a man, not a ten-cent hero like that Fred Fearnot character in *Work and Win* magazine. It made Moses a little testy to know, while Hattie had no problem believing the worst of *him* at times, her precious Jake was forever inviolate.

But it was senseless to hold a grudge against Murdock. The man hadn't asked for Hattie's single-minded devotion. And, hell, Moses *liked* Jake. He liked him a lot. So, as he'd done many times before when Hattie began raving about her hero, he changed the subject. "My folks got me a timepiece, too." He pulled it from his pocket and passed it to Hattie to admire. He hesitated a moment, knowing he'd regret telling her this, but it was too exciting to keep to himself. And Hattie wasn't like most females. She neither wanted nor appreciated being sheltered from life's steamier aspects. "My old man also promised to take me to Mamie Parker's place."

"What!" Hattie sat up like a puppet whose strings had been jerked. She stared at Moses with huge eyes. "When?"

"I couldn't pin him down. Sometime soon."

"You must promise to describe it to me in detail once you've been there!"

"Describe what, exactly?" Moses had visions of being expected to describe all the sweaty details of his sexual education before Hattie's relentless quest for knowledge was satisfied.

"You know! How it's decorated, what the harlots wear, what they look like, everything! I have seen the outside, of course, but never the inside."

"Okay, yeah, I can do that."

"Well, that's something, I suppose. But it's not like seeing it for myself." She tossed her head. "I'm going to sneak out there and see it on my own some night, I declare I am."

"The hell you say!"

"You can't stop me, Moses Marks. If you won't take me, I'll simply go on my own."

"Fine! You do that! For God's sake, *sneak inside* one day? No wonder they talk about you in town the way they do. No decent girl would ever suggest the things you do!"

He wished the words back as soon as they left his mouth, even before glimpsing the look of betrayal on her face. He reached for her, but she shook off his hand and stalked through the high grass to where they'd left the tandem bicycle.

It was a struggle to see the handlebars through her tears, but by the time Moses reached her, Hattie had the bike upright and herself under control. She felt as if she were bleeding inside, but she wouldn't give him the satisfaction of seeing her cry. Never! Ignoring every apology he attempted, she helped him push the bicycle through the grass to the road. When he offered her the forward seat, she declined with cool courtesy and climbed on the rear one.

"Hattie, I didn't mean it," he tried once again. She refused to look at him. "Sometimes I just get so frustrated I say things without thinking."

"Could we not talk, Moses?" she requested quietly. "I want to go home."

"Listen," he said desperately. Her politeness was killing him. Hattie yelled and screamed and called him names. She didn't resort to cool social manners. "I'll take you by Mamie's place, okay? We'll take the shortcut and go by there right now."

"Why?" She nearly screamed the question. She did slug him between the shoulder blades. "Because I'm not a decent girl, so it really doesn't matter where you take me?" She hit him again and the bike swerved as Moses brought it to a halt. "Just take me home, you hypocritical sonovabitch!" Hating that she couldn't prevent it, she burst into tears.

Moses froze. He'd seen Hattie spitting mad and he'd known the talk that followed her wherever she went had to hurt, though she rarely let it show. But never, in all the years he'd known her, had he seen her cry. And in typical Hattie fashion, she didn't cry in half measures. No, sir, no dainty sniffling for her. Huge tears spilled down her cheeks, her eyes and nose reddened, and her entire body shuddered with the force of her emotions.

Unable to bear watching it any longer, Moses plucked her off the bicycle seat and carried her to a downed tree alongside the road. Sitting, he set her beside him, murmuring soothing words and awkwardly patting her back. Turning, Hattie wrapped her arms around him and clung, sobbing for every insult and slight she'd ever received, every untrue word ever said about her.

The worst part? Hattie knew in her heart Moses wasn't wrong. While she hated the unfair judgments people made about her, she also knew she possessed an unthinking tendency to say outrageous things at times. Of *course* she was never going to sneak into a cathouse. But, Lord love her, she sometimes wished she had been born a male. Their lives were so much freer and worlds more interesting than women's were.

"You know I didn't mean it," Moses kept muttering. "You're my best friend. You know I didn't mean it."

"Then you shouldn't have said it," she finally muttered, raising her likely red-rimmed eyes to look at him. But she was incapable of holding a grudge, and her anger washed away with her tears. Besides, Moses was her best friend and she knew she sometimes drove him to the limit, thus bringing out his counterattacks. She summoned a half smile. "After all," she murmured, "I'd never say anything so mean to you if I didn't mean it."

Moses snorted. Raising a hip, he dug a handkerchief from his back pocket and passed it to her. "Here. Blow." Once she did, he mopped up the remaining puddles beneath her eyes with a clean edge and said, "What about the time you swore Florence-May Jordan told you I reminded her of a big blond gorilla?"

"Well, *that* hardly counts. Who in their right mind would believe

Florence-May would ever tell me a blessed thing? We both know what her opinion of Hattie Taylor is. You, on the other hand," she said, fluttering her eyelashes and speaking in a thick, sugary accent in an exaggerated imitation of Miss Jordan, "are *Just so big and strawng!*'"

"At least she's got that right," he agreed and flexed his biceps. When Hattie pretended to swoon and cried, "Oh, Mistah Mawks!" Moses stood up. "You wanna go home now?"

"Yes. And we can take the shortcut by Mamie Parker's place. If I'm late coming home again, Aunt Augusta will make me wax the stair rails. And that takes forever."

"Hattie, with all the talk going around about you, even you must see it's a bad idea if you're seen anywhere near Mamie's establishment. You've got a lighted torch in both hands, girl. Don't go beggin' a dance on a powder keg."

"We've used the shortcut behind it for years, Moses. I hardly think I'm chancing the ruin of my reputation by pedaling past Miss Mamie's stable!"

"Okay. But don't say I didn't warn you if this blows up in your face."

And it usually does, Hattie admitted silently. She almost did the smart thing and told Moses to take them the long way home. But she was serious about her aunt's threat. Augusta had promised Hattie exactly that if she came in late again. And if Hattie knew nothing else, she knew Aunt Augusta kept her word. If Hattie failed to show up when she said she would, she *would* be waxing those railings.

As they drew closer to the infamous establishment, Hattie wished she'd thought to trade places with Moses. He informed her as they crossed the railroad tracks that they were going to whip through the shortcut—and if she didn't like it she could just lump it.

She'd accepted his conditions. But like it had been on the trip earlier, her visibility was restricted by Moses' shoulders. When they suddenly stiffened, Hattie knew he must have seen something truly scandalous, and she feared she was going to miss it.

"We're going home," Moses said flatly, and started to turn.

"What is it? What'd you see?"

"Nothing."

"Moses, what is it?" She rose to stand on her pedals, unmindful that her skirts were dangerously close to the bicycle's spokes. She stared over his shoulders at the stable, which looked deserted and mundane at this hour of the afternoon. For pity's sake, there was nothing scandalous there. Why, there wasn't a blessed thing to see aside from . . .

"No." Her legs losing strength, Hattie collapsed back onto the bicycle seat.

The only thing to see was an old saddle on the corral fence. And, beneath it, the colorful saddle blanket Hattie had given Jake Murdock two birthdays ago.

11

Murdock Ranch

FRIDAY, JUNE 29, 1906

JUST WHEN JAKE thought his life couldn't possibly become more com-plicated, it did. He didn't know what happened. He'd looked for-ward to having Hattie spend the summer at the ranch. She was the only person who still regarded him with unquestioning approval. Lord knew his own wife didn't, and it ate at him. It also turned him cynical at in-appropriate moments, a recently acquired quirk that threatened to affect his relationships with others.

Jane-Ellen's view of him kept changing. One moment she treated him like a harmless friend. The next she regarded him with such revulsion it turned his blood cold, staring at him as if he were a ravening animal with-out the decency to leave her be. Or failing that, to at least confine his conjugal visits to the dark hours, suitably clothed so only the essentials touched. He invariably left her bed feeling like a sweaty, insensitive clod. As a consequence, he'd reduced his visits to almost nil. Hell, given how infrequently he'd made demands, it was a wonder she'd ever gotten preg-nant.

But the pregnancy was a blessing to both of them. Jane-Ellen's joy might stem in part from the fact that he no longer joined her in her chaste bed. Jake just flat out couldn't wait until his child—this miraculous life he had helped to create—was born. His baby was going to be someone he'd love unconditionally, who would love him in return. Until then, he'd looked forward to Hattie's company, to her quick wit, laughter, and adoration, expecting it to soothe his lacerated ego and soften his new-found cynicism. But something had changed her.

Her laughter wasn't as frequent these days, at least with him. In fact, she seemed to apply great effort to avoiding him. Since coming to the ranch, she'd spent most of her time with Jane-Ellen. That was unusual in itself, given how difficult it had been coaxing Hattie indoors during her past visits. And while Jake had heard her husky laughter once or twice from the other side of a door, he'd given up trying to intrude on her visits with his wife. His entrance into any room Hattie occupied invariably caused her merriment to evaporate like morning mist under the rising sun.

He didn't doubt she harbored some deep-seated anger toward him. What he didn't know was why. What the hell had he ever done to her? And why didn't she just come out and say what was bothering her? It wasn't like Hattie to be so reticent. This was a young woman who yelled when she was angry and never hesitated to hurl accusations. Christ, she was sometimes outspoken to a dangerous degree. Yet she'd been at the ranch for nearly three weeks and had tried and convicted him of only God knew what.

Had she bothered to level any charges? Hell, no. Instead, she looked through him rather than at him. Left rooms when he walked in. With-held her laughter. She punished him for a crime she wouldn't identify. Jake didn't know how to deal with her when she refused to present him with one tangible grievance he could address. And what was infinitely worse, her antagonism inexplicably incited him to notice her as a woman.

Like things weren't bad enough. He had a wife who scorned his touch and his visits to the local whorehouse left him empty and emotionally depleted. But, dear God, to suddenly notice Hattie's enticing curves? It would be ironic if it wasn't so damn horrifying. He had loved that kid like a sister for years and she'd worshipped him in return. He'd adored the gutsy little girl, the fearless young woman. Appreciated her candor and her laughter, her unique way of looking at the world around her. And he loved her for the way she made him feel ten feet tall when the rest of his life left him feeling like shit. But he had *never* loved her the way a man loves a woman. Hell, before this visit, he hadn't even noticed Hattie's female attributes, except for the acknowledgment she was growing up. Now, this summer, everything had suddenly changed, including the way Jake viewed Hattie. And he feared there'd be no turning back.

She used to be kind of funny-looking. Hell, she still wasn't beautiful in the current fashion. But there was something about that flaming mass of hair, those exotic amber eyes, that mouth. And, God, her body . . . Whatever happened to her sturdy little freckled chest? Or even the barely developed breasts she'd had when she was twelve, which was probably the last time he had noticed anything physical about her.

Jake began avoiding Hattie as assiduously as she avoided him. He couldn't imagine making an improper advance toward her. Yet, sometimes he looked at her across the dinner table and the impulses running through his mind were so carnal in nature it nailed him to his chair.

Scared him to death. He wasn't exactly overburdened with faith in his self-control these days. And the compulsion to frequent Mamie's wasn't half as compelling as what his imagination all of a sudden envisioned.

He began spending even longer hours than usual tending to ranch affairs. For the past eight days, he'd only come into the house to eat and sleep.

If this had been an ordinary summer, instead of hiding in the stables he would have cross-examined Hattie like a hostile witness until she broke down and told him why she was so mad at him. But he doubted anything would ever be ordinary again. His loneliness was exacerbated by these feelings for Hattie he had no business feeling and the need to police his actions for fear of doing something to blow this family apart.

Jake had a sinking feeling it was going to be a long summer.

HATTIE PICKED UP the telephone and removed the earpiece from its switch hook. The instrument was still new enough to give her a little thrill as she cradled the black receiver to her ear and raised the candlestick body until its mouth horn was a scant half inch from her lips.

"Central."

"This is Murdock Ranch. Marks' Barbershop, please."

"One moment, please." The line went silent—then blared with static, background voices, and Moses' father's voice snapping, "Confounded contraption. Still makes me jump whenever it rings. *Hello!* Marks' Barbershop."

Hattie jerked the earpiece from her ear. Mr. Marks always yelled into the mouthpiece, convinced the other party wouldn't otherwise understand him. Hearing his voice, overloud and warm-toned, made Hattie visualize him in his shop as clearly as though she stood outside his big glass window. Snugging the receiver back against her ear, she said, "This is Hattie, Mr. Marks. Is Moses available?"

"Hello, young lady," Mr. Marks yelled with his customary cheerfulness. "How are you? Hang on, missy. Moses is out sweepin' the sidewalk. Moses!" he bellowed. "Call for you, son."

Hattie barely took the time to greet Moses when he picked up the receiver. "Can you meet me at the creek? I've gotta get outside for a while or explode."

"Sure."

"Thank you! How long before you can get free?"

"Hold on. Dad? You need me anymore this afternoon?" Hattie heard a blurred exchange of words; then Moses' voice once again grew clear and strong. "Hat? Meet you in about twenty minutes."

"You, my friend, are wonderful. Bring your suit."

"Yes, ma'am," he agreed with a laugh. And broke the connection.

Hattie practically skipped to the creek. Lordy, it felt delightful being out of doors. She loved and admired Jane-Ellen dearly, but sometimes Hattie was so bored with their conversations she felt she would shatter and be blown to the four corners of the earth if she didn't get out.

Hattie had been the subject of too much gossip to enjoy speculating about other people's foibles and possible indiscretions. And interesting as fashion could occasionally be, she figured one could say all there was to say about it in thirty minutes flat.

She loved speculating about Jake and Jane-Ellen's baby, however. One day Jane-Ellen's entire stomach abruptly rolled to one side. It was the bulliest spectacle Hattie had ever witnessed. She would've dearly loved to jump up and rest her hand atop Jane-Ellen's enormous stomach to feel the movement. Shame that Jane-Ellen was so reticent about physical contact.

Hattie knew she and the older woman had little in common, likely because even when Jane-Ellen and Jake still lived in Aunt Augusta's house they hadn't spent the sort of concentrated time together they were spending these days. Hattie was accustomed to reading the paper, then carrying on lively debates about the issues at mealtimes with Aunt Augusta—and before this summer, with Jake. Jane-Ellen didn't read the paper because it made her hands dirty. Neither did she like conversations about ranch business.

In fact, if Hattie wasn't so disgusted with Jake she would almost feel sorry for him, for it was quite obvious Jane-Ellen didn't appreciate the way he tracked ranch dirt through the house or occasionally appeared in her immaculate parlor in his sweat-stained work clothes.

Hell's bells, Jane-Ellen and her guests had nearly swooned the afternoon Jake disrupted their luncheon party by barging through the dining room clad in work-worn Levi's and an unbuttoned shirt that flapped behind him. He'd made some attempt to wipe blood from his forearms, but it must have been pretty darn slapdash because rusty brown smears still adorned his arms from wrist to elbow.

He explained a bit tersely that he'd just delivered a foal. The mare had suffered through a particularly difficult labor, but Hattie had a feeling she was the only one who understood why he might like a tot of whiskey to celebrate with his foreman. And given Jane-Ellen's own advancing pregnancy, he probably could have put a little less stress on the labor difficulty. All told, however, Hattie had secretly wondered which offended the good ladies more, Jake's open shirt and blood splatter or his lack of temperance.

Later that night, in her room down the hall, Hattie had heard Jake yelling as he'd defended his interruption of the afternoon entertainment. Jane-Ellen's voice had been indistinct, but Hattie didn't doubt the other woman was giving him the very devil over his lack of decorum.

Not that he didn't deserve it, but . . . Was nothing ever quite what it seemed? Why was it, this summer, that everything appeared to be just slightly off-kilter?

Jane-Ellen was perfect, wasn't she? The feminine ideal. She walked, talked, and dressed with elegance and decorum, a splendid example of social success, according to Aunt Augusta. Why, then, did Hattie know it would drive her purely simpleminded if she had to live with her full-time?

Not that it in any way excused what Jake had done. Hattie had always considered him the strongest, the most honorable man in the world. But what he did was wrong. Totally, absolutely wrong. So, why didn't he seem to care what she thought of him? He had at first; she could tell. But lately, he was never even around to ignore, and when he was around, *he* ignored *her*.

Confusing, confusing, confusing.

Hattie beat Moses to the rock pool. She went behind a tree and removed her shirtwaist, walking skirt, and petticoat and draped them over a bush. She sat down to remove her shoes and stockings, which left her clad only in a chemise and a pair of boys' swim trunks, which she'd convinced Moses to purchase for her in Norton's Mercantile. She couldn't get enough of the sense of freedom her skimpy attire afforded her, especially when it came to gliding through the water. It didn't occur to her how immodest it was. The only person to see it, after all, was Moses.

It occurred to Moses. It was a shock to circle a large boulder and see Hattie sitting in the sun, wearing only what amounted to her underwear. Jeez, she wasn't even wearing the flannel shirt with the ripped-off sleeves she usually wore.

His father had finally come through on his promised graduation excursion to Mamie Parker's place, and Moses was no longer ignorant of the ways of men and women. He was, in fact, a dedicated convert, having taken to the sins of the flesh like a cat to cream. He thought about it constantly, remembering and reliving that astounding night and those that followed. And pausing in the shade of the boulder to covertly eye Hattie, he had to admit it was disturbing that she'd willingly flaunt herself in front of him like he was some harmless gelding. Didn't she realize he was a man now, and therefore dangerous to appear before dressed in next to nothing?

Wait a minute. This was Hattie. His best pal. Nothing was going to happen between them, regardless of how stupid her clothing choice was today.

That would have been the end of Moses' thoughts, and their afternoon would have been spent like a hundred before it, if only Hattie had worn her old flannel shirt. Or at least kept her chemise dry.

JAKE WASN'T THRILLED to be chasing after two teenagers when there was work to be done. But Jane-Ellen's pregnancy gave her notions, and it was easier to indulge them than argue with her. And a call from the operator at Central had given her the notion that Hattie and Moses Marks were swimming together down at the creek.

Jake had a hard time comprehending what all the fuss was about. Those two had been swimming together for seven years now. He doubted they were doing so nude. Hattie was a well-bred young lady, after all, and God knew, he thought cynically, well-bred young ladies were encased up to their virtuous eyebrows in maidenly modesty. So, he was rocked back on his heels to walk out of the woods and find Hattie's maidenly modesty nowhere in sight. She was wrapped in Moses Marks' brawny arms, their mouths fused together in a manner that, although lacking style, lacked shit-all in passion.

And although Hattie hadn't been swimming naked, she may as well have been. For she wore nothing more than a skintight pair of boys' swimming trunks that faithfully displayed her shapely ass, hips, and thighs, and a chemise so wet it was transparent.

Hattie was never quite certain how it happened. One minute she and Moses were horsing around in the water the way they'd done dozens of times. Then the next, as they surged to their feet in the shallows where they'd been pulling themselves along the creek bottom with their hands, they found themselves standing only inches apart. And everything changed.

Moses suddenly looked different to her. Bigger—even though he'd gained his height years ago. More . . . male. Maybe it had to do with the adult expression in his blue eyes looking down at her. Whatever it was, when he reached out to touch the cloth clinging to her breasts in transparent wrinkles, when he pulled it away from her skin, then watched as the heat of her skin sucked it back into place when he let go, she didn't slap his hand away. She didn't yell or blush. She just raised her gaze from where it had been following his fingers' actions and met his.

Lifting his hand, he ran a finger down her cheek. Then he kissed her. It was like a Fourth of July explosion. Suddenly, their healthy bodies were pressed together in earnest yearning. Sensations jolted through Hattie at the feel of Moses' tongue touching hers. She stood on tiptoe and wrapped her arms around his thick neck, pressing herself against him.

Then self-consciousness struck. The same thought flashed simultaneously through both minds. What are you *doing*? This is Moses. This is Hattie. Your *friend*.

Their lips parted. Hattie's arms dropped to her sides. Moses loosened his grip on her waist, and they both stepped back. Sheepishness drew identical half smiles on their faces, a tacit recognition this would never happen again. And without speaking they turned toward the shore.

Where Jake Murdock stood.

Shock, embarrassment, and shame where none existed before jerked their frames, and the teens stood rooted in place, standing in the creek bed up to their calves in icy, burbling water. Abruptly aware of their lack of clothing.

Jake, too, stood stock-still, afraid to move. Consumed with rage, his mind echoed with whispers of ribald comments overheard at Mamie's.

The whores murmuring that Moses Marks was the most prodigiously endowed male in all of Mattawa. Maybe in all of Oregon. The lusty laughter as they confided the kid might be an amateur, but he was a gifted one, loaded with raw talent. Had the talented amateur been sharing his gifts with Hattie?

"Step away from her, boy," Jake commanded, and his voice sounded as if it hadn't been used in a century.

Moses didn't argue with that voice or the look in Jake's eyes. He might be ten years younger, four inches taller, and thirty pounds heavier than Jake, but there was the promise of mayhem—and a distinct possibility of death—in Murdock's eyes should Moses not do exactly as ordered. He stepped away.

Feeling more exposed with Jake's eyes on her than she had when Moses plucked at her chemise, Hattie desperately wished she were dressed. She was confused, embarrassed, and mortified right down to her numb toes. *Ashamed*. The latter emotion infuriated her, and she glared at Jake. She had done nothing to warrant this feeling. All right, maybe it hadn't been too bright to swim in only a thin chemise instead of the flannel shirt she generally wore. But that was foolishness, not wickedness. Her and Moses' reaction to finding themselves in such close proximity in a state of undress had been unexpected and unforeseen.

But they'd silently called a halt to the resulting emotions before anything got out of hand. Knowing Moses had seen her practically naked was awkward—yet it hadn't seemed dirty until she discovered Jake watching them. Before that, without discussion, they had both known they weren't willing to sacrifice their long-standing friendship for what was likely only a momentary urge to experiment. It was Jake's reaction that made everything seem so awful. But who was he to judge them?

"Get your clothes on, Hattie," Jake commanded roughly, and the sound of his voice galvanized her into action. She stomped past him to the bushes holding her clothes and struggled into them.

"I ought to kill you, boy," she heard him say. "How long has this been going on?"

Hattie whirled around, buttoning her shirtwaist and stuffing it into the waistband of her skirt. "Leave him be!" she snapped. "We didn't plan this, Jake; it just happened. And I'll tell you something else. It didn't seem nasty until you came along and made it that way!"

Jake almost sagged with relief, because Hattie would never bother to lie, not even to save her own stubborn hide. But he was still furious at what could have happened. "You think it's acceptable behavior to parade practically naked in front of a grown man?" he demanded in cold fury, whirling to face her and grateful to see she was finally decently covered.

The question threw Hattie into a state of confusion. "I . . . I never thought of him as a grown man," she confessed in a stammer. "He's always just been my friend, and then—" She glanced over at Moses in confusion. Then, looking back at Jake, she shrugged helplessly. "He's still my friend."

"It won't happen again, Jake," Moses said quietly, pinning Jake with a steady gaze.

Jake recognized sincerity when he saw it, and it was obvious Moses was sincere. It should have calmed him. Somehow, it exacerbated the tension knotting the muscles in the back of his neck instead. "You're damn right it won't," he said with cool finality. "Because you won't be seeing her anymore."

Jake observed the shock dilating Moses' pupils, but it was Hattie's response that drained the blood from Jake's face.

"You hypocrite," she said in a bitter little voice, striding over to confront him eye to eye. Her finger punched into Jake's chest in time to her next words. "You sanctimonious, horrid hypocrite." Then her arm dropped to her side as she tipped her head back to stare at him.

"Moses kissed me one time and we both told you it won't happen again. But don't you go flattering yourself it's because of anything you had to say." She stood toe to toe with him, staring up at him with contemptuous eyes. "It won't happen because we don't want to jeopardize our friendship. But who are *you* to judge, anyway? Moses is free and single, and I'm of marriageable age if that's what we're of a mind to do, which we aren't. If Moses tells you he won't do something, then he won't. He's honorable. He's not a married man consorting with whores behind his wife's back!"

"Hattie!" Moses' voice was a disappointed reprimand behind her.

Stunned, Jake didn't utter a word to defend himself or refute her accusation. He simply stood in front of Hattie, still as stone, feeling sick to his soul. God, how had she found out? This, then, was the reason she had been so cold since the beginning of the month.

He felt as though he'd swallowed a boulder. Somehow, it was worse having Hattie discover his guilt than if Jane-Ellen had been the one to stand there accusing him. Hattie had always treated him like a hero, and he hadn't realized until he lost it just how much he'd treasured her unwavering faith in him. Jake tore his eyes away from her contemptuous stare and glanced over at Moses, the sickness he felt showing in his face.

"I didn't tell her, Jake. I swear."

Jake looked back at Hattie. There was anger in her big, whiskey-colored eyes. But, worse than that, there was disillusionment. He wanted to tell her there were extenuating circumstances. He wanted to assure her he hadn't wanted it to happen in the first place and it wouldn't happen again. But he couldn't. He turned and walked away.

Moses watched Jake's back until he disappeared from view. Then he turned to face Hattie. "Well. Do you feel better?" he inquired. "You finally lanced the wound. I've watched it fester in you since you saw Jake's horse blanket at Mamie's place, but now the poison's all drained, isn't it, girl? Do you feel better for it?"

"No." Hattie gripped her stomach against a very real pain. She shook her head and discovered with some surprise her legs no longer desired to hold her weight. She sank down on the gravel shore and hugged her knees to her chest. "No, I feel perfectly horrid." She looked up at Moses. "I thought I would, Moses. I thought I'd feel perfectly righteous if I ever confronted him with his . . . with his—" She couldn't think what to call it. "But I guess nothing is ever the way you think it's going to be, is it?

Criminy, I never thought he'd look so lonely and defeated. And I certainly never thought confronting him would make me feel like yesterday's horse droppings."

She looked around the clearing, breathing in the scent of dusty evergreens under a hot noonday sun. Both arms wrapped around her middle, she turned her face to Moses. "Nothing is ever going to be the same now, is it?"

"I don't know."

Studying Moses' profile as he hunkered at her side staring across the creek, Hattie couldn't reconcile the feelings observing him created. He was at once familiar and alien. The almost-white blond hair and the thicket of pale eyelashes narrowed against the sun's glare were the same. He had the same twelve freckles across the bridge of his nose, his eyes were still blue, and the same heavy muscles strained against the rolled-up sleeves of his shirt. Just like yesterday.

Yet he wasn't the same. She wasn't the same. Everything had changed. Moses wasn't just her friend anymore. He was a man now, different from the boy of a thousand yesterdays.

"I've never been kissed like that before." She was silent for an instant; then a wry, self-deprecatory smile tilted one corner of her mouth. "Heck. The truth is, I've never been kissed at all." *And I'm gonna keep to myself how much I liked it.*

Moses turned his head, meeting her gaze head-on. He feigned surprise. "What's this? The girl rumored to have the easiest virtue in all of Mattawa has never been kissed?"

"Yeah. Kinda funny, isn't it?"

" 'Funny' is not the word I'd use to describe it, Hattie-girl." Moses hitched his rump over until he was sitting hip to hip with her and draped his arm around her shoulders.

Hattie let her head droop onto his chest. "I'm sorry I didn't wear my flannel shirt today." She tilted her head back to look up into his face. "I guess I've been taking you too much for granted lately, haven't I? But I didn't mean to start anything. Honest."

Tucking his chin into his neck, he smiled down at her. "I know that. I expect we're both getting too old to run around half-dressed in front of each other." His smile suddenly stretched into a grin. "You kiss real good, though, for a beginner."

"Why, Mo-ses Marks!" She slugged him in the chest and leaped to her feet. Hands on hips, she scowled down at him in mock indignation. "You are a shameless bounder."

"Aw, shucks, ma'am. That's what all the ladies say."

"I bet they do," Hattie murmured to herself, brushing the gravel from her skirt as she trailed him to the path through the woods. "I bet that is *precisely* what they say."

12

Murdock Ranch
TUESDAY, JULY 17, 1906

HATTIE HAD NEVER known time to drag on so long. The passage of
time from that horrid day at the creek made poured molasses look
like a raging waterfall.

Fall hadn't seemed that far away when Augusta first set out for San
Francisco. Hattie's festering disappointment in Jake might have chipped
at their relationship, but having righteousness on her side had made time
fly. With her new doubts over her right to pass judgment on his actions,
however, the days dragged unbearably.

It didn't help that Jake wasn't even around to revile. That at least
would have sped up the tempo of her days; she was sure of it. But less than
a week after their confrontation, he accepted an increasingly rare case
from an old client, and it took him away from the ranch to the county
seat. He'd been gone for a little under two weeks now. And she missed
him. She was still furious with him, and she still despised his lack of fidel-
ity to Jane-Ellen. Yet, she missed him.

Dang, she hated to admit it. After all, with Jake out of the way, she
was finally free to once again roam the stables and barn. Naturally, she
took full advantage of the opportunity. She thoroughly enjoyed having
the run of the ranch for the first time this summer, instead of being
cooped inside with Jane-Ellen for hours on end. And yet . . .

Below the surface of her enjoyment lay a restlessness she couldn't shake, couldn't soothe, could not *control*. She found herself watching the ranch road at odd moments, searching for his return. She'd give a bundle to convince herself she was merely anxious for him to get back so she could tell him to go whistle in the wind. Except that hound wouldn't hunt, as Doc Fielding liked to say. Aside from little social niceties like stretching the truth to save another's feelings, Hattie had a lifelong habit of not lying. Neither to herself, nor to anyone else. She couldn't wrap her mind around starting now.

What Jake did was wrong—dead wrong. And her *knowing* about his infidelity created a giant rent in the once-golden fabric of high regard she'd long held for him. A rip, moreover, she wasn't certain could be mended. Yet, the longer he was away, the more Hattie wanted back her old laughing Jake. She wanted back the man who had teased her and rumpled her hair. The man who had listened to her opinions seriously, with every indication her thoughts on an issue *mattered*. As if they were, perhaps, actually every bit as important as those of the men with whom he conversed.

She rued the day she and Moses had pedaled down the shortcut past Mamie Parker's stables. If Hattie had the ability to turn back time, she would have one hundred percent handled things differently. She would've taken the long way home that day, as Moses had suggested.

Wishing for the impossible was a radical departure from Hattie's usual approach to life, and had anyone told her weeks ago that ignorance was bliss, she'd have screeched a denial. Now she wasn't so sure. She sure as shootin' didn't care for the situation as it currently stood. And against her better judgment, she longed for a return to her old, uncommonly close relationship with Jake. She *hated* their new, stiff formality and had no idea how to relate to the man whose hazel eyes were newly cool. His lanky appearance was as familiar to her as her own. Yet he was suddenly a stranger who treated her with impeccable politeness—and not a speck of his old breezy warmth.

It was all such a dreadful mess. Nothing was the same as it had been a few weeks back. Would it ever be again? She no longer possessed the conviction that it was her God-given right to feel righteous indignation in the matter. That, at least, might have warmed this frigid hole of loneliness carved in her chest. *Did* she have the right to pass judgment on Jake? She'd thought so, the day after commencement. Heck, she had taken one look at Jake's horse blanket and saddle—damning proof his horse was in the local bawdy house stable—and felt it as an instinctive right to judge and try him. Her hero turned out to have feet of clay, and she couldn't have been more disappointed or disillusioned if he'd been *her* husband instead of Jane-Ellen's. She had been angrier, in all probability, than Jane-Ellen would be, did she know what Hattie knew.

She still was. It was disgustingly clear the men of Mattawa were cognizant of Jake's infidelity. Moses had known, even before that day. Even through her own shock, Hattie had recognized his lack of surprise. And her suffragist heart had rebelled.

She was not a radical, chain-yourself-to-the-courthouse-pillar suffragette. She was, however, genuinely outraged by the inequality existing between the sexes, and she'd never hesitated to say so or tartly state innumerable examples. The tendency had alienated her from half the people in Mattawa.

Well, if *this* wasn't a prime example of inequality, she didn't know what was. Not that she would breathe a word of it to anyone, for to do so would shame Jane-Ellen beyond bearing. But, dang, it made her blood boil! A man's unfaithfulness had the effect of grouping men together to protect one of their own. Boys will be boys and all that rot.

But just let a *woman* be unfaithful in the exact same manner as Jacob Murdock, and she would be labeled a whore and forever ostracized. Now, there was equality and justness for you.

With that lack of fairness factoring into her reaction, Hattie had taken one look at Jake's horse blanket at Mamie Parker's stable that day and made an immediate, instinctive judgment.

She had judged, tried, and convicted her once hero—and felt perfectly justified in doing so.

And yet . . . *Judge not,* the Bible preached.

It wasn't a passage Pastor Stone dwelt on at Sunday services, being more of a hellfire-and-brimstone sort of preacher. But Hattie knew her Bible, and that had always struck her as the essence of Christianity. Hadn't she herself run afoul of unjust judgments, of character assassinations hastily made and too numerous to count? Didn't she know how it hurt? Still . . .

Lest ye too be judged. Well, there you were, then. *She* would never be unfaithful to her husband. So, she could judge away. Which wasn't actually the point, though, was it?

Lord, she was confused. As she went over it again and again in her ever-whirling mind, watching for Jake's return—wishing he would come back to the ranch, wishing he'd stay away indefinitely—what Hattie wished for more than anything was for Aunt Augusta to come home.

A futile hope, that one, since Augusta's return wasn't scheduled until the end of next month, two weeks prior to Hattie's own departure for normal school. But it would surely be wonderful if, for whatever reason, Aunt Augusta cut her trip short.

She rarely even had Moses' company these days to alleviate her grinding loneliness. Ever since that day at the creek, they had seen darn little of each other. Only three times in the past two weeks. Compared to what time she was accustomed to spending with him, it wasn't much.

For a while she'd thought a bit of distance between them was just as well. Two of the times they'd managed to spend together were filled with painful awkwardness. She'd always found solace in Moses' company, but in both of the recent encounters, he'd spent most of the time they were together telling her he really should get going. Hattie didn't understand what was happening between them. She was used to being unwelcomed by a lot of people. She had never expected to feel that way with Moses, and it hurt. *Every*thing hurt these days.

But then the last time she'd seen him, it had been as if nothing had ever come between them. And she'd thought things might be all right after all. But it had been several days now since she'd seen him. Twice she had called him on the telephone to ask if he wanted to come out to the ranch, or if she could come into town to see him. He'd had an excuse both times for putting her off. His rejection, on the heels of believing their relationship had finally regained its normal steady footing, hurt something fierce—even worse than before.

She felt so darn alone. For seven years, she'd pretended she didn't care what the inhabitants of Mattawa thought of her, a self-deception difficult enough when Aunt Augusta, Jake, Mirabel, and Moses were her only champions. They were the solid core of people who hadn't disapproved of her at one time or another. Four people who knew all her faults intimately, and loved her anyway. Out of all the individuals in the world, four wasn't an overabundance of friends. Yet it had been enough. Until now.

Because now she feared she might only have two. And they were out of town.

13

Murdock Ranch
SATURDAY, JULY 21, 1906

"COME ON, JANE-ELLEN—be adventuresome. It'll do you good to breathe some fresh air."

"Hattie, it poured yesterday. The ground between the rosebushes will be solid mud."

Hattie handed Jane-Ellen her gardening hat. "I've already dragged a chair out there for you," she cajoled. "You needn't get even a speck of dirt on you." She aimed her best grin at the petite blond woman, tilting her head toward the open window. "Listen to those birds! C'mon. Please. All that's required of you is sitting in a comfortable chair and holding the basket. Pretend you're a queen holding court. I'll pick the flowers, and you know *I* don't mind a bit of dirt."

Jane-Ellen smiled. "No, I daresay you don't." She plopped the straw hat on her head. "Cut flowers would be charming in the parlor."

"Exactly. And the weather is splendid. I believe you'll love it."

Jane-Ellen rather felt like the queen Hattie mentioned by the time the younger woman had her settled in the shade of the large old lilac tree. Its flowers long since had given way to the summer heat, but leafy greenery still lent welcome dappled shadows. Not only had Hattie brought out the most comfortable porch chair for Jane-Ellen to rest in; she'd provided a cushion atop an upside-down bucket on which to prop her feet. A tall glass of lemonade from the icebox sweated frostily on a small wicker table. "You're spoiling me shamelessly."

Hattie laughed. "You're a mama-to-be. You deserve a little spoiling!"

Jane-Ellen rested a hand on the huge swell of her stomach and sipped her cold drink as she watched Hattie putter among the rosebushes. She truly was a sweet girl. It was a pity the women of Mattawa couldn't see this side of her. Maybe then they wouldn't judge her so harshly.

Jane-Ellen was perfectly aware of the scandalous regard in which the town held Hattie. She, too, was often appalled by Hattie's outspokenness and disregard for convention. Yet Jane-Ellen harbored a sneaking admiration for the girl's daring and refused to let her friends speculate about the Murdock ward in her presence. In all the time she had known Hattie, Jane-Ellen had never once heard her utter an unkind word behind anyone's back. Hattie at times lacked tact to a regrettable degree. But she didn't simper sweetly to a person's face, only to turn around and verbally stab them in the back, like some in their social circle Jane-Ellen could name.

"Can I get you more lemonade?" Hattie dumped several cut roses into the flower basket at Jane-Ellen's side.

"No, thank you. I still have a bit left." She smiled up at Hattie. "This is lovely."

"Told ya." Grinning, Hattie turned back to the garden, humming a lively tune beneath her breath. Jane-Ellen laughed as she watched the younger woman roll back her sleeves and sit in the damp dirt at the base of a rosebush. Hattie weeded vigorously, as if routing personal enemies.

What must it be like to eschew an entire town's opinion of oneself? Jane-Ellen cared far too dearly what others thought of her. There must be a wealth of freedom in not caring one whit.

Watching Hattie as she paused to brush a forearm across her forehead, leaving a smear of dirt in its wake, Jane-Ellen also wondered what it must be like to not always feel a burning need to make sure the façade one displayed to the world was impeccable at all times. She truly did envy Hattie's disdain for convention sometimes. Observing the full curves shifting freely beneath the faded cotton of Hattie's oldest dress with the girl's every movement, Jane-Ellen reflected wryly that it had taken a pregnancy for *her* to discard her corsets.

Hattie's adamant refusal to wear one most of the time was a great affront to the women in their strata of Mattawa society. In truth, Jane-Ellen knew that Hattie, in deference to Augusta's feelings, did bind her breasts with winding gauze when going to town or an event. And Jane-Ellen had learned these past few months how marvelous it felt not to have her own breasts and torso cinched tightly by whalebone. So, who was to say Hattie didn't have the right idea? Jane-Ellen rather thought a good deal of the vitriol aimed at the young woman was nothing more than envy over Hattie's daring to do what they all secretly wished they had the nerve to do.

Of course, much as she envied Hattie's freedom, Jane-Ellen knew perfectly well she would go back to wearing her own corset, and all its attendant discomforts, as soon as the baby was born. Coward that she was.

She was so tired of being afraid of everything. She avoided the workings of the ranch because she abhorred the dirt, the noise, the smells. And the horses frightened her. The most adventurous she ever got was picking flowers from the garden in the summertime. She was afraid to speak her mind when she heard an unjust piece of gossip, for fear it might result in not being liked, or—shameful, petty thought—being left off an important guest list. The only time she stood her ground was when someone censured her family to her face.

She was afraid of the marriage bed, and consequently, her husband quite despised her. Oh, Jacob was unfailingly polite. She wasn't a fool, however: she knew he no longer loved her. She regretted that. She remembered the flushed, wonderful feeling when Jake looked at her with those marvelous, hazel-green eyes of his, back when they were full of adoration. And in truth, some of her female acquaintances simply glowed when their husbands were around. Jane-Ellen wished she knew their secret.

She was also terrified of her approaching birthing. Her friends who were mothers related such horrendous stories. Still, she clung tenaciously to Augusta's tranquil reassurances. Having babies, the older woman promised serenely, was normal, natural, and happened every day. She assured Jane-Ellen that even the women who complained of utter misery during the delivery of their children were proud mamas once the birthing was behind them.

Observing Hattie wave a droning bee away from her face, then scratch the tip of her nose, Jane-Ellen marveled at how instinctually tactile the young woman was. Jake, too, was like that. They touched people in the course of conversations, as though underscoring the point they were making. Or perhaps it was simply to include the other person in the process. It was an automatic gesture, not a matter either gave a second's consideration. Both also possessed the ability to hug and be hugged without feeling the least bit graceless. Jane-Ellen stifled a sigh. She always felt stiff and awkward when she was embraced by others. In that respect, however, she did look forward to the birth of her baby. She was convinced she'd finally lose her awkwardness, would freely give and receive affection from her child.

She studied Hattie again. "Are you nervous about going to school in Seattle?"

Hattie pushed back to sit on her heels. "A bit. My acceptance letter said I might have a roommate." She gave the clipped rose in her hand a wistful smile. "It would be lovely if she liked me." Then, clearly realizing she'd bared a vulnerability Jane-Ellen hadn't even realized the girl harbored, Hattie straightened her shoulders. "Well, she either will or she won't, I suppose. And mostly, I'm looking forward to learning how to teach."

"Well, I think you're very brave. Much braver than I." *And if my baby is a girl,* Jane-Ellen thought with sudden fierceness, *I want to raise her to be a happy mixture of myself, Jake, and Hattie.* Not that she wanted her daughter to be a hellion. But Jane-Ellen couldn't bear it if her daughter turned out afraid of her own shadow like her mother. And if her little girl should sometimes be tactless in her public behavior? Jane-Ellen was going to bury her own embarrassment and be just like Augusta. She planned to look the recipient of her daughter's transgression squarely in the eye and silently dare that person to mention her child's misstep.

And if her baby was a boy . . . Jane-Ellen smiled and closed her eyes, resting her head against the high back of the wicker chair. She absorbed the birdsong overhead, the lazy drone of bees, Hattie's tuneless humming, and felt content. For once she was able to look beyond the fast-approaching certainty of giving birth in favor of daydreaming about the end result: her and Jake's baby. It left her feeling amazingly content.

She must've dozed, for the next thing she knew she started at the sound of hoofbeats pounding up the drive. She opened her eyes, slightly disoriented. Muzzily blinking and yawning behind a politely raised hand, she looked over at Hattie to ask what all the commotion was about.

Hattie was resting back on her heels in the middle of the rose garden, a hand raised to shade her eyes from the sun as she squinted down the lane connecting the ranch to the county road. She was uncharacteristically still, and, curious as to what could provoke such a reaction, Jane-Ellen followed her gaze. Well, heavens, it was only Jake. He was galloping up the drive at his usual breakneck speed, and Jane-Ellen experienced the confusing mixture of pleasure and disapproval she felt whenever she saw him.

Spotting her and Hattie in the yard, he veered away from the stables—his obvious destination—and slowed his horse to a canter, then to a walk. He covered the remaining yards with a sedateness even Jane-Ellen could approve of. Saddle leather creaked as he dismounted in front of the house and threw the reins to the stable boy who had come out to attend to the horse.

"Rub 'im down good, Davey," he instructed. "He's had a long, hard ride."

"Sure thing, boss." Patting the horse's sweaty neck, Davey led the animal to the barn.

Entering the garden, Jake tipped his hat to the women, then removed the dust of his travels from it by slapping it against his thigh. "Afternoon, ladies." He grinned. "Miss me?"

He crossed to Jane-Ellen, leaning over to kiss the cheek she presented. She gave him a welcoming smile. Then he looked over his shoulder at Hattie and raised one eyebrow.

Hattie snorted, hoping her furious heartbeat wasn't obvious. Turning back to the few remaining weeds, she listened as Jane-Ellen inquired about Jake's trip and filled him in on the day-to-day events he'd missed. She praised Hattie unstintingly for this afternoon's arrangements, regaling Jake—in long, boring detail, to Hattie's way of thinking—with everything she had done to ensure Jane-Ellen's comfort.

Jake made himself comfortable on the ground next to Jane-Ellen's chair. Ankles crossed and forearms draped over his pulled-up knees, he listened to Jane-Ellen's chatter and watched Hattie from beneath the brim of the hat he'd put on again and pulled low over his eyes. *How typical,* he thought, *to come home and find her mucking about in the mud.*

Jake had given his and Hattie's relationship a great deal of thought while he was away. He missed having her unquestioning approval; he freely admitted it. But he'd finally concluded he couldn't spend the rest of the summer hiding out in the stables just to avoid facing her new, gut-registering disapproval. He understood her reasons for being disgusted with him, and God knew Hattie was passionate in the execution of her emotions. He could never justify his lack of faithfulness in her eyes. Hell, he couldn't justify it in his own.

But he refused to let her sit in judgment of him for the rest of her stay here. His private life was none of her damn business. So he intended to act like nothing had changed between them. He would treat her exactly as he always had.

Except for the part where he was very, very careful never to touch her.

He watched as Hattie vigorously pulled weeds from the rose bed and tossed them aside. Her hat hung by its ribbon down her back, and her hair, untidily escaping the fat braid draped over her right shoulder, formed a nimbus around her head, glowing in the sunlight like a glimpse of hellfire. Curly tendrils clung to her flushed cheeks and forehead. Her arms and face were streaked with dirt, and perspiration spread under her arms and down the spine of her shirtwaist. She shouldn't have been the least bit appealing. Yet, he couldn't look away.

Until this summer, Jake had never been faced with a need to restrain his physicality around her. He'd handled her in any number of ways in the past without a thought. But he knew touching her now was nothing short of perilous. For simply gazing at her, merely *thinking* of laying hands on her, sent jolts of lightning through him.

It was against all reason, and while away he had almost convinced himself he'd inflated her impact. Deep down, however, he knew he hadn't—and the idea of not being able to control this unwanted attraction disturbed him. He could, however, avoid it. And his best bet was going back to treating her like a little sister.

By the sudden quizzical silence, he realized Jane-Ellen had asked him a question. He thumbed his hat to the back of his head, leaned back on an elbow, and looked up at her. "Sorry, I was woolgathering. What did you say?"

"I only wondered if you'd like a glass of lemonade. It's quite refreshing, and you must be parched after your trip."

Jake felt a flare of his old affection for her and, sitting up, reached for her hand. Bringing it to his lips, he bestowed a gallant kiss upon her fingertips. She was a sweet lady and the fault wasn't solely hers they'd turned out to be less compatible than either expected when they'd wed. "That sounds great, but I'm too lazy to move at the moment. I'll be going in soon to clean up. I'll cadge a glass from Cook then."

"Very well." She smiled down at him. Then in a rare moment of physical contact, she reached out to brush a hank of his hair off his forehead. She studied his face, feature by feature, then spent a moment staring into his eyes. "I am glad you're home, Jake."

"I'm much obliged to hear it, ma'am. I'm happy to be here."

Hattie suddenly stood, twisting to brush patches of clinging dirt from the seat of her dress. She crossed over to the pair. "Do you mind if I steal your bucket, Jane-Ellen?" she inquired. "I need something to carry the weeds to the compost."

Jane-Ellen slid her feet off the overturned bucket. "Of course not, dear. I should take these roses in and arrange them before they wilt."

Hattie accepted the bucket Jake handed her, giving him a belated word of thanks. She didn't half comprehend the snake's nest of emotions roiling inside her. Her first reaction when she saw Jake thundering up the lane was joy at knowing he was home. She'd been happy to see him. Now she felt a compulsion to hug her anger to her breast, to *nurture* it against once again succumbing to hero worship. She wished she could either hate him or love him. This seesaw of emotions was exhausting.

Jane-Ellen's small cry of distress interrupted Hattie's bleak ruminations. The other woman had pricked her finger on one of the muddy thorns adorning the rose stems.

Removing the basket of flowers from Jane-Ellen's hands, Hattie leaned over to inspect the wound. There wasn't much to see, only a welling drop of blood. "You best wash that immediately," she advised. "The stems are filthy."

"It's nothing," Jane-Ellen demurred. "It actually startled me more than anything."

"Nevertheless," Jake instructed firmly, helping her to her feet, "you will do as Hattie said. Go on in and wash it thoroughly. I'll find a strip of gauze to wrap it."

"For pity's sake, you two," Jane-Ellen protested. "It's only a prick."

"Humor us." Jake flashed his old devil-may-care grin at her, his cheeks creasing attractively. "Expectant mothers deserve special pampering."

"Very well," Jane-Ellen agreed and laughed self-consciously. "But I must tell you I feel a bit foolish about all the fuss." She nevertheless set off for the house.

Jake and Hattie, following behind her, kept a carefully wide space between them.

14

Murdock Ranch
THURSDAY, JULY 26, 1906

JAKE HAD STARTED cutting back on his horse-breeding operation this summer to expand his cattle stock, but it was his carriage horses Roger Lord had arrived to inspect today. The two men were in the stable yard discussing the finer points of a pair of dapple grays when several ranch hands drove a herd of cattle past. For a few moments the noise and dust were overwhelming.

Jake watched Roger observing the cattle's progress and had to swallow a smile. He didn't know how Roger managed it, but he appeared to be looking down his nose even as his chin remained perfectly level and his eyes focused straight ahead. Maybe it was the slight purse of his lips or the supercilious flare to his nostrils as he listened to the lowing cows and swearing cowhands. It didn't matter. Roger was his guest. Yet Jake couldn't help but smile. Just a little. Because the man was so full of his own consequence.

Roger noticed Jake's smile. He considered it quite common but ignored it the same way he'd ignored the other man's quick once-over of Roger's clothing.

As if he didn't know how to dress, for God's sake. He'd known damn well he was coming to a ranch—of course he wore the appropriate garb. Granted, it wasn't the sweat-stained chambray and worn denim Murdock had on—Roger hadn't lost all sense of propriety. But if his shirt and pants weren't anything he would be caught dead wearing in town, they were certainly heavy-duty enough for tramping around a barnyard.

He looked down at his boots. He'd had them polished up by the servants, for a man had to maintain some standards. It didn't mean he felt the need to watch his every step as he tramped after Murdock. What difference did it make if shit got on his boots? Or even if he tracked some into his rig or his house? That was precisely what servants were for. The help was there to take care of the unpleasant aspects of life. It was their *job* to deal with it.

As Roger stroked a hand down one of the horse's shoulders, he looked over the animal's withers at Jake. Roger prided himself on his knowledge of horseflesh, and the dappled grays were prime animals. "You're an unusual man," he stated coolly. *And a fool,* he privately tacked on, but kept the thought to himself. "First, you give up your lucrative law practice to breed horses. That was almost understandable—it is at least a gentlemanly pursuit. But to give up breeding these fine animals to enlarge your herd of cattle—?" *Incomprehensible.* But he bit back the word and managed not to shake his head.

Jake had no difficulty reading Roger. And why the other man thought Jake owed him an explanation baffled the hell out of him. But aloud he merely said, "Automobiles."

Roger turned to him with eyebrows raised. "I beg your pardon?"

"If automobiles keep gaining in popularity at the rate they've been doing, horse breeding won't remain as viable an enterprise."

"Rubbish," Roger snapped. "Those noisy contraptions are nothing but an abomination!" He looked down his nose at Jake. "I'm surprised at you. You don't strike me as a man who would disrupt his entire financial structure for the sake of a passing fad."

"You may be right," Jake agreed easily, stroking the velvety nose of the gray poking its head over the corral railings. The horse blew down the front of his shirt, making his lips quirk. "There aren't many here in Mattawa. And the ones that are seem to be constantly breaking down or in need of tire changes. They're a rich man's toy."

He moved the horse's head aside and met Roger's contempt with a level gaze. "But damned if I'll risk my entire fortune on the assumption that's what they'll remain. I met a judge over at the county seat who showed me his Peerless. He had a catalog from a New York store called Saks & Company. The thing was two hundred and seventy pages long and devoted exclusively to motoring garb. Two hundred and seventy pages, Roger. Can you imagine a catalog of that size selling nothing but clothing for a person to wear motoring? There is something about automobiles that's catching everyone's fancy. And you can't discount American ingenuity when it comes to overcoming obstacles. I wouldn't be surprised if someone finds a way to improve the quality of these machines. At this point motorists also have to be mechanics. But if enough vehicles are sold, repair stations may eventually be set up along the main roads to service them. Or," he said with an indifferent shrug, "you may prove correct and the rage will die a natural death. In which case I can always build up my breeding operation again."

Roger knew Jake to be an idiot. A gentleman to his fingertips, however, he refrained from saying so. The talk turned once again to the finer points of the two carriage horses he seriously considered purchasing.

Hattie picked her way carefully past steaming mementoes left by the cattle and halted a few feet from the men, waiting for a break in their conversation. Roger Lord noticed her first and she experienced a frisson of unease at his unblinking regard. Criminy, he was a chilly man. Feeling foolish for the uneasiness he inspired, she was still relieved when Jake looked up.

"I'm sorry to interrupt," she said. "But Doc is here, and he'd like to speak to you."

Jane-Ellen had been feeling under the weather for several days, and this morning she'd complained of a stiff neck, tight jaw, and some difficulty swallowing. Jake insisted, against his wife's weak-voiced protests, on calling her father to examine her.

He turned to Roger. "If you'll excuse me," he said quietly. "My wife has been ill. I'll get back to you as soon as I can."

"Certainly," Roger agreed urbanely. He eyed Hattie thoughtfully. "I have a few more questions. Perhaps Miss Taylor can answer them for me."

"When it comes to the horses, Hattie knows almost as much as I do," Jake agreed, already moving away. As he strode past his ranch manager, however, he slowed down to direct the older man to stay close enough so Hattie and Roger didn't appear alone together. No sense supplying something else for people to gossip about her. Once past the corral and across the drive bisecting the ranch, he broke into a lope.

Hattie watched his departure, then reluctantly turned to Roger Lord.

She didn't like the way his gaze traveled over her whenever they met. It was never anything she could put a finger on or point out to others. But if another adult wasn't present, he stared freely at her breasts and hips. Other men had been known to do that occasionally, of course. Yet there was something particularly unnerving about Lord's appraisal.

Which sounded ridiculously melodramatic. Even so, she felt threatened, almost. She also resented the way he talked down to her, as though she couldn't understand words longer than two syllables. But she answered his questions politely, then offered him refreshment in the house when he indicated an interest in purchasing the horses under discussion. She couldn't repress a small smile, however, when he stepped in a fresh pile of horse droppings. She tried to not let him see her amusement as she watched him scrape it off on the grass at the side of the road but feared she was less than successful when he looked up suddenly to catch her watching. Still, if a fella doesn't bother to take his nose out of the air long enough to watch where he's stepping, he gets what he deserves.

Passing Jake's office moments later, she glanced in and saw him in intense conversation with Doc Fielding. Their discussion looked so grimly serious she slowed down, hoping to overhear a bit of it. Jake glanced up as she went by with Roger in tow, and without a word he closed the door in her face.

Well, how rude. Stung, Hattie led Roger into the parlor and invited him to make himself comfortable while she ordered a pot of coffee and a platter of small cakes from the cook.

She was running out of things to say to Jake's guest by the time Doc and Jake emerged from the office and joined them in the parlor. Jake's face was set in grim lines and Doc seemed distracted, slopping his coffee and cussing a blue streak. He didn't even bother excusing himself, which wasn't like him. Usually, he took special effort to not swear in Hattie's presence, and when he did slip he always followed his curse with a "Begging your pardon, missy."

Hattie grew increasingly uneasy and excused herself as soon as she could, hurrying up to Jane-Ellen's room. The men's preoccupation was making her worry about the state of Jane-Ellen's health. Alarmed to see the other woman looking worse than she had earlier, Hattie carefully schooled her expression to hide her dismay. She laid a cool hand on Jane-Ellen's forehead. "How are you feeling?"

"Not very well." Jane-Ellen's blue eyes appeared darker than usual in her too-pale face. "I hurt all over." She licked her dry lips. "I thought perhaps I was having the baby early, but Father said no." She passed her tongue over her lips again without noticeable satisfaction.

Hattie spied a tray containing a glass and pitcher on the dresser. "Want some water?"

"Please."

Hattie poured her a glass and carried it back to the bed. Helping Jane-Ellen to half sit up, she held the glass to the other woman's lips.

Jane-Ellen took three tiny sips and sagged back onto the pillows. "'S good," she murmured. "Thank you."

"I wish I could do more for you."

"I'll feel better tomorrow, I'm sure," Jane-Ellen whispered, and her eyelids slid closed. "Know what I miss?" she murmured. "I miss hearing you play the piano."

Hattie smiled at her. Her musical abilities had improved over the years. Playing the piano still wasn't her favorite activity, but she'd gained expertise since she'd stopped resisting Augusta's insistence on daily practice. "I'll play for you tomorrow, if you feel well enough to come downstairs."

"'A Bird in a Gilded Cage'?"

"Yes. And sheet music for a new one came in the mail yesterday—I meant to tell you earlier but forgot. Aunt Augusta sent it from San Francisco. It's called 'Meet Me in St. Louis, Louis.' I haven't tried it yet, but I've read the music and it's quite lively. I think you'll like it."

A small disturbance of air, something not quite an actual sound, made Hattie glance at the doorway. Jake stood there, his hands clutching the doorframe with enough force to turn his fingertips white. The grief etching new lines in his face frightened Hattie, and she turned away, smoothing the counterpane over the large mound that was Jane-Ellen's stomach. "Jake is here," she whispered. "I'll leave you now, but I'll be back later to see how you're feeling."

It wasn't until suppertime that Hattie was informed of Doc's diagnosis. It had been a grim and silent meal as the three of them moved food around their plates, arranging and rearranging it to disguise their lack of appetite. She didn't know the nature of Jane-Ellen's illness, but she knew from Doc and Jake's actions all afternoon it was bad. Finally, she pushed back her plate and looked at them. "Jane-Ellen is very sick, isn't she?" *Is she going to die?* She longed to ask the question aloud, but fear of the answer stopped her. Clenching her fists in her lap, she awaited a reply.

"She's contracted tetanus," Doc replied. "From the rose thorn that punctured her hand."

"Tetanus? I've never heard of that." Relief washed over Hattie. If it was only a little infection from a prick to her finger, it couldn't be too serious. Thank goodness—

"Lockjaw, Hattie."

"No!" Hattie's chair screeched across the hardwood floor as she shoved back from the table. She stared at Doc pleadingly, woozy from the blood deserting her head. She tried not to show her horror, but her inability to dissemble likely played her every trepidation across her face. There wasn't a person above the age of five who hadn't heard of lockjaw—and knew it was deadly.

"But that was a week ago," she argued. "And it wasn't a rusty nail or anything. It was only a rose thorn and we washed it out really well—" She turned to stare beseechingly at Jake. "Tell him, Jake."

"I told him, Hattie," Jake replied impassively. "But Doc says the symptoms are unmistakable."

Hattie stared at him and saw only his apparent lack of feeling. For a moment, she forgot the grimness she'd glimpsed earlier, the grief she had witnessed in Jane-Ellen's room. All the rage she'd suppressed this summer abruptly boiled over. "It's your fault," she said in a flat voice and glared at him, her eyes no doubt full of the fury and fear icing her innards. She saw him recoil as if she'd struck him, saw by the look in his dark eyes he had already accepted the guilt in his own mind. Momentarily, it filled her with a savage sort of satisfaction. Then she remembered the rose. "No," she contradicted herself. "Oh God, it's mine. I encouraged her to come out while I gardened. She didn't want to at first, but I talked her into it."

"Stop it!" Doc roared, and he, too, pushed back from the table. He planted his fists on the highly polished surface. Amid abandoned china and silverware, he rested his full weight on his knuckles as he leaned over to glare at Hattie. "Goddammit to hell, just stop it this instant! The fault lies with no one, missy. Not Jake, not you, not even Jane-Ellen. It happened. It just happened." Tears began to leak out of the corners of his eyes. "Blaming yourself or blaming Jake will not help my baby girl now. And it won't help her child."

"Dear God, the baby." Hattie's fingers trembled as she pressed them to her lips. Involuntarily, her eyes sought Jake's. His were devastated. "Will the baby—?"

"There's nothing we can do," Doc said flatly and knuckled the tears from his leathery cheeks. "Except make Jane-Ellen as comfortable as we possibly can."

Hattie turned and ran from the room. She slammed out of the house but stopped indecisively on the front porch. Leaning her forehead against one of the cool pillars supporting the porch roof, she whispered a litany, not quite a statement, nor exactly a prayer. "Oh God, oh God, oh God."

She stayed out there for quite a while, hearing the nightly chorus of crickets and frogs but unable to derive her usual pleasure from it. Finally, she let herself quietly back into the house and walked over to the telephone. Picking up the receiver, she requested the Marks residence.

When Moses answered, Hattie clung tenaciously to her composure to prevent her distress from climbing through the lines to his ears. "Could you come out to the ranch for a while?"

"Hattie? It's pretty late, girl."

"Please?" *Don't cry,* she told herself. *Do. Not. Cry.*

In his family parlor, Moses fought his private demons. She sounded a little desperate. And he was consumed with guilt for how he'd been avoiding her lately. Still, it really was for the best. He simply couldn't act natural around her this summer. It seemed so easy, that day at the creek, tacitly agreeing they'd not attempt taking their relationship beyond friendship. And in that moment, he had meant it. She was his best friend and he didn't want to mess with that.

But he hadn't reckoned on the power of his dreams. He hadn't suspected that day how he'd be tormented by visions of her on a near-nightly basis.

And what visions. He was haunted by resurrected memories of the way she'd looked barely clothed. He wasn't an innocent boy anymore. He knew what pleasures could be found in a woman's body. And, much as he tried banishing the memories of Hattie's magnificent body in her wet chemise and boys' swim trunks, in his nocturnal fantasies the images refused to be vanquished.

It was so damn confusing. Twice, he'd gone out to see her. And in the daylight hours, she was just the same old Hattie. Yet, shameful memories of those dreams had interfered with his ability to act natural in her presence. He'd felt on edge every minute they were together, anxious to be away, afraid she'd somehow read his mind and know about his dreams. It didn't matter that she failed to inspire his lust when they were face-to-face. If she knew about his dreams, she'd be appalled.

Then the dreams had mercifully disappeared. He'd waited awhile, until he'd finally felt it would be safe to start seeing her again. And the last time he'd seen Hattie, it had been just like old times. But that very night, forbidden images of her paraded behind his eyes in even more explicit detail, jerking him awake, leaving his body one sweaty, pulsating ache.

Shit. Hattie was his friend. His mind knew it. Even his body knew it—as long as he was awake. He missed her. And it sounded like she needed him now. Yet he couldn't bring himself to go. He just plain could not look her in the eyes these days. He thought it smarter altogether to avoid her the rest of this summer, after which she'd leave for teachers college. By the time she came home again, these fucking dreams were sure to have faded. Their relationship could regain its old, steady footing. Consumed with guilt but feeling it necessary, he invented an excuse to not go out to the ranch that evening. It sounded feeble, even to his own ears.

And before he finished, Hattie hung up on him.

15

DRIZZLE FELL INTERMITTENTLY outside the open bedroom window as Hattie helped Doc lay out Jane-Ellen's body. Although Hattie's emotions were numbed by fatigue, she experienced a dull sense of relief that Jane-Ellen was finally at rest. Her death three hours ago had been a merciful release from an ordeal progressively more agonizing and ugly.

Within a day and a half of Doc's diagnosis, Jane-Ellen developed difficulty opening her mouth, the symptom from which lockjaw got its name. It was followed by difficulty swallowing. Her muscles became rigid and subject to excruciating spasms. Convulsions followed, and Hattie feared she would relive Jane-Ellen's ragged efforts to breathe in her dreams for a long time.

By the time Jake returned from the barn with a ranch hand and the plank to transport Jane-Ellen's body to the icehouse, Doc and Hattie had finished washing and dressing it. Hattie looked away as the men transferred Jane-Ellen's forever stilled body from the bed onto the board. She simply could not bear seeing the large mound of Jane-Ellen's stomach where her unborn child still resided. Every time she glimpsed it, she was reminded of the day the baby abruptly stopped moving, all prior signs of life erased.

Jake's reaction was the exact opposite. Compulsively, he stared at the shrouded mound. That was his child under there, forever barred from entering the world. He'd never know if it was a boy or a girl. He would probably wonder for the rest of his life.

He felt like he was bleeding to death, deep inside where no one could see. He'd dreamed sometimes of being free of this marriage in which his touch caused his wife to cringe. But not like this. Shit. Never like this. Jane-Ellen hadn't been the right woman for him. But she'd been sweet and decent, undeserving of the inhuman agony she'd suffered from the first tetanus symptoms to her death. They'd both awaited the birth of their child eagerly. And, dammit, they would have made good parents. He felt it in his bones.

The icehouse door creaked when the ranch hand opened it. As they maneuvered the burdened plank through the opening and onto the sawdust-covered ice blocks, Jake thought it seemed a lonely place to leave Jane-Ellen's body. But they didn't have much choice in the matter.

The day Doc informed Hattie and Jake of Jane-Ellen's condition, they sent a telegram to Augusta. One couldn't, however, simply fly like a bird between San Francisco and Mattawa. Augusta had wired back to inform them that she and Mirabel had missed last week's sailing but were booked on a steamer ship scheduled to leave tomorrow for Seattle and from there they would catch a train home. With a little luck and reasonable weather on the Pacific Ocean, they would arrive Sunday evening around five fifteen. Jake had talked to the pastor and scheduled the funeral for late Monday afternoon.

He gathered a couple more ranch hands to help him return the piano to the parlor. The day after Doc gave them the news, Hattie insisted they bring it upstairs to the room next to Jane-Ellen's. Between bouts of nursing her, Hattie had played tirelessly. It was the only thing that helped alleviate Jane-Ellen's pain—and then, only temporarily.

Doc materialized at his shoulder, haggard and thin, looking five years older than last week. "I'm going now, son," he said wearily. "I've been ignoring my practice since Jane-Ellen fell sick. More 'n likely, there's a load of patients after me like hounds after a bitch in heat."

Jake shook his father-in-law's hand, reaching out to squeeze Doc's forearm with his free hand. "I'm sorry, Doc."

"I know you are, son." Doc's eyes filled with tears, but he blinked them back. "I am, too."

"Where's Hattie?"

"I sent her to bed. She's worn herself to the bone, but I couldn't get her to sleep for more 'n two, three hours at a stretch before now." Raising his eyes to meet Jake's, he sighed. "Don't be a stranger, now, boy. No matter what the future brings, I will always think of you as a son." He walked away, loneliness stark in the slump of his shoulders. He had just lost his last blood kin.

HATTIE EMERGED SLOWLY from a deep, dreamless sleep. Finding it dark outside, she peered at the clock on her bureau to check the time. Her brow pleated. That couldn't be correct. It was much too dark for seven a.m. Sitting up and reaching for her wrapper, she stared at the clock as though it might suddenly reveal the correct time. Then she realized the pendulum was still.

Of course. She hadn't wound it during the not quite two weeks since hearing Jane-Ellen's diagnosis.

Hattie used the necessary and brushed her teeth. Barefoot, she groped her way down the stairs. Using the moonlight through the kitchen windows to find her way around, she stirred the embers in the stove, added a couple of sticks of wood, and put on the kettle. While she waited for it to heat, she prepared the teapot and cut herself a wedge of cake.

A short while later, feeling stronger for her sleep and the snack, she opened the back door and stepped out into the cool early morning air. It was the first time she'd been outside since Doc said Jane-Ellen's illness was fatal, and Hattie drew a deep breath. The boards of the porch were damp with dew against her bare feet.

Beneath the normal nocturnal noises, a harsh sound whispered on the wind. Hattie stepped off the back porch, trying to pinpoint the source. It sounded like it originated in the front yard, and she picked her way carefully over the damp lawn. Stopping at the corner of the house, she strained to see into the front porch shadows. The sound she'd heard was that of a man crying—harsh, deep, gut-wrenching crying.

Her eyes adjusted to the nighttime gloom and she stood at the edge of the flowerbed, distressed, uncertain. Rubbing one bare foot atop the other, she pondered how to help Jake, who sat on the porch floor, hunched over his pulled-up knees, head pressed against his kneecaps and shoulders jerking beneath the force of violent sobs.

Hattie had never seen a man cry like this before and she didn't know what to do. Should she slip away and allow him to grieve in private? Should she offer comfort? Oh God, which was the least destructive option? In the end, she simply couldn't walk away while he tore himself apart. Not trying to help was unthinkable. She climbed the stairs and crossed to squat next to him. Reaching out, she touched his shoulder. "Jake?"

He raised his head, and his eyelids were swollen and rimmed with red. The sound he made deep in his throat when he swallowed mid-sob made Hattie's throat ache in sympathy. Then he reached out for her, pulling her into his arms with a force that knocked her off her feet.

She fell half across his lap, her knees striking the floor of the porch. She gasped for air as he clutched her with a strength that made her ribs creak. Carefully, she adjusted herself to a semicomfortable position. One of her feet struck a nearby bottle, sending it rolling, and she smelled whiskey as it splashed across the floorboards. Hattie wrapped her arms around Jake's neck, tunneling her fingers into the soft layers of his hair as she pressed his face into the contour of her neck. Tremors wracked his body with each muffled cry.

"God, Hattie, I loved her so much when we got married."

"I know."

"It could have been so good," he mumbled into her neck. "Dammit, it could have been perfect. Except she couldn't stand me touching her. I loved her so much—and it repulsed her when I touched her." His chest heaved with the force of his grief.

"Shh." Hattie managed not to freeze in shock at the unexpected revelation. But she simply held Jake, rocking him and whispering mindless platitudes that hopefully soothed.

Jake gradually found comfort in Hattie's embrace. She was soft and resilient, her arms holding him securely in an ultimately calming way. When the force of his crying gradually diminished and he finally pulled away, they were both overheated and damp from the combination of warm evening air, body heat, and tears.

"When you first announced your plans to marry Jane-Ellen," Hattie said softly, "I was prepared to hate her." She watched Jake wipe his nose on his shirtsleeve like a little boy before he recollected himself and pulled a clean handkerchief from his pocket. "I wanted you to wait for me to grow up, you see, so I could marry you myself." She smiled softly when his startled gaze flew to hers. "You ruined my plans, Jake. I wasn't about to like your fiancée."

Jake reached for the whiskey bottle, contemplating it for an instant before setting it aside. He looked at Hattie crouched a few feet away, her hair a wild tangle leached of color in the darkness, her white nightgown billowing around her. Rising to his feet, he dragged over a wicker chair. "Here, sit." When she did, he sat at her feet cross-legged. "I never knew that. About you planning to marry me."

"Well, of course not. I had my pride. But the point is, I was prepared not to like Jane-Ellen." Tears rose in her eyes. "Only, I discovered it was impossible. She was always so nice to me. We were so different and she could really irritate me sometimes. The way she constantly worried about everyone's opinion."

He nodded. Jane-Ellen had definitely done that.

"But she was sweet and good to me," Hattie went on. "Even when she acted as if her corsets were laced too tight."

A snort of laughter escaped Jake, taking him by surprise. For a second he was appalled he found the least bit of humor in this situation. But, tears standing in her eyes, Hattie's mouth cocked up on one side in a self-deprecatory grin, and he knew it was okay. They weren't being disrespectful. And it wouldn't do to idealize Jane-Ellen just because she was gone.

Gone. How euphemistic. Still, it sounded less final, somehow, than "dead."

"She did do that, didn't she? It was as though she needed to be absolutely perfect at all times." Jake was silent for a moment. Then, suddenly, his fist smashed down on the floor of the porch. "Dammit, Hattie, she shouldn't've had to die that way!"

"I know. It was so unfair."

"Hell, yes, it's unfair. And my baby—" His voice suddenly cracked in the middle of the word and he looked up into Hattie's stricken eyes with angry, helpless grief. "I will never know, now, whether I would have had a son or a daughter."

Dawn was just beginning to replace the darkness with a less impenetrable gray as once again they cried.

16

THE BARBERSHOP WAS more crowded than usual, the simultaneous conversations louder, when Moses came in that afternoon. He wondered what hot gossip had triggered this.

Then he shrugged and strode past the men in the front room. Hell if it had anything to do with him. So, when his father walked into the back room seconds after Moses went to grab the broom, he looked up in surprise. "You left your customer?" His dad never did that. Never.

Gerald Marks rubbed the back of his neck. "I wanted you to hear this from me, son. Jane-Ellen Murdock died yesterday."

Shock reverberated through Moses like a struck gong. "That can't be right! Hell, you know how the men can be. They're worse gossips than women." It couldn't possibly be true; it—

"Jake told me himself," Gerald interrupted gently. "When he was in town arranging for a coffin."

And suddenly Jane-Ellen's death was a cold, hard fact wishful thinking couldn't alter. Moses' shock morphed to guilt. Hattie must have called him the minute she heard Doc Fielding's diagnosis. But had he been there for her? Hell, no.

Bitter self-blame hammered him, and he refused the luxury of clutching his own out-of-control emotions as a mitigating factor. Situations were either honorable or dishonorable. Black or white—no shades of gray.

Hattie had called and he'd avoided her with an excuse lamer than Henderson's old mare. This wasn't the first time he had let her down. But it was sure as hell the worst.

Moses viewed his failure as his worst betrayal yet, and figured Hattie did too. It mentally berated him in an endless loop as he rented a bicycle and haunted the road between town and the Murdock Ranch. Twice, he got as far as the gate to Jake's ranch, determined to offer Hattie his sincerest apologies and what solace he could. Both times he lost his nerve.

He turned away the second time, and his shoulders slumped in defeat as he dispiritedly pedaled back to town. He knew he wouldn't ride this way again. It was too damn late. He had callously turned her down when she'd called specifically asking for his help. His face was the last one Hattie would want to see now.

"I APOLOGIZE FOR intruding on your privacy, Jake, but I wanted to offer my condolences."

Jake's head snapped around in surprise. Roger Lord was the last person he'd expect to defy Mattawa's convention of leaving families to their bereavement until the funeral. Only very close friends were allowed to ignore the custom.

Jake finished fishing a stone from Thunder's shoe, then unclamped his knees to let the stallion's hoof drop. After swatting the horse's rump, he swept up the hobbling reins and led Thunder to a clean stall. Reemerging moments later, he wiped his hands on his worn, clean dungarees and extended his right to Roger. "Thank you, Roger. It was right neighborly of you to make a special trip." *Sure as hell wish you hadn't, though.* He kept that thought to himself.

Roger exchanged meaningless platitudes with Jake for several moments before working the conversation around to his true reason for going out of his way to make this trip to the Murdock Ranch. During the past months, he'd become obsessed with the idea of forcefully relieving Hattie Taylor of her virginity. The idea had consumed him since the afternoon he'd overheard her conversation with the Marks boy outside Armstrong's Livery. Knowing the perpetration of such an act against Hattie Taylor could carry serious repercussions for him rarely entered his consideration. And when it did, it was brief blips he found easy to brush aside. Hell, he was an elite personage in this town, above the laws governing lesser mortals. Besides, who would believe the slut's word over his? Everyone whispered that she was a girl of loose character.

His paramount concern was the need to strike soon. Not only was she leaving town in a few weeks, but given her outspoken, free-spirited nature, he doubted she'd long remain a virgin to despoil. It would be just like the lush little baggage to freely bestow her virginity on the first smooth talker to come her way. And that wouldn't do. Roger was determined the mouthy bitch forever remember her deflowering as the most degrading moment of her life.

It was such a pleasurable way to teach a woman her rightful place in this man's world.

He'd heard people say the grief accompanying the loss of a loved one was mind-numbing. It was a sentiment he didn't understand, for a person of superior intellect didn't allow extraneous nothings to interfere with his thought process. Still, the minute he heard about Jane-Ellen's death, he realized the confusion of such a time was a golden opportunity for him.

He never doubted he would achieve his objective. He was accustomed to getting his way—it was the only just outcome. Of *course* preeminent men such as himself were rewarded.

"It must be difficult to keep everything running smoothly at a time like this," he murmured in the sympathetic tones he'd heard others use. "Handling your ranch. Taking care of your ward."

"I'm getting by."

"When is Augusta due back in town?"

"Sunday, if all her means of transport run on schedule."

"If it would help," Roger offered, concealing his excitement, "Hattie is welcome to stay with Gertrude and me until Augusta's arrival. It would give you one less thing to worry about, and it might be easier for Hattie to be in town."

Jake wasn't prepared for the rush of panic Lord's suggestion unleashed in him. Hattie leave? She was the only reason he'd remained relatively sane. Face impassively stoic to conceal his thoughts, Jake leveled a look at Roger Lord and tried to keep his voice neutral when he said, "No. I appreciate the offer, but Hattie has been a great comfort to me, and she needs to be where she feels helpful. It was a generous offer, though. I'm much obliged."

No? Roger was nonplussed. And furious. Hell, yes, it was a generous offer! Who did Murdock think he was to decline? It had never occurred to him that Jake wouldn't jump at the prospect.

Not understanding people's apparent need to forge bonds with friends and family, Roger was left at a loss over Jake's refusal. His wishes were supposed to be instantly gratified. It was his *right*. Enraged, but unable to express it, he made polite conversation for another few minutes before taking his leave. His brain, however, worked at a fever pitch.

By the time he turned his buggy onto the county road and clicked at the horses to pick up their pace, he was already turning ideas over in his mind, looking for an alternate means to achieve his goal.

17

Murdock Ranch
FRIDAY, AUGUST 10, 1906

IT WAS GROWING late and Jake's still-sweltering office hosted the only light on downstairs. Contemplating the level of whiskey left in his bottle, he sat tilted back in his chair, his damp shirt stuck to his skin and his bare feet propped up on the desk. He knew he'd been knocking back too much liquor the past couple of days. Shrugging, he poured himself another shot.

He'd already drunk more than he should, but it was the only way to guarantee himself a reasonable night's sleep. Besides, it wasn't like anyone was around to see or care if he got a little drunk. Cook always withdrew to her room behind the kitchen shortly after the dinner dishes were washed and put away. And Hattie had already retired.

At least he assumed she had; she'd disappeared upstairs earlier in the evening and he hadn't heard a peep from her since. Which was just as well. He was on the verge of losing control and he sure didn't need her to see him like that. On the other hand, if she'd stayed for their nightly conversation, it might have staved off this god-awful loneliness. He had discovered his best defense against the bleak night hours was a heated debate or quiet conversation with Hattie.

During the day he handled things reasonably well. Not even death excused ranchers from tending their spreads, and the nonstop demands of the Murdock spread kept Jake occupied mind and body for ten to twelve hours at a stretch. Not that he didn't have a perfectly competent foreman willing to take the burden of running the ranch off his shoulders. But Jake needed to work, to burn off the restless energy, the seething emotions.

In contrast to his rigid daytime control, the early hours after midnight were a nightmare. Sleep was all but impossible unless he drank himself stupid. He tossed and turned until the sheets were a damp jumble more constrictive than a spider's web with a fresh fly. His mind refused to rest. For the past two nights, his brain had spun with relentless feverishness, battling unrelated emotions. Anger at God for taking his wife and child in such a terrible manner, unbearable grief, unspecified rage at the unfairness of life. And most horrifying of all, now that the first shock of Jane-Ellen's death had worn off . . . a niggling sense of reprieve.

Jake's feet hit the floor with a thump and, swearing roundly, he staggered slightly as he pushed away from his desk. He hated himself for those fleeting moments of a sense of freedom. Swaying slightly and eyeing the whiskey with a caustic look, however, he acknowledged booze wasn't the answer. It helped dull the edges, but it didn't begin to address the problem. Thinking it did was a sure road to ruin. He'd wind up like old Doc Baker if he wasn't careful. Putting the bottle back in the bottom drawer of his desk, he turned off the light and left the office.

He had nearly reached the top of the stairs after securing the house for the night when the bathroom door down the darkened upstairs hallway suddenly opened and flooded the surrounding area with light. His breath caught in his throat as Hattie stepped out into the hall.

Clearly, she'd been bathing and washing her hair, for she was briskly rubbing her wet hair with the towel draped around her neck. To Jake's mind, the activity was too little, too late. She sure as hell hadn't been quick enough to prevent her hair from dripping onto her thin wrapper. A wrapper that currently clung damply to her skin in several places.

He couldn't tear his gaze from the silky material plastered to the upper curve of her right breast. His body responded with an erection, hard, painful, and immediate. Infuriated, with drunken logic he laid the blame on Hattie. What was she thinking, running around the house half-naked? That her room was only steps away from the bathroom and she had obviously not expected to encounter anyone never occurred to him. "What the hell do you think you're doing?"

Hattie jerked to a halt mid-stride, slapping a hand over her heart. She peered into the darkness at the top of the stairs. "Jacob Murdock, you scared me to death!"

Jake pushed away from the newel-post that had been supporting him and advanced on her. Even as he loomed over her, however, he was very careful that they didn't touch. "Get in your room and put some clothes on!"

Hattie's eyes widened and hot color washed up into her cheeks. The hand still resting over her heart gathered the lapels of her wrapper together, clutching the two sides closed near her throat. "That's where I was headed," she said coolly. Then her nostrils flared, clearly catching the scent of whiskey Jake imagined pumped off him with all the subtlety of Bigger's Saloon's floor on a Saturday night. "You're drunk!" she snapped.

He grabbed her wrist and hauled her the few feet to her door. He kicked it open with a force that caused it to slam against the bedroom wall. "I said, get in your room."

"Jake!" Hattie protested indignantly and twisted her arm free of his grip with one strong yank. Planting her hands on her hips, she snarled, "Keep your stinkin' hands to yourself. What's the matter with you, anyway?" Her movement loosened her wrapper. Now gaping, what had been a respectable if slightly damp covering exposed a generous expanse of lightly freckled cleavage.

Jake saw red. "What's the matter?" he sneered, staring at her. "I'll tell you what's the matter! You running around out here with your tits hanging out for all the world to see."

Hattie didn't know what tits were, but following the direction of his hot-eyed gaze, she could make a darn good guess. Blushing with furious embarrassment, she tugged the parted sides of her wrapper back into place and tightened the sash at her waist. "How dare you," she spat, glaring up at him. "*What* world? I thought I was alone, and I sure as heck wasn't expecting to see you! And what do you mean, running around? I was going from the bathroom to my bedroom."

"Y'like flashing it and getting the men all excited, Hattie?" he demanded insolently. "Y'like seein' how many of the poor suckers you can give a straight shooter to?"

"Maybe I do," she yelled, incensed beyond reason. "You tell me what any of this has to do with giving guns to men and I'll let you know."

Jake barked an abbreviated laugh. "I'm not talking about guns, damn you." He grabbed her hand and yanked her forward, pressing her palm against his erection. "I'm talking about this straight shooter. *This*, Big-eyes."

"Jacob!" Hattie whispered, shocked down to her bare toes curling into the thin runner on the hardwood floor. But she didn't attempt to pull her hand away. She was too eaten up with curiosity. Lashes lowering, she looked down, staring at her hand and what it covered. Even through the material separating them, it was extremely hard and warm against her palm, and her fingertips pressed into something soft and shifting at its base. Her palm was imprinted by a thick, rigid length she'd swear wasn't there before.

It wasn't her habit to look at men's private places, of course, but surely she couldn't have missed seeing an appendage of such size had there been one to see. Maybe it was like the stallion she'd once seen covering a mare. She looked back into Jake's glittering dark gaze. "How do you do that?" she whispered in awe. "Does it grow?"

"Ah, Jesus, Hattie," he muttered, pressing hard against her hand before gaining control of himself and snatching it away. He swayed a bit as he stared at her. "You're supposed to run screaming from me." He reached out gentle fingers to trail down her smooth cheek. "But you never have done the expected, have you? You've always had such big, curious eyes." He bent his head and pressed a kiss against each of her eyelids. Then he pulled back a bit to look at her.

God. He was drunk, and he shouldn't be here. He needed to get the hell out before he did something he'd regret.

But her cheeks were flushed and her lips were lush, a pearly sheen of white teeth showing behind them. The uppermost layer of her hair had begun to dry, curling crazily about her pale skin. And, groaning, he leaned into her, slipping a hand around her neck at the base of her skull and tipping her face up to his descending mouth. Just one kiss; then he'd go.

It didn't enter Hattie's mind that what they were doing was improper. Jake's mouth was warm and gentle; then it was hot and a little rough. And when he indicated by deed she should part her lips, she did so unquestioningly. His tongue tasted not unpleasantly of whiskey, and it was aggressive and mobile against hers, demanding a response.

Flooded with new sensations, Hattie responded with a vengeance, using her own tongue to imitate Jake's actions, standing on tiptoe and holding his face between her splayed fingers. She pressed her body into the hard warmth of his.

Jake lost what little control he'd managed to exert upon his reeling mind. He backed her fully into her bedroom until the backs of her thighs bumped against the high mattress and they overbalanced to sprawl across the bed. Rolling on top of her, he pushed up on his left forearm while his right hand slid between their bodies to wrestle with the knot of her sash. His kiss was harsh and out of control, pressing Hattie's head into the pile of small satin pillows. Her doll, Lillian, tumbled from its place atop its decorative perch, rolling to the edge of the mattress.

Jake finally managed to untie her sash, and he brushed the silky material aside until it pooled beneath her. Dragging his mouth away from hers, he kissed the smooth, soft skin of her cheek. Kissed beneath her ear, then worked his way down the warm column of her neck before raising onto his elbow again to stare down at her. His breath whistled harshly through his teeth. "Pretty," he said in a low, gravelly tone. "Lovely, beautiful . . . Jesus, God, you're perfect."

He liked that, although Hattie trembled, she let him look at her. His eyes made a thorough survey, not missing a single voluptuous inch. Starting at her shoulders and rounded arms, his gaze slid down to where her long fingers clutched the bedspread. He started counting the freckles on her chest but kept losing track and gave up to trace the rising slope of her breasts. They were full and round and set high on her chest, capped with ruddy, puffy aureoles and tiny jutting nipples. Even while she lay flat on her back, her breasts remained arrogantly upright.

"Uppity," Jake murmured and flashed her a smile when he tore his attention away long enough to glance briefly into Hattie's smoldering eyes. "Why am I not surprised?" He was dying to touch them but feared once he did he'd never get around to the rest of his visual inspection.

And he wanted to see everything. *Now.* All summer long, he had tried not to imagine her naked. He'd tried hard, without success. Neither, however, had his imagination conjured anything remotely as spectacular as the bounty sprawled out in front of him. Beneath her pretty breasts, Hattie's rib cage was narrow, then dipped into a slim waist before flaring into full, round hips. Her legs were surprisingly long, given her less-than-impressive stature, and holy shit they were shapely—all firm muscle beneath smooth, creamy skin. They culminated in feet small and high arched.

Bringing his gaze back up her legs, Jake's inspection ground to an abrupt halt. For there, at the apex, where plump, firm thighs joined her torso, was a triangle of fiery ginger-copper curls. God help him, she was just luscious all over.

After impatiently unbuttoning and removing his shirt, he rolled back to gather Hattie in his arms, his chest flattening her breasts as he held her tight. Heart pounding faster than it had as a teenager smooching his first girl, Jake kissed her with escalating passion. And his breath grew more ragged with every enthusiastic, generous response she returned.

Pulling his fingers from Hattie's tangled, drying curls, Jake smoothed his hand down her throat, trailed his fingers over her collarbone, and lightly rubbed them down her satin-sleek chest before cupping her breast. The feel of its full resilience made him expel an abrupt breath into her mouth, and he broke the kiss to slide down her body. Cupping both breasts in his hands, he pushed them together, his thumbs reaching to stroke her velvety nipples into fine points as he licked the deep valley he'd created between them.

Moaning, Hattie arched her back. "Oh, Jake," she whispered. "Oh my, oh, Jake, *oh my*!" She'd never dreamed such sensations existed. As his mouth surrounded one tight nipple and sucked it into the hot furnace of his mouth, she clamped her thighs together, trying to subdue the flood of feeling causing a riot deep inside her private place. It didn't help. To distract herself, she asked, "Are my bosoms what you were talking about when you said 'tits'?"

Jake froze in shock, suddenly feeling stone-cold sober. Hearing that word he never should have exposed her to, inquired about with innocent curiosity, was like being thrust into the icehouse on a steamy summer day. Goose bumps broke out over his flesh and shame shot through him. He rolled away from her and sat on the side of the bed. Hunched over the elbows he'd braced on his knees, cradling his head in his hands, and rocking in misery, he fought to regain control. His body raged with unspent needs even as guilt scorched his mind. Dear God, what had he nearly done to her? His wife hadn't been dead two full days, Hattie was an innocent virgin left in his care, and *this* was how he behaved?

Even now he wasn't above finishing what he'd started, he discovered when Hattie sat up and touched his shoulder with a soft hand. "Jake?"

His body throbbing with needy awareness, he shook her off with a near-violent shrug. "Don't touch me! Jesus, Hattie, if you value your virginity, don't touch me. Get your robe on."

Hattie pulled her wrapper tightly around her and fumbled with the tie. "Did I do something wrong, Jake? I'm sorry. Tell me what I did wrong and I'll try to make it better."

Her words, her apologetic tone, were red-hot nails skewering his self-esteem to the wall—and he cracked. "Shut up!" he snarled. "Dammit, Hattie, just shut up! Don't you see what was happening here? I was about to fuck you right through the mattress!" *Oh, nice, Murdock; that's just great. You've added a slew of obscenities and two vulgar expressions to her vocabulary tonight. When you do something, you really do it up right. Big improvement, now you've found the honor not to violate her body, to violate her mind instead.* He picked up his shirt and surged to his feet.

Careful to keep a distance between them, he turned and looked down at her. Seeing her full bottom lip wobbling and tears magnifying those sun-shot whiskey-brown eyes as she met his gaze in miserable confusion was a knife to the gut. "I'm sorry," he said through a throat that felt lined with broken glass. "This never should have happened. It's all my fault— none of yours—and I'm sorry. Lock your door, girl, and don't let me back in, you hear?" Even now, he wasn't positive he could trust himself to stay away from her. "Tomorrow evening, you'll go stay at Roger Lord's house."

"What?" She launched herself from the bed, horror in her eyes. "No!"

Jake hurriedly backed away to maintain a safe expanse between them. "I'm not arguing this tonight, Hattie. Just lock the damn door behind me!"

"I won't go to Roger Lord's! I don't like the way he looks at me."

She didn't like the way Roger *looked* at her? "Dammit, girl, don't you get it?" he snarled. "Looks can't hurt you. What I'd do to you, given half a chance, is what you need to worry about. I can't be trusted to keep my hands off you!"

"You would never force yourself on me, Jake," Hattie whispered with utter confidence. *"Never."* She wasn't so sure about Roger Lord, but since she didn't have a shred of evidence to back up her suspicions, she didn't say so aloud.

Wanting nothing so much as to throw Hattie back down on the bed and finish what he'd begun, Jake found her statement nearly laughable— or he would have, had he been in the slightest mood to find amusement in anything. "Just lock the door now." He stepped out into the hall and pulled her door closed behind him.

He didn't relax the rigid restraints he'd imposed upon himself until he heard the click of the bolt sliding home.

SATURDAY, AUGUST 11, 1906

Hattie stayed in her room the next day. She was mortified by her active encouragement of the liberties Jake had taken the night before. At the same time, she couldn't stop thinking about the way he'd made her feel. *What is the* matter *with me? A nice girl would be horrified to be caught in her nightclothes. But not only have I flaunted myself the next best thing to naked in front of two men; I have—*

Hattie felt herself blushing all over and dared not recall the depth of her disappointment when Jake called a halt to things last night. But, Lord, it had felt amazing before he did! Was she every bit as wicked as the gossips in town declared? Surely, no moral woman would think the things she thought. She feared her boldness was responsible for the new distance in her friendship with Moses. And now Jake was threatening to send her away. Hattie shuddered at the thought of being subjected to Roger Lord's hospitality. Augusta was due home tomorrow. Surely, if she kept out of Jake's way, they could manage one more day.

Jake grimly ignored the pain of his hangover and spent the day driving himself to the point of exhaustion. He, too, tried to convince himself one more night couldn't possibly make a difference. But . . . no. The memory of Hattie's wholehearted response to his advances kept interfering with his vow to keep his distance.

He'd ignited something last night that never should have been lit. All summer long, he'd told himself he wasn't really attracted to her. Knowing in his gut it was a lie, he at least thought he had enough self-control not to do anything about it. Then to get drunk and force her to touch his cock?

Jake knew he couldn't be trusted to spend another night in the same house with her. His actions and language in the deep dark of the early morning were an outrage. Yet Hattie hadn't been scared or offended. He knew damn well he'd shocked her, but curiosity and eagerness overruled even that.

He couldn't stop thinking about her reaction. It was too close to what he'd expected of Jane-Ellen on their wedding night for his peace of mind. And every time he thought of Hattie's big eyes looking down at her hand on him, then lifting her gaze to stare at him with such awe—

He had to get her out of the house. A locked door wasn't a sufficient deterrent to prevent him from taking what he wanted. He knew he could tempt her, and the excitement the knowledge created appalled him. No matter how far he had diverged from the man he'd always believed he'd be, he drew the line at seducing a trusting young virgin left in his care.

Still, it didn't have to be Lord; maybe he could find someone Hattie would be happier going to. He placed a couple of calls, but his onetime golden luck had turned to shit.

And at three p.m. he left the ranch and rode over to Roger Lord's house.

"No!" Hattie stared at him in horror when he informed her of his plans. "I won't stay with that man."

"You will."

"No! If you insist I leave, then I'll stay with Moses."

Jake wasn't prepared for the jealousy that engulfed his reason at Moses' name. The memory of him and Hattie in the creek made him say with deliberate cruelty, "Moses hasn't been beating a path to your door lately. What makes you think he'll welcome you now?"

He hated himself when he watched pain flicker in her eyes.

Hattie's chin tilted stubbornly. "I'll stay with Doc, then."

"Doc is out at the Whitfield place. I did call him, Hattie, but his receptionist said he'll likely be there all night. And before you ask, I also called Aurelia Donaldson, but she's shopping in Eugene for the next couple days." Jake drew himself up, gave her an "I mean business" look, and made damn sure his tone was final when he said, "I have already made the arrangements with Lord, and that is where you're going."

"But Roger Lord's wife is an invalid. That's pretty much the same as him being a bachelor. It's not proper."

Jake snorted. "That's rich, little girl. Since when have you worried about what's proper?"

"I hate you," she whispered. "If you make me go to Mr. Lord's I will never forgive you."

Jake's stomach twisted in knots, but he replied coolly, "I'll just have to learn to live without your forgiveness, then. Go upstairs and pack."

The ride to town passed in tense silence. Stopping only once, at the dressmaker's to pick up Hattie's funeral apparel, they soon arrived at Roger Lord's house. Hattie sat staring a moment at the ornate façade before she finally turned to face Jake. "Please, Jacob," she begged. "Don't do this."

Steeling himself against her plea, he handed her the dressmaker's box and her portmanteau. Hattie shuddered as she accepted them, and the look she gave Jake as she shunned his assistance from the buggy looked like full-out hatred.

Jake felt sick. Not even when she'd discovered he was unfaithful to Jane-Ellen had she looked at him with such loathing. He was ready to relent and take her back to the ranch. But following her up the walk, he noticed her dress. She was wearing one of three garments she'd dyed black, and its drab appearance reminded him his wife had died three days ago and already he was overpoweringly tempted to turn an eighteen-year-old innocent into his chippie.

God forgive him, for a moment he considered taking her home anyway. Then the front door was opened by Roger Lord himself, and it was too late for second thoughts.

HATTIE WATCHED JAKE'S buggy depart and barely contained the desperate urge to run after him. He'd refused Roger's offer of refreshments, retreating in an indecent rush, and Hattie was overwhelmed by a feeling of something horrid about to happen.

Later, at dinner with Roger, she silently admitted she was wrong. She could certainly think of more comfortable ways to spend this hour, but nothing untoward had occurred.

"I suppose after the funeral, you will spend your time searching for a husband," Roger said out of the blue, looking up from his glass of wine.

Excuse me? Hattie's ire rose, but she managed a polite, "No, sir. I'm leaving next month for the Seattle Normal School."

He gave her one of those supercilious looks she despised. "What on earth for? You're a young woman of consequence." His gaze dropped to her breasts for a moment, making her long to cross her arms over them. "You have no need to work. You should be thinking about an advantageous marriage."

"And yet I am looking forward to an education."

"Preposter—" He broke off as an older woman entered the dining room. She stopped just inside the door until Roger snapped his fingers at her, then tapped his pointer finger twice against his temple. Shooting a nervous look in Hattie's direction, the servant crossed the room. Roger cocked his head as the woman leaned to whisper in his ear.

Snapping his fingers again, he waved the servant away. Roger stood as she sidled out of the room. He turned to Hattie. "You'll have to excuse me; my wife needs me."

Then he turned and left the room. So, she was wrong. Nothing horrid going on here. Just the opposite, in fact. The man was upstairs devoting time to his invalid wife. Alone in Lord's dining room, Hattie felt foolish for imagining melodrama where none existed.

Fine. She smiled. Perhaps she would forgive Jake after all. She had truly feared Roger would make improper advances and had been on guard from the moment she was dumped on the man's doorstep. But while Lord spoke to her as though she had all the brain function of a stump, Hattie admitted he had been an acceptable, if condescending, host. While he made Hattie edgy as a cat stroked from tail to head rather than vice versa, the problem was clearly with her, not him.

But Hattie's relief faded as she gazed at the dregs in her teacup, a bone-deep loneliness taking its place. She was accustomed to being surrounded by females. They *talked* to each other in her aunt's house. The sheer silence of the Lord household unsettled her. Since her arrival, Hattie hadn't heard a solitary laugh or so much as a snippet of chatter among the household staff.

Hearing the muffled clatter of dishes through the door at the far end of the dining room, Hattie collected her cup and saucer and rose. She crossed to the closed kitchen door but hesitated upon hearing faint murmurs on the now-quiet other side. Finally, along with a deep breath, she pushed the heavy swinging door open with her hip.

Two older women, one in a clean, worn dress covered by a splattered apron, the other dressed in dowdy but slightly more fashionable apparel, sat at a worn worktable, steaming cups atop its scrupulously scrubbed surface. The apron lady, whom Hattie surmised was the cook, scrambled to her feet.

"Miss!" She wrung her hands. "Be you needin' more tea, dear? I'm so sorry, let me jes' get you some!" She dashed over to remove the cup and saucer from Hattie's hands. "Please," the older woman added, "make yerself comfortable in the dining room. I'll bring you a fresh cup right smart-like, along with a nice slice o' cake."

Returning to that large, empty dining room was the last thing Hattie wanted. "Might I stay here with you for a few moments?" she asked. "I'm used to having my evening tea with my aunt Augusta in the parlor, or with Mirabel in the kitchen. I barely know Mr. Lord, so it feels odd to be sitting in such solitary splendor in his big dining room."

The women exchanged uneasy glances and Hattie braced for their refusal.

The aproned woman, however, merely said, "Whatever you like, miss."

Hattie caught a flash of what looked suspiciously like fear crossing the other woman's face. But that made no sense, and when Hattie blinked and reexamined the woman's expression, she decided she must have been mistaken.

Her tea and cake were set before her. "I be Mrs. Morton, the cook," the older woman said gruffly. She indicated the other lady. "This here be Mrs. Bryant, the housekeeper."

"How very nice to meet you both," Hattie replied sincerely. "I'm grateful for the company."

Mrs. Bryant studied her. "It's not my place to say, miss, but I'm rather surprised you weren't taken to a more female-leaning household to spend this night."

"Oh, I agree wholeheartedly," Hattie admitted. "But my aunt and Mirabel are out of town and unfortunately so is Aurelia Donaldson, with whom I would ordinarily stay."

Instead of prompting more conversation between them, her explanation seemed to grind it to a standstill. Mrs. Morton and Mrs. Bryant were perfectly polite and respectful, but Hattie could see her presence in their domain unsettled them. What conversation she could coax from them was stilted, and while they seemed to avoid looking directly at her, Hattie caught them exchanging worried glances.

Accepting that she was unwanted in the kitchen, she finished her tea and rose. "Thank you for the refreshment and your company. I'll retire to my room now."

She tried not to let their patent relief affect her.

Upstairs, Hattie undressed, neatly hung her gown and underclothes in the wardrobe, then donned her night rail and turned out the light. She climbed under the neatly folded-back counterpane and pulled the covers up around her shoulders. She had clearly discomfited the women in the kitchen and wondered if it was her reputation—if it had preceded her. Well, either that or her barging into their territory had affronted their sense of propriety. Hattie wouldn't be surprised to learn Roger had strict rules about interaction between the classes. That would account for the . . . trepidation that seemed to encircle the two servants.

Trepidation. Hattie shivered, although the room was comfortably warm. It was an unnerving word, yet try as she might to tell herself she was too imaginative, she felt unsettled. Unease was an itch at the back of her neck. She could not relax, but rather tossed and turned, while continuously flipping her pillow in search of some soothing coolness. Finally, however, sheer exhaustion tugged her into agitated slumber.

She was twitching in restless sleep when her bedroom door silently opened.

18

DOC FIELDING WAS warming a pan of milk when he heard the scratching at his kitchen door. What the hell?

It was after two a.m. and he groaned, hoping Mrs. Worley's time hadn't come. He had only been home ten minutes, following a particularly hard delivery at an outlying ranch. Mrs. Whitfield and babe were fine, but it had been touch-and-go for quite some time. Moving the milk to the back of the stove, he went to answer the door.

Hattie stumbled into the room when the door supporting her opened. She stood barefoot, swaying unsteadily. "He hurt me, Doc," she whimpered, gazing up at him with dazed eyes.

Doc stared at her in horror. She was dressed only in a once-white ripped nightgown. He saw a bruise on her arm beneath the torn sleeve and her bottom lip was split. Trembling visibly, she hugged herself with one arm. The other arm clutched a dressmaker's box to her side.

Doc swore long and imaginatively. He stepped forward to give her a comforting hug, but she flinched away, and it produced an unthinkable suspicion. Gently grasping her arm, he led her to a chair, glancing at the back of her night rail as he seated her. There was blood on it around her thighs, and Doc felt sick. "Who did this to you?"

"I begged Jake not to . . . but he wouldn't listen to me," she mumbled through chattering teeth.

"Jake?" Doc went cold with shock, then hot with rage. "*Jake* did this to you?"

"What? No." Hattie's eyes didn't quite focus as she stared in confusion at Doc Fielding, and he realized she was in shock. She was so pale her freckles stood out like cinnamon on cream.

"Don't move," he ordered and sped from the room. Returning in moments, he draped her in a wool blanket and poured the warm milk he'd been preparing for himself into a cup and added a generous shot of whiskey. "Here, drink this."

Hattie held the cup between shaking hands and brought it up to her mouth. Her teeth rattled against the cup as she took a sip. She choked and coughed as the whiskey no doubt burned a path down her throat, yet Doc knew when its heat reached her stomach, for it restored a measure of color to her face.

He pulled up a chair and sat facing her. "Now, tell me: is Jake responsible for this?"

"Yes—no." She shook her head. "He made me go there, but he would never . . . he didn't—" The chattering of her teeth and shaking of her hands intensified, and she set the cup down on the table before she dropped it.

"Easy, girl," Doc said soothingly. "It's all right now; no one's gonna hurt you again." He picked up her hand, and after an initial resistance, she allowed him to smooth his thumb over her long fingers. He waited patiently for her eyes to meet his. "Where did Jake make you go?"

Her trembling increased. "R-Roger Lord's."

"Why?"

"B-because, Jake kissed me and t-touched my bosoms. He was drunk and upset about me being in the hall wearing only a wrapper. But I knew he wouldn't hurt me. He stopped after a couple minutes, but he was angry with himself and he said it wasn't . . . wasn't safe for me to stay at the ranch with him." Hattie began to laugh hysterically. "Isn't that fu-funny?" Her laughter turned to a storm of weeping, and cautiously, Doc eased her into his arms, rocking her gently.

His reaction to hearing his son-in-law had initiated an intimacy with Hattie was mixed. It hadn't angered Doc when he'd first discovered Jake had started frequenting Mamie Parker's girls after four years of marriage. He'd assumed Jake went there to spare Jane-Ellen from unwanted attention. Doc knew his daughter was a rigidly moral young woman, and he'd suspected she didn't like the marriage bed. Jake was an earthy young man and, overall, he'd been a good husband. But, dammit, his daughter had been dead less than four full days! And Hattie was only a kid . . .

As she shuddered in his arms, Doc reminded himself she was eighteen, an age when most girls her age were married, some already with a child or two. She also possessed a figure that probably brought a throb to more than one young buck's loins. To be fair, from her few faltering words it sounded as though fear for her virtue was what had driven Jake to make arrangements to remove her from his reach. He must have thought he was delivering her to safety.

Instead, he'd delivered her into the hands of a goddamn rapist.

"Missy?" Doc drew back until he could look into Hattie's eyes. "I'm going to ask you some questions, dear. Then I'll have to do an examination. Do you think you can bear with me?"

Hattie nodded uncertainly. She wiped her eyes with the back of her hand, watching Doc rise and go to the icebox. He chipped some ice from the block in the bottom of the oak cabinet and placed it in a clean dishcloth. Returning to her, he placed it gently against her split lip and instructed her to hold it.

"Did Roger Lord do this?"

"Yes," she whispered.

"Did he rape you, Hattie?" At her blank look, he realized she'd probably never heard the word before. He cleared his throat. "Did he force his . . . man part . . . into—"

"It *hurt*, Doc." Her voice verged on hysteria, and the ice pack fell from her hands as she used them to push away an unseen attacker. "I tried to make him stop, but he kept hitting me and shoving that . . . Oh criminy, it was so painful. He said, 'You're not s-such a fast talker now, are you, you little bitch?' and something about teaching me to kn-know my place, and, oh God, it hurt, it hurt, it *hurt*!" Shaking violently, she stared at Dr. Fielding with dazed eyes. "I hurt him, too, Doc. I s-stabbed him with a pair of embroidery scissors."

"What?"

"I just wanted to make him stop. I struggled and I fought, but it didn't seem to make any difference. I scratched his neck with my fingernails, and he called me a filthy name and hit me so hard I skidded partway off the side of the bed."

She shuddered and hugged herself, rocking back and forth, back and forth. Closing her eyes, she felt again that unholy agony pinning her hips to the mattress, and her eyes snapped back open. It was easier if she concentrated on the remembered pain of her arm cracking against the corner of the night table before it slid across the furniture's surface, sweeping off everything in its path.

"I tried to grab the edge of the table for balance," she whispered, "but my hand kept sliding across its top. Then I felt a pair of scissors and . . ." She made a stabbing motion in unconscious illustration. Her hand dropped limply into her lap and she stared at its empty, widespread fingers. "Oh God, they were sticking out of his arm and he just looked at them. It wasn't until the bleeding started that he pulled them out. And I shoved him as hard as I could and ran."

The next half hour was a nightmare for both Hattie and Doc. The examination he insisted upon was one more trauma she had to endure, and he felt sicker to his soul and so goddamn *furious* with every new bruise he unveiled.

Ordinarily, he would've awakened his housekeeper to attend Hattie during an examination of this nature. In this instance, however, he didn't dare. Mrs. Higgins was a fine woman and a soothing presence for the ladies when a pelvic examination was indicated. But she dearly loved her gossip. The personal nature of the exam was difficult for Hattie, but luckily, she was still mostly numb with shock. Growing grimmer with each new discovery, Doc wished he, too, could submerge his emotions.

Using his new Brownie camera, he recorded the evidence of abuse to her face. Then he pulled her nightgown up here and down there, rearranging it carefully in order to record as much of the damage to her arms, legs, and chest as he could, while still preserving her modesty. He knew he'd have to take the film into the county seat to have it developed. Word would spread like wildfire if he developed the photographs in Mattawa. And until he knew what Augusta wanted to do, he planned to protect Hattie's privacy.

It was a relief to finally dose her with tincture of opium and tuck her into the bed in Jane-Ellen's old room. Doc felt like crying when she revealed that the dressmaker's box, which she insisted on keeping with her, held her attire for Jane-Ellen's funeral. He sat with her until she went to sleep, then went into the kitchen and poured himself a stiff drink. Sitting at the table, Doc wrote notes on Hattie's condition while they were fresh in his mind. His brain churned with a dozen emotions as he thought about his daughter's death, Jake Murdock, Roger Lord, Hattie's brutally stolen innocence, and Augusta's homecoming. He cradled his aching head in his hands.

Christ Almighty, what a mess.

EARLY SUNDAY EVENING

Doc closed his office early to meet Augusta's train. His expression carefully bland, he directed Mirabel and the stationmaster to collect the women's luggage and transport everything to Augusta's house. Then he assisted Augusta into his car. Ordinarily, he'd have helped Mirabel himself, but he simply could not summon the patience today. And regardless of how close Augusta was to her companion, this was a conversation best delivered privately.

He wanted to drive while he delivered the dreadful story. At least then, he wouldn't have to see Augusta's horror when he broke the last news she'd want to hear. He also wanted his child back and Hattie untouched, the way she had been yesterday. But all the wishing in the world couldn't make that happen—so he cranked up the car. And started talking.

No, no, no. Augusta thought coming home to bury her daughter-in-law and grandchild was the worst thing that could happen. But this! Her darling Hattie viciously violated?

Dear, dear God. "What should we do?" She pressed her knuckles against her trembling lips. "God in heaven. Roger Lord cannot be allowed to get away with this outrage. I dearly want to call the sheriff and have that man dragged away in chains." Her eyes burned with a fierce light when she stated, "I want to see him either hanged or spending an eternity in jail—I don't care which." She met Doc's eyes. "And I understand perfectly well if I take steps to ensure that, Hattie will be ruined."

"I know, Augusta." Swearing, Doc ran his fingers through his thinning hair. "That's why I didn't do anything before you got home. I have enough evidence to ensure Roger Lord spends a good long time in jail. But it would mean a trial. And despite the pictures I took, or giving testimony in which I swear Hattie was relieved of her virginity in a most violent way, or even the fact that she struggled to the point of causing him bodily harm, she will never again be accepted in polite society. Jesus, Augusta, she is sometimes barely tolerated now, even under your protection. If it becomes known she no longer possesses a maidenhead, Mattawa's upstanding citizens will turn their backs on her entirely—I guarantee it. Men will make improper advances, women will cross the street to avoid having their skirts brush against hers, and all of them will feel perfectly justified in doing so. Hattie's been too outspoken in the past, and that girl is a born fighter. She isn't the type to kill herself over this, and—bet your bottom dollar—she won't be forgiven for rejecting death over dishonor." He rubbed his temples. "And if it ever came out at a trial why Jake sent her to Lord's house in the first place—" He shook his head.

He hadn't wanted to tell Augusta that part, but the first question she'd asked when the initial shock wore off was why Hattie hadn't been at the ranch.

"I'm terrified of Jacob's reaction if he discovers the truth," Augusta admitted. "Not just his guilt over knowing he was responsible for sending her there; maybe he deserves that. But if he finds out Roger raped her, he will kill him."

"The man deserves to be killed," Doc replied flatly.

"You think I don't *know* that?" Augusta sat stiffly erect on the edge of her seat. "But his richly deserved death will be a cold comfort, indeed, if my son expends his youth in jail."

"Augusta, there is not a jury in the land would convict him."

"Which brings us right back to a trial."

Doc rubbed his temples harder. "Yeah. Which brings us back to a trial. Son of a bitch." He didn't tack on his usual apology for his language.

Although it was Hattie's future they were deciding, neither thought to ask her opinion on the matter. Doc had left her resting in an uncharacteristic state of inertia in Jane-Ellen's old room while he'd met Augusta's train. He'd kept Hattie fairly sedated all day, but even without the opium he doubted she'd be fully functional. Her emotions had sustained too many shocks in too short a period of time and were temporarily deadened.

Not that she would have been consulted had she been her normal, feisty self. Their generation didn't consider it necessary to ask a female's wishes before rendering a verdict affecting her future. A young woman's parents or guardian made all the decisions in her life until she married. Then her husband took control.

"We cannot let her life be ruined," Augusta finally said. "But how can we live with ourselves if we let that monster go free? God forgive me, I want to destroy him."

"Maybe we can . . . without involving Hattie," Doc said slowly.

Augusta snapped ramrod straight. "How?"

"First, I want your permission to talk to the sheriff." Augusta shifted involuntarily and he hurried to say, "Jacobson's a fair man. He's also close-mouthed and he's nobody's fool. He'll understand the need to keep this private. At the very least, he'll keep an eye on Lord."

"Very well. But that will hardly ruin Roger."

"No. It won't. But rumors might."

"Rumors? I fear I don't understand."

Quietly, Doc outlined his plan, and as she listened, a small, tight smile of pure vengeance curved Augusta's lips.

19

"M Y DARLING GIRL," Augusta said as Doc ushered Hattie through her front door. She looked at Hattie's split lip and held her arms out, wishing the lip was the worst of it. "I'm so sorry this happened to you."

For the first time in Augusta's memory, Hattie walked into her arms, clung to her, and wept. It was rare to see her cry at all, and the deep, wrenching sobs shaking her frame broke Augusta's heart into a million pieces and nearly brought her to her knees. She smoothed her hands down the luxuriant wealth of Hattie's hair and held her tightly.

Doc set Hattie's dress box on the foyer floor and gestured that he was leaving. Augusta mouthed her thanks. The door closed behind him and they were left alone at the foot of the stairs.

"I am so sorry I disgraced you, Aunt Augusta," Hattie sobbed into the powdered contour of her guardian's neck.

Augusta stiffened and, clamping Hattie's shoulders in her hands, stepped back to hold her niece at arm's length. "I don't *ever* want to hear such talk from you again, Hattie Witherspoon Taylor," she commanded, staring into her ward's red-rimmed eyes. "What happened to you should never happen to any woman—and you certainly could not control it. I absolutely refuse to let you be shamed by it. What that man did was criminal, and if it wouldn't ruin you in the process, I would see to it he was punished to the full extent of the law."

She put an arm around Hattie's shoulders and ushered her up the stairs, continuing fiercely. "Do not think Roger Lord will be allowed to get off scot-free, though, my dear. I have already placed a call to him."

Hattie's amber eyes flared with sudden panic and she stopped in the middle of the hall. "Oh, Aunt Augusta, I wish you hadn't done that." She was ashamed of her craven desire to keep her attack private, but she simply didn't think she could bear it if it became public knowledge. "Central always listens in."

"I know they do, dear." Gently, she urged Hattie down the hall. "I counted on it. Don't worry, darling, your name was never mentioned. I simply informed Roger he was most unwelcome at Jane-Ellen's funeral tomorrow and that his services were no longer required as my lawyer." Her heart still accelerated with fury at the remembrance of Roger Lord's surprise. Had he thought he could just abuse her ward in the vilest manner possible and have it overlooked? "That will start the grapevine humming."

"*Good.*" For the first time since her attack, Hattie felt a faint semblance of her old fire. "I hope they conclude you've discovered something truly awful about him. I hope he is shunned in the streets." As she would be if the truth came out.

"Oh, I intend to make sure of it," Augusta said resolutely as she turned down the spread and helped Hattie into a clean night rail and into bed. "Doc gave me the idea. We're going to bury him in rumors. It's only fair that for once they be directed at someone who truly deserves it. The only thing that worries me is Jacob will hear of it and want to know what is going on. Well!" She waved that away. "We will worry about that when and if we come to it."

Hattie's reborn fire cooled considerably at the mention of Jake. It was largely thanks to him she was no longer pure. Now the very thing the gossips had speculated about this past year was true. Not that she was a girl of easy virtue. But she'd always had the knowledge of her own virginity to bolster her when the rumors flew. Now, however, thanks to Jake's refusal to listen to her, her claim to purity had been ripped from her. "I don't care whether he hears or not," she said flatly. But even as she said it she knew she cared terribly. "Yes, I do," she admitted with her usual honesty. "I think I would die if he knew."

Augusta, tenderly sweeping a tendril of hair from Hattie's forehead, thought this was the first time she'd ever heard Hattie utter words that sounded like something her peers would say.

"Aunt Augusta?" Hattie shifted uncomfortably. "What if I quicken?" The violent act Roger Lord had forced on her had not been anything like what she'd imagined when Jake explained procreation to her. But the mechanics were the same. She was very much afraid she might bring shame to the Murdock name after all.

"That won't happen, dear." Augusta stilled the perturbed movements of Hattie's fingers as they plucked the embroidered doves on the pillowcase. "Do you remember when you were twelve and Jacob explained about the seed and the egg?" At Hattie's nod, Augusta forced herself to continue levelly even as her face grew hot. "Well, Doc said he found no evidence of Roger Lord's seed, so you clearly used those scissors in a timely manner. There will be no child."

Hattie sagged with relief. "Oh, thank God. I was worried."

Augusta sat with Hattie until her ward's eyelids began to droop. Not until the young woman fell into a deep sleep did she go downstairs. Mirabel came into the parlor wiping her hands on a tea towel seconds later, and Augusta filled her in on the details. Not sharing this latest tragedy never occurred to her—Mirabel had been her confidante for more than forty years, and she'd suffer untold torture rather than divulge a Murdock secret. Also, Augusta knew good and well Mirabel loved Hattie every bit as much as she did.

They had only begun to sip their cooling tea when the front door banged open, then was slammed shut. Augusta met Mirabel's eyes and her friend made a discreet exit. Augusta set the other woman's cup and saucer on the service tray as Jake stormed into the room.

"Where's Hattie?"

"Keep your voice down, Jacob," Augusta remonstrated. "She's asleep."

"Doc said she was ill when I called to ask him to meet your train." Jake ran a hand through his hair. "I was delivering a foal or I would have been here sooner. Is it serious?" He'd been a wreck all afternoon, worrying.

"It's a female problem, Jacob," Augusta said repressively.

He sagged with relief as he sank into a chair. "Yeah. That's what Doc said." But his father-in-law's voice had been uncharacteristically cool, and Jake had wondered if he was trying to shield him from the knowledge of a more serious ailment. "Do you have another cup? I could use some of that." He hadn't touched a drop of alcohol since the night in the hall.

"Certainly." Augusta poured. She watched while he devoured several of the dainty sandwiches she couldn't swallow. When he lounged back in the corner of the davenport with his second cup of tea, she said, "While I was gone, Jacob, I did some thinking. I would very much like it if you would take control of the family affairs."

Jake slowly eased upright and set his cup on a nearby table. Praying the timing wasn't too obvious, Augusta rushed to say, "I always intended to turn everything over to you, but when you dropped most of your practice—"

His clear, dark eyes studied her face intently. "You're not ill, are you, Mother?"

"Oh, darling, no!" She hated that he worried but was relieved he'd jumped to the wrong conclusion. Better than asking why she was suddenly intent on dropping Roger Lord. She patted his hand. "I suppose seeing so many Witherspoons in San Francisco made me think of family."

"What about Roger?"

Augusta poured every ounce of iron discipline into maintaining her facial expression. "I'm sure he will understand, dear. I did warn him, years ago, you would one day handle all my affairs. But if it's too much?"

"No, of course not. I'll see to it next week."

"Good, because I already called to tell him as much."

They talked for a short while longer before Jake got up to leave. He asked to look in on Hattie before he went, but Augusta vetoed the idea. It was probably the first time in her life she was relieved to see her son leave her home. Blowing out a sigh, she turned away from the door. Rubbing the ache in her temples, she echoed Doc's sentiments.

Dear Lord. What a god-awful mess.

20

First Presbyterian Cemetery
MONDAY, AUGUST 13, 1906

"ASHES TO ASHES, dust to dust . . ."

Hattie stood on patchy parched grass next to the newly dug plot. It looked raw as a fresh wound against the late summer landscape, and during the service she'd deliberately stared at the hazy hills on the horizon to avoid seeing the gleaming coffin sitting before it. Occasionally, a whiff of the fresh-cut flowers blanketing Jane-Ellen's coffin spiraled on the wind.

Hattie tried to marshal her thoughts into some sort of order, but it was hard. All she could seem to do was *feel*. A hard, tight knot of misery lodged behind her breastbone as she gazed through the shield of her veil at the large crowd gathered in the cemetery to pay their last respects to Jane-Ellen Murdock. Hattie wondered with some bitterness how many of them would have attended had it been *her* funeral.

Her need to get out of this town began to border on desperation. It was hard enough before, knowing herself to be despised. Then, at least, she'd had Moses and Jake and Jane-Ellen. And she hadn't had this grinding sense of betrayal and violation. Standing very still, she tried by sheer force of will to subdue the fine tremors rippling along her nerve endings.

"Are you all right?"

Hattie started as Jake took her arm and she realized the service was over. Growing cold all over, she tugged in panic against the hand under her elbow. "Don't touch me."

Jake stiffened and dropped her arm. He wished he could see her face, but it was a pale, insubstantial shadow behind her veil. He'd felt the tremors vibrating through her and there was an air about her warning of nerves stretched to the breaking point. He wanted to hold her until she calmed, then take her somewhere where they could talk. The way she kept her face slightly but perpetually averted from him, however, discouraged any attempt on his part to get close to her. He stuffed his hands in his pockets.

Hattie thought she would come unhinged during the impromptu reception line staged near the line of black-draped carriages. Everyone wished to pay their respects, and naturally she was expected to stand next to Augusta, Doc, and Jake as part of the family. It was difficult to find the correct responses to murmur back to people who under ordinary circumstances would be dissecting her reputation behind politely raised hands. Regardless, she did her best. The wind whipped up and she concentrated on the shadows racing across the cemetery as clouds sped across the blue sky.

Someone tapped her arm. "Doc tells me you worked your fingers to the bone while Jane-Ellen was sick."

Hattie turned her attention to Aurelia Donaldson, who stood in front of her. "I only did what anyone would have done, ma'am," she murmured. "Jane-Ellen was always very good to me and I wanted to help in any way I could."

Aurelia peered intently through her lorgnette for an endless moment. Finally, she harrumphed and reached her gnarled hand out to pat Hattie's. "You are a good girl," she said decisively and moved on.

The unexpected praise did what nothing else had been able to do that horrid day. Scalding tears rose in her eyes and her mouth began to quiver. She didn't even see Moses until he stepped close, blocking the sun.

Her heart lightened to see him after such a long absence. But when he reached out to hug her, she forgot for an instant this was her friend, who, despite his great size, would never hurt a fly. She felt only his massive strength, absorbed his masculine scent, and she flinched away.

Her reaction infuriated her. She was not going to let Roger Lord's violence and bitterness poison her—she wasn't! This was *Moses*. Not all males were intent on violence the way That Man had been. She reached out to grasp her friend's hand, but it was too late.

Ever since learning the reason behind Hattie's reaching out the night he declined to see her, Moses had been eaten alive by guilt. She'd needed his support and he'd let her down for his own selfish reasons. So, assuming she wanted nothing further to do with him, exactly as he'd feared, he quickly turned to Jake with a few muttered condolences. Then he turned away, feeling cold and lonely.

It was a relief when the line finally broke up and they could go home. Hattie's split lip was still noticeable, so she went upstairs and stayed in her room to avoid questions. Augusta let it be known to the gathered mourners that Hattie had only climbed out of her sickbed long enough to attend the funeral.

Hattie lay in misery all afternoon, listening to the soft murmur of voices drifting up the stairs and through her open window. It seemed forever before people began to leave. Jake was the last to go, and by then it had grown quite late.

SHE SPENT THE next weeks trying to piece her life back together while she prepared for her move to the teaching college up in Seattle, Washington. Her lip mended and her bruises faded, but her confidence and sense of self-worth sustained wounds she despaired of ever healing. Mattawa was her home and she dreaded leaving it. Conversely, she could hardly wait to go.

Finally, on Monday, September 10, Hattie stood on the platform with Augusta and Doc, awaiting the train to Seattle. Doc talked with the stationmaster while Augusta drilled Hattie with last-minute reminders for checking in to the hotel where she would stay this evening, as well as additional warnings and advice.

Hattie only half listened. Her eyes roved over her stacked luggage and past it to the countryside beyond the depot. She'd tried committing every familiar detail to memory as they had driven from home to the station.

Just as the train came roaring around the bend, Jake raced down the platform. He rocked to a halt in front of Hattie. "You were going to just leave?" he demanded breathlessly. "Just like that, without saying goodbye?"

"Goodbye, Jake."

"Dammit, Hattie! You've refused to see me for four damn weeks. Haven't I been punished enough?" He reached for her arm, but she hastily drew away. "When are you going to forgive me?"

The roar and rattle of the train as it pulled into the station drowned out her reply. Jake watched Hattie observe her luggage being loaded into the luggage compartment. Then she turned to kiss Doc and Aunt Augusta goodbye. She clung to Augusta, as if loath to let her go.

Jake stepped closer. "What did you say?" He'd watched her lips move, but he hadn't heard her answer—and it sure as hell couldn't be what he thought he saw. Jesus, he could not believe she'd carry a grudge this far. He had sent her to Lord's for her own protection, dammit. She had to know that.

Hattie stepped up onto the train without replying.

"Dammit," Jake roared at her back. He shook off Doc's hand when the older man attempted to pull him away. "Answer me! When are you going to forgive me?"

Hattie turned back and looked him in the eye, making Jake jerk his head back. What the—? Her eyes were empty of life when she finally acknowledged his question. In her vast array of expressions, Jake had never seen that one. Not once.

Yet, it was like a blow to his heart when she said with flat finality, "When hell freezes over."

21

Seattle, Washington
TUESDAY, SEPTEMBER 11, 1906

H ATTIE ARRIVED IN Seattle physically mended but emotionally battered, her innate confidence nowhere in sight. Instead, she was angry, lonely, and subdued.

It was a measure of how stubborn her depressed mental state was that, during her check-in interview, when the school matron glared over the top of her steel-bowed spectacles at Hattie's figure and peremptorily ordered her to purchase a corset, she meekly agreed. The matron, who appeared braced for an argument and seemed pleasantly surprised not to get one, unbent so much as to reluctantly mutter she supposed there was nothing that could be done about the color of Hattie's hair. Issuing a room assignment, she dismissed her.

Hattie's shared room on the top floor of the teachers college was half the size of her bedroom back home. It was furnished with two narrow beds, two plain dressers, two chairs, and a wardrobe. There was barely room to move. As soon as her trunks were delivered, Hattie began to unpack.

She had the room to herself the first night—an unforeseen bonus she appreciated. Returning from the washroom down the hall, she retired early, clutching Lillian for comfort as she attempted to fall asleep.

But sleep wouldn't come. She tried thoughts of learning to teach. It didn't help. She had been so desperate to leave Mattawa that this current wrenching homesickness caught her by surprise. She was in a strange city where she didn't know a soul. She missed her room at home. She missed the freedom of the ranch. She missed Augusta, Doc, and Moses.

She didn't miss Jake, she assured herself.

There was nothing in the unfamiliar room to take her mind off the debilitating assault that was her constant companion. Scalding tears streamed silently down her face, and she began to shake so hard her narrow bed rattled. Wrapping her arms around herself, she held on tightly, grinding Lillian into her chest. She bit down hard on her lip to keep from sobbing aloud. Then, realizing this was likely her last night alone, she allowed herself the luxury of doing just that.

She wanted to go home. She wanted to regain control of her life. She wanted her virginity and her old inviolate self-confidence back. *OhGodohGod*. She wanted to turn back the clock and do a hundred things differently. Yet, in truth? She had no idea what would make this awful pain go away.

Her normal optimism surfaced when she awoke the following morning. Perhaps it wouldn't be so bad here; she'd get used to it. Hadn't she hankered to be independent since she was sixteen years old? She thought of her mama, who had given up an opulent life in a prestigious family because she loved Hattie's father. If her mother could do that and remain true to herself, then Hattie could darn well learn to succeed in *her* new situation.

Breakfast was served at long tables in a large, drafty hall on the first floor. The food was filling, if not particularly flavorful. As Hattie ate, she surreptitiously inspected her fellow students and was amazed at how young they were. An eighth-grade education was the single admittance requirement for normal school, and it appeared very few of the girls here had advanced beyond that.

She didn't know why this surprised her. Even in Mattawa, only about twenty percent of the students she'd begun with went on to graduate. Children from the outlying farms and ranches in particular were hard-pressed to finish their education when there was so much work demanding attention at home.

Yet, she was flabbergasted. Most of these girls looked no older than thirteen. How well could they teach the older students, if they didn't understand the material themselves?

An unexpected smile curled her lips. Because that's why they were here, wasn't it—to learn how to teach.

Classes didn't begin for another two days, and Hattie requested and received permission to go to town for her corset. She had naively thought Mattawa was cosmopolitan. Compared to the city she saw today, it was a one-horse town. Seattle was enormous and bustling—she'd seen a bit of that on her hansom cab ride from the King Street train station. Her innate sense of adventure was piqued as she boarded a trolley for town. Head constantly turning, she attempted to absorb all the sights along the way. Upon disembarking the novel mode of transportation, she wandered through Seattle's shopping district with wide-eyed amazement.

There were several department stores, and she finally settled on Mac-Dougall and Southwick on Second and Pike. Smiling as she wandered its massive first floor, she thought the mercantile and dressmaker's shop at home would both fit quite handily into one small corner.

The clerk was helpful when Hattie expressed her aversion to being strapped into corsets. The woman chose a lighter-weight corselette for her to try and laced it just tightly enough to lend support without restricting Hattie's breathing. It was certainly handier—and prettier—than the gauze Aunt Augusta had her bind herself with to keep from—Augusta's words—"jiggling in everyone's face."

Hattie was highly conscious of the undergarment she'd elected to keep on. But during the ride back, she decided perhaps growing accustomed to it wouldn't be too horribly hard. As long as she relinquished all thoughts of ever bending over again.

The dormitory lobby was surprisingly deserted when she arrived, and Hattie wondered where everyone was. Reaching the landing at the top of the stairs, she discovered the answer. A gaggle of speechless girls crowded around her open doorway, those in the back standing on tiptoe to peer over the shoulders of those in front. Hattie worked her way through the crowd until she stood just inside the room. And stared in dismay at the chaos.

Open trunks occupied every inch of floor space between the furniture. Clothing draped over the backs and seats of the two uncomfortable-looking wooden chairs and lay strewn across both beds. A young woman mumbled to herself as she leaned into the open wardrobe.

Conditioned by years of receiving nothing but disdain and ridicule from her female social peers back home, Hattie took a deep breath. She might as well fire the first volley in what would likely be a two-year war. Standing in the doorway, she said clearly, "Pardon me, miss. Are you sure you have enough clothing?"

It was rather feeble, but half of that wardrobe space was hers. And, honestly, where did this woman plan to wear the four exquisite evening gowns draped across Hattie's bed?

Emerging from the wardrobe, the new roommate turned around. Hattie and the other girls were rendered speechless.

The girl sharing Hattie's space for the next two years was probably the most beautiful woman she'd ever laid eyes on. Hair as black as a raven's wing, dark eyes velvety as pansies, and skin like cream, this stranger was also the tallest female Hattie had ever seen.

"Isn't it awful?" The exquisite apparition agreed with a cheeky grin. "But it was either bring it all with me, or have my sister, Lizzy, wear everything I left behind. And when Lizzy helps herself to your wardrobe, she returns it in rags." She stepped forward, elegant hand extended. "How do you do? I'm Nell Thomesen."

Warily, Hattie shook hands. "Hattie Taylor."

"Hattie Tay . . . my roommate? Oh dear, I am sorry! I'll have this mess cleared out momentarily." Looking at all the clothing, she added weakly, "I hope."

Hattie picked her way across the floor, cleared a small area off her bed, and sat down. She cast surreptitious glances at her roommate, at the girls silently crowding the doorway, and back at her roommate again. What on earth was a woman such as this doing at a teaching institute? She looked as if she should be planning charity balls in one of the mansions on First Hill Hattie had heard about. Hattie momentarily forgot that she, too, could have chosen to live comfortably on the trust fund Aunt Augusta had given her on her eighteenth birthday. She had no financial need to earn a living. It would have driven her slowly insane to sit around, doing nothing, but the option was there.

"Perhaps," she finally suggested after watching Nell struggle to find room for everything, "you should pick out what you think you will need most. You could leave the rest in the trunks and have it taken down to storage. It's quite safe, you know. They lock it up."

Nell smiled brilliantly and Hattie's wariness tripled. Experience had taught her to look for a trap when girls her own age displayed that kind of friendliness.

But all Nell said was, "What an excellent idea!" And did what Hattie suggested. In short order, she'd tidied the room and summoned the custodian, who grumbled about taking the trunks back down when he'd just brought them up. Smiling gently, Nell closed the door on a number of awed faces and turned to Hattie. "Thank heavens that's taken care of! My goodness, you have beautiful hair."

"Thank you," Hattie said charily, bracing herself for the stinger. Compliments on her hair were always followed by *Pity about those freckles* or *Who do you call to put out the fire?*

But no insult was issued.

And so the day progressed. Nell was friendly, complimentary, and curious, while Hattie held herself guardedly aloof. She politely answered questions, but in the briefest manner possible—and without expressing any reciprocal curiosity of her own. She kept her distance, wary of trusting. She'd been poked by too many verbal barbs from the snide girls of the upper echelon to voluntarily walk into that trap.

Finally, day faded into evening, evening into night, and they turned out the lights and climbed into bed. But like they had the night before, Hattie's homesickness and general wretchedness returned. Once again, she hugged her doll and clamped her bottom lip between her teeth while she silently cried herself to sleep. The pattern was to repeat itself for the next two weeks.

Classes began, and as long as it was daylight, Hattie was reasonably content. But the instant she lay down to sleep, pain and a bone-deep feeling of worthlessness crept up to knock her flat. Night after night, she curled in a rigid fetal position on her narrow bed, shuddering helplessly and soaking her pillow in silent misery.

Nell pretended to be oblivious. She feigned sleep each night, but, staring into the darkness, she ached for a way to alleviate her roommate's pain while simultaneously preserving her privacy.

Curiosity consumed Nell. Hattie was so mysterious and fascinating. Her exotic appearance—all vivid coloring and bold features—suggested ancestors from faraway places. Her striking looks weren't fashionable, yet were so much more compelling and infinitely more interesting than insipid prettiness. Then there was the contrast between her bold appearance and leery attitude. To look at her, Nell would've thought she'd be aggressively confident. Yet whenever Nell spoke to her, Hattie's shoulders tensed, as though braced for an attack. She was an enigma—chin held high, looking people squarely in the eye during the day, then crying herself to sleep each night. And something both defiant and vulnerable in her eyes made Nell yearn to know what caused such deep heartache.

She doubted she'd ever find out, for from what she'd seen thus far, Hattie refused to let anyone get close. To be sure, she had beautiful manners and was unfailingly polite. Yet, no matter how hard Nell tried, the wall surrounding the redhead was impenetrable. So, Nell listened to the muffled sobs each night and wished she could help. Yet she honored the other woman's firmly posted No Trespassing signs. Until, after fifteen straight nights of trying to ignore Hattie's anguish, Nell could stand it no longer.

More vibrations felt than actual sounds heard, Hattie's sobs were still enough to make Nell silently rise from her bed. She knelt in the narrow space between their beds and reached out to stroke Hattie's hair. Her other hand rubbed at the tense muscles at the base of Hattie's neck as she bent over her. "Shh," she murmured softly. "It'll be all right. Shh, now."

Hattie jerked once, then cried harder, harsh, throat-scouring sounds escaping in spite of her best efforts to contain them. Not only for what was, but for all that had never been and never would be.

Nell bent closer and continued to croon, to touch, to reassure. Finally, Hattie rolled onto her back and peered up at her roommate through swollen eyes. She rubbed the back of her hand inelegantly across her lips and nose.

"It won't be all right," she whispered in a flat, tired voice. "You just don't understand."

Nell's face held no judgment that Hattie could see. Twisting away for a moment, the other woman extracted a handkerchief from beneath her own pillow. Offering it to Hattie, Nell merely said quietly, "Tell me, then, so I do understand."

To Hattie's horror, she did. She didn't know what made her do it, but she told this young woman she barely knew everything. Maybe it was the genuine concern she sensed, reminding her of her lost friendship with Moses. Maybe it was the tender care of Nell's touch. Whatever the reason, Hattie talked for a long time, pouring out her heartbreak and confusion, her sense of betrayal and rage. "I feel so worthless," she finished dully. "So unclean and worthless."

"No!" Nell surged up, pulling Hattie upright as well, until both sat on the edge of their respective beds, their knees touching. She held Hattie's hand tightly. "No, you mustn't. Look at me. *Look!*" Reaching across the small space, she grasped Hattie's chin and their eyes locked. "Now." She enunciated each word clearly. "You are *not* worthless."

Miserable, Hattie snorted. "Didn't you hear a word I said? I have done things no decent woman ever would. With Moses and with Jake. Then Roger Lord ruined me for good. I must give off a scent or something telling men I'm easy." She laughed, but it was a bitter sound. "Ask anyone in Mattawa!" She waved the soaked hanky in a dismissive gesture. "Practically the entire town would rush to tell you there's something bad in Hattie Taylor."

"Your little town sounds perfectly horrid, if you ask me. The world is full of narrow-minded people, Hattie, and Lord help the unfortunate who doesn't fit in their mold. But maybe not everyone is intended to fit into a tidy little slot. Do you believe in God?"

"Of course."

"Well, He created you just as you are for a purpose. Perhaps you're supposed to view the world differently than most. As for the other, you should place the blame where it belongs."

Hattie sniffed and swiped at her eyes with the back of a wrist. "What do you mean?"

"Just because you experimented with your friend—who incidentally doesn't sound like much of a friend to me—or lost your head with Jake, it doesn't necessarily follow that therefore Roger Lord had a perfect right to forcefully relieve you of your virginity. It sounds to me like you did everything in your power to keep from being overcome by the man, and the only reason you weren't successful was because he had brute force on his side."

Dismally, Hattie nodded, but added, "Whether I fought him or not, the end result is the same. He goes free and I'm ruined if it ever becomes public knowledge. Even if it came to a trial and he was put in jail for the rest of his life, I would still be ruined. What does that tell you?"

To her surprise, Nell answered vehemently, "That women get the short end of the stick. We can't vote, we lose any right to handle our own money if we marry, and we can be set aside in a marriage if we are unfaithful, yet aren't offered the same option if our husbands stray. But just because a bunch of oh-so-self-important *men* say something is so, it doesn't make it right. And while you may have made a few unwise choices, you haven't done a thing to justify being made to feel worthless."

No one had ever talked to her this way, and Hattie experienced a new lightness as some of her burden lifted. She managed a wobbly smile in the darkness. "Thank you. I'll keep that in mind."

"You do that," Nell commanded and scooted back into her bed. "I hope you can sleep now."

For the first time in a long while, Hattie did exactly that.

22

WHEN HATTIE AWOKE the next morning, she regretted every word she had uttered the night before. *What* had possessed her? Sure, Nell had been extremely nice to her last night. But was Hattie so starved for affection she just offered a weapon with the power to destroy her to the first person with a kind word? *What have I done?*

She'd already dressed and was fumbling with her hairbrush when Nell came up behind her. "Your hair is incredibly lovely," she said. "It looks so alive. May I brush it?"

Hattie handed over the hairbrush warily. "If you want."

Nell placed one palm on the crown of Hattie's head and stroked the brush firmly through the unruly mass. It crackled as tight curls, pulled through the bristles, leaped into full, deep waves. "It even feels alive," Nell said in amazement. Noticing how stiffly Hattie sat beneath her ministrations, Nell paused in the middle of a stroke, the bristles buried in the abundant curls. "You're sorry you talked to me last night, aren't you?"

Hattie shot her a wary glance over her shoulder and Nell swallowed a sigh as she completed the brushstroke. "You needn't be, you know. I'd like to be your friend and I shan't ever repeat anything you tell me. I know what it's like to be different, Hattie. I've been five foot ten since I was twelve years old, and my family is what is known as the genteel poor."

"But you're beautiful!" Hattie twisted around to stare up at her roommate in amazement. It had never occurred to her that Nell, too, might suffer from self-doubt.

Nell smiled with delight. "Do you think so? I've been as tall as or taller than practically every man I have ever met for as long as I can remember. Do you honestly think I'm pretty?"

"Not pretty, Nell, *beautiful*. I think your height is elegant. It's better than being a dumpling like me with too much bosom and hip. And my face is all eyes and mouth." She grimaced.

"You underestimate yourself considerably," Nell disagreed. "If we stood side by side at a cotillion, you would be the one with the full dance card. I'd be the beanpole wallflower in the corner."

"Don't be ridiculous," Hattie said and laughed. It was the first time she'd done so in a very long time and it felt marvelous.

"It happens to me all the time. Only the tallest men dare dance with me. And if none are available, I either sit with the matrons or suffer through mercy dances with men whose wives badger them into it when it becomes obvious no one else is going to." She completed brushing Hattie's hair and deftly twisted it into place, anchoring it with hairpins.

"Well, that's just incomprehensible," Hattie said, standing up and leaning forward to admire Nell's handiwork in the spotted mirror above her dresser. "Imagine anyone passing up someone as exquisitely beautiful as you simply because you stand eyeball to eyeball with him. Men are such fools. Maybe I should introduce you to Moses. He's huge."

"Your erstwhile friend? No, thank you. It seems to me if he had been there when you needed him, your Jake never would have sent you to Mr. Lord's house."

"He's not *my* Jake, and as far as I'm concerned *he* is solely to blame for sending me there. I don't care what he said his reasons were. They were ludicrous—Jake *never* would have hurt me. But he was so bound and determined to follow his own course he ignored every attempt I made to tell him how nervous Roger made me. I don't know if I can ever forgive him for that." She looked at Nell over her shoulder. "Don't blame Moses,

Nell—I certainly don't. My immodesty was responsible for ruining our friendship."

"Well, it sounds to me as if he took full advantage of your immodesty and when he was through enjoying it, he cast you aside." Nell found Jake's attempt to save Hattie's virtue from his ravening lust rather romantic—sort of like star-crossed lovers from a Shakespearean play. But for a *friend* to turn his back on her in her time of need . . . that was unforgivable.

Hattie rather thought Nell was being overly hard on a person she'd never even met. But because Hattie was awed that this woman genuinely sought her friendship, an act so unique and lovely it wrapped Hattie in an unaccustomed blanket of warmth, she let it go.

That morning was the beginning of a healing period for her. Being in an environment where no one had preconceived notions of her was a revelation. Her friendship with Nell grew deeper every day, and there was something liberating about confiding her thoughts to a female her own age. She could tell Nell anything and be understood in a way she'd never been before. Even with Moses, whom Hattie loved like a brother, certain subjects were taboo. With Nell, there were none. When she said as much, however, Nell merely sniffed. She persisted in holding a grudge against Moses.

To Hattie's further amazement, she discovered she was regarded as a leader. She and Nell were the oldest students and the best educated. Studies came easily to them, and socially, they were of the "first water," as one student constantly commented. Soon the younger girls were coming to them for help with their schoolwork or to solicit advice on clothing, manners, and etiquette. Being held in high regard was a first for Hattie—one she found seductive.

Free time at the normal school was limited. Students were only allowed to leave during daylight hours, in well-chaperoned groups. But Nell had been raised in the upper strata of Seattle society, and although her father's earning capability died with him, spelling the demise of most of her family's wealth, the association still carried weight with the school's matron. Nell's family might be considered poor by their former standards, but they were still on society's fringe. Because of it, occasionally Nell gained permission for herself and Hattie to spend the weekend with her mother and sister.

Mostly, they spent their weekend quietly visiting with Nell's mother, a soft-spoken woman baffled by her newly demoted position in society, and her sister, Lizzy, who was as tall and as beautiful as Nell and cheerfully determined to marry a rich man. They clearly loved Nell even if they didn't understand her desire to make her own way. Hattie, who understood perfectly, enjoyed spending time with them.

Hattie's two years in Seattle passed rapidly. The memory of her violation at Roger Lord's hands was an easily aroused specter, but she learned to relegate it to the back of her mind, and its impact faded over time. Doggedly avoiding going home during holiday and summer breaks helped. Except for Nell, no one here knew what had happened to her, and it was amazing how much being unreservedly admired and respected bolstered her sense of self-worth. Her confidence grew daily.

Nell taught her tricks to help her stop and consider her words and actions instead of reacting with rash thoughtlessness. They became valuable tools she tried to practice daily. To Hattie's pleasure, although she occasionally backslid, her skills continued to grow.

In return, when she saw Nell did indeed grow quiet and diffident around men, stifling her sense of humor as she tried to blend into the woodwork, she taught her friend the art of light flirtation. There weren't many opportunities for Nell to practice her budding wiles, but twice last summer they'd gone to the dance pavilions on Alki Point. Almost ten months later, Nell was still talking about her success in gratified amazement.

Seven weeks ahead of graduation, before she had a chance to send out her first application, Hattie received an offer of employment from the Mattawa school board. She was stunned. And quite positive Aunt Augusta had something to do with it.

"Are you going to accept?" Nell asked after reading the letter Hattie handed her.

Hattie's first inclination was to reject the offer out of hand. "Why should I?" she demanded. "Until I left Mattawa I never realized people could actually like me or that other girls my age might actually look up to me. Why subject myself to more of Mattawa's character assassination when I can go somewhere I won't be prejudged before I even set foot in town?"

"Because you miss your home?" Nell suggested gently. "Because you're lonely for your aunt and Moses and Doc and Mirabel, and even Jake? Because letters from home and spending your holidays with my family haven't been enough?"

Nell sat next to Hattie on the bed. "Aren't you the one who's complained for the past two years that you can't hire a decent mount in this town? That you're tired of riding streetcars and long to race the wind on your horse, Belle?"

It was true. For all Mattawa's faults, it was still her home and she missed it.

Yet, it wasn't that simple. "I don't know if I can face Jake, Nell. Or Roger Lord."

"I know. In a town the size of yours, I imagine it's inevitable you will run into Lord sooner or later. But why wouldn't you be able to face Jake? I thought you'd finally forgiven him."

"Sometimes I think I have. But other times . . ." It had taken her nearly the full two years here to reach an uneasy peace with her feelings for Jake. She resented him bitterly when recollections of her violation exploded past her guard. Yet, with the newly adult part of herself, she tried to put herself in his place and understand his reasons.

Plus, she couldn't forget that night in her room and the way Jake had made her feel. Yes, he was responsible for sending her to Roger Lord. Conversely, he was also responsible for her knowing what Roger did to her was not the way the private act between a man and a woman was supposed to be. "I can't decide this immediately," she finally said, looking down at the letter in her hand. "I need to give it some thought."

The next day, Hattie was in their room when Nell entered. She looked up to greet her and was struck by the strange expression on her friend's face. "Are you all right?"

"Yes. It's just . . ." Nell's voice trailed away. "Hattie, have you reached a decision about taking the teaching position in Mattawa?"

"I keep bouncing between being sure I wanna go home and equally sure I don't. Why?"

Nell pulled a letter from her skirt pocket and handed it Hattie. Perusing it swiftly, Hattie felt her jaw sag. Snapping her teeth together, she looked up at Nell. "They're offering you a position, too." She handed Nell the letter. "This *has* to be Aunt Augusta's doing. She knows how much you've come to mean to me." Reaching out, she grasped her friend's hand. "Oh, Nell, not to have to go our separate ways."

And so it was decided. Hattie might have been able to ignore the lure of home, but she was utterly helpless in the face of the opportunity to keep her friend with her. Hattie and Nell wrote the Mattawa school board that evening, accepting the positions.

She was going home.

PART
2

23

Northern Pacific Cascade train
FRIDAY, JUNE 12, 1908

A LLLL ABOARD—FINAL call!"

Staring out at the station platform through a rain-drizzled train window, Hattie mentally willed the ticketholders on this trip to shake a leg. Mere moments later, the exterior door nearest her clanged closed, and she perked up. Finally. Then she swallowed a sigh when the porter escorted an older woman to the seat next to hers. "Here you go, madam," he said.

Drat. She had been so close to that seat remaining empty. Hattie looked up at the plump, smiling woman standing next to the aisle seat beside hers.

Oblivious to her disappointment, the woman flashed her a cheery smile. "Hello, dear. I am Mrs. Whelan. It appears you and I will be seatmates."

"Yes, ma'am. I'm Hattie Taylor."

"Lovely to meet you." The train jerked, and as it began its slow chug away from the station, the older woman hastily took her seat. Her heavily embroidered waistcoat rustling beneath her long jacket, Mrs. Whelan settled. "Which is your stop, dear?"

"Mattawa, Oregon, by way of Portland." She half attended as her seatmate regaled her with her closer destination and the family she'd be visiting. Hattie could not shake the tension in her shoulders. If she hadn't been in such a burning hurry, she could've been traveling back with Aunt Augusta right now. That would have made this return far less stressful.

When she'd left Mattawa almost two years ago, Hattie had desperately needed the distance, yet once having made the decision to accept the offer of employment, she'd all but champed at the bit to go home. She suddenly missed everything she'd been so anxious to leave behind. So, Hattie had impulsively wired Aunt Augusta to forego the graduation ceremony. If she picked up her diploma but skipped the ceremony, she'd explained, she could catch a train to deliver her home a full day and a half earlier.

It never occurred to her she might suffer a complete reversal of her frantic optimism the instant the train departed King Street Station. Yet, five minutes ago, she could barely wait to get home again. Now actually on her way, she questioned the wisdom of going back at all.

"How about you, dear? Is Mattawa your hometown? Do you have family there?"

Hattie shook off her messy ruminations and after what felt like a long pause but she hoped was not, said, "Yes, ma'am, to both. I was born elsewhere, but have lived with my aunt in Mattawa since I was a youngster." That Aunt Augusta was actually Hattie's too-many-times-removed cousin for anyone to keep it straight didn't need to be shared. In Hattie's heart, Aunt Augusta was precisely that: her most beloved aunt.

"Have you been on a shopping trip to the big city?" Mrs. Whelan inquired.

"Oh no, ma'am. I just received my diploma from the Seattle Normal School. I'm taking a position at the schoolhouse in Mattawa." In truth, she was still a bit rattled that she'd accepted the position. As the miles from Seattle dissolved beneath the steel wheels of the locomotive, she asked herself why she had.

Because she missed Augusta grievously, and Mirabel and Moses too? She even missed Jake, God help her, and heaven knew their relationship was rife with ups and downs. But, of course, Mattawa was her home. Which led her back to—

"Where did you go?"

Hattie jerked and realized she'd drifted into thoughts of home mid-conversation with the very curious Mrs. Whelan. "I got so caught up in the idea of going home I'm afraid my mind wandered. What did you ask?"

"I . . . Well, my question was actually quite rude of me and truly none of my affair."

Channeling Aunt Augusta, Hattie raised her chin to an imperious angle and pinned the older woman with a steely "then don't ask" gaze.

And darned if it didn't work. Mrs. Whelan slapped her hands together and rose briskly. "I believe the dining car is calling me to have tea. Would you care to accompany me?"

"Thank you, no. Even though it's early days yet, I'm still preparing mentally for the upcoming school year."

Mrs. Whelan nodded. "Then I shall see you in a while." Rising, she stepped into the aisle and made her way down the car.

Hattie's mind promptly returned to her interrupted thoughts. Since her unexpected offer of employment, she'd given her relationship with Jake a lot of thought. And finally concluded it was time to let her anger go. Knowing he'd sent her to Roger Lord that awful night still made her stomach churn. Jake had been upset and hadn't given any real credence to her protests. To the unease she'd felt . . . Yet, she knew in her heart he had no reason to suspect what would happen. Even her discomfort around Lord had been feelings, not knowledge. She hadn't suspected anything near the terrifying violence he'd inflicted upon her. Plus, she and Jake had once shared a special bond. It might not still exist, but at the very least she could be civil.

Hattie locked the subject in a far recess of her mind. Her forgiveness, or whatever this was she was attempting, was a work in progress. Watching the landscape flash by outside the train window, she considered instead the upper echelon of Mattawa society, of which the Murdocks were an esteemed part.

It was ironic, really, to recall how most of those people seemed to believe she didn't care about their collective opinions. She'd cared, all right.

She had cared a great deal. Only Aunt Augusta and perhaps Moses ever understood how much. And neither of them, much as they might have wished otherwise, had the power to help her. Hattie had known, even as a headstrong teenager, that she was the only person with the ability to reverse the town's opinion of her. And it had been beyond her capabilities then to pretend to be someone she was not. No matter how much she'd desired to fit in—and there had been times she'd ached with the need— her tongue had possessed a mind of its own.

During her time away from Mattawa, she'd come to realize much of the disapproval she'd garnered was not, perhaps, entirely unfounded. Accepted the fact she'd often been the author of her problems. Her behavior had been far from exemplary. She was defensive in response to her peers' dislike of her and tended to say far too much instead of prudently keeping some thoughts to herself. And what impulsively emerged from her lips had far too often simply reinforced her detractors' unfavorable opinion of her. She hadn't yet accepted the wisdom of considering her response before actually uttering it.

Thanks to Nell, she'd learned to play by society's rules. The hardest lesson had been accepting that life wasn't always fair. Once she quit expecting every situation to be so, she had made amazing strides. Good heavens, under Nell's tutelage Hattie even mastered her unfortunate, impulsive tendency to speak first and think second. Most of the time, anyway.

Hattie stared out the window at the ever-changing landscape as the train left the sunlit valley to barrel into shaded woodlands. She all but pressed her nose to the less-than-pristine window, hoping to see something recognizable. Nothing was.

She wished Nell had accompanied her today but understood her friend's desire to stay in Seattle awhile longer. For Nell, the move to Mattawa meant leaving everything she knew. Of course, she was eager for her family to see her graduate. And following the ceremony, she planned to spend a few weeks with her mother and sister.

It sometimes slipped Hattie's mind that her friend didn't have the same financial resources Hattie did. Nell shouldn't have had to gently remind her that teachers weren't paid with overwhelming generosity. Or that Nell had no idea when the next opportunity to see her family would arise. It was important she see as much of them as she could before her employment began. Hattie felt so selfish, wishing Nell were with her instead.

She would likely come up against old attitudes and prejudices again and wouldn't always have a buffer. *So, please, Lord,* she fervently prayed, *let my brain act more swiftly than my tongue.*

In her first female friend's absence, Hattie simply needed to remember the lessons Nell had drummed into her head. And her way of relating to folks would, most definitely, be different this time. She was more mature, less hotheaded these days. And surely a shade more tolerant.

Yes, she admitted as she watched Mrs. Whelan approaching, she was still a bit suspicious. It was part of her character—a part embedded right down to her bedrock during those final weeks before leaving for school in the summer of '06. But she would, by golly, work on overcoming her suspicions.

In her heart, Hattie thought she did, in fact, understand her reasons for accepting this unexpectedly offered position. Mattawa was her home and she had much to prove.

What she didn't know was what had driven the decision to extend an invitation to join the staff. She was pretty certain, however, she detected the fine hand of Augusta Witherspoon Murdock behind her and Nell's surprising appointment by the school board.

Regardless of how it came about, she had been given an opportunity to make Augusta proud. She was determined to play the game by society's rules and all the slippery edicts that had eluded her in the past. She would grasp her temper in both hands and not let go. No matter what.

If she knew the guiding forces in Mattawa's top social circle, they had her dismissal already prepared before she even got to town. It was probably all neatly written up on one of those new typewriter machines, just waiting for her to provide them with the opportunity to ride her out of town on a rail.

Well, she hoped they didn't hold their breath. Because she was going to be so even tempered, so blessed schoolmarmish this go-around, it would make Mattawa's collective heads spin.

Just wait and see.

24

Mattawa
HOURS LATER

H ER TRAIN ROARED out of a patch of woods and Hattie blinked against blinding sunlight. She recognized Six Tree Bluff. It was a familiar sight not far from town, a rocky bluff topped with trees stunted and molded by the wind. Her heart kicking up its pace, Hattie sat straighter. She smoothed her shirtwaist, shook out her skirt, and rubbed the toes of her new shoes against her stockinged calves to remove the dust of travel. She drew a deep breath as the whistle blew a long, plaintive note.

Then the train rattled around the corner, and there, suddenly up ahead, was Mattawa. Hattie had to grip the edge of her seat to keep from pressing her nose against the window in order to see everything at once. Oh mercy. All her doubts faded. She was home.

Remember decorum, she instructed herself as the train chugged into the station. Then she spotted Aunt Augusta and Jake. She saw them before they saw her, both scanning each window as it passed their position on the station-house platform. Jake was searching with single-minded intensity; Aunt Augusta was smiling and clutching a fluttering handkerchief in the delicate fist pressed to her breastbone. And decorum flew out the window.

The moment the train came to a complete stop, Hattie bolted from her seat. She sped down the narrow aisle to the nearest door, excusing herself breathlessly as her portmanteau bumped off a shoulder or two.

The step box was not yet in place to bridge the gap from stairwell to platform, and she nearly tumbled out of the car. Clutching the metal poles framing the opening, she leaned out, a huge, no doubt unseemly smile stretching her lips. "Aunt Augusta! Jake!"

Augusta and Jake saw her, and for an instant both froze in wonder. She seemed to glow in the shadowed recess of the train doorway, from her shining eyes and jubilant smile to her pale, lightly freckled skin and the glimpses of fiery hair beneath the pale green confection perched atop it. Then, growing impatient waiting for the conductor to bring the step, she picked up her skirts and leaped to the platform, and their paralysis was shattered. Jake whooped and set off at a dead run. Augusta whispered, "Oh, my darling child," and trotted as quickly as her middle-aged bones would carry her. There were few people at the station, but she wouldn't have cared if the entire population of Mattawa was lined up to observe Augusta Witherspoon Murdock's unladylike behavior. She had honored Hattie's need to put a physical distance between her and anyone reminding her of that horrid time two summers ago. But the years were exceedingly long with only letters to sustain her—and her dear child was home at last.

Jake reached Hattie first, and he snatched her up and whirled her around. "Welcome home, Big-eyes," he shouted, then laughed, a Jake Murdock special, his head thrown back, dark eyes narrowed, and the creases bracketing his mouth deep, smooth slashes. "Welcome home." He held her much too tightly as the mad whirl eased into slow circles.

Hattie wrapped her arms around his neck and buried her nose where strong neck curved into shoulder. Her feet dangled above the station platform and her breasts were crushed by his too-tight grip. She didn't care. She'd feared she would never again be able to look Jake Murdock in the eye. Perhaps, once the first flush of homecoming was over, all her problems reconciling their relationship would return, despite her decision. But now she simply clung to his familiar lanky frame, feeling his warmth and strength as he held her in a grasp threatening her bones. She inhaled his distinctive, never-forgotten scent: part horse, part soap, part sunlight, a hint of bay rum . . . and all Jake. His soft brown hair must have been slicked back in her honor since she'd only ever seen him wear it like that at weddings, funerals, and dances. She smiled widely and sniffed the added aroma of pomade.

Then Augusta was there and Jake released her and she whirled away to become engulfed in her aunt's embrace. It, too, was scented with sweet, powdery familiarity, and Hattie knew she was truly home at last.

"Where's your friend?" Jake asked when the women finally pulled apart.

"She'll be here in two weeks. She's spending time with her family." Hattie turned to Augusta. "I don't know how you did it, but I'm delighted you did. Nell is very dear to me."

"Did what, dear?"

"Talked the school board into hiring both of us. I was so surprised when they offered me the position. But when Nell also received an offer . . ."

Augusta looked blank.

"It was you, wasn't it?" Hattie had simply assumed—

"I'm afraid not, dear."

"But who . . . ?"

"Why does it have to be anyone? You and Nell graduated top of your class. Why wouldn't the school board want the very best?"

"Because it's me," Hattie said quietly. "And this is Mattawa."

Augusta searched Hattie's face. Finally, she inclined her head in agreement. "Very well. If you insist someone put in a good word, my guess is Aurelia Donaldson. She's been singing your praises ever since you began writing her, and she is on the school board."

Hattie smiled. She hadn't considered Aurelia, but that made sense. The older woman had sent her a nice note and a box of chocolates shortly after Hattie began normal school. Touched by the unexpected gesture, she'd replied. And what started out as a simple thank-you note grew into a letter full of her impressions of Seattle, her classes, her teachers, and her new friend, Nell.

She had nearly torn it up and penned a bread-and-butter thank-you instead, but with a shrug she'd mailed it to the elderly woman. Aurelia's gift was likely nothing more than a polite gesture when a young woman left home. Hattie probably wouldn't hear from her again. It was still awfully nice of Aurelia to go to the effort, and it made Hattie feel a little less lonely in the new town. It turned out from that exchange a budding correspondence had grown.

When he saw her soft smile, Jake had to bite his tongue to keep from demanding why she'd never written him. Despite her words at this station the day she'd left Mattawa, he had waited to hear from her, certain she was constitutionally incapable of holding a grudge—especially one so ridiculous. Hattie had too much common sense not to comprehend he had only done what was best for her. He had been wrong.

It took Jake months to comprehend that Hattie really wasn't forgiving him. To this day, he didn't understand why. He had been on the verge of storming to Seattle to have a showdown over the matter, but his mother put the kibosh to that plan. She told him in no uncertain terms Hattie needed this time away from Mattawa to make the transition from a schoolgirl to an adult who would teach other schoolgirls. She said it was Hattie's turn to stretch her wings and come into her own—and Jake would, by God, leave her alone to do so.

Given that, Jake had no idea why Hattie appeared glad to see him today. But he would simply thank his lucky stars and leave it be.

He arranged to have Hattie's trunks sent to Augusta's. Carrying Hattie's portmanteau, he ushered the women through the station house to his black Packard.

"What—?" Hattie smiled hugely. "Oh, Jake, a motorcar! Is it yours?"

"Yeah." Jake tried to swallow his pride as he ran his sleeve over the hood, removing a speck of dust. "Whataya think?"

"It's awe inspiring. I've only ridden in one automobile—and it was a taxi, not nearly as nice as this." She smiled crookedly. "Very fawn-cy."

"Here, put this on and climb in." He handed her a dustcover and a long piece of netting. Hattie grinned and donned the voluminous duster, then draped the netting over her hat and tied it beneath her chin. "We'll take her for a spin out in the country," Jacob said, giving the car's handle a crank. "Hit the starter button, Mother."

"Oh dear," Augusta said faintly, but she did as requested and smiled when the motorcar rumbled to life.

Hattie allowed Jake to hand her into the back seat. She laughed aloud at the vibrations against that unmentionable spot she sat on, as well as radiating down her limbs and up her spine. Sitting forward on the edge of her seat, she rested her arms on the front seats' backrests and poked her head between Jake and Augusta. "This is so exciting."

"At my age," Augusta murmured, "I could do with a little less excitement." But she smiled at Hattie's unabashed enthusiasm and Jacob's possessive pride in his shiny new machine.

They rattled and shimmied slowly down the main street of town. An occasional horse shied away from the noisy contraption, and people either smiled or scowled at them, depending on their inclination. Hattie saw Moses Marks, wearing a black leather apron, in the courtyard of Armstrong Livery. He glanced up at the sound of the approaching motorcar.

"Oh, wait!" Hattie called over the engine's noise. "I want to say hello to Moses."

Jake frowned, but dutifully pulled into the courtyard and killed the engine. He drummed his calloused fingers on the steering wheel as Hattie clambered out of the car. "Moses!"

Moses shaded his eyes with his hand. "Hattie? Is that you, girl?"

"Yes. Oh, look at you!" She walked right up and slapped him on the biceps straining his thin cotton shirt. Tilted her head back to peer up at him. "Mercy me, I do believe you've grown again. Aunt Augusta wrote and told me you'd apprenticed with the blacksmith. I suspect your mama must be worn to a frazzle trying to keep you fed."

He reached out to touch a strand of her fiery hair beneath its fashionable covering, but drew his hand back when he noticed the blackness of his fingertips approaching her pristine features. Lord, she looked so cool and ladylike . . . but her actions and her words were the same old Hattie. A lump rose in his throat. "Girl, I started to write a hundred letters to you. But I tore 'em all up."

"Why?"

"Because I was ashamed. And jealous."

She reached out and laced her clean fingers through his forge-blackened ones, squeezing his tough-skinned hand when he instinctively started to pull away. "Tell me."

"I let you down. First when Jane-Ellen was sick and you needed my support, and then when she died. I'd like to tell you why." He glanced over at the motorcar and saw Jake's expressionless stare. "But not now."

Hattie nodded. "All right, yes. I wish I could say your defection didn't hurt, Moses. But it did, so I really would like to hear why you did it. But what on earth could you be jealous of?"

"I hear you have a good and great new friend."

"Nell?"

"Yeah, that's what they say her name is. Listen . . ." He pulled his hands away and ran one through his hair. "I'm glad for you, Hat, truly I am. But I can't help being jealous of your relationship with her. I know it's not rational and probably petty as hell. But I was always your best friend. And even though I'm the one responsible for messing it up . . . Oh shit, I don't know."

"You will always be my friend, Moses." Hattie reached out and squeezed his arm. "You and I have a history that goes way back, and nothing and no one can change that. You were my friend when no one else wanted to know my name. But I love Nell, too." Her face lit up. "Wait until you meet her, Moses! You'll love her, too, wait and see. And don't you think it's possible for all three of us to be friends?" She conveniently forgot Nell's unreasonable antagonism whenever Moses' name was mentioned.

"Sure," he replied as convincingly as possible. "Sure it is." But in his heart, he wasn't sure at all.

"ISN'T THAT THE Taylor girl over there talkin' to Marks? Heard she was comin' back."

Expression bland, Roger Lord played out his hand. Then he said, "Deal me out," and pushed back from the table. Casually, he wandered over to stand at the side of the saloon's swinging doors.

It was her. Unconsciously, he touched the small scar on his arm, feeling its raised texture through his shirt. Trouble-making, bad-luck bitch. Shit. Her and the whole damn Murdock clan.

Watching her talking and laughing in Armstrong's Livery across the street, seeing Jake lounging behind the wheel of his Packard and Augusta patricianly erect beside him, Roger was filled with cold rage. Ever since that night, his life had turned upside down.

He still didn't understand how his plan to dominate and use her had gone so wrong. The bitch should have cringed and cried and begged for mercy, and at first, she had. Infused with power, he'd shoved into Hattie Taylor's tight young body to teach her a female's place in the natural order of the universe. Then out of nowhere she had stabbed him, the no-account bitch, and he hadn't been able to complete what he'd begun. Compounding her offense, she had escaped into the dark summer night.

And he would never know what she'd told her aunt, or why the old biddy believed the ravings of such a suggestive little piece. But whatever was said, Augusta had conspired to ruin his good name. Shortly after the red-haired witch left town, his clients began deserting him. Oh, not all of them, of course, but it might as well have been, for his practice was based on serving the finest families in town. They were the only people who mattered.

Yet, what was he reduced to now? Handling the affairs of merchants, for Christ's sake.

Judging by the way Jake interacted with him the few times their paths converged, no one had informed him of Hattie's deflowering. Sometimes the temptation to tell Murdock himself, to whisper how Hattie had cried and scratched and fought, was almost overpowering. Roger wanted to see Jake's expression when he discovered his little princess was soiled goods. But he held his tongue. Savored his delicious little secret.

Though wealthy and educated, Murdock was as unpredictable as the joker in a deck of cards, so it was impossible to anticipate what he might do. A gentleman by right of birth, he squandered much of his privilege with unfortunate leanings. Roger had witnessed it more than once during the younger man's apprenticeship with him. Instead of maintaining his position high above the laborers, farmers, and other nonentities, Jake had instead gotten down in the dirt with them and worked to resolve their complaints. Tarnishing his own impeccable standing.

Roger had abhorred Murdock's tendency, even then, to idealize women. Females were placed on earth to serve men. But did Murdock subscribe to the inarguable ideology? He did not.

So, while the blame for Hattie's object lesson that night should have been placed squarely where it belonged—with the woman who repeatedly advertised her need to be shown her proper place—there was no predicting Jake's reaction. Not knowing forced Roger to remain silent. And he resented Murdock a little more each day for the need to do so.

He'd bide his time, he vowed as he watched Hattie rise on her toes to kiss Moses on the cheek. But he didn't have all the time in the world; he was finding it more difficult to maintain the type of life he deserved. His wife's money wouldn't supplement it forever.

He watched Hattie sashay back to the motorcar. The time rapidly approached when he would make his move. Then they all would pay.

The motorcar broke down miles from town. Hattie restlessly paced the country road, darting frequent glances at Jake, who was hunched over the engine. When he'd first started searching for the problem, she had hung over his shoulder, asking questions and trying to help. But he'd become unbelievably testy and finally she had stalked off. Augusta was serenely patient as she rested on a blanket beneath a shady tree yards off the road.

Hattie, however, found it impossible to sit still. She'd removed her duster and hat and unfastened a few buttons on her shirtwaist to allow vagrant breezes to cool her throat. But she simply could not sit and do nothing. So, she paced.

On one of her circuits, she passed near the automobile and reluctantly halted. If Jacob was just going to snap at her again— She stood for several moments without speaking. Finally, she nudged a tire with her toe. "Not very reliable, is it?" she asked and was embarrassed by her petulant tone. "Not like a horse." Well, if she sounded sullen, too bad. His crankiness hadn't been necessary; she'd only been trying to help.

To her surprise, Jake turned his head and grinned at her. The sun shining in his eyes turned them a truer green than the muddy hazel they normally appeared, and there was a smear of grease alongside his long, bony nose. "Guess you wouldn't be interested in learning how to drive one, then, huh?"

Hattie's eyes immediately lit with enthusiasm. "You'd let me drive it? Truly? I wouldn't know what to do. But you could teach me, couldn't you?"

Jake studied her face, taking in each feature in turn. His gaze dropped for a moment to the pulse in the exposed hollow of her throat, then returned to her eyes. "Yeah, sure. Provided I ever get 'er running again."

Hattie edged up to the bumper. "Let me help. Look at all this stuff—" She indicated the box of tools and motoring paraphernalia. "I can hand it to you as you need it. Surely that would save time."

Jake seriously doubted it, but he acquiesced just to have her near. As he suspected, it took longer to describe what he needed—and wait while she searched for the tool—than it would to find what he required himself. But she was so sweet in her earnestness to help that he reined in his impatience.

In time, he discovered the problem and corrected it. Eyeing Hattie, he decided her wide smile of prideful accomplishment over the once-again-running-smoothly motorcar was almost worth the hindrance of her assistance.

It was damn good to have her back home where she belonged.

25

T ELL ME WHAT it's been like since your return." Nell tested the mattress in the room Mirabel had prepared for her, then grabbed Hattie's hand to pull her down beside her. "I want to hear everything."

Hattie was happy to make herself comfortable next to her friend. She, Augusta, and Moses had met Nell's train, but in the flurry of introductions, unpacking, and settling in, this was the first moment they'd had alone since her arrival. "Mostly positive," she replied thoughtfully. "Being home, being able to ride a decent horse again. And, of course, being with my family and seeing Moses and Doc." She laughed a shade breathlessly. "Even the townspeople seem less critical. It has felt rather miraculous. I met with the school board, and everyone was cordial. I think that's mostly due to the influence of Aurelia Donaldson. Did I tell you Aunt Augusta believes it was she who was responsible for our contracts?"

"I thought you said it was your aunt's doing."

"I believed it was. But she says not."

"Well, mercy me."

"Oh, and you'll never guess. Jake is teaching me to drive a motorcar!"

"No! Honestly?" Nell sat upright, her dark brown eyes wide and just the tiniest bit skeptical.

Hattie grinned, happy Nell was finally here, astounded she'd actually forgotten how lovely her friend was in the two-plus weeks apart. "Cross my heart and hope to die," she vowed. She wriggled with excitement. "Oh, Nell, it's so thrilling! You simply cannot imagine the speed. Why, on a straight stretch of road, provided the automobile doesn't break down, we've gone as fast as twenty-five miles an hour!"

"My Lord," Nell said faintly. "I can't wait to meet your Jake. He sounds a most unusual man." She studied Hattie's expression. "Your relationship isn't as awkward as you feared, then?"

"He's not my Jake, Nell. At least, not in the way you mean." Hattie hesitated, searching for words to explain. "It's almost as if we've both gone back to the way it was before the summer of aught-six—only not quite. He treats me the way he used to, but sometimes he gets this look in his eyes I can't explain. Except to say it's not the way a man looks at a little girl. And except for the first day, he doesn't touch me. As for me . . ." She gave her buffed fingernails a careful inspection. "Most of the time he's the same old Jake, and I'm so happy to be in his company. But then I'll wake up in the middle of the night, caught in the aftermath of a bad dream about that night and, oh, Nell, I resent him so much. I want to scream at him in those moments, to accuse and revile him. I want him to know what he's responsible for."

Nell squeezed her hand in understanding, and Hattie met her friend's gaze. "In the clear light of day, though, I know something in me would curl up and die if he learned about that night. It is so confusing, Nell—and I honestly have no idea where we stand."

"Have you seen Roger Lord?"

"No, and I thank God every day that passes without doing so. But I know sooner or later I will have to face him." She had spent a lot of time thinking up ways to handle the inevitable meeting. Since the awful night he raped her, she hadn't left the house without the little razor-sharp dagger Mirabel gave her tucked into her petite leather handbag. She'd also armed herself with a sharp hatpin, which on the rare occasions it wasn't used to secure an actual hat, she wove into an inconspicuous fold in her skirt.

But this was their reunion, so Hattie determinedly shook off depressing thoughts. "I am just grateful it hasn't happened as yet. And changing the subject, what did you think of Moses?"

It was hard catching Nell's gaze when she kept it locked on a flower on Hattie's quilt she outlined with a fingertip. "He seems nice," she said stiffly.

Hattie sighed. The meeting between her friends had been pretty disastrous. She'd nagged Moses into accompanying them to the depot, certain once he met Nell he would love her as much as Hattie did. And Nell would love him in return.

It hadn't worked that way. When introduced, Moses said, "Nice to meet you," properly enough. Except he'd all but tugged his forelock in a farm-boy-meeting-the-grand-lady-of-the-manor way. Nell already thought he'd let Hattie down, and his attitude made her poker up. So, Moses had stuffed his work-blackened hands into his trouser pockets and disassociated himself from their small gathering. The sideways look he gave Nell after helping the stationmaster with her myriad trunks had been downright snide, making her grow even more formal and self-effacing. It reminded Hattie of the night she'd first discovered how truly uncomfortable her friend was in the company of men. And she'd wanted to scream. She had finally gotten her two best friends together, and they'd acted so unacceptably stupid she had barely recognized them.

Well, she would be darned if she pretended to either of them the other did not exist. They could just blasted well learn to get along.

Hattie flipped onto her side and stuffed a pillow under her cheek. "Moses and I had a long talk last week," she said with dogged persistence. "He told me the reason he wasn't there for me when Jane-Ellen became ill. And, Nell, it was quite an . . . unexpected . . . explanation."

"Oh?"

Hattie ignored the lack of encouragement in Nell's voice. "I told you about the time down by the river before I left for school, right? The day I didn't wear my flannel shirt over my make-do swimsuit, and Jake caught us sharing our one and only kiss?"

Nell nodded at the bedspread, in which she was apparently greatly interested.

The long-ago stupidity hadn't been easy to share the first time around, and what Hattie had to share today was even more difficult. But she thought it was necessary for Nell to relinquish the notion that Moses wasn't a good friend to Hattie. And when better than now, in the privacy of her room? "Apparently, Moses was fine with me during the days after that. But at night he began having these lurid—um—sexual dreams." Word for word, she related her conversation with Moses, directing most of it to the bedspread, but glancing up often enough to observe Nell's face growing pinker and pinker with every word.

"My Lord, Hattie," Nell said faintly when her friend finished her tale. "That was . . . He said . . . ? No." Peering at her friend suspiciously, she perked up. "You are making this up."

"I'm not."

"You must be. Men simply do not tell women things like that." Nell fanned her face with both hands. She felt inordinately flushed just thinking about it. Imagine that enormous man dreaming such vivid, naughty dreams, then telling their star the lurid details! She'd known the moment they were introduced he was a bold one. But this was beyond anything in Nell's experience.

"You don't understand," Hattie said earnestly. "Moses is not a man to me; he's just . . . Moses."

"Not a man! Are you mad?" Aside from once saying he was quite gigantic, Hattie had never really described Moses. Nell had been unprepared and stunned by his physical presence. Even without the added burden of his obvious contempt for her, she would have found it difficult to combat all her old feelings of inadequacy.

"Well, I know he's been going to Mamie Parker's fancy house since shortly after we graduated from high school. But it's not the sort of thing we ever discussed, except for him to satisfy my curiosity about the place's furnishings and what sort of fashions the soiled doves wore. It never occurred to me to consider what he actually did there."

"My goodness, Hattie, what did you feel . . . how on earth did you react when he told you he'd been having those kinds of dreams about you?"

"I was . . . flattered. Kind of." Then she blurted with her habitual honesty, "Oh criminy, Nell, mostly I was embarrassed. So was he. You've met him, so you know how fair he is. Well, he was red as the roses in Aunt Augusta's garden the entire time. We both were. He stammered a lot and I blushed and looked at my toes like they'd sprouted diamonds. I don't think either of us has been so uncomfortable with the other in our entire lives! It was all we could do to make occasional eye contact. He didn't want to tell me at all but said it was the only way I would truly understand why he wasn't there when I needed him."

Nell pulled her heels onto the bed and hugged her knees to her chest, resting her chin on her kneecaps. The fabric of the comforter under them felt luxurious through her thin stockings, and she slid the balls of her feet against it. She tried not to think too closely about what she was hearing, for it made her feel—oh my goodness—rather, well, squirmy.

"The truth is, he's right," Hattie continued, her head rising from her own apparent study of the bedspread. "I never held him accountable the way I did Jake, but I was awfully hurt by his defection. And I don't believe our friendship would've regained its old footing if he hadn't explained."

Nell tried to imagine him embarrassed and couldn't. She climbed from the bed, swept up her shoes, and sat back down on the edge of the mattress to don them. "Does he still have those dreams?"

"No. Mercy, what a relief, huh? Moses and I . . . Well, we've always shared a special friendship. But it was never that kind of a friendship. Our one venture into romance nearly ruined it entirely. So, no matter how mortifying that conversation was, I'm glad he told me what drove him away."

"I suppose he squires quite a few women to the local events," Nell said casually, extending her leg and rotating her foot the better to admire her new half boot.

Hattie sat up and admired them as well. "Those are pretty," she said.

"Is that what your mama bought you for graduation?" At Nell's nod, she returned to the prior conversation. "I don't think Moses is squiring anyone at the moment. At least no one he's mentioned to me."

"Hmm," Nell said. And changed the subject to their upcoming school year.

26

HATTIE CHOSE TEACHING because she wanted a measure of independence and knew there weren't a great many options available to a woman. Given free rein, she'd choose working with the Murdock horses. But fat chance Jake would turn that over to her, even if the herd had been substantially reduced these past few years. Teaching struck her as the next best thing. She found the process of learning exciting, and generating a thirst for new ideas in others was more appealing than the prospect of being a salesgirl, librarian, or typist.

She was nevertheless apprehensive about her ability to perform her job satisfactorily. At night during the week before the start of the new school year, she lay wide awake in bed, fretting. Was she prepared? She was going to have fourteen students. What if she failed to command their respect or control her class?

The school had three classes. Nell got the younger children, whose ages ranged from six to nine; Hattie had the ten- to thirteen-year-olds; and Jack Dalton was assigned the older students since he had the seniority, experience, and additional education required to teach high school.

The Friday before school opened, the teachers, along with Mirabel; Jack Dalton's doting landlady, Mrs. Wilson; and a ranch hand Jake sent over, moved the desks out into the yard and cleaned the three-room schoolhouse top to bottom. They knocked down spiderwebs, swept and scrubbed floors, whitewashed the walls, washed windows, blacked the potbellied Wetter's Comfort stoves, cleaned blackboards, and pounded erasers free of chalk dust. Mirabel left early to prepare dinner, and by the time Hattie and Nell trudged for home, they were exhausted but pleased with the results. Their sparkling classrooms were ready for occupation.

The big barn doors of Armstrong's Livery stood open as they passed by, and on impulse, Hattie grabbed Nell's arm to pull her to a halt. "Let's say hello to Moses," she suggested.

Nell was horrified at the prospect and glanced down at her grubby apparel. She wore her oldest dress, and her arms, hands, and probably face as well were smudged with dirt. Half her hair had slid out of its neat pompadour. But Hattie hadn't waited for an answer and was across the courtyard by the time Nell gathered her wits about her.

Hattie turned at the big double doors. "Come on!" With a sigh, Nell grudgingly followed.

They found Moses at the forge, pounding out a long piece of iron with a glowing red end. The heat was overwhelming and he'd removed his shirt, wearing only a leather apron to protect his chest from flying sparks. Sweat plastered his hair to his head and trickled down his sides, back, and chest. His forearms above his grimy leather gloves were blackened with soot, and his muscles flexed and slid smoothly with every movement beneath the oiled sheen of his skin. Nell stared in fascination while he was still unaware of their presence. Lord above. She had never seen such a virile man.

Her inspection was cut short when he set aside his mallet and shifted the iron from the anvil into a bucket of water by his side. Hattie moved forward. "Hey," she said.

Moses' head swung around, a white smile splitting his face. "Hiya, Hat." His smile grew wider yet when he saw her disheveled appearance. "What in tarnation y'been doing—cleaning somebody's chimney?" Then he spotted Nell in the shadows behind her, and his smile dimmed as he suddenly became aware of his filthy appearance. He reached up and tugged a lock of his hair, inclining his head. "Afternoon, Miss Nell."

"Moses," she said coolly, stepping forward with her regal posture, her chin elevated.

"We spent the entire day being scullery maids," Hattie explained. "We've been preparing our classrooms, and, oh my, do they shine!"

Moses smiled at her with affection but shuttered his gaze into something more mocking when he turned to Nell. Looking her over from her shining black topknot, sitting askew on the crown of her head, to the scuffed toes of her shoes, he paused deliberately at every smudge in between. Hoping to hell it would erase this god-awful yearning in his gut. "It's a right proper look for you, Miss Nell. Scullery work suits you."

Nell was tired to begin with and uncomfortable in his presence. It was overheated and stuffy in this corner of the livery and smelled of overworked man and horse. The sight of so much unclad muscle and skin was unnerving, and to her abject horror, tears rose in her eyes. Blinking rapidly, she turned without a word and left the livery.

Moses felt sick at the sight of her tears. He turned from watching her retreating ramrod-straight back and looked straight into Hattie's contemptuous eyes.

"My God," she said softly. "It's one thing if you simply don't like her. I suppose I can learn to live with that. But I have never known you to be deliberately nasty."

He shrugged his big shoulders uneasily. "No one in their right mind would ever believe that girl was designed for scullery work. Even in dirt and rags, she looks like some princess come to inspect the stable boy's work. Can't she take a joke?"

"Oh, were you joking? Forgive me, I guess I missed the punch line." She slugged him in the arm. "You listen to me, Moses Marks, and pay attention because I'm only going to say this once. Nell isn't some rich society woman working for a lark, and she's not looking down her pretty, patrician nose at you, so you can just save your 'Aw, shucks, I'm nothing but a country rhubarb' routine for someone who actually deserves it. It's not only not funny, it's cruel. She doesn't have two pennies to rub together and she's shy around men. It took me a long time to convince her just because she's inordinately tall for a woman, it doesn't mean she's unattractive."

Moses looked at her incredulously and Hattie said, "That's what she used to think, you know—at least around men. I'm surprised at you. You have been too good a friend to me for too many years to make me believe you made a value judgment based on her looks. If that was the case, why didn't you run screaming from me when the entire town condemned me as a loose young woman of easy virtue? After all, they formed their theory based on the way I looked."

"I knew you," he muttered.

"Well, heaven forbid you should get to know Nell. If you did, you just might have to justify it to yourself when you let loose that mean streak. If you're bound and determined to be a bully, Moses, then go pick on someone your own size. Leave my friend alone." She turned on her heel and strode for the door.

"Hattie."

She halted at the sound of his voice but didn't turn to look at him. "What?"

He stared at her rigid back as she stood in the open doorway, her hair beneath its coating of dust blazing in a shaft of sunlight. He admired her defense of Nell and was shamed by it. She had more guts than ten men put together. She'd stood up to him the way he should have stood up to others on a number of occasions when it had been Hattie under attack. "You're the best of friends," he said softly. "And I'm sorry, girl."

"Good—but don't tell me." Glancing over her shoulder, she met his contrite gaze with a steely one of her own. "Tell Nell."

27

HATTIE SAT BEHIND her desk, watching her students as they filed through the doorway. Her nervousness began to melt away as she observed them. Not much had changed, apparently, since she was a student here.

The children from Mattawa's first families were easily identifiable by their fashionable clothing. The rest of her students could be classified into one of two groups: those from town and those from the outlying ranches and farms. All were scrubbed clean, but the farm kids tended to wear clothing that had seen a little more service than their town-bred counterparts, and their complexions were ruddier from a life spent more outside than in. In the few moments before the bell rang, conversations buzzed, two farm boys horsed around in the back of the room, and several girls sat with their heads together, whispering and occasionally giggling.

Out in the schoolyard the bell rang. Hattie rose from her chair and crossed the room to close the door. Hearing footsteps thundering down the hall, she paused and was nearly bowled over when a large boy threw his shoulder against the closing door and barged into the room.

"Sorry, miss," he said, his tone both belligerent and contrite.

He appeared older than the rest of her students, so Hattie surmised he'd been assigned to her class to make up missed schooling. She found it difficult to tell if he was town or country. He was large and like the farm kids had weathered skin. But he lacked their well-fed look and scrubbed appearance. He had clearly made an attempt to clean himself up, but there was a line of grimy skin near his collar where the soap had stopped. His clothes were ill fitting: too short in the leg, too loose on his big-boned, gangly, underfed frame. And while passably clean, they were inexpertly pressed, as if he'd laundered them himself. He had the vulnerable, defiant look of a misfit, and Hattie felt an empathetic shift deep in her stomach. "What is your name?" she asked.

"Jonathan Semp, miss."

"Welcome to class, Jonathan. Please take a seat." She closed the door and returned to stand behind her desk. "Good morning," she said. "My name is Miss Taylor. I would like to begin by attaching names to your faces, so I can get them straight in my mind. As I call your name for attendance, please stand, say 'here,' and seat yourself." She leaned down to open the drawer of her desk to retrieve her attendance book.

The drawer had been pushed in unevenly and she had to wriggle it before it slowly slid open. Pulling it open, she glanced down, and her heart kicked hard against her rib cage. Uncoiling from a dark back corner was a good-sized garter snake.

Hattie stifled a smile. Her students didn't give a darn about who she used to be. They just wanted to see what their new teacher was made of.

A shrill, short scream echoed faintly from Nell's room next door. In response, a nervous titter erupted from the middle of Hattie's room, and she held the snake down with two fingers while she slid her attendance book out of the desk and closed the drawer. A small smile curved her lips as she glanced at the class.

All the students sat unnaturally still. Most of their faces contained expressions of bland innocence; a few couldn't hide their anticipation, and one girl had her head averted, a hand clamped over her mouth. Hattie picked up her attendance book and circled the desk. Leaning against its oak edge, she flipped the pages open and calmly read, "Amundsen, Katherine."

As one, the students shifted. There was a moment of silence as they exchanged uneasy glances. A girl of about twelve surreptitiously raised her feet off the floor. "Amundsen, Katherine," Hattie repeated. "Please stand and say 'here.'"

One of the younger children hesitantly climbed out of her seat. Blushing furiously, she straightened her skirt, cleared her throat, and said, "Here." The tension began to dissipate as one by one, each student rose in response to the attendance call. Hattie studied them, trying to memorize something about each to help her remember their names. When the last name was called, she circled around her desk once again and took her seat.

"I had planned to begin your studies with a reading assignment," she said clearly, and the corner of her mouth tilted up in a half smile. "But there's been a change of agenda. I think we'll begin with a little science lesson, instead." She opened the desk drawer, reached in, and removed the snake. Resting her elbows on her desk and holding the reptile stretched out between her hands for all to see, she continued, "Who can tell the class what species of snake this is?"

JAKE LEANED AGAINST the warm boards of Norton's Mercantile, whistling softly. Glancing often up the block, he rhythmically tossed an apple up in the air and caught it in one hand. Tossed it and caught it. He'd stolen it from Henderson's orchard outside of town and polished it on his thigh all the way to Mattawa, until it gleamed with deep ruby depths.

Suddenly, he straightened, the foot he'd propped against the store wall dropping to the sidewalk. He tucked the hand holding the apple behind his back. Sashaying up the street, skirts swinging, came Hattie. And hot damn if she wasn't alone for once. He stepped into the recessed doorway of Norton's Mercantile and peered around the edge to monitor her progress.

When she was parallel to the doorway, he stepped onto the sidewalk in front of her. Tipping his hat, he grinned. "Howdy, Teacher, ma'am. How was your first day of school?"

"Jake!" She tilted her head back to look up at him, her face aglow with delight. "It was so wonderful I can't describe it! I was kinda scared about how I would do, but it was simply marvelous. I have a great class."

He wondered if her delight was in the unexpected meeting or in her day's achievement but decided it didn't matter. "I bet the boys in your class are all giving thanks tonight for having such a pretty schoolmarm." He admired the sun shining on her upturned face and how it turned her hair to flame, her freckles to gold, and her eyes to the clear, glowing amber of good whiskey. "I know my teachers never looked nearly as fetching as you." He brought his hand out from behind his back, offering her the apple. "This is for you. I always wanted to be teacher's pet, but since I had Miss Wicket for seven years and she was uglier than a pan full of worms, it wasn't worth the effort. If I'd had someone like you, I would still be attending school today."

"Oh, Jacob, for me?" Hattie stared at the apple as though he'd given her rubies. Her smile dazzled him right down to the ground as she plucked it off his palm. Pressing it to her breast, she reached up to palm his cheek with her free hand. "Thank you."

He grinned, curving a calloused hand over her smooth fingers and turning the side of his face more fully into her touch.

When he smiled, Hattie felt the soft skin rising on either side of the crease in Jake's cheek. It gave her a bolt of unadulterated pleasure. She'd be hard-pressed to say why his gesture meant so much to her. It just did, and she had a sudden desire to rise on her toes to kiss him.

My goodness, what was she thinking? They were downtown, in broad daylight. To distract herself, she said, "Did you steal it?"

He stepped back, all affronted male. "Hattie Taylor! What do you take me for, some Cheap Charlie? Do I look like I can't afford to buy you a crummy apple?"

Oh, she wanted to hug herself and spin in a circle. Laughter bubbled out of her as she teased him. "You did, didn't you? You wouldn't protest so much otherwise. Ooh, I'm gonna tell your mama. I bet I know where you got it, too. Henderson's orch—"

"Afternoon, Jake. Miss Hattie."

Hattie froze, the remainder of her words stuck in her throat. She knew that voice—it was the sound of her nightmares. Tension shot up her spine, and for an instant, she was plunged into a blinding-white abyss where nothing existed except burning pain, degradation, and that voice mouthing unspeakably cruel words as he forcefully stole her virginity.

"Afternoon, Roger," she heard Jake say without enthusiasm, and gave herself a brisk mental shake.

She was prepared for this, dammit. Ever since she'd received the letter offering her a job, she had known she would have to face Roger. But this wasn't the way she'd planned it . . .

Still, she would not let that bastard reduce her to this: to some craven, cowardly little mouse who retreated to quiver mindlessly in its burrow, waiting for danger to pass. Pride stiffened her spine. "Mr. Lord," she said coolly, inclining her head in the same regal manner she'd seen Augusta display. Chin tilted up proudly, Hattie turned and let her eyes, carefully clear of expression, meet Lord's dead on.

She expected to see an animal gratification that he'd bested her, forcing her to admit her helplessness to prevent this public conversation. Instead, she encountered surprise and impotent rage. With a small jolt of satisfaction, she realized Lord hadn't bargained on her unwillingness to run. This poor excuse for a man clearly counted on her making a fool of herself by scampering away, or at the very least by stammering and looking down. The bastard! He thought he could toy with her like a cat with captured prey, and knowing she'd bested him, she surprised herself by feeling downright confrontational. "How is your law practice, sir?"

"Doing nicely, thank you," Roger replied with stiff politeness, while inside he burned with rage. Hell-bound daughter of a whoreson! He'd kill her. He would wrap his hands around the ripe little bitch's throat and squeeeeze until he felt the fragile bones snap beneath his fingers. And while he was doing it, he would tell that smirking jackass Murdock exactly how it had felt to rip into her tightly guarded virginal body. He actually took a step forward before he caught himself. Not here. Not now. He tipped his hat. "Well, I must go. I just wanted to say hello." He had a new parlormaid at home. A redheaded parlormaid. And tonight, he intended to pay her a visit.

"Afternoon," Hattie murmured at his retreating back. "Well, that went well," she whispered.

"What?" Jake demanded, warily watching her watch Lord walk away. "What went well?"

She turned a startled gaze his way. "Oh, nothing important," she replied, but he didn't miss the way her eyes shuttered.

Simmering with frustration, Jake could have put his fist through the nearest wall. Here he'd had a nice little conversation going—almost as free and easy as in the old days—and unblemished for once by the myriad black clouds marring the summer his wife died and Hattie left for school. Then Lord had to show up. Son of a bitch, of all the people in this town!

Jake could never fathom why Hattie resented him so much for sending her to Lord that night. She knew he'd done it to protect her from *him*. He'd lost control when he should have been the adult, but, dammit, he'd caught himself in time not to cause any permanent damage. Hattie told him she'd never forgive him for sending her to Roger, both before and after the fact, and, by God, for two long years she'd stuck to her word. Since her return, her attitude had softened, yet by no means had it regained its old easy give-and-take. The two of them still displayed tendencies to tiptoe around each other.

The conversation between Hattie and Lord began and ended so quickly, Jake wasn't sure what to make of it. He searched her expression for a sign her fury was returning and supposed he should be grateful she didn't regard him with those unforgiving eyes she'd turned his way before leaving for school in '06. That was a soul-chilling expression he would not forget if he lived to be a hundred. But dammit to hell!

In fact, Hattie did experience a flash of resentment toward Jake, but she stomped it dead. She knew she couldn't continue holding him to blame and not tell him why. And *that* she would never do. Just the thought of Jake knowing what that son of a bitch had done to her made her break out in a cold sweat. Silence surrounded them.

Jake broke it when he asked, "Where's your sidekick this afternoon?"

"Nell?" Hattie's tension slowly ebbed at the change of subject, and she smiled slightly. "She had a few things she needed to do and it was much too nice an afternoon to wait around indoors, so I left ahead of her."

"In that case, please allow me to escort you to a champagne supper to celebrate your first day of teaching." Jake offered his arm.

Knowing he was pulling her leg, she regarded him with a lifted eyebrow. "A champagne supper? Ooh, la-di-dah. And how I deserve it." Taking his arm, she elevated her nose as if she accompanied ruggedly handsome men to champagne dinners all the time. She allowed Jake to usher her down the block to his shiny black Packard parked between a farm wagon and a high-wheeled buggy. Never let it be said that Hattie Taylor couldn't play along. Even if it was just a silly game of make-believe.

Perhaps especially then.

28

JAKE HADN'T BEEN kidding about the champagne supper. Augusta's celebration included Doc Fielding, Jack Dalton and his landlady, Moses, Nell, and Aurelia Donaldson. They sat around the dining room table as the three teachers regaled them with the events of the day.

"Tell them what you did with your snake," Nell commanded Hattie, and Jack Dalton grinned as he pushed his plate away.

"Yes, you have to hear this," he informed the assembled guests. "Our students planted a garter snake in each of our desks this morning. And Miss Hattie here . . . well, you tell them."

Hattie did so, delighted by the warm laughter her story generated.

"I wish I could have been so coolheaded," Nell confessed. "I'm afraid I screamed to wake the dead and it took me ten minutes to regain control of my class."

Moses, sitting on her right, said, "You can't blame yourself for that, Miss Nell. You didn't have the benefit of Hattie's experience." He smiled in reminiscence. "She and I planted our fair share of snakes in teachers' desks."

Nell was surprised he'd excused her cowardice. She'd expected him to take the opportunity to make her feel out of place. Before she could give the matter more thought, Hattie was speaking. Nell straightened in her seat so she no longer gave Moses her shoulder while dancing attendance on Doc Fielding to her left.

"I must admit, seeing that snake gave me a shock," Hattie said. "My heart jumped right up my throat." She smiled over her shoulder at Mirabel, who was removing her dinner plate and replacing it with a portion of caramel custard. "Thank you," she whispered. "This looks lovely." Then raising her voice, she said to the guests, "It's been several years since I handled a snake." A thought occurred to her and she turned to Jake. "Do you know a family called Semp?" she asked.

"That would probably be Big John Semp," Doc answered while Jake was still searching his memory. "Herds cattle at Smyth Dooley's place. He's a hard-drinkin' sonovabitch—beggin' your pardon, ladies. Stays sober on the job, but I'll lay odds his pay voucher goes to liquor and gambling."

"I have his son in my class, and, Doc, I don't think he's getting enough to eat. He's a big-boned boy, but so thin. I think if he were eating properly, he might be as strapping as Moses."

Nell was extremely aware of how strapping Moses was when his large shoulder jostled hers at the table. Out of the corner of her eye, she saw his left hand resting by his plate. It was obviously strong and looked as if it had been scrubbed with a wire brush to remove the forge grime—all raw-looking and so big it could probably wrap around the back of her head from temple to temple. The thought made her shift uncomfortably in her seat.

"Perhaps the young man is going through one of those growth spurts boys are prone to," Aurelia Donaldson contributed, peering at Hattie through her lorgnette. "I recall my own Edward looking so hollow he was nearly transparent, while simultaneously driving Cook to distraction trying to keep the pantry filled."

"I wish I could believe that were the case," Hattie said glumly. "But today at lunch, he only had two apples to eat and those were probably stolen from Henderson's orchard." Involuntarily, her eyes sought Jake's and one corner of her mouth tilted up in a secret smile when he arched an eyebrow at her.

"I shared my lunch with him, saying I had much too much food for one person, which was true enough since Mirabel packs enough to feed a stevedore. But I fear I shan't get away with the ploy indefinitely. He gobbled that food up like a starving hound, but he's a proud boy and just stubborn enough to view accepting food more than occasionally as taking charity."

Nothing more was said that evening, but Hattie was surprised to find Jake waiting for her in the schoolyard during lunch one day the following week. She crossed over to him, aware of all the eyes that watched their every move. "Hello," she greeted him. "What are you doing here?"

"I came to meet Jonathan Semp."

Her eyebrows shot skyward, but obediently she led him over to Jonathan, who was devouring his apples in an isolated corner of the schoolyard. "Jonathan," she said, "this is Jacob Murdock. He'd like to speak to you."

"What for?" Jonathan climbed to his feet and regarded Jake warily. He stuffed his hands into his overall pockets and hunched his shoulders defensively. "I ain't done nothing."

"I haven't done anything," Hattie corrected.

"Yes'm. Haven't done anything."

"I understand you know a little about working with cattle," Jake said, offering his hand. It was a stab in the dark he hoped was correct. But if the kid had grown up around cattle operations, chances were he'd absorbed some knowledge. He mentally winced at the boy's thinness. Hattie hadn't exaggerated.

Jonathan didn't think to question where the man in front of him might have heard that. He just shook the proffered hand hesitantly and said, "Yes, sir. I been around cattle all my life."

"Have been," Hattie interjected, and Jake shot her an exasperated glance.

"Give us a moment alone, Hattie."

"Oh. Certainly. See to it that Jonathan is in class when the bell rings." She was all starch as she spun on her heel and walked away.

Jake grinned. "Hattie's real big on proper grammar usage. But a conversation with her correcting every word that pops out of our mouths will take all day."

Jonathan stared at Murdock in awe. He'd called Miss Taylor by her first name and ordered her away like he was mayor of Mattawa. Then the man looked at him, suddenly all business. "I need an extra hand but don't have enough work for a full-time man. How would you like to work for me after school and on Saturday mornings? I pay two bits an hour and meals. I know it's a long way from town, so I'll throw in the use of one of my cattle ponies. But know this, boy. You only get the unskilled work until you've proven yourself. We got ourselves a deal?"

Jonathan swallowed hard. Meals? And two bits an hour? Cripes, his old man made that and he'd been punchin' cattle for twenty years. Plus the use of a pony? He'd be rolling in clover! "Yes, sir. When do you want me to start?"

"Today. I'll talk to Miss Taylor and have her bring you out after school. Then you'll know the way and it will be up to you to get yourself there promptly after school. Understood?"

"Yes, sir!"

"Good." The bell began to ring, signaling the end of the lunch recess. "Get to class. I'll see you this afternoon. Oh, and tell Hattie I'll have a hand bring out the buggy so she can deliver you to the ranch." Jake turned and strode away.

After school, Hattie had her work cut out to keep from grinning like a ninny on the ride out to Jake's ranch. Jonathan sat beside her on the buggy seat, leaning forward as if he could urge the horse to greater speed. Hattie's heart galloped as she thought of Jake. Oh, that man. That splendid, marvelous, ingenious man! This absolved him forever for his part in her downfall at Roger's hands. This was the Jake Murdock she had known and loved as a child: generous to a fault, kind, and concerned about the welfare of those less fortunate than himself.

He was waiting for them in the driveway when they pulled up, a sweat-stained, battered hat shading his eyes. He extended a hand to assist

Hattie from the wagon seat and, accepting it, she grinned and jumped to the ground. Releasing her, he turned to Jonathan. "Go into the kitchen and tell Cook to give you a meal. When you're done, go on over to the bunkhouse—it's the building over there with the big porch. Happy will assign you your rig. I'll see you in the north pasture when you're all set." He gave succinct directions and watched the gangly youth until he disappeared around the corner of the house. Then he turned back to Hattie.

She flung her arms around his neck and squeezed. "Jake Murdock, I adore you." She planted a quick peck of a kiss on his lips, then whirled away. "I'm going to take Belle for a ride as long as I'm here. It seems an age since I've ridden." Then she was off and running toward the stables.

Jake stood still as a stone, staring at her retreating figure. Every vein in his body felt scalded by the sudden rush of hot blood pulsing through it, and he closed his eyes for a moment, drawing in a deep breath. Christ Almighty. He had to forcibly restrain himself from following her into the stable. This was not the time. He had plans and was following a strict timetable. But many more incidents like this would shoot to hell all his careful planning.

Hattie best not get too cocky, though, thinking she could say things like that, thinking she could just kiss him and run away. For his patience was a fragile thing—and already worn thin. And whether Hattie Taylor knew it or not, their time was coming.

29

TEACHING REWARDED HATTIE in ways she'd never imagined. She had looked forward to the challenge it represented but hadn't dreamed of the inroads it would make into her acceptance by the community. It was a continuous source of delight to discover her students liked her.

She felt validated by their attentiveness in class, their bright minds and fresh outlooks. Their personalities and backgrounds ran the gamut, as did individual desires for knowledge. Yet, as a class, there was a uniformity to their efforts to achieve, and Hattie told anyone who bothered to ask that her students couldn't be topped. It never entered her mind it might be her enthusiasm for the world and events around her firing their imagination, her firmness and unique methods that brought wandering attention back to the lesson at hand. She only knew she was blessed with an exceptional class.

Her students talked about her at home. Beginning with the snake episode on the first day, parents began to hear Miss Taylor said this and did that. Hattie had no way of knowing her name was bruited about with increasing frequency across supper tables, in stables and barns during chores, in parlors over embroidery lessons, and in ranch kitchens while busy hands prepared meals. It seemed out of the blue when parents began consulting her about their children's progress.

She loved talking about her students. It became a familiar sight in town, Hattie Taylor's face alight with enthusiasm, her mobile mouth smiling as she regaled any parent who took the time to ask with detailed instances of their child's academic achievement. She would halt whatever she was doing wherever she was: in Norton's Mercantile, outside the bank or the *Mattawa Clarion*, or simply walking along the streets of town, to uninhibitedly block an aisle or a sidewalk while she praised and discussed her students.

Only gradually did it dawn on Hattie that, with those very conversations, she was being accorded a measure of respectability in return. When the realization finally sank in, her first reaction was surprise. After all, except for her two years in Seattle, respectability wasn't an attribute applied to her.

Her newly gained acceptance tickled her pink. She'd probably never marry. How could she, when the specter of explaining her lack of virginity haunted potential relationships? But she felt content envisioning a life spent teaching. It represented personal independence and Hattie thought she could do a lot worse. After all, she earned forty dollars a month, had work both challenging and steady, and was carving a place for herself here in Mattawa.

And she got to work with Nell. Making friends with another female later than most, she especially valued her relationship with her fellow schoolmarm. As she'd predicted, Mattawa embraced Nell wholeheartedly, and Hattie was as proud as a mother with a cherished only child. They loved her friend's impeccable manners and obvious breeding, her gentleness with their young ones. Of the whole town, only Moses seemed to feel the need to hold himself aloof.

He was no longer actively hostile since Hattie blew up at him in the livery, yet he stubbornly maintained a cool-eyed reserve around Nell. Hattie wasn't thrilled with his attitude.

But the fault wasn't solely his. Nell's demeanor didn't defuse the situation. Instead, her attitude had just the opposite effect and simply inflamed the stance Moses had taken with her.

Nell was consistently stiff around him. Her usual ebullience evaporating when Moses was nearby, she became awkward and formal.

Hattie harbored a secret urge to grab them both by the scruffs of their necks and knock their heads together. It made her want to swear—and normally only conversations with Roger Lord could make her do that. The two of them were the funniest, warmest people she knew with everyone, *anyone*, else. Watching them with each other made her want to scream.

But she'd made up her mind that as long as they weren't actively at war, she would bite her tongue and stay out of it. They needn't think, however, that because she wouldn't interfere, she'd help them promote their idiocy. She talked about each to the other incessantly, as though bearing the news of one cherished friend to another.

The curious thing was, she could almost swear they hung on every word—but conceded that particular notion was likely a cross between wishful thinking and an overactive imagination.

Buchannan Hotel
FRIDAY, DECEMBER 18, 1908

For weeks, the teachers had been helping their students rehearse for the annual Christmas pageant. Now rehearsals were finished and pageant night was upon them. Her stomach aflutter with nerves, Hattie paced behind the stage curtain in the ballroom where the pageant was being held. Had she forgotten any crucial instructions? She bet she had. For all she knew, she'd neglected an entire vital segment of the production. As a result, the darn thing would probably be ruined, and it would be all her fault. "Lord, would you look at that rain come down," she muttered and dropped the curtain on the small backstage window to shut out the lashing rain on a hard-blowing wind. "It's coming down in sheets! What if no one comes?"

"Peek out the stage curtain," Nell suggested. "The room is already filling."

"Where's my music? Oh no, I've lost my music!" Hattie began pawing frantically through the heaped coats, umbrellas, and overshoes.

"For heaven's sake, it's right here where you left it." Nell handed her the sheaf of sheet music. "Please, put it on the piano so you'll know where it is, then go check on your students to make sure everyone has everything they need. That should calm you down." Nell shook her head in amusement as Hattie raced off. She'd never seen Hattie so unhinged . . . and over a school pageant, for pity's sake.

As Nell predicted, working with the students—correcting last-minute problems, locating lost props, and adjusting costumes—settled Hattie's nerves. By the time Jack Dalton signaled her, she had her class lined up in the wings in the order in which they'd appear. With a smile and a firm nod, she took her place at the piano. Flexing her fingers, Hattie listened to Jack welcome the parents, families, and guests of the student body. There was a shuffle of feet backstage. Then, slowly the red velvet curtain opened and she launched into the first tune, smiling encouragement as the first group of students began to sing.

As with all school pageants, there were forgotten or misquoted lines. One of Hattie's students, carried away by his moment in the limelight, used an extravagant arm gesture that knocked a crown off of one of the three wise men. One of Nell's little ones forgot the words to her song and hummed until she came to a part she remembered. A high school student tripped, staggering halfway across the stage before he regained his balance. The audience didn't care. They applauded each effort generously, laughed when they were supposed to, and managed to conceal their laughter at some of the more outrageous mistakes. The play was a roaring success.

The noise level during the post-performance reception rose steadily. Chairs were moved to the perimeter of the ballroom. Cakes, pies, and cookies, brought by the parents and deposited on a table near the entrance, were unwrapped and arranged. Urns of coffee and tea were brought from the kitchen to flank either end of the desserts, and a huge bowl of punch was placed on a small table nearby. The students were still in a high state of excitement as they accepted praise from their guests. The little ones chased each other, their shrill laughter bouncing off the vaulted ceiling as they dodged between the milling, shifting groups of adults.

Miss Eunice Peabody buttonholed Hattie. She cleared her throat nervously. "I . . . um . . . wanted to commend you for whatever it was you did to convince my niece to perform onstage tonight."

Hattie's eyes lit up and she smiled widely. "Yes, Cora is very shy, isn't she? But she put so much effort into overcoming her nervousness, and wasn't she simply wonderful?"

Moses watched Nell watch Hattie. Nell's dark eyes were soft and her lips curved up in a small, satisfied smile, and against his better judgment he crossed the room until he stood just behind her. Leaning down, he said softly in her ear, "That woman talking to Hattie? She's always been one of her biggest critics. Was convinced Hattie was bound for hell from the moment she stepped in town—and didn't mind sharing her conviction with the rest of Mattawa."

Nell tilted her head back and smiled at him over her shoulder. It was a natural smile, free of her usual constraint. "But she's winning her over, isn't she?" She laughed with sudden exuberance. "One by one, she's winning them all over."

He looked down into Nell's face. God, she was so damn pretty. And her soft black hair, brushing his chin, smelled sweeter than Henderson's orchard in March. "Yeah," he agreed in a slow drawl and tore his gaze away to look across the room at Hattie again. "She is by God winning them over." With a final inhalation of her sweet scent, he straightened and moved away.

Nell watched him go until her attention was commandeered by a student's parent. But in a corner of her mind, she wondered: Was Moses in love with Hattie? Did he still have dreams of her, those torrid, impossible-to-imagine dreams she had heard secondhand from her friend?

The father talking to Nell found her sudden blush quite charming.

Across the room, Aurelia Donaldson tapped Jake's shoulder with her lorgnette. "I don't believe you're paying attention to me, young man," she said crisply.

Jake pulled his eyes away from Hattie and grinned at the woman his father had grown up with. "Not paying attention? Nonsense! Who could ignore the prettiest girl here?"

"What horsefeathers." Her faded blue eyes glowed with amusement. "I swan, if you aren't your father's son all over! Luke Murdock was the only other man I ever met could spout such folderol and almost make a woman believe he meant every word of it."

She scanned the room, then brought her gaze back to Jake's face, her eyes sharp as they peered at him through her lorgnette. "You warm the cockles of this old girl's heart, Jacob Murdock, so I'm doing you a favor in return. Look what Hattie Taylor is standing under. I see the high school students have been up to their usual Christmastide tomfoolery."

Jake searched the room until he spotted Hattie. He looked at the arched doorway over her head and breathed, "Hot damn." A huge smile creasing his cheeks, he bent down and gave Aurelia a noisy buss on the cheek. "Thanks, Aurelia. I owe you."

"Indeed you do, sonny," she replied and reinstated her stern expression. She couldn't help but smile, however, as she watched him head for the red-haired teacher in the doorway.

Crossing the floor, Jake noticed several high school boys covertly watching the archway where Hattie stood chatting to Augusta. He raised an eyebrow at one of them as he swept up to her. "Nice program, Hattie." He turned to Augusta with an impeccable half bow of acknowledgment. "Mother."

"Jake!" Hattie's face was flushed with her students' triumph as she turned to him. "Didn't it turn out well? These kids are so darn talented!"

"Mistletoe!" a raucous cry interrupted her words. "Hey, Mr. Murdock, Miss Taylor's standing under the mistletoe!"

Jake pretended surprise as he glanced up. Hattie's confusion was real and she glanced around to find herself the cynosure of almost every eye.

She turned back to Jake with a wary expression, her face flushed. "Oh dear."

"Gotta be a sport, Hattie."

"Now, Jacob," Augusta said. "Don't you go embarrassing her."

He gave his mother a smile of assurance, then bent down, one hand reaching out to lightly cup the side of Hattie's face. He was highly aware of the callouses on his hand compared to her soft, smooth skin. He slowly lowered his head while Big-eyes stared at him like a deer caught in the light of a poacher's lantern. His lips hovered just above hers for an attenuated moment but didn't touch down. Then, with the softest of touches, he pressed his mouth against her cheek at the corner of her mouth, his parted lips nearly but not quite touching hers. He rubbed his thumb once across her cheekbone; then his hand slid away and he straightened. The high school boys stomped and hollered their approval; the adults smiled, pleased with his decorum, and the noise level rose again as conversations resumed.

For Hattie, it wasn't quite as easy to regain her equilibrium. She, too, was pleased he hadn't turned it into a spectacle. And yet . . . For an instant there, feeling his breath wash over her lips, she'd wanted him to kiss her—really kiss her. It was madness, of course, but remembering how his one kiss had felt resurfaced for a moment with incredible force, slamming through her body, making her want . . . well, making her want—she didn't even know what. Darn it, she was just beginning to make a place for herself in Mattawa, so, truly, anything other than the peck he'd given her would have been ruinous. And yet . . .

All she knew was the kiss he'd bestowed upon her left her feeling unsettled.

ACROSS THE ROOM, Nell tried to gauge Moses' reaction to the public kiss, but his expression gave nothing away. Irritation with herself itched like scratchy wool. What possible difference did it make? Even if he didn't love Hattie, he had made it plain he didn't even like her, so why did she keep trying to assess his every response to Hattie's actions?

Good grief, can you act any more like a fool? Nell knew she wasn't the type of woman who inspired men to dream lusty dreams. It had only been in the past year she'd managed to inspire a few to ask her to dance! And it wasn't as if she aspired to be that type of woman anyway. Right? More than anything, she'd like to talk to Hattie about her utterly confused emotions regarding Moses Marks. Yet, how could she? How on earth would she phrase it? *I'm experiencing all these new emotions for your oldest friend and I don't know how to deal with them. And, oh, by the way, is he in love with you?* Hattie was so oblivious to her own appeal, she'd probably reject the question out of hand without giving it so much as a moment's consideration. But, merciful Lord, these feelings! Nell shivered. How was she supposed to navigate all these unfamiliar feelings if she couldn't talk to someone about them?

She didn't have an answer to that, so in the weeks after the Christmas pageant, she simply locked them deep inside and pretended they didn't exist. Yet they were ever present, causing her to become even more desperately stiff and correct in Moses' company. Perhaps in retaliation, he dropped the cool politeness he'd adopted and went back to baiting her with faux sycophancy.

Nell had never been so unhappy in her life. This was a hurt that struck much deeper than simply being overlooked—and God knew feeling invisible had been bruising enough to her not-so-stalwart ego. But this . . . No one had ever actively disliked her before.

She tried not to let them, but her rampant emotions impacted her relationship with Hattie. She fought a niggling resentment she didn't understand yet couldn't seem to control. Hattie asked more than once if something was bothering her, but Nell couldn't bring herself to unburden herself of all the emotions building inside her. Until an evening of rare balminess at the end of February, when they finally had words.

30

S CHOOL WAS CLOSED for Washington's birthday. It was crystal clear, sunny, and unseasonably warm, with temperatures rising to the mid-sixties—a bonus spring day in the dead of winter—when Jake stopped by Augusta's unannounced. Nell watched Hattie look up in delight when he burst into the dining room, where they'd just finished their luncheon.

"Hey," he said cheerfully. "I had to come to town to pick up some feed and thought the two of you might like to join me for a spin in my motor-car first."

"Oh yes!" Hattie responded enthusiastically. "That sounds like a mar-velous way to celebrate a rare day off." She turned to Nell. "Don't you think?"

"I do," Nell agreed with a smile, and after collecting their dustcovers and hats, they joined Jake at the automobile he was in the midst of pre-paring for ignition. Nell felt the moody angst that had been haunting her dissipate.

Then Hattie ruined the "marvelous celebration" by waiting until they were on their way before suggesting they stop by the Marks home to see if Moses cared to join them as well. By then, of course, it was too late to back out, and from the moment Moses climbed into the back seat with her, it went sideways. He didn't say a word to her—not even so much as

Great weather today. And he gave her those awful sardonic smiles that never touched his blue eyes.

It felt like an eternity before they finally dropped Moses off back at his house. Once they returned to Augusta's, Nell raced up the stairs ahead of Hattie, wanting only to escape to her room, where she could bawl her eyes out in private. She could not bear the thought of having to talk to anyone, and luckily Augusta was visiting a friend. Since Hattie usually spent several moments saying goodbye to Jake, Nell felt safe in fleeing.

HATTIE WAS FED up with Moses' and Nell's attitudes and seethed in anger. She said goodbye to Jake in record time and followed practically on Nell's heels, entering her friend's room behind Nell and firmly closing the door. "What is the matter with you two?" she demanded hotly. "Good grief, can we not have one simple drive without you and Moses acting like a couple of cats with one fish? Separately, you're both so funny and fun and just plain nice. But together? Nell, if you had fur instead of skin it would be standing permanently on end in his presence. And Moses spits and snarls like his tail is caught in a wringer."

Nell neither acknowledged her presence nor said a word in response, and frustrated with having to talk to her back, Hattie grabbed her by the arm and whirled her around. "Will you look at me when I'm talking to you?" She went still with shock, sighting the torrent of tears cascading down her friend's cheeks.

"He hates me!" Nell sobbed. "It's so easy for you because he thinks the sun sets and rises on you, but he hates me and I can't bear it. You think I don't know how I act when I'm around him?" Her words crowded each other as she spoke faster and faster, clearly choking on her tears as she angrily faced Hattie. She dashed her forearm across her eyes in an ineffectual attempt to stem the flow. "I know perfectly well I must look and sound like an old-maid prude. But I can't stop because I know he can't s-stand the sight of me, while I'm aware of every darn thing about him.

Like how he's so robust. And how I feel c-crowded and can't breathe when he's around. And how big his hands are and what I feel when I look at them. But he's in love with you, and he thinks I'm a pompous prig, and I want to die, all right? So why don't you just save your lectures. In fact, get out of my room and leave me alone!"

Hattie stared at her friend in stunned silence. She had never seen Nell so out of control, and Hattie's first reaction was incredulity. Nell liked Moses? She had an odd way of showing it!

Then Hattie was ashamed of herself. Who knew better than she how confused emotions could affect one's actions? Gently, she reached out and touched Nell's flushed face, deciding to deal with the obvious first. "Moses isn't in love with me."

"I knew you would say that!" Nell jerked back in fury. "I knew it! You are so damn blind, Hattie, it makes me want to scream. What will it take before you open your eyes to the truth—does he have to fling you down in the dust and have his wicked way with you? Would that get your attention?"

Hattie froze in shock, a surge of nightmare memories flooding her senses. Nell must have belatedly realized what she'd said, too, because looking horrified, she immediately stepped forward to pull Hattie into her arms. Hattie stood stiffly, not responding.

"Oh, Hattie, I am so sorry," Nell said. "I truly didn't mean that the way it sounded. I forgot—I didn't think. Please. I didn't mean to make you remember that time. I'm so, so sorry."

Hattie shuddered once, then slowly relaxed the unnatural rigidity of her posture. "It's all right," she said dully and stepped out of Nell's embrace. "Really. It just caught me unaware, that's all." She sat down on Nell's bed. Nell sat beside her and they both stared at the wall for a moment, each lost in her own thoughts. Finally, Hattie turned and faced her friend.

"You have been privy to darn near every private aspect of my life, Nell. So why haven't I heard a word about how you've been feeling in return? Why have you kept it all to yourself?"

"I don't know." Nell wouldn't return her look. She continued to stare at the wall, hesitated an instant, then admitted, "Because I've been jealous, I guess, and the subject is so embarrassing. Because I feel as if I'm losing control of my life and I don't know how to get it back."

She gave a short, mirthless laugh. "I thought I knew everything before I arrived here. I had a picture in my mind and I was convinced I knew exactly what kind of person Moses was. But I certainly wasn't prepared for the impact of the flesh-and-blood man." She turned to look at Hattie. "I haven't kept this to myself from a desire to exclude you from my private life, Hattie. I've wanted to talk to you about it—so, so wanted that. At the same time, I resented you. I know it isn't fair and it doesn't make sense, but I don't know how to explain it any clearer."

"Try," Hattie whispered.

Nell stared at her in entreaty. Sucked in a breath, then blew it out. "Okay. First off, I have been horribly confused. I could not begin to figure out how to broach the subject when I'm deep-down scared to death Moses is in love with you. I suppose, too, I didn't want to look like a fool in your eyes."

"Oh, Nell, how could you possibly think you would?"

"I don't know, Hattie. I'm out of my depth. So many of the little things you take for granted simply throw me."

"Like what?"

"Like . . . your ease with men. You never have to search for things to say. You're comfortable, especially with Moses, whereas I . . ." She let that trail off. Shook her head. "And you never seem to notice his size. How can you not notice that?"

"I grew up with him," Hattie replied, meeting her friend's dark eyes. "I'm used to it."

"I expect that does make a difference, but I find it intimidating. I have never been around a man that large in my life. And God knows I have no experience with a man who regularly visits fallen women and has dreams the likes of which I never even dreamed *existed*, let alone thought I would hear about because he described them to the woman they were about. I don't know how to act around him, and that's the plain truth. So, I react instead."

She looked away, staring at the wall before looking down at her hands clasped in her lap. "It's clear he detests me. He's pegged me as a snobbish, know-nothing prig who thinks she's too good to associate with a blacksmith. He mocks me and infuriates me to the point where I find myself acting exactly the way he expects me to act, and I can't seem to stop myself. The truth is, I'm scared and tongue-tied every time I see him, but I can hardly admit that, can I? I feel so exposed around him, Hattie."

She turned to face her redheaded friend more directly. "Have you ever had that dream where you're caught naked in the town square?"

Hattie nodded. She hadn't had that exact dream, but she'd had ones that were similar—mortifying dreams from which it was such a relief to awaken.

"Well, that's how I feel in Moses Marks' company."

"Maybe if you explained this to him, you two could start over again."

"I couldn't. I simply could not. What if I summoned the nerve to admit it and he turns around and uses my fear against me? I'd be destroyed. It's hard enough feeling the way I do when he so patently cannot abide me." She shrugged. "I muster all the protective armor I can. I stick my nose in the air and put starch in my spine and pretend his dislike of me is beneath my notice or simply too plebian to mention. I don't like myself very much for it. Yet I can't seem to stop."

She looked up from studying her hands and met Hattie's eyes. An unamused smile that likely looked bitterly unhappy, if it was even close to what she felt, twisted her lips. "It's pretty ironic, isn't it, Hattie? All those lessons I gave you, trying to teach you to think before you respond in order to prevent just this type of act-and-react situation. Turns out I can't take my own advice." More tears welled in Nell's eyes.

Hattie reached out and stroked her hand. "He is not, I repeat, not in love with me, Nell. I can't change the fact that he's a man and I'm a woman, and I don't know whether I would if I could. Moses was the only friend I had growing up, and I suppose a result of having a boy for a friend is I've heard and experienced a number of things most girls don't know exist. Plus, men have been less judgmental, so I'm comfortable in their company. I'll tell you right now, having his friendship was just another black mark against me in this town, but no matter what anybody ever says, I shall always be grateful Moses was my friend. It would have been terribly lonely without him."

Swiveling around to a more comfortable position, she used her toes to ease off her low-cut shoes with their newfangled expandable elastic side gussets. Then she raised her head to face Nell squarely. "I do know his feelings for me are only those of one friend to another," she said earnestly. "And that's the honest truth. He never would've told me about those dreams had they still been part of his life. For a short period of time, they interfered with our friendship. But they're gone now. And if he loves me, it's as a sister, not a lover."

"Why does he hate me so, Hattie?"

"I wish I knew. I have never seen him act this way with anyone, and I don't understand it any better than you do. To tell the truth, I don't think I understand men, period." Hattie pulled her heels up on the bed, swept her skirts up to prevent an immodest display of her limbs, and hugged her knees to her chest. Resting her chin on her kneecaps, she studied the carpet's pattern. "Big revelation," she said with glum sarcasm. "Most of the time I don't even understand myself."

Nell was surprised. "You don't? I thought everything was finally beginning to work out for you."

"It is. Which is what makes the past few weeks so difficult to understand. The two years I spent in Seattle meant the world because they taught me that without a history shadowing me, I could be valued just for myself." She smiled lopsidedly. "More than anything, I have always wanted to command the same sort of esteem right here in Mattawa." She shrugged. "Well, for the first time in this town, I am gaining a measure of acceptance, and I like it. I have you and Moses and Aunt Augusta and my students. I think I'm actually beginning to be liked by some of their parents as well. Heck, I'm even getting along with Jake. Everything should be bully." She watched her stockinged feet as her toes curled and straightened beneath her skirt.

"What's the problem, then?"

"I don't know, Nell! That's just it, I don't know what I'm fighting. Most of the time, everything is fine. So much better, in fact, than I dreamed it could be. But lately I've felt so . . . restless. Not during the day so much, but at night?" She gazed numbly at Nell, her confusion clear. "It's as if something beneath my skin itches, except it's not a real itch because when I try to scratch it, there's no satisfaction. No matter what I try the darn itch remains just out of reach, and I have no idea how to make it go away. At first I got relief when I fell asleep. Now, it interferes with that, as well." She blew a stray curl off her forehead. "Criminy, Nell, there are nights when it's all I can do to simply lie still. I'll see the moon or hear the wind in the tree outside my window and I get this overpowering urge to run away to the ranch, saddle up Belle, and just ride as fast and as hard as I can until I'm at peace again."

Nell absorbed her words in silence. Finally, she asked with hesitant softness, "Are you in love with Jake, Hattie?"

"No, of course not!" At Nell's level-eyed stare, Hattie squirmed. "I don't know," she qualified more honestly. "Maybe. I don't want to be."

"Whyever not?"

"Because it's pointless. It could never go anywhere."

"Not even if he loved you, too?"

Hattie's heart threw in an extra beat, which made her defensive. "I don't see how. Say he did love me. What then—marriage? He'd want to know why I wasn't a virgin. All men expect virginity in their brides. You know it; I know it; every female over the age of twelve knows it. What possible explanation could I give for my lack?"

"Maybe that would be the time for the truth."

"I will never tell him what Roger Lord did to me. Never."

"Why, though? I cannot believe Jake would—"

"I will not tell him."

"But why?" Nell looked into Hattie's eyes and was shocked at the shame reflected there. How could she be ashamed? Hattie wasn't responsible for what Lord did. And she had certainly done everything she could to prevent it!

"Because it made me dirty," Hattie said in a fierce, low voice. "I will never be truly clean again, but I've learned to live with that. What I cannot live with is Jacob knowing. I don't ever want to look into Jake Murdock's eyes and see he finds me unclean. Ever."

"But he wouldn't!"

"*Ever*, Nell." Hattie climbed off the bed and walked straight out the door.

31

THE FOLLOWING DAY, Nell sought out Augusta. Relating her conversation with Hattie, she attempted to capture the exact shade of hopeless shame coloring Hattie's eyes, her voice. "What can we do?"

Augusta sat in silence for several moments. When she finally met Nell's eyes, she looked weary. Older. "Nothing, I'm afraid. This is clearly something Hattie must work out for herself."

"But she hasn't, Augusta! That's the problem in a nutshell. For some reason, she holds herself responsible when she wasn't the least bit so. The last thing she should feel is shame. Anger, certainly, embarrassment, perhaps, but shame? I hate this. She was forced into a situation not of her making and most emphatically not her fault."

"You're absolutely right: she was that man's victim," Augusta agreed. "But, darling, neither you nor I suffered through her experience. Therefore, we cannot say with any degree of certainty how we would feel were we in her place. Emotions don't always conform to what is right or wrong. They aren't tidy. You know Hattie well enough to understand she isn't victim material. She's spirited, strong-willed, and quick with words and emotions. She is also too intelligent not to realize somewhere inside she couldn't possibly have prevented that monster from doing what he did. Yet, she feels ashamed anyway. Doesn't that tell you something?" Augusta could see by the frustration on Nell's pretty face it did not. Slowly, Augusta tried to put her own theory into words.

"I believe that, more than anything, this has to do with Hattie's convoluted feelings for Jacob. He and Hattie have always shared a unique relationship. From the first day she came to live with us, she adored the ground he walked on. And I think her adoration made him feel ten feet tall. Yet, something happened between them that summer before Hattie left for school."

Nell moved involuntarily, and Augusta said, "Ah, I see you know what it was. Don't squirm, dear, I, too, know the circumstances, so I shan't be asking you to break any confidences. But if Hattie confided in you, then you must also know the reason Jake sent her to Roger Lord's house."

Nell's face burned with embarrassment. "Yes."

"In that case, perhaps you can understand what I'm trying to say. She loves Jacob; she hates him. But never is she indifferent to him. Clearly, the mere thought of him learning about her ordeal is different than her knowledge that you, I, and Doc know. It's untenable."

"But—" Nell hesitated, then, feeling her way, said slowly, "Doesn't she have to face it eventually? I mean, knowing why Jake sent her away that night and seeing them together now . . . Can you truly envision them continuing through life with the same relationship they had when Hattie was a kid?"

"No."

"Then—?"

"She still has the right to handle any explanations she gives him in her own way and on a timetable acceptable to her. It may be easier than she believes it's going to be, or it may be incredibly painful. Either way, nothing you or I say to her will ultimately make a difference. This involves Hattie and Jacob. Their emotions. They are the ones who have to work it out. In their own time, in their own way."

"I don't like it," Nell muttered.

Augusta patted her hand. "I know, dear." The older woman's voice brimmed with sympathy, but the look she leveled at Nell was commanding. "And yet?"

Nell sighed. "I suppose it doesn't amount to a hill of beans whether I like it or not. I am not the one fighting demons"—at least not ones so deep and dark—"so I also suppose I will therefore keep my opinion to myself unless Hattie asks my advice."

"That's my girl," Augusta murmured, and gave Nell's hand another gentle pat.

FRIDAY, APRIL 30, 1909

Hattie was furious with Jake. For two days in a row, Jonathan Semp had missed school.

Jonathan had changed since the first day of school. Regular meals and physical work had filled out his large, previously underfed frame, and he was now nearly as strapping as she'd suspected he would be.

She knew Jake was responsible not only for issuing Jonathan clothes that fit properly but for seeing to the ranch cook supplying the boy with lunches to bring to school. She had nothing but admiration for the attention and care Jake had subtly bestowed upon the neglected teen. Jonathan's size and his new confidence prevented him from becoming the butt of the other students' jokes, and he had even forged a few friendships among the farm and ranch boys.

But Jake had agreed with Hattie that schooling must come first, and now he was reneging.

That evening, Hattie arrived at the ranch seething. Arrangements had been made some time ago for her, Nell, and Aunt Augusta to spend the weekend at the Murdock spread. It was one of the ranch's many overworked periods, so Jake was too busy to come into town. The women planned to ready the gardens around the house for planting.

Their visit was also designed to give Nell a glimpse at life on a working ranch, Hattie the opportunity to ride to her heart's content, and Augusta some time with her son when he could snatch ten minutes here or grab a cup of coffee between chores there. Hattie had been looking forward to the visit for weeks, as there was nowhere else she'd rather be. Her anger over Jake's cavalier disregard of their agreement, however, chafed the edges of her anticipation.

Jake was occupied when they arrived. It wasn't until supper was concluding that he finally joined them in the elegant dining room. He strode in still attired in his dusty work clothes, but freshly scrubbed and hair combed.

"Ladies." He grinned hospitably as he dropped into a chair and saluted them with a finger to his forehead. "I apologize for not being here to greet you when you arrived."

Hattie was ready to erupt by then, but she was proud of controlling her temper and taking part in the conversation during coffee and dessert. As they were leaving the dining room, however, she waylaid Jake. "I'd like to speak to you," she said with cool crispness.

"I'm all ears." He grinned down at her attentively but sobered quickly when she returned his smile with hostile silence.

"In your office," she said flatly.

Scratching his temple, he gave her a puzzled look. Then the look so promptly smoothed into something she couldn't read, she could only conclude she had imagined the bafflement. He indicated that she should precede him down the hall.

If she didn't know better, Hattie would almost swear Jake was staring at her hips as she marched before him. Her skin temperature ratcheted up a couple of degrees. Waving the thought aside as bonehead mad, Hattie whirled to face him when the door closed behind them. He regarded her through narrowed eyes as he lounged back against the rich wood panels of the door. He looked so free and easy, while she . . .

Well, she badly wanted to smack him. "You went back on our deal."

"What deal?"

"You assured me Jonathan's schoolwork would always come first," she replied through clenched teeth. "Yet you have kept him out of school for two days!"

"What?" His amusement vanished, and jerking upright, he pushed away from the door. "Wait here." He strode from the room with Hattie on his heels. Striding straight out the front door and onto the porch, he hailed a passing cowhand. "Tell Semp to present himself in my office. Pronto!"

"Sure thing, boss."

Jake turned and noticed Hattie had followed him. "I told you to wait."

"Oh, you actually thought I was paying attention to your snapped orders?" She gave that absurdity the snort it deserved, then shrugged. "I'm not your lackey, Jake Murdock."

"Go wait in my office!" he commanded in a tone she seldom heard, and she whirled on her heel and stalked back to the office. Burrowed into the corner of the leather couch moments later, her arms crossed militantly over her breasts, she watched him through narrowed eyes as he took his seat behind the desk.

Jake returned her look calmly. Without taking his eyes off her, he picked up a pencil and tapped its eraser end on the desktop. Sliding his fingers down its length, he lifted the pencil off the desk until gravity flipped it over and the lead point touched the smooth surface. Slid his fingers down its length again and kept repeating the motions with hypnotic regularity. All the while watching her.

There was a tap on the door and Jake bid the caller to enter. Jonathan Semp stepped into the room. "You wanted to see me, Jake?"

"I thought you told me you had Miss Taylor's permission to miss school."

"Yeah. Uh . . ." A movement in his peripheral vision caught Jonathan's eye and he turned his head. Heat burned up his neck when he saw his teacher sitting on the couch, tapping her foot and staring at him. "Uh . . . hi, Miss Taylor." He swallowed hard. Oh boy. He was in for it now. He rushed to explain. "Jake needs my help, Miss Taylor. Y'see, it's calvin' season and—"

"You want to keep working for me, boy?" Jake interrupted coldly.

It was hard to swallow past the sudden constriction in his throat. "Yes, sir."

"Then I would advise you not to lie. I told you when you started here school comes first, and I meant it."

"Yes, sir." Jonathan turned to Hattie. "I'm sorry, Miss Taylor."

"I want that in writing, Jonathan. One hundred times. You will write 'I will not miss school and I will not lie.' Have it on my desk first thing Monday morning. Understand?"

"Yes'm."

Jake opened a desk drawer and pulled out several sheets of paper. He extended them to Jonathan and handed him a pencil. "Get started."

Face burning, Jonathan accepted the supplies and backed out of the room, leaving silence in his wake. Hattie had built up a full head of steam, and discovering she'd wrongly accused Jake only made her angrier. Ungraciously, she muttered, "I apologize for my erroneous assumption," and stood up, nose elevated. "I promised Aunt Augusta I would play a few pieces on the piano. I better join her and Nell in the parlor."

Jake stood also. "That's it?"

"What's it?"

"I'm sorry for my erroneous assumption?" His mimicry of her sullen tone was right on target, and Hattie's cheeks burned. "That's it?"

"I'll write it out a hundred times."

He was around the desk in a flash. Towering over her, he gripped her elbows and drew her onto her toes until they were standing eyeball to eyeball. "Don't get cute with me or I'll—"

"What?" Hattie wrenched free and backed up. Hopefully only she knew her heart was pounding to beat the band. "You'll do what, Jacob? Smack my butt so hard I'll be eating off the sideboard for a week?" It was a threat he'd used several times when she got out of line as a kid.

His whole body jerked and his eyes darkened, the lids appearing suddenly weighted. "Is that what you'd like, Hattie?" he whispered hoarsely. "My hand on your bare butt?" He reached out and ran his hand over her hip, sliding it around to follow the curve of her buttock.

Suddenly sinking his fingers into the resilient fullness beneath his hand, he pulled her forward until less than an inch separated them. He leaned over her, his face suddenly so close she felt his breath on her lips. "Because I'd be more than happy to oblige you, Big-eyes, if that's what you're angling for."

"Get your hands off me." Hattie placed hers on his chest and shoved him away. Ignoring the wretchedly persistent, tickly feeling between her legs, she clenched her fists and stated coolly, "I've said it once and I'll say it again: I am sorry I jumped to the wrong conclusion. If you don't like my tone of voice, I'm sorry for that, too. But don't go thinking that entitles you to take liberties with me, Jacob Murdock. It doesn't. Not with me or any other woman." She whirled away in a red-hot fury and, reaching for the doorknob, wrenched the portal open. She stormed out, then slammed the office door closed behind her.

A few moments later, Jake heard her taking out her temper on the exterior door as well.

32

Murdock Ranch

LATE SATURDAY NIGHT, MAY 1, 1909

THE SCREEN DOOR squeaked softly as Jake pushed through to the front porch, then shut behind him with a quiet slap of wood on wood. The wicker chair he dropped onto creaked a protest. He barely registered the latter sound, he'd heard it so often. With a sigh of pleasure, he swung his stocking-clad feet atop the porch railing, making himself comfortable. Except for the usual nocturnal rustlings and calls of distant night creatures, the house and surrounding ranch were quiet. Just the way he liked it. Weary of wrestling his sheets, he'd come downstairs to see if a drink and a dose of the early spring night air might help him relax. His body was bone weary, but his brain was more awake than a kid before the county fair.

He shouldn't have grabbed Hattie that way yesterday. It was a tactical error. What was it about her stubborn anger and sassy mouth that made him lose all reason? He didn't think of her as a little girl anymore. Hell, he hadn't for a long time. So, when she'd thrown his old threat of a spanking in his face, it had been like waving a flag at a bull. He hadn't even tried to resist the overpowering urge to demonstrate just how adult he considered her. Still, he couldn't blame her for being angry. You don't treat nice women like that. He had no excuse.

But, damn. This timetable shit was a helluva lot harder than he'd figured it would be.

When Hattie left Mattawa for school, Jake tried hard to put her out of his mind. It was all he could handle dealing with his grief over the deaths of Jane-Ellen and his baby. Disgracefully harder was the guilt clawing him for not being able to repudiate his rampant desire for Hattie. The same damn desire that laid waste to his control a mere two days after his wife's death.

But Hattie's departure had left him hollow. And rather than diminishing, the pain of her furious leave-taking and her refusal to see, write, or talk to him had spread like cancer inside him. A situation not helped when he'd tried to see her at school on a trip to Seattle and the matron informed him it was against school policy to allow males to visit a student unless specified by the student's parent or guardian. A list his name was not on.

Not being able to see Hattie on that trip gutted him. It also made his guilt over her not coming home for holidays, or for so much as a visit since she'd left, worse than it had been before. He knew damn well Augusta, Mirabel, and Doc missed Hattie, too, and Jake didn't doubt for a minute her absence was his fault. It didn't seem to matter that he didn't live in town. Evidently, Hattie had no intention of coming back to Mattawa as long as he was anywhere in the county.

Guilt or no guilt, however, it didn't erase the way Hattie had responded to him that night up in her room. No way in hell had he been able to forget the hot sensuality of her in his arms.

He'd thought, given time, she would forgive whatever it was he'd done so wrong. But she hadn't written him and she wouldn't talk to him when she called. All news of her had come to him secondhand through the letters Hattie sent to his mother. And as the end of her schooling grew closer, he'd begun to feel desperate. What if she never came back at all? That was when he'd talked to Aurelia Donaldson. And in exchange for her help, he had made a promise.

"Ideally, we try to hire male teachers," the older woman had told him as they sat in her dimly illuminated, heavily furnished parlor. "Once a woman marries, she is, of course, disqualified from teaching. And in the past few years we've seen far too many of them come and go. Now, as you clearly know, the positions are available. But your request goes against every decision we've recently approved. You're asking me to hire not one, but two young women." She lowered her lorgnette and looked away with a sigh. "That's going to be difficult to get past the rest of the board."

"You owe it to her."

Aurelia's head snapped around and she raised her lorgnette to look down her nose at him in her most imperious manner. "Do I?"

Jake met her gaze levelly. "Yes. The whole damn town does."

"Perhaps you're right," she conceded. "I've discovered she is an incredibly sweet child. I never gave her credit for that in the past. Her outspokenness and the way she ran around with the Marks boy led me to believe she was a hellion."

She looked around her large, elegant parlor. "I began to realize I may have misjudged her when Jane-Ellen died. Doc told me the lengths Hattie went to in order to make his daughter comfortable. And her letters have brightened this old woman's life. She has an honesty that tickles me—she doesn't give a fig about my money or the power I wield in Mattawa. Why, she actually wrote me a letter specifically to disagree with a decision about which I had written her. Her argument made sense, too."

Jake smiled wryly, knowing Aurelia had most likely first been offended, then been delighted by Hattie's effrontery. But he sobered quickly. "Offering a position to her friend is the only option I can think of to guarantee having Hattie come home."

Aurelia's face softened. "Yes. Her letters are full of Nell."

"If anyone can do it, you can," he pressed.

Her lorgnette had lowered, but Aurelia brought it up again to peer at him. "Why is it so important to you, Jacob?"

Jake hesitated. Then he admitted with stark honesty, "Hattie's special. You're just beginning to realize it, but I've known it from the minute she first stepped off the train in ninety-nine."

He thrust his fingers through his hair. "I used to be special to her, too, Aurelia, but when she left here she was furious with me. I think I know why, but if it's what I believe it is, it doesn't make a lick of sense."

He shrugged, then admitted, "I can't tolerate the way things between us stand much longer. She never writes to me, she doesn't ask about me in her letters to Mother, and she's refused to talk to me the few times she's telephoned when I've been at Mother's house. God only knows where she may accept an offer of employment. It could be anywhere in the state, and I will never know for certain what I did to make her cut me out of her life. I need the chance to know."

Aurelia looked at Jake sitting there, determined and ruthlessly honest as he stated his case. He was at ease in the stiff, formal ambiance of her home. He'd arrived unannounced in the parlor where few guests ever dared drop by uninvited, and she admired his boldness. She liked a person who knew what he wanted and was unafraid to go after it.

"Very well," she said. "I'll get it by the board. And I will do my best to ease her reemergence into Mattawa society. In return, I want your promise you will give me a year's worth of work out of the girl before you go interfering in her life."

It had seemed a simple request to honor at the time.

Jake became aware of his feet slowly turning into clumps of ice. The days had been lengthening and they'd enjoyed a few days in the high sixties. But when the sun went down, the temperature dropped a good twenty degrees and evenings quickly grew chilly. The night sky was clear and black, with stars thick, brilliant, and low overhead. Jake dropped his feet to the porch floor, threw back the remainder of his wine, and surged up out of his chair.

He had his boots in his hand and was reaching for the screen door when he heard the jingle of a bridle. Rubbing one stockinged foot against his shin to restore a little warmth, he hesitated, listening hard. There! There it was again, and now he heard a quiet clip-clop of shod hooves as well. Stepping into a shadow, he searched the road for the source of the noise.

Hell, it was Saturday night—no doubt one of his men was returning to the bunkhouse after a night at Bigger's Saloon or Mamie's cathouse. And yet—

This had a feeling of stealth at odds with the habits of his men. Regard for others' sleep wasn't a general consideration when they were liquored up and racing up the road, anxious to grab a few hours' shut-eye before having to roll out of bed again to start another workday.

Jake used the marginally successful warming motion on his other foot. Whoever it was definitely seemed to want anonymity. The rider kept to the shadows and avoided the areas where starlight cast skeletal fingers of illumination. It wasn't until the horse walked out of the lane and into the stable yard that Jake recognized it. And knowing the horse, he knew the rider.

Anger rose in him like the creek during flooding season. Swearing beneath his breath, he yanked on his boots and vaulted the porch railing. He was across the yard seconds after the stable doors closed behind Hattie and her horse.

Hattie hummed to herself as she loosened the cinch beneath Belle's stomach. She didn't remember the last time she'd felt so relaxed. After nights dreaming of racing her horse, she'd finally been in a position to do so. It had been everything she imagined it would be, too. Her nerves had settled and those nameless, relentless urges, which lately had increasingly plagued her—were gone. She felt wonderful.

Until the door slammed open. "What the hell do you think you're doing?" Jake demanded.

She'd been removing her saddle, but startled by Jake's arrival, she lost her grip. The saddle tumbled to the stable floor, making Belle sidestep nervously. Hattie grabbed the reins and patted the mare's glossy brown neck in reassurance. "Easy, girl," she whispered. "Eeeeasy, now." She looked over her shoulder at Jake. Clearly, from the tone and volume of his voice, he was furious. Seeing his face merely confirmed it. "Will you kindly lower your voice? You startled me to death and you're upsetting Belle."

Muscles in Jake's jaw jumped ominously. "Oh. Well," he said through clenched teeth. "We mustn't upset Belle."

She shrugged.

Jake did a slow burn while Hattie ignored his sarcasm and hefted her saddle onto a railing as though this were a perfectly acceptable time of night to be performing her post-ride chores. She put the rest of the tack in the tack room, then reached for a brush and quickly groomed the mare. Finally, she tossed a blanket over Belle and led her to a clean stall.

Jake watched every move through narrowed eyes. Hattie's appearance was quite the change from the spit-and-polish schoolmarm she'd shown the town since her return to Mattawa. He inspected her loose, wild hair spilling over her shoulders, breasts, and back. And while Hattie was covered in a respectable blouse, split skirt, and boots, she wore no corset. Displaying every bit of sensuality she'd suppressed these past eleven months.

What the hell was going on here? The instant she reemerged from the stall, he pushed off the post he'd leaned against. In two giant strides, he stood in front of her. "Now," he said with implacable command, "I want to know what the hell you were doing out on a horse on a deserted country road in the dead of night."

Jake's tone made her hackles rise, but Hattie resisted her immediate inclination to respond in kind. "I was riding," she said and congratulated herself on her neutral tone of voice.

"No shit," he replied, making her promptly bristle. If he was going to spout obscenities, he could just . . .

"Well, gol-ly," he drawled with heavy-handed mockery, "I wonder why I didn't figure that out for myself?"

Taking exception to his country-bumpkin sarcasm, she whirled away.

Instantly, his hand clamped down on her wrist and she was whirled right back. "Where the hell you think you're going?" he demanded, his voice rough and his hayseed impersonation forgotten.

"In the house," she snapped. "I don't have to put up with this from you."

"Ah now, that's where you're wrong," he disagreed smoothly. "You don't appear to get the big picture, Big-eyes. I'm not offering you a choice here. I'm bigger than you, so until I say otherwise, you're not going anywhere. Not until I get to the bottom of this."

"To the bottom of what, exactly?" Hattie planted her free fist on a round hip, impatiently shaking her hair behind her shoulders as she stared up at him. "Is there supposed to be a mystery? I couldn't sleep, so I went for a ride." Her chin jutted toward the rafters. "Nobody was hurt by it."

Involuntarily, his fingers tightened around her wrist. "Which makes you damn lucky! It's Saturday night, or had you forgotten? Payday for every cowboy and farmhand in the county. There are any number of drunks out at this time of night, making their way back home. They would just love running into a tasty little tidbit like you."

Hattie tried unsuccessfully to yank her arm free. Nerves finally soothed were once again jinglejangling, and the darn unable-to-scratch itch in that embarrassing spot between her legs was back with a vengeance. "Darn you, Jake! Why do you have to ruin everything? All I wanted was one midnight ride. I've been dreaming of this for months." Her frustrated gaze met Jake's irritated dark hazel-green eyes, and for a moment, she couldn't look away.

Neither, from the looks of things, could he.

"It's really none of your business," she finally said, "but I've been so restless lately. My nerves have been so on edge I can't bear it. I can't explain it because I don't understand it myself, but what I do know is the one thing that's helped me through too many sleepless nights is the thought of racing Belle." She shifted in agitation. "Well, tonight I finally had an opportunity, and it was wonderful until you had to go rain on my parade. I was nice and calm and tired enough to sleep. In short, I felt magnificent." Her blood ran so thick and fast under her skin, she'd put money down her freckles were drowned beneath the red bloom on her chest, throat, and cheeks. She tried once more to tug her captured wrist free, but he held it firmly. "Now you've got me all riled up again, and I'll probably never get to sleep."

Jake went very still. Christ. Of course. It explained everything: the lack of foundation garments, the tangled hair. The meaning behind her words struck at a vital hidden nerve deep inside him and he forgot his anger, his good intentions, and every previously given promise. Slowly, he reached out and tunneled the fingers of his free hand beneath the thick wavy hair at the nape of her neck. It flowed through his fingers with crackling vitality. "I know what you need to take care of those restless urges," he whispered roughly as his fingers tightened on her neck and the wrist he still held, exerting pressure to bring her closer. "And, Big-eyes, it isn't a horseback ride." The corner of Jake's mouth tipped up as Hattie's eyes grew round . . . and aware.

Oh my God, oh my God. Hattie wondered if Jake could hear her heart pounding in her chest. He looked as if he knew the effect he had on her. And, good God Almighty, his voice. It was as raspy as a cat's tongue, licking a message up her spine. She shivered beneath the goose bumps cropping up in the wake of the ghostly communication.

She could read Jake's intent in his eyes and instinctively, knowing if he kissed her she'd lose all will to resist, she ducked her head. Why hadn't she run for safety the moment she realized she was alone with him? Now it was too late. Jake's hand twisted in her hair, wrapping it around his fist, and tugged, forcing her head back until her neck arched. She closed her eyes against the helpless longing assailing her as his head lowered.

His mouth was urgent and hot, and it rubbed her lips apart before she knew what was what. She was conscious of the roughness of his stubble abrading the soft skin around her lips. But when his tongue slid across her teeth and plunged, wet and determined, into the recesses of her mouth, all rational thought dissolved. He released her wrist and her freed hands twisted in the material over his chest, using it as leverage to pull herself up on tiptoe. Pressing herself against him. Striving to get closer.

Hattie reveled in the low sounds rumbling in Jake's throat and in his rough-skinned hands sliding down her back until his calloused fingers gripped her resilient bottom. He pulled her up, and as her feet left the ground, instinct had her spreading her legs, then clamping them tightly around his hips as he backed them into an empty stall. Without releasing her or breaking their kiss, he scraped clean straw into a pile with the side of his boot. Then his legs folded and he knelt with her still astride his lap.

An unidentifiable unit of time later, Jake broke the kiss, plunging his fingers into her hair and holding her head erect as he kissed his way down her throat.

Hattie's response was unthinking and incontrovertible. Clutching Jake's shoulders, she moaned her pleasure and tilted her pelvis to feel more of the hard heat barely nudging that space between her thighs.

Then before she could string two thoughts together, her blouse was on the stable floor, her chemise was pulled down around her waist, and Jake's mouth was moving with damp suction over and between her breasts. His hands pushed her loose-legged split skirt high up her legs. Warm, hard, fingers gripped the back of her thighs and paced her slow, mindless rocking motion, rubbing her back and forth against the warm thickness straining behind the fly of his pants. Hattie's head dropped back and her eyes slid closed. She panted softly between parted lips.

Jake pulled his face from Hattie's lush cleavage and looked at her. His breath hissed sharply between his teeth. Oh God, if he didn't have her soon . . . Leaning over, he eased her onto her back atop the piled straw. Kissing her from throat to waist, he wrestled off her skirt and her cotton step-ins, leaving her wearing a twist of material around her waist, polished riding boots, and white stockings held up by the pink garters above her knees.

Jake kicked off his boots and only managed to get his pants as far as his knees before lowering those same knees between her thighs. Holding himself in one fist, he watched as he rubbed his erection between the soft, giving folds of Hattie's pretty cunny.

Oh Jesus, Jesus, she was so wet. Hunching over, he pulled a distended nipple into his mouth and milked it with eager lips. A small moan rattled in the back of her throat and her legs parted. Carefully, he aligned his cock and pushed with slow care, mindful of her virginity.

There was no barrier to impede his progress. He sank into her in one smooth, gliding thrust. Stilling, he stared at her in shock. Who—?

Hattie's eyes were closed, her expression lost in wonder. He wanted to know who she had given her virginity to; he needed to love her; he—

Oh hell, he couldn't deal with this right now. Hattie's face was flushed with desire, and her beautiful eyes were prominent even behind closed lids. Her teeth were startlingly white against the natural red of her lower lip. And inside, surrounding him, she was hot and wet and, God, so unrelentingly tight. He couldn't look at her, could not feel her sheath gripping him, and still be expected to think. Slowly, carefully, he began to move. He brushed her nipple with his lips and felt her contract around him. Oh hell, yes. Later. Hands planted on the dusty floor next to her shoulders, elbows locked, Jake slowly thrust in and out of her.

Hattie had never dreamed anything could feel this good. Her legs spread farther and her hands reached to grip the backs of his thighs, her fingernails sinking into the muscles standing out in hard relief. Little whimpers issued from her throat as something deep inside of her began winding more and more tightly.

Then . . . Hattie had no idea if it was the sounds, or the sight, or the feel of her woman parts wrapped around his man part that got to Jake. Whatever it was, it seemed to push him beyond all restraint. His straight arms unlocked and his chest suddenly crushed her breasts. His body was clearly in control now, his hips moving fast and rough, slamming into her.

Hattie hadn't connected this emotion erupting between them with her rape. But with Jake's sudden weight pinning her down, the sweet, exciting feelings his touch garnered were abruptly buried in an avalanche of terror. She couldn't breathe. Dear Lord, she was suffocating and there was material against her breasts, in her mouth . . . just like That Night. Worse, once again there was a pounding, pounding, pounding between her legs. The lack of pain didn't register, only the abrupt violence of his movements.

"No! No, stop it!" She began to fight him, her hands trying to push him away, her fingernails reaching for his eyes.

Jake was stunned by her sudden attack, by the tears standing in her eyes and the stark terror where only moments ago there had been desire. His body was a senseless beast knowing it was seconds away from a climax and had no desire to follow his command to pull out of her. But, Jesus, that look on her face! Gritting his teeth, he jerked back.

"Oh God, oh fuck," he said as he pulled out. But he wasn't completely free when he started to come. "I'm so sorry, baby," he whispered as he ejaculated some of his seed in her before fully extricating himself to spill the rest on the ground. He shuddered as every bit of his strength drained from him and sat back heavily on his heels, his head hanging in shame.

Next thing Jake knew, he was lying on his back, looking up at Hattie, who had kicked him there. He didn't think he would ever, as long as he lived, forget the look in her eyes as she scrambled away from him, hitching up her chemise and snatching up her skirt and blouse.

He'd never seen such terror or disgust in his life. She stepped into her clothes but didn't take the time to fasten anything, holding the skirt's waistband closed with one hand and the button placket to her blouse bunched together in the other. She headed for the door.

He wanted to stop her, to find out what the hell had gone so wrong. He wanted to know why she'd been so willing one moment, so frightened the next. He wanted to stop her for a hundred good reasons. But mostly to apologize, to say he was so sorry he didn't stop the very instant she got scared.

Instead, he was appalled by the words that left his mouth even as they halted her flight. "Who did you give yourself to before me, Hattie?" he demanded. White-hot jealousy, that anyone could have seen her, felt her, the way he had, ate at him. But, God, why did those particular words have to come out now?

Hattie whirled in the doorway. Her face was stark white, lacking even the minutest drop of color. "Give myself?" she said in a low, rusty voice. "I didn't give myself, you sonovabitch. I was handed over on a silver platter. The man didn't ask, and I didn't offer. He took."

Jake jerked in shock. But before he could say a word, she was gone.

33

JAKE SAT FOR almost a full minute, wrestling with the implications of her words. Some man raped her? One minute Hattie had been clinging to him, all sweet, soft cooperation; then the next she was fighting him off in obvious terror—and she said she'd been *raped*?

Ah, God, please. Tell me I've misunderstood.

But Jake knew he hadn't misinterpreted, misread, or misconstrued a damn thing. Murderous rage pumped through his veins, while nausea churned acid in his gut. He jumped to his feet and yanked his pants up, dancing cautiously in place as he buttoned them. Christ. He'd learned the hard way about lockjaw, yet here he was running around stocking-footed in a stable? It seemed the instant he'd recognized Hattie as his mystery rider, his common sense took off for parts unknown and his emotions and damn traitorous body ruled each subsequent move.

Out in the yard, Hattie kept darting panic-stricken glances over her shoulder as she raced for the house. But Jake wasn't in hot pursuit as she'd feared. Knowing didn't dampen her roiling emotions. She flew up the porch steps and slipped inside the kitchen, maintaining just enough restraint to resist slamming the door behind her. She maintained enough wits as well to step over the third riser in the staircase to avoid its telltale creak, though God alone knew how, given her state of mind. Moments later she closed her bedroom door behind her. She stood in the middle of her room, chest heaving as she panted for breath. Oh Lord, she had to get ahold of herself. She was so far out of control—

Her door whipped open.

Hattie screamed. Clamping a hand over her mouth, she cut it off mid-cry.

Jake stepped into the room and closed the door. Leaning against it, he worked to get his breathing under control. His instinct was to grab Hattie and shake some answers out of her. He retained just enough good sense to know approaching her at all would be a mistake. Her eyes were huge with near hysteria, and she looked like she'd fly to pieces if he took so much as a half step in her direction.

"Did I understand you correctly?" he asked with forced softness. His skin felt as though it might split at any moment trying to contain all the emotions swelling and clawing inside him. "Some man forcibly relieved you of your virginity?"

Her eyes grew impossibly larger and she didn't say a word behind the fingers pressed to her lips. But she didn't have to; he read the truth in her face. His last hope that he'd somehow twisted her words to mean something other than what she'd intended sank without a trace. "Who?" he demanded in a raw voice and took a step toward her.

She removed her hand from her mouth and pointed her finger at the door. It shook badly. "Get out."

"Hattie, please . . ."

Her voice rose hysterically. "Get out!" She was trembling all over.

"All right," he said in a placatory voice. "It's okay, baby, don't be upset. I'm leaving." He backed toward the door, reaching behind him to fumble for the knob. "We'll talk tomorrow."

Her voice was expressionless, her eyes icy. "We will talk never."

Jake paused, wanting to argue the point but knowing this was not the time. Hopefully she'd be calmer in the morning and he could get some answers then. He opened the door and turned to leave.

Only to very nearly bowl over Augusta, who stood on the other side of the threshold.

For the first time in his life, Jake saw no vestige of warmth in his mother's eyes. She looked at him as if he were a stranger—and not one she cared to know.

Then her gaze went to Hattie. She pulled her bedtime braid from the collar of her robe and tugged her lapels tighter across her chest. "Are you all right, dear?" She turned to Jake. "You will wait for me in the parlor," she said with cold authority and turned her back on him, crossing the room to take Hattie in her arms. Hattie immediately clung to her guardian.

Feeling sick, he stared at them an agonized moment before obeying his mother's order.

It felt like he waited hours, even though he only had time to build up the fire and down a thimbleful of brandy before Augusta joined him. She accepted a sherry but the look on her face when she regarded him spread a chill throughout his entire system. "How is she? Is she okay?"

"Of course she is not."

"Maybe if I go talk to her—"

"No," Augusta interrupted firmly. "You have done quite enough for one night."

Jake winced. "Look, I can explain."

"Can you, Jacob? I should like to hear."

He opened his mouth to defend himself, then realized, in truth, he could not.

Augusta watched him for a moment, growing progressively angrier as she thought of the girl upstairs she had just bundled into a fresh night-gown. Finally, she asked coldly, "Can you explain the straw in Hattie's hair, Jacob? Or her swollen mouth or the whisker burns on her face and her—" She couldn't bring herself to say the word, but the hand she swept across her own chest and breasts said it for her. It was a measure of her fury that she did not blush one iota when she finally did speak the un-speakable. "Can you explain your seed upon her thighs? Will you still be explaining in a month or two if she swells with your child?"

The thought of Hattie carrying his baby jolted something deep and primordial within Jake. But before he could respond, Augusta said with implacable authority, "This isn't the first time you've dallied with that girl, Jacob Murdock, but it is, by God, the last."

Shock tightened all his muscles. He was so staggered learning his mother had knowledge of that other shameful episode following Jane-Ellen's death he nearly missed her next words. Then he went cold all over with another kind of shock when he tuned back in to hear her say, "—will post the banns at church in the morning. You will marry the girl in three weeks."

Jake did not respond well to orders. Before he gave himself an instant to measure the wisdom of replying out of frustration, hurt, and pain, he'd already uttered the unforgivable. "Isn't that demand usually reserved for the man who takes a girl's virginity?"

The force behind Augusta's openhanded blow turned Jake's head. "Don't you dare be flippant," she said in a low, venomous voice. "Hattie did not offer her virginity—it was forcibly taken from her. If you think I would place her welfare in the hands of a man who delighted in brutalizing her, then I did a pretty poor job of raising you."

Jake felt as if he were being torn into a thousand pieces. "I'm sorry, Mom," he said in a raw voice. "I'm a little confused. How long have you known about this, and who the hell else knows? I can't believe nobody bothered to tell me." His work-roughened hands clenched helplessly at his sides. "Christ, how could she have been raped? How could she have gone through something so life changing without me knowing? How did I not suspect a thing?" he demanded raggedly. "You've known for some time, clearly, but this is all new to me. It *kills* me to know she has been brutalized this way. And I don't know who . . . or even when."

"What would you have done had you known?"

Jake's dark hazel eyes met his mother's squarely. "I'd have killed him."

Augusta looked at her handprint welting red against her son's bloodless cheek as he thrust his fingers through his hair. "Which is precisely the reason you were never told," she replied, and responded to the uncomprehending anger in his eyes with rage of her own. "Do you think you're the only one who would like to see this animal punished—who wants revenge? But at whose expense, Jacob? Win, lose, or draw, Hattie is the one who pays. Not me, not you: *Hattie*. If it comes out she was raped, she'll be ostracized. It won't signify that up until the moment he brutally rent it apart, she possessed a maidenhead. Won't matter that by the time he was done she was bruised, battered, and terrorized. It won't even matter that before he could conclude the act, she sank a pair of sewing scissors into his arm. She will be ruined regardless."

She looked directly into the eyes of the son she'd always taken such pride in and said, "I could not do anything to correct the wrong done to Hattie before. But I damn well aim to see the right thing is done by her in this instance. You had your pleasure on her this night—"

"Please, Mom, let me talk to her. Let me make this right. I know her scream is probably what woke you, but I swear I did not force myself on her." Had he? God, she had been so willing, but then she'd suddenly been so afraid . . .

"If I thought for one moment you had, Jacob, I would shoot you myself and weep while I reported it as a rifle-cleaning accident. Hattie told me the responsibility was equally hers. I find that difficult to believe— you're eleven years older and worlds more experienced than she. Would you have me believe she seduced you?"

"No." Only by her responsiveness.

"Then I can only conclude you took your pleasure without giving a moment's consideration to the repercussions it might have for Hattie. Such being the case, you will damn well accept the consequence of your actions. You will marry her in three weeks' time."

34

THERE WASN'T A weapon to be found in the church, yet it felt like a shotgun wedding to Hattie. She was petrified she was making the worst mistake of her life. One way or another she'd loved Jake for what felt like forever, so this should be a happy, joyful day. It wasn't. Maybe if she felt their marriage was what Jake wanted, instead of something he'd been forced into because of that night in the stable— But she was nobody's fool and she still remembered Jake's wedding to Jane-Ellen. He had been all smiles that day—so different from the solemn man standing by her side in the crowded church today. Jake possessed a streak of responsibility a mile wide. In the past, it was one more quality she'd admired. Today it made her want to bawl like a baby.

Quietly repeating her vows, Hattie wondered how they would possibly make a life together. The problems they were starting out with felt insurmountable.

She had seen very little of Jake in the past three weeks. The day after their encounter, he'd informed her grimly of their upcoming nuptials. He'd also told her in flat, unemotional tones that theirs would be a real marriage in all respects, adding in an angry undertone that he'd be damned if he'd have another wife who shunned his touch. Hattie understood exactly what he was saying about a real marriage, and the rush of emotions rattled her so much she couldn't define her reaction to save her

soul. Was it anticipation or anxiety that had her stomach in this perpetual state of nerves? With everything that happened the end of the summer of aught-six, she'd all but forgotten him telling her about Jane-Ellen
being repulsed by his touch. And if the conversation scratched at the back
of her mind at all, she'd assumed it was because the other woman had
learned of Jake's trips to Mamie Parker's place.

Unfortunately, he brought up Jane-Ellen when Hattie's own temper
was flaring, so she'd informed him she had a condition of her own. She
would be a real wife, she agreed with commendable coolness—but in return he had better plan on being a faithful husband. Maybe, she'd added
a bit snidely, Jane-Ellen wouldn't have shunned his touch if he'd stayed
away from Mamie Parker's.

Jake had gone very still. She could still hear his cool voice saying,
"You've got that backwards, Big-eyes," which promptly shut her up.

For herself, Hattie had mixed emotions about the intimacy Jake was
determined they'd share. She was mortified about the way she'd acted
that night in the stable. Not only had she encouraged him in what they'd
done; she was doubly embarrassed by the way she'd suddenly gone stark
raving mad midway through it. In her heart, she knew there was no comparison between her brutal deflowering by Roger and the way Jake took
her. At the same time, the thought of what he expected from her tonight
caused her heart to beat far too hard and fast in apprehension.

Another part of her was just the teeniest bit eager to experience Jake's
brand of loving. She would give a bundle to deny it, but an insistent corner of her mind wouldn't let her forget how he'd made her feel before
terror swamped all those luscious sensations. If he took her in anger, however, Hattie didn't think she would survive. And Jake seemed awfully
angry these days.

Her inability to dissemble sure hadn't soothed his temper. But upon
the announcement of their betrothal at church, Hattie, being inherently
honest, found it difficult to act all happy and bridal when she was actually
scared to death. In her defense, it had been a traumatic night before. Add
to that the way Jake had just told her she'd better be prepared to share his

bed, and the thing about Jane-Ellen, which Hattie could have died happy never knowing. Plus, he was so moody and grim, and . . . well.

The few times they'd seen each other between the two postings of the banns and today, Jake had barely talked to her except to hound her for her rapist's identity. Her stony refusal heaped more coal upon the flames of his ire.

Irritation tightened the muscles in Hattie's neck. Well, too bad. She simply could not talk about it, especially to him. Just knowing he knew shamed her to the bone. Naming names would serve no purpose she could see beyond exacerbating an already volatile situation.

Was respectability even worth this? Okay, most of her instincts cried, *Yes!* About all she had in the world was her good name, and in truth that was so newly bestowed on her, the thought of losing it terrified her. But if the price she paid was having Jake hate her—

She should have stuck to her guns when she'd argued heatedly he needn't marry her until they knew for certain if that night in the stable had borne fruit. But Jake had insisted, Augusta had insisted, and secretly, her own greedy heart had insisted. Given the way she so readily capitulated, then, it was all the more perverse that she nursed a little seed of resentment.

But, hell's bells. It wasn't only Jake's life being turned upside down; hers, too, was every bit as topsy-turvy. She felt cheated. Her one and only wedding was being ruined by worry, fear, and wildly fluctuating emotions. Why did other people's lives seem to flow so smoothly, when hers hit every damn snag life had to offer?

This was her wedding day, which was supposed to be the happiest of her life, right? Instead, it was shaping up to be the most painfully confusing. God, what a mess.

NELL KEPT AN eye on the bride and groom as she mingled with the guests at the reception. Jake had a grip on Hattie's hand, and everywhere he went, he pulled her along with him. There was no separate mingling, with the bride chatting with one group of guests while the groom chatted with another. His attitude was so proprietary, in fact, the men at the reception shied away from demanding the traditional kiss or dance from the bride. And even though Hattie smiled and chatted with whatever guest was near, she was pale, not flushed with the exuberant triumph or happiness Nell expected.

It bothered Nell so much, she did something she had never done before. She voluntarily approached Moses.

He was talking and laughing with one of the few women who still treated Hattie as though she were the social misfit she'd been before her return to Mattawa: Florence-May Somebody. The woman was pretty enough, if you liked the dainty-Dresden-shepherdess look. But in Nell's opinion, Florence Whosit was a no-class floozy who had a nerve looking down her nose at Hattie. From everything Nell had heard, Florence-May hadn't done one worthwhile thing in her own life except marry some old man with pots of money who had recently died. If you asked Nell, the way the other woman was hanging on Moses' brawny arm and gazing up at him with limpid eyes, it looked as though old Flo was looking to change her luck this time around by latching onto a young, virile specimen. Maybe Florence wanted a man who could help her spend her money and still give her what her old fool of a rich husband couldn't. Not that Nell was entirely certain what that might be or why she should care. "Moses?"

Moses' head whipped around, Florence-May immediately forgotten at the soft sound of Nell's voice. He gave her a quick visual once-over, then recollected himself with a cynical smile and a tug at his white-blond forelock. "Miss Nell."

"Could I speak with you a moment?" Nell glanced at Florence-May pointedly. "Alone?"

"Yeah, sure." He extricated his arm from Florence-May's grip. "Excuse us, won't you?" Ignoring her irritated glare, he grasped Nell's arm and led her to a semiprivate corner. "What can I do for you?"

Now that Nell had his attention, she wasn't quite sure where to begin. She fidgeted with the sash to her dress for a moment. "I need your advice."

He smiled at her with skeptical amusement. "What's the matter, princess, the champagne not chilled to your specification? Want me to beat up the waiter?"

"Please," she whispered. "Could we, just once, not snipe at one another?"

Something in her tone gave Moses a visceral jolt, and he sobered. Involuntarily, his hand reached out to touch her cheek before he caught himself and dropped it to his side. "All right. What do you wanna know?"

"Does Hattie seem happy to you?"

"What?"

"I said—"

"Yeah, I heard you. I just couldn't believe the question. Why wouldn't she be? It's her wedding day and she's always believed Jake Murdock hung the moon."

"I know. But . . . does she seem *happy*? You know her enthusiasm when everything is going right. Wouldn't you expect her to be racing around, all flushed and excited, talking and touching and laughing with everyone?"

Moses looked across the room at the bride and groom. "Damn," he murmured. "She is kinda pale and subdued, isn't she?" Then he turned his attention back to Nell. "You do know there's nothing you or I can do about it if she is unhappy, don't you?"

"But . . . I thought you loved her."

"I do. I love her like a sister, but it doesn't give me the right to interfere in her marriage unless she asks for my help. And you know Hattie—that's not likely to happen. Jake and Hattie will be fine. It's probably just bridal nerves."

"Like a sister?" Nell had hardly heard anything after Moses said that. "But you had those dreams about—" She clapped her hand over her mouth, but it was too late. The words, beyond her ability to recall, hung between them like a black cloud.

A red flush crept up from beneath Moses' collar. "I don't believe this . . . She told you about the dreams? That's just goddamn grand." He about-faced and stalked out the nearest door.

Nell caught up with him on the terrace. She grabbed his arm, but he jerked it away and glared down at her. "Please," she said, touching his forearm with conciliatory fingertips. "Don't be angry. She didn't deliberately disclose your confidence. She was defending you, and . . ."

Moses grabbed her by the shoulders and backed her up against the hotel wall. Hemming her in with his body, he bent his head until their noses nearly touched. "You want to know who I dream about these days, Miss Nell?" His big, hard hands quite gently encircled her throat, tough-skinned thumbs pressing beneath her chin to angle it up. "You wanna know whose lily-white body rolls naked across my bed when I close my eyes at night? I'll give you a clue." He crowded in until his large body brushed down her entire length. "It's not Hattie."

Nell couldn't control her trembling, and she bet her eyes were the size of saucers as she stared up at him. "Please," she whispered helplessly. *Don't be angry,* she wanted to say again, but the words wouldn't come. Instead, she licked her lips.

Moses whispered a curse. And kissed her.

It was the first time any man had done so, but Nell knew it wasn't the sort of kiss a respectable girl ought to be receiving. It was all hard lips, bold tongue, and heated, pressing bodies, and she knew she should put a stop to it. Immediately.

Instead she tried her best to emulate his actions. She'd dreamed of him, dreamed of this. Standing on her toes, Nell slid her arms around his muscular neck, clinging and attempting to get closer. She offered up her mouth and shy advances of her own tongue.

Moses groaned and pressed her harder into the hotel wall with his body before he abruptly ripped his mouth away and pushed back, reaching behind his neck to disengage her hands. His wide chest heaved as he dragged air into his lungs. "Good . . . God . . . Almighty," he said hoarsely.

Nell watched him eye her breasts, which heaved as she, too, tried to catch her breath.

Then he suddenly raised his pale blue eyes to pin her in place. "You a virgin, Nell?"

Nell blushed but said truthfully, "Certainly."

"You're not gonna remain one for long, you keep kissing like that."

She smiled in delight. "I did all right?" Moses stared at her in incredulous silence, and she rushed on, "I mean, it was my first kiss, and I wasn't sure I was handling it properly."

"Who you trying to kid? That wasn't your first kiss!"

"It was so." She lowered her eyes and admitted with painful honesty, "Men don't generally find me attractive. I'm too tall."

He snorted. "Bull. You're a dainty little thing."

"Compared to you, Goliath would be a dainty little thing."

Moses rolled one of his massive shoulders. "You gotta know you're beautiful."

She gazed up at him uncertainly. "I'm gawky."

He swore. Ran his fingertips from her cheekbone down to her waist, not missing a curve or hollow in between. "No, you're not." He swallowed, then said sternly, "I'm a blacksmith, girl. Ain't ever gonna be a fancy banker."

"I'm a schoolmarm. Not ever going to be a fancy socialite." She looked down at her shoes, wondering if she—just plain old Nell Thomesen— would be enough for him.

Moses hooked his fingers beneath her chin, raising it. "Look at me," he commanded when Nell's delicate eyelids remained lowered. When her gaze finally rose to meet his, he leaned over, kissed her chastely, then straightened to his full height. "You wanna be my girl?"

"Yes," she breathed. "Oh please, yes."

Moses' heart beat like a kettledrum. He could not believe his luck. This woman had robbed him of more sleep than he could keep track of, and here she was, letting him kiss her and acting like he was honoring her with an offer of courtship. Amazing. "First thing we gotta do is go in before people start tossing your name around."

"All right." Nell straightened her dress and self-consciously patted her hair.

"And we gotta stay out of dark corners." She gazed at him with those big, innocent eyes and he explained, "I want to do more than hold hands and exchange chaste kisses, Nell. I will, too, given half a chance. So, we avoid temptation, y'got me?"

"Yes, Moses." She rather liked the idea of courting temptation. But since it was her reputation he was trying to protect, she supposed the least she could do—

Moses grinned. "You always gonna be this docile?"

"No, Moses."

He laughed. "That's what I thought." He leaned down and kissed her once more. Then he grabbed her hand. "C'mon. Let's get in there before the good people of Mattawa start gossiping."

HATTIE'D HAD QUITE enough. She was angry, hurt, and at the end of her patience. "This hasn't been a wedding," she suddenly said in a low, vehement voice when she found herself temporarily alone with Jake in a corner of the big ballroom. His head whipped around and she looked him squarely in the eye. "This has been a circus." Holding up her hand, she stared pointedly at his grip on her wrist—a grip he hadn't relinquished since they walked out of the church. "Which I guess makes me the trained bear."

She pried his fingers up until she could jerk her hand free. "The entire town will be counting on their fingers after the unseemly haste in which we wed—I don't need to be shackled to your side on top of it. If you want to create a spectacle, go do it by yourself." She turned and walked away.

Jake watched her go, curbing his first impulse, which was to snatch her back and force her to stand by his side, where she belonged. He rubbed the tense muscles at the back of his neck. What the hell was the matter with him? He'd been angry for three solid weeks. Normally an easygoing man, he wasn't accustomed to these bitter emotions eating at him.

Well, hell, he thought, trying to justify his less-than-heroic behavior, *I got a right to be angry.* He was a grown man being ordered to marry like the callowest of youths. Naturally he resented it.

Then why, that same voice whispered, *were you angrier still when Hattie argued against the marriage?* Shit. He was all messed up.

He could not get the knowledge that she'd been raped out of his mind. His gut held a constant, leaden weight at the thought of some faceless man brutalizing her. Augusta's words kept coming back to haunt him and he'd developed an unfortunate penchant for conjuring vivid pictures of Hattie struggling and scared to death. She was violated over and over again in his mind's eye.

Why wouldn't she tell him who had done this to her? Had it happened here in Mattawa or had some city-bred rat slunk out of a Seattle alley one night? And what the hell had she meant when she said she was handed over on a silver platter? He'd been so absorbed in his own emotions, he hadn't stopped to consider hers. Until now.

The unvarnished truth was he'd spent the past weeks sulking about being forced to do exactly what he most wanted. He might rebel at being commanded to wed like an errant kid, and his timetable sure enough had been blown to hell. But this was what he'd planned ever since going to see Aurelia Donaldson about getting Hattie back in town. How many hours had he spent while Hattie was in Seattle, thinking about her, debating the pros and cons of a relationship between them? God knew he'd drummed up damn few cons. Shit, it hadn't even been a question of maybe; it had been more a matter of how, given her anger at him, and when. As for her most recent accusation, he doubted the good people of Mattawa would waste time counting on their fingers. Hattie appeared to be the only one in town who was unaware that he had been courting her for a good eleven months.

Thinking about the look on her face a moment ago, he wished he could go back and change his behavior these past weeks. He'd gone about this all wrong. Ceremonies of this sort were important to women, and his anger and possessiveness had ruined it for her. He was sorry, and he'd like to tell Hattie that. Yet how could he explain his behavior to her when he didn't really understand it himself? He desperately wanted their marriage to work. If they could just get past these bollixed-up misunderstandings, he knew it would be something special.

Watching the doorway to the women's powder room, where Hattie had disappeared, he decided the most important step he could take toward rectifying the mess he'd made was to quit demanding her rapist's identity. He'd been reacting to the knowledge of her attack in terms of how it affected him—and giving pretty short shrift to what was best for her. Every time he badgered Hattie for a name, he most likely forced her to relive a nightmare. His mother had tried to tell him something of the sort, but he hadn't been ready to listen. Now he got it. He had reopened Hattie's wounds, and by poking at them, he was refusing to let them reheal.

Forcing himself to turn away from the ladies' room entrance, Jake threw himself into the festivities. He would give his new wife room to maneuver. Hattie had a fierce independent streak and he couldn't chain her to his side just to satisfy some misguided notion that it was the only way to both stake his claim and keep her safe.

Hattie nursed her confusion and indignation in the powder room as long as she dared, but eventually she had to come out. She expected Jake to be haunting the entrance as she emerged, ready to take possession of her hand again. Instead, he was dancing with Aurelia Donaldson. When the song ended, he escorted the fierce old woman to the chairs against the walls and invited another woman to dance. He didn't so much as glance in the powder room's direction, and much to Hattie's chagrin, she discovered that instead of relieved, she felt rather nettled. Not that she wanted to be chained to his side again; she didn't. But he sure as heck lacked consistency.

Crossing the room to where Moses was standing, she invited him to dance with the bride. Generally observant where her friends were concerned, she barely even noticed the unusually friendly conversation she interrupted between him and Nell.

The reception began to wind down. Finally, the orchestra announced the last dance. For the first time since she had pried his fingers away and retreated to the powder room, Jake materialized at Hattie's side. He extended his hand. "This is my dance, I believe."

She placed her hand in his and let him lead her to the dance floor, where he pulled her into his arms and held her much too closely as the band struck up a waltz. They circled the floor in silence, gazing at distant points over each other's shoulders.

Their refusal to talk or look at each other should have been uncomfortable. But for the first time in three weeks, tensions eased, coiled knots unwound, and resentments faded. Jake's arms tightened around her; Hattie rested her head for a moment where his chest met his collarbone before recollecting the impropriety of such a posture. As they moved across the dance floor, they both silently absorbed the heat and scent of their partner and felt comforted.

Silently, Mr. and Mrs. Jake Murdock separately arrived at the same conclusion. This was where they were meant to be.

35

HATTIE SAT AT the dressing table in the Buchannan suite, brushing her hair with long, hard strokes and pretending she wasn't nervous.

A short while ago, Jake had carried her over the threshold, kissed her like a sister, poured her a glass of champagne, and drew her a bath. She'd tried to relax in the hot water but finally decided she'd just as soon face the music as hide in the bathroom worrying herself half-sick over the ways this night could go. When she'd emerged from the bathroom, Jake went in, sparing her a single swift glance—but one that traveled from her not-yet-brushed-to-a-fare-thee-well hair to the tips of her bare toes. She heard his movements now behind the closed bathroom door.

Hattie met her reflection as her brushstrokes slowed. She hated being a coward. Once she hadn't been afraid to meet challenges head-on. Not that she believed, had Jake not sent her to Roger Lord's house that night, she wouldn't still be a bit apprehensive tonight. But she might not be frightened so fiercely of what was going to happen any moment now.

People said ignorance was bliss, and she didn't disagree. She wished to heaven she was ignorant of the terror that could be unleashed upon a woman by a body part Hattie had yet to even see.

The bathroom door opened and Jake stepped out, wrapped in a black dressing gown that ended just below his knees. Clearly it was all he wore, and the atmosphere between them suddenly seemed thicker than molasses. Wondering if he'd order her summarily to bed, she kept a wary eye on her new husband's reflection in the mirror.

Barely glancing in her direction, Jake crossed the sitting room. He stopped at the ornate ice bucket containing the champagne he'd ordered and reached for two clean long-stemmed flutes. Seconds later, tiny cheerful bubbles from the fizzy beverage he poured popped and disappeared above the flutes' crystal rims.

Hattie continued working the bristles through a tangle at her nape as she watched Jake in the mirror, the stemmed glasses incongruously fragile in his work-roughened hands. But even seeing his approach, she started nervously when his hand, offering the flute, appeared over her shoulder. She reached to accept it with the hairbrush still in her hand. "Oh," she murmured in consternation, feeling like a dolt, and set the silver-backed brush on the dressing table.

"Wait," Jake said and pressed the champagne flute into her right hand. When he reached around her left shoulder to place his own glass on the dressing table, his arms momentarily surrounded her. Heat pumped off him, and Hattie was aware of his clean, soapy scent.

Picking up the brush she'd abandoned, Jake knelt behind her. She watched his reflection, noticing the way his newly shaved jaw gleamed beneath the room's soft lighting. The creases alongside his mouth when his reflection smiled at her were particularly shiny and soft-looking. "Let me," he said in a low, husky voice.

Hattie cast him a wary glance over her shoulder. He pressed a gentle kiss into the wing of her eyebrow. "Drink your wine," he ordered. "Close those big eyes and relax. I just want to brush your hair."

She took a sip of her champagne. Then, cradling the glass against her breast, Hattie did as requested and closed her eyes. As Jake pulled the brush through her hair from scalp to waist, some of her anxiety faded. The only sound in the room was the static crackle of her curls being tamed into loose waves in the brush's wake. His fingers occasionally skimmed her neck or cheek, and their rough texture against the softness of her skin spread slow warmth through Hattie's veins. Without opening her eyes, she raised the wineglass and took another sip.

"Your hair is beautiful," he said in a low voice. "I've thought so since the first day you came to live with us." He buried his nose in it and inhaled.

The rhythm of Hattie's heart picked up an extra beat and her eyes opened. "Jacob?"

Draping coppery waves over a shoulder, he kissed the skin he'd exposed. His gaze met hers in the mirror. "I'll never hurt you, Hattie," he whispered with husky-voiced sincerity. He pressed his parted lips as well to the curve where her neck flowed into her shoulder. His gaze remained steady on hers in the mirror's reflection. "Never, Big-eyes. I swear it."

Hattie trembled as another emotion replaced her fear. Cautiously, she tipped her head to one side, exposing a wider expanse of bared skin. And closed her eyes.

Jake couldn't prevent the sound rumbling up his throat, and he gathered up Hattie's hair in both fists, tugging it to tip her head back as he kissed his way up the side of her neck. He stretched out his torso and twisted her head to one side, guiding it against his shoulder. Torqueing his own around, he rocked his mouth over Hattie's soft, full lips. Sucking lightly at them, he groaned when they parted. It was the opening Jake sought, but the position was too awkward for follow-through. Reluctantly, he raised his head, then moved so swiftly, Hattie's eyes had barely begun to flutter open before he pulled her chair away from the dresser and circled to crouch in front of her. Removing the flute from her lax fingers, Jake set it on the dressing table. Then he framed her face in his hands. "Come to bed, Hattie-girl."

To his amazement, she let him lead her to it. He pulled back the spread and she climbed in, but averted her eyes when he dropped his robe to the floor. An instant later, he slid in next to her. She stared up at him as he eased her onto her back.

He braced himself on one elbow, perched over her. Finding a stray curl escaping the mass to tumble over her forehead, Jake wrapped it around his finger and studied her in silence for a moment. Her big golden eyes stared back at him. They were wide and wary but contained a spark of curiosity in their amber depths.

That trace of interest shot delight through Jake. Hattie was all his, sanctioned by church and state. Under the law, he could do anything he wanted to her, but what he wanted was to show her she had nothing to fear from him. And that meant he needed to be exceptionally careful in his handling of her tonight. To facilitate that, he'd taken care of himself in the bathroom to prevent his own needs from outstripping his caution.

His long abstinence—Jake having sworn off Mamie's girls as soon as he learned Hattie was coming home—was partially responsible for his shameful seconds-long hesitation before stopping that night in the stable. But he would, by God, see to it he stayed in control on their wedding night. For once, he'd woo his woman the way she deserved. He took it as a good sign when Hattie didn't ask to have the lights doused.

Tugging on the curl still wrapped around his finger, he lowered his head. Her mouth was warm and incredibly soft beneath his, and he parted her lips. His tongue traced the slick inner lining and he stiffened slightly at her responsive, shuddery inhalation.

He teased her with light kisses, never allowing his tongue to trespass farther than her lips. Hattie began to shift restlessly beneath him. Lifting her chin, she offered her mouth for a more complete kiss, then licked her lips in frustration every time he raised his head to change angles. Her arms wrapped around his bare neck and finally, upon feeling his mouth once again leave hers, she gripped the back of his head in both hands and forcibly held him to her while her own tongue slid into his mouth, seeking the satisfaction he'd denied her.

Approval rumbled up Jake's throat and he gave her what she wanted: deep, drugging kisses with nothing held back. Sliding a hand between their bodies, he began to slip the tiny buttons running down the front of her night rail through their loops. Reaching the end of the row, he pushed up on his elbow.

Hattie murmured in protest at the loss of Jake's kiss and slowly opened her eyes. She felt the front of her gown separate, then begin sliding off her shoulders. "Jake?"

"I want to look at you, Big-eyes."

Embarrassed modesty sent scalding heat coursing through her entire body. Instinctively, Hattie covered her bared breasts with her hands, spreading her fingers wide to conceal as much as possible. Jake tossed back the covers and rolled onto his knees to straddle her. His hands reached out to grasp her wrists and she tightened her grip, expecting him to remove her protective fingers any moment now.

Instead, he guided her hands in circular motions against the fullness of her breasts. "Don't be shy with me," he whispered and hunched over, lowering his head to lick . . . everywhere. His mouth was in constant motion, pressing kisses against anything her hands failed to conceal. His tongue probed along the perimeter of her wrist, licked upward to the tip of her thumb, slid between her fingers.

He smiled up at her and said, "Married people are allowed to see each other naked." Then he pried up a finger to run his tongue between it and her breast. He angled his head to suck her finger into his mouth, rubbing his smooth cheek against the full swell of her bosom.

Hattie's fingers went lax and she didn't resist when he brushed them aside, replacing them with his hands. Her skin had always been almost milk white, but now she noticed that not even the generous sprinkling of freckles across her chest and breasts lent much color against the weathered darkness of Jake's wide-palmed hands.

"They're so pretty, Hattie," he whispered hoarsely. "So perfect. Look."

She followed his gaze, and a soft sound escaped her throat, knowing Jake was also looking at and comparing the textures and colors of his skin against hers.

"Someday," he said, and something in his voice pulled her eyes away from his hands to meet his gaze, "I want to see our babies nursing here." Maintaining eye contact, he lowered his head and opened his mouth around a ruddy nipple.

Hattie's womb clenched at Jake's reference to future babies. But his dark eyes staring up at her, his lean cheeks hollowing as he drew as strongly on her nipple as might the babes he mentioned, and the tug sending heat lightning straight to that private place deep between her legs drove rational thought from her head. Crying out, she squeezed her thighs together and fought free of the nightgown sleeves still tangled around her elbows. Reaching for him, she dug her fingers into the smooth skin of his shoulders.

Jake released her nipple with a soft, suctioning pop and rolled onto his side. Pillowing his head on his arm, he breathed heavily as he stared at her. Christ. So much for easing himself earlier. He wanted to gobble her up.

Hattie rolled to face him as well. "Why did you stop?"

"You've let me look at most of you. I thought maybe you'd like to look at me." His free hand reached out to stroke her from the sharp dip of her waist to the rounded curve of her hip. His palm rasped to a halt at the top of her thigh, where her nightgown still bunched at an angle across her lower abdomen.

Hattie was thoroughly intimidated but tried to act as though seeing a completely naked man for the first time was an everyday event. Tossing her hair over her shoulder, she made herself look. And ho-ly cow.

Jake's shoulders were wide and muscular. She already knew this, but somehow, seeing her new husband without his usual shirt felt new. With a fingertip, she traced the curve from his neck to his shoulder, to the point where the shoulder curved again into his upper arm. The hard muscles there were rounded, unlike those in his chest and stomach, which were longer and—not flat, exactly, but they weren't as bulgy, either.

Jake didn't have an abundance of body hair, but what he had was surprisingly dark. His chest was smooth, but black hair feathered his forearms and lightly dusted his lower legs. It grew in tangled tufts under his arms and feathered around his navel before arrowing straight down his hard belly to explode lush and thick around his— "Oh . . . my . . . God."

She'd been following the visual path with one hand, lightly skimming his biceps and forearms, her fingertips gliding across his chest and stomach—but she jerked back her hand as if burned. She could not, however, tear her eyes away from that thing jutting at her from a pelt of hair more wiry-looking than the rest. She was both horrified and unwillingly fascinated by the appendage's thrust. It looked . . . savage . . . unlike anything she'd ever clapped eyes on.

"I'll never hurt you with it, Hattie."

She pulled back a little, looking up at him with troubled eyes. "It looks so . . . angry."

"Nah," he whispered and picked up her hand, guiding it down his flat stomach. "Merely excited." Carefully, he wrapped her fingers around him, then, keeping them captive beneath his own, moved them up and down a few times.

Involuntarily, Hattie smiled. "Oh my goodness, how strange. It's like hardwood wrapped in velvet." Her fingers moved of their own accord in the manner Jake had just demonstrated. She marveled at the way the hot skin beneath her fist shifted fluidly over the inner rigidity.

"Yeah," he said hoarsely and pulled her hand away. Rolling her onto her back, he pushed up onto his palms above her, then bent his elbows to hotly kiss her.

All the sensations that had dulled to a simmering throb in Hattie boiled over once more as Jake's urgent tongue thrust and withdrew. His hands returned to her breasts, pressing, kneading, plucking at her nipples. Then one glided down, down, until it cupped the bright triangle of feathery curls between her legs. "Jake," she protested, squeezing her thighs together.

He removed his hand, but it hovered only inches away. "Don't be embarrassed, baby. It's all right. We're married."

"But I'm all . . . wet." She was scarlet with mortification having to confess it. But if he touched her there, he'd discover it for himself.

"Oh God!" Jake's eyes slammed shut and he shuddered, yet even in her inexperience, Hattie could tell it was excitement motivating him, not revulsion. His eyes reopened and he leaned to kiss her fiercely. Raising his head, he said, "That's good in this case, sweetheart. Wet is exactly the way it's supposed to be." Persistently, his hand returned.

Hattie was far from convinced and kept her legs firmly pressed together as she protested once again. But when Jake's rough-skinned fingers delved into her secret curls, found a slick, hidden little pearl, and strummed it, a world of sensation filled her. And in a different tone altogether, she sighed, "Oh, Jacob," as her thighs went lax.

His fingers slid up and down, crafty in their knowledge, and Hattie began to pant, to arch, her hips swiveling, reaching, searching for . . . she had no idea what. But it would be something *huge*—she was sure of it.

Jake knew precisely what Hattie sought. Rolling to cover her, he gently kneed her thighs apart. Pushing up on his hands, he slowly penetrated his new bride, giving her time to accommodate to his length and girth. Hattie's inner heat expanded to encase, then clasp his cock. He watched her for signs of panic. Her eyes grew enormous, but as he sank into her she shuddered with pleasure, not fear. Her eyelids slowly slid closed, and biting back a groan, Jake began to move.

Hattie whimpered deep in her throat as Jake slowly thrust and withdrew. With each pump, it felt . . . Oh mercy, it felt so . . . She spread her legs, first just a bit, then wide, then finally wrapped them around his waist. Jake slammed into her convulsively, then stilled.

"God," he whispered rawly, "I want to move faster . . . love you harder." He did so for several uncontrolled strokes before forcing himself to stillness. "So tight," he muttered. "Does it hurt? Am I scaring you?"

"No . . ." she whispered. Her husband—*husband!*—began to move again with that same rough force, making her moan. "Feels so . . ." She sighed. "Oh, Jacob, it feels . . . so"—tilting her hips, she drove him deeper—"amazing."

"Shit," he muttered and lowered his head to feather one pouting nipple with the flat of his tongue. She contracted sharply around him and he pumped his hips faster, unable to help himself. The new pace made it difficult to reach her breasts at the same time. "Oh God, Hattie, I can't—" His tongue swept the air just above her nipple, missing by centimeters. "Help me, baby, please."

She didn't think twice. Arching her back, she cupped the underside of her breast and pressed it up. When Jake's lips suddenly clamped around her distended nipple and sucked, she cried out at the explosive, shattering sensations detonating deep inside her, a convulsive, rippling clench and release around that hard man part of his. Thrusting her hips up, she froze, whimpering helplessly. Jake continued pounding into her, and the life-altering inner explosions went on and on, her body jerking slightly with each one. A bit mortified by her near-violent reaction, she opened her eyes.

And saw Jake didn't appear to mind. In fact, it seemed to drive him over an edge of his own. Mouth going slack around her nipple, he straight-armed his upper body to hover above her, his head thrown back, his teeth clenched, and his eyes squeezed shut. He buried himself in her with a final rough surge of his hips, and Hattie clutched his forearms as she watched the same powerful force that had driven her overtake him. Guttural sounds forced past his strong white teeth as he shuddered in release. Then seconds later his head dropped forward. Bending his elbows, he lowered himself gently atop her.

Hattie wrapped her arms around his neck, holding him in a fierce embrace, grateful when his strong arms slid under her to grasp her in return. He was heavy, but Hattie didn't care. She was too dazed by what had just happened.

Jake rolled them both over, and Hattie found herself lying atop him almost before she had time to realize what he was doing. Raising her head, she gazed down at him, her hair spilling to the mattress to form a private cave around their heads.

Jake rubbed his hands up and down her bare back. "You all right?"

"Yes." She hesitated, blushed furiously, then admitted with her usual forthrightness, "I had no idea it could be like that. When I lost my . . . on that awful night . . . well, thank you. You've shown me a marvelous aspect of this business I never suspected." She didn't have the words to express what he'd restored to her.

Jake tightened his hold. The temptation was strong to press her again for the identity of her rapist, but he hung on to his resolve. Instead, he said lightly, "My pleasure."

Unexpectedly, she giggled. "Yes, it was, wasn't it?" She buried her face in his neck, still laughing.

Jake thought his heart might have just exploded. God, she was a marvel. "Hattie?" He threaded a hand through her hair and tugged her head up until he could see her face. "I'm sorry about the honeymoon."

It was a busy time on the ranch, and because the end of the school year was almost upon them, Hattie had been given special dispensation by the school board to finish teaching out the term. Consequently, their honeymoon had been reduced to this weekend. She smiled a little wistfully but merely said, "That's all right. It's not your fault."

It wasn't, but he'd taken a perverse pleasure in her disappointment when he'd informed her it was impossible to get away, which shamed him now. "I'm still sorry. As soon as I can free up some time, we'll take a belated one. Anywhere you want to go."

She smiled radiantly. "Oh, I would like that."

A long curl fell across his mouth when she moved her head and he picked it up, inhaling its scent before tucking it behind her ear. "Will you miss teaching?"

"I will. I truly love it, and it was my first taste of being a part of the community." She gave him a little smile and ran her fingernail up and down the crease in his cheek, eyeing him from beneath her lashes. "But maybe you'll let me help with the horses? That would help ease the crushing disappointment."

"Maybe," he said, knowing if she kept smiling at him as she did now, if she gave him more loving like tonight's, he would probably let her do anything her heart desired.

His cock had been shrinking inside her for the past several moments and suddenly slipped out. A rush of warm liquid followed.

"Oh!" Hattie's face registered profound shock and she tried to disguise her embarrassed dismay at the flow of liquid on her thighs. Jake roared with laughter. He lifted her off of him and settled her on her back on the mattress. "Stay there. I'll get something to clean you up." He rolled out of bed, unconcerned with his nudity as he walked to the bathroom.

When he emerged, Hattie tried her best to get an eyeful without seeming to be looking at him at all. She remembered how she used to think he was skinny. Boy, had she been misled! He looked lean and lanky in his clothes to this day, but out of them . . . Well, he was still long-boned and lean, but far from scrawny. Muscles moved under his skin with fluid precision, in his shoulders, his arms, his legs, all appearing carved in bold relief. Her eyes darted to his man place for a quick peek and she bolted upright, unmindful of her own nakedness. "Why, it's teeny-tiny!" she blurted, staring openly. "What on earth happened to it?"

Jake snorted and dropped down beside her on the bed. He flipped back the covers, which had pooled around her waist, and gently used the warm cloth he'd brought from the bathroom to wipe away all traces of his loving from her thighs. As he looked up from his self-imposed task, one corner of his mouth tilted up in an ironic smile as he met her wide, curious eyes. "I don't think there's anything quite so deflating as having a woman point to a man's pride and joy and proclaim it 'teeny-tiny.'"

Pride and joy? "All right," she corrected, "not really. But it sure is a lot smaller than the last time I saw it, and it looks so soft and defenseless now. Before it looked sorta mean. How do you do that?"

"For heaven's sake, girl, you've been around the breeding pens enough to know—"

"Oh, certainly," she interrupted, "as if you ever allowed me near any animal being bred." Briefly, she remembered the time she'd seen a stallion covering a mare, but it had been so many years ago now, the details had blurred.

"Okay, fair enough." His smile was wry as he regarded her, torn between chagrin at having his cock considered small by the woman whose admiration he desired above all others, and amusement at her lack of tact.

One thing he'd always known about Hattie Murdock was she would say whatever popped into her mind. She was curious and outspoken about things certain to send another girl into a swoon. It was one of the first things he'd loved about her. "In any case," he declared firmly, "I want you to repeat after me: Jake Murdock has the biggest damn straight shooter you have ever seen—"

"Jake!" Hattie blushed crimson, but she had to press her fingers to her lips to hide a delighted grin. "Do men actually care about that sort of thing? I retract the 'teeny-tiny'; it's really not all that small. It's just, compared to the way it was before . . . Well, believe me, it was certainly large enough then! In fact, I was kinda worried it would be far too big, but it fit quite . . . well, you know." Heat pulsed in her cheeks and she wished she'd taken a moment before speaking.

Jake enjoyed watching her, knowing she was embarrassed by her words, yet unconscious of her nudity as she sat in the middle of the rumpled bed, dressed only in blushes. He wanted to keep her unaware, to prevent her from diving for her discarded nightgown. So, he picked her hand up in his and placed it on his thigh, inches from the quiescently curled product of her scrutiny. "Want to make it grow?"

"Ja-cob Murdock," she breathed, shocked, but oh-so-clearly tempted.

"Hat-tie Murdock," he mocked, sitting very still, watching her.

She stared down at her fingers on his hard, warm thigh and the object they almost touched. "That is a scandalous suggestion."

"I've got a million of 'em." He grinned when her whiskey-eyed gaze flew to meet his in interested speculation. She blushed and ducked her head again. "C'mon," he urged. "It'll be educational."

"It certainly would be that," she muttered. Her fingertips itched with the temptation. "I shouldn't."

"Sure you should. It's allowed. We're married."

"Well, that's true." Tearing her gaze away from the object under discussion, she glanced up at his face, half-afraid he was making sport of her. But his expression was hopeful, not mocking at all. Hesitantly, she stretched out her fingers.

"It feels different like this," she whispered, "so . . . sweet." She stroked it experimentally and it pulsed. "Oh!" She snatched her fingers back, but rampant curiosity trumped modesty and her hand returned to carefully grip him. His . . . straight shooter . . . pulsed again, its contours rapidly losing any semblance of sweetness. Then again.

"Ho-ly," she breathed in awe. The corners of her mouth tilted up, and feeling wicked and daring she looked up into her groom's face and whispered, "Jake Murdock has the biggest darn . . ."

"Oh, Hattie, girl—" Jake pulled her into his arms and held her in a grip that nearly squeezed the breath out of her.

Hattie could live with that. Because her big strong man's voice was half moan and half laughter. And he was putty—er, steel in her hands.

36

B Y THE TIME Jake and Hattie checked out of their suite, neither remembered their wedding-day qualms. The closest reminder their
union was different from some was when Jake cut himself with his
straight-edge razor and allowed the blood to drip on the hotel sheet
as they were packing to leave the room. His dark eyes met Hattie's puzzled gaze. "People talk in this town," he murmured in masterful under-
statement.

Two weeks later, school closed for the summer. Hattie bid her students
a final farewell and went home to the Murdock Ranch to take up man-
agement of the ranch house. When that didn't take up enough of her
time, she worked in the garden. Gradually, Jake also found chores for her
involving the horses, and she spent her days in a haze of happiness so intense it was almost scary. Surely, feelings this wonderful could not last.

She had always held strong feelings for Jake. She'd loved him for rarely
treating her like a child even when she was one, and for his conversation,
which had never been condescending—despite her female status and lack
of years. She'd loved him for showing respect to her opinions, and for his
sense of humor. Not in her wildest dreams, however, had she expected
him to restore her confidence as a woman.

Hattie always knew she wasn't a beauty. Occasionally she'd wondered
if the town's opinion of her might have been different had she been. Per-

sonal doubts of that nature were rare, however. Mostly she'd simply possessed a headstrong confidence originating from something other than a pretty reflection in the mirror. Then Roger Lord assailed her unassailable sense of womanliness and stole something from her more precious than her virginity.

Jake gave it back. He made her feel wanted with an intensity she'd never experienced. Made her feel needed. He talked to her. He listened to her. He made her laugh. His desire for her was insatiable and honored no timetable.

Hattie assumed when they returned to everyday life, lovemaking would be reserved for the hours after dark. Jake quickly disabused her of the notion. With the feeblest pretexts, he often returned to the ranch house in broad daylight and once there didn't even bother maintaining the charade. He just grabbed her by the hand and hauled her up to their room. He woke her in the morning with his mouth and his hands; he loved her at night. Praising her all the while.

For the first time in her twenty-one years, Hattie felt it was desirable to have red hair, because Jake thought it beautiful and constantly said so. He extolled the beauty of her eyes, the desirability of her lips. He paid tribute in embarrassingly frank detail to her body. He flattered her outrageously, yet with a patent sincerity that made her feel like the loveliest woman on earth. His words, his hands, and his body healed what another man had wounded.

Through Jake's brand of loving, she discovered sex between a man and a woman could sometimes be violent. But it was a leashed violence comprised of shocking words, gripping hands, escalating sensations, and a demanding mouth with no apparent boundaries. Never from a desire to hurt. Even at Jake's most uncontrolled, he was aware of their differing strengths.

Hattie was secretly convinced that many of the things he did to her were assuredly sins. They were simply too bold and felt much too good to be otherwise. Jake, however, insisted they weren't. And when she questioned the propriety of a touch or the placement of his mouth, he had a way of just forging ahead and finishing what he'd begun. And it felt so good—felt so right—she never questioned him twice. After all, as he so often whispered, it was allowed. They were married.

Truly, though, who did he think he was fooling? She doubted a quarter of the married people in Mattawa did a fraction of the bedroom things Jake dreamed up.

Jake believed he was fooling Hattie. Not making a fool of her—hell, never that. But rather simply taking advantage of her naive trust. God, she was a miracle, so honest and genuine. And so. Damn. Enthusiastic.

Hattie believed she was plain, but Jake found her a feast for the eyes, unequaled by the greatest beauties in the world. And her responsiveness when they made love was the biggest miracle of all. Her experience with the rapist could have scarred her for life. God knew, Jane-Ellen had feared and repulsed Jake's advances with far less reason. But Hattie turned into his arms at the slightest touch. She kissed him back; she denied him nothing. He knew he'd shocked her more than once in the ways he touched her. Yet as soon as he told her it was allowed, they were married, she offered herself up with renewed gusto.

It made him grin and feel cagey as a fox in a henhouse. Hell, he had dozens of new ideas to make her explode in pleasure, and eventually he'd use them all, with his handy refrain readied for backup should she fear once again it was sinful. His standard justification was so perfect, because who was she going to ask? Luckily for him, women didn't discuss sex with each other. Or so he thought. Until the day he came back to the ranch house for a little unscheduled loving and found Hattie and Nell deep in discussion in the parlor.

He stopped unseen in the doorway when he realized Nell was there, battling disappointment. Then he shrugged it aside. There was always later, and Hattie had missed her friend's company. He watched them for a moment.

Their heads were together, cups of tea untouched on the table in front of them, while Nell, her expression a curious mixture of disbelief and rapt wonder, hung on to every word Hattie whispered to her. Hattie was using her hands to illustrate her words, spreading her thumb and index finger wide of each other as though to demonstrate a measurement. Then she added something in a low voice and her two hands spread about a foot and a half apart, looking for all the world like a fisherman describing the one that got away.

Nell looked downright horrified and Jake's curiosity got the best of him. He strolled into the room. "What in tarnation are you ladies discussing? Looks mighty interesting."

Two heads whipped in his direction, hot color staining faces that were a study in consternation. Nell's glance skittered nervously off the front of his pants, then quickly rose to stare unseeingly over his shoulder. And comprehension exploded in Jake's brain. By God, his wife was telling her friend how his cock changed size when he was aroused—and giving more credit to his hard stage, he might add, than he fairly deserved.

For the first time in an age, Jake blushed. And he couldn't even look at Nell. "Hattie?" he croaked. "Uh, could I see you out in the hall for a moment? Excuse us, won't you?" he added to the top of Nell's downcast pompadour.

"Of course," Nell murmured in reply, speaking to her cup of tepid tea, which she'd picked up from the table in front of her. *My goodness, it must be true then.* She thought Hattie was funning her, until she'd seen the look on Jake's face when he realized what they were discussing. *Perhaps she and Moses should reconsider their marriage plans.*

Then again, Hattie did say it was the most marvelous experience. And she was clearly happier than Nell had ever seen her.

Hattie grinned at her husband's embarrassment as she trailed him out into the hall, quickly attempting to wipe the smile from her face when he whirled to face her.

"You were discussing our *sex life*?" he demanded in a low voice choked with disbelief. He ran his fingers through his hair, staring down at her. "Good God Almighty, Hattie!"

Hattie looped her arms around his neck and leaned into him, pressing her breasts into his chest. "Shouldn't I?" she whispered innocently, then added with wicked emphasis, "Isn't it *allowed*?" She raised her head to press a soft kiss on his lips. Pulled back. "After all, we are married."

Jake had a hard time thinking straight when she did things like that, but a wry grin finally twisted his lips. She was onto that, was she? He should know better than to underestimate her. He ran his knuckles down her smooth cheek. "We are, Big-eyes, but Nell's not."

"No, but she and Moses are talking about getting married sometime in the not-too-distant future. I just thought I'd give her a little information so she wouldn't be as unprepared as I was."

"Oh, I don't know," he said in a low voice, his hands on her backside pressing her closer to him. "You were a pretty quick study. If Moses is half as lucky as I am, Nell will be too." He pulled away before he gave in to the temptation to drag her into the closet beneath the stairs. "I have to get back to work. Try to confine your conversation to something innocuous while I'm gone, will you?"

"Why, certainly, Jacob," she agreed demurely. "Whatever you say."

Jake didn't believe her demure act for a minute. If he knew his Hattie—and he was learning more about her all the time—she'd be back in the parlor within seconds of his departure, imparting all sorts of scandalous facts. In boundless detail, no doubt.

37

JAKE STOPPED DEMANDING the name of Hattie's rapist, but he hadn't forgotten about it. Since it seemed important to her peace of mind, he made an honest attempt to erase it from his memory. And because he was happy, he was mostly successful. Yet, out of the blue sometimes, the look on Hattie's face that night in the stable would flash before his eyes and he would hear the bitterness in her voice again. *I didn't give myself, you sonovabitch. I was handed over on a silver platter.*

What the hell did that mean? During odd moments, he dissected her words over and over, worrying them like a dog with a bone. And he was no closer to understanding them. *I was handed over on a silver platter.* The words stuck in his craw. To be handed over had connotations of someone purposefully colluding to deliver her into the hands of a rapist. Yet that made no sense. No one in their right mind willingly dispatched a helpless virgin into the hands of a vicious debaucher.

Unless it was unintentional. While pitching fresh hay into the newly cleaned horse stalls early one evening, he decided accidental made more sense than anything else he'd considered. If a person didn't have an inkling of an acquaintance's or even a friend's perversions, then it was entirely possible that arrangements were made all unknowingly for Hattie to meet or dine with someone, or even spend the night in a home recommended by a friend. Folks made such arrangements quite often, and in the case of an unattached female, she had little choice but to comply. Hell, he himself had—

I was handed over on a silver platter . . . handed over on a silver . . . handed over—

"No." It squeezed up through the breath-stealing constriction in his throat like the croak of a faraway frog. God, please, please, please. *No.*

But truth was being caught in a burst of fireworks, and pitiless, savage shards of agony flayed his nerve endings. His legs buckled and his hands slid down the shaft of the pitchfork as he crumpled to his knees on the ground. The tool toppled unnoticed as he doubled over until his forehead ground into the packed-dirt stable floor.

Oh Christ. It fit. It all fit. Her refusal to see him after the night he'd nearly relieved her of her virginity up in her room. Doc's coolness. Her vow to hate him until hell froze over. His mother's request that he assume responsibility for the family's legal matters. Lord's inexplicable fall from grace with the town leaders. Augusta's knowledge of his dalliance with Hattie that night. Hattie's refusal to write, to speak, to— It was him. He was responsible for the brutal theft of her virginity.

Jake vomited on the dirt.

Twilight lengthened and shadows crept across the floor as he knelt in the stall, unaware, in his unbearable pain and guilt, of the passage of time. He didn't hear the creaking of the outer door opening, but he stiffened all over when Hattie's voice called softly in the gloom, "Jake? Are you in here?"

He didn't answer, but her footsteps grew progressively nearer, halting momentarily outside each stall. "Jake?"

"Where is he?" she muttered only moments before reaching his stall. Then she was at the entrance. The smell of sickness and his crumpled posture must have registered, because Hattie rushed in, crouching down at his side, reaching for his forehead. "Jake?"

"Don't touch me!" He knocked her hand aside. God, he was so unclean; let her not be contaminated by him.

Hattie drew her hand back. "What is it? Oh God, not influenza. Everyone knows how deadly that can be."

Jake blinked at her, not really absorbing what she was saying as his mind spun in sick turmoil. But he saw her shake her head.

"No, that doesn't make sense," she murmured. "No one's reported it this summer." She stretched a hand toward him once again.

Jake struggled upright. Wiping his mouth with the back of his hand, he backed out of her reach and stared at her. She was his pure, beautiful, redheaded bride, and he . . . Hell, he was the filthy procurer for her rapist. His eyes slid away, too ashamed to maintain contact with hers.

"It was Lord, wasn't it, Hattie?" he asked of the space somewhere beyond her right shoulder. His voice was low and as dead in tone as he felt. "He raped you the night I made you stay with him. The night you begged me to send you somewhere—anywhere—else. The night I handed you over on a fucking silver platter."

Hattie's body jerked in shock. Then the hand extended to touch Jake dropped to her side as she went still as a stone. She felt as though all the blood was draining from her head. Oh God, he knew. How did he know?

It didn't matter. What mattered was Jake wouldn't look at her, he didn't want her to touch him, and clearly, she literally made him sick to his stomach. She *knew* this would happen when he learned what Lord did to her! Somewhere deep inside, she had always known she must guard the identity of her attacker for her and Jake to be happy. Yet somehow, he'd found out. And now it was too late.

"Wasn't it?" Jake insisted in a harsh near growl, and Hattie stared at him in sick helplessness. He stood rigidly, his hands fisted at his sides. He was tightly clenched all over: the veins in his arms, his hands, his neck, all standing in stark relief. The small muscles along his jaw bunched, and his eyes stared past her.

"Yes," she whispered. She wanted to say something to make him look at her and see *her* again, instead of used goods. But she couldn't find the words. And feeling lost, she turned and walked away.

Back in their bedroom, she waited for Jake to come to bed, but he never did. She eventually fell into a restless sleep sometime before dawn, only to toss and turn beneath dream after disturbing dream.

———————

JAKE EASED OPEN the door to their bedroom and tiptoed in. For a moment, he allowed himself to stare hungrily down at his wife. She was curled on her side amid tangled bedclothes, her hair a wild mass of tumbled curls blocking her face, her left leg exposed where her nightgown had ridden up to twist around her hip. She whimpered softly in her sleep and her legs moved fitfully. The nightgown twisted around her even more.

Forcing himself to turn away, he swiftly pulled his clothes out of the wardrobe, then let himself out of the room. After leaving instructions with his foreman, he drove from the ranch. The sun had just cleared the horizon when he parked in front of his mother's house.

He went around to the back door. Through the window next to it, he saw Mirabel, who replaced Cook for the breakfast meals. He tapped softly on the glass before letting himself in.

Mirabel turned from the stove where she was replacing a pot of coffee. "Jacob! My, you're out early." Then she looked closer and saw his grim expression, the paleness beneath his habitual tan, his swollen, reddened eyes. "Are you all right? Nothing has happened to Miss Hattie, I hope." She began to worry in earnest when Hattie's name produced a spasm of pain across Jake's features.

"I need to speak to my mother," he said in a gritty voice. "Please. I know it's early, but it's important."

"Certainly. I'll go wake her."

"That won't be necessary." Augusta stepped into the room, tying her wrapper's belt. "I heard Jacob's automobile." She crossed the room. "What is it, son? Has something happened to Hattie?" Not even when Jane-Ellen and the baby died, not even when he learned of Hattie's rape, had Augusta seen Jake so devastated.

"I happened," he said in raw agony. His posture was rigid as he stood in the middle of the kitchen. "I handed her over to Roger Lord on a silver platter. Oh God, Mom, how can I live with this? She was so honest and giving and innocent, and I hand delivered her to that, that—"

Augusta sank onto a kitchen chair. "How do you know this?"

"It just came to me." He raked his fingers through his hair. "I kept thinking about something she'd said, and suddenly I just ... knew. I can't believe I didn't realize the moment I learned she'd been raped. It seems so damn obvious now."

Augusta stared at him. His voice had the raw hoarseness of vocal cords strained beyond endurance by sustained bouts of throat-ripping, gut-wrenching sobbing. "Sit down, Jacob," she urged. "Mirabel, pour him some coffee." When Jake automatically responded to her command, she reached across the table and laid her hand over his tanned fingers. "When did you last eat?"

"What?" He looked at her as though she spoke a foreign language.

"When was your last meal, dear?"

"I ..." He shrugged impatiently. "Dinner, I guess."

"You need to eat." She looked to her housekeeper and companion. "Mirabel, perhaps some eggs?"

Mirabel nodded and pulled out a skillet.

"I'm not hungry. I doubt I'll ever have an appetite again."

"Don't be self-indulgent, Jacob. I realize this has come as a shock to you, but you can only wallow in your own guilt for so long. You have an excellent mind, son. You need to use that, not your emotions."

He stared at the tabletop as if she hadn't spoken, and she squeezed his fingers until he raised his head to look at her.

"Roger Lord raped Hattie three years ago, Jacob. It's a fact that cannot be changed. You are partially responsible by sending her there in order to keep from seducing her yourself. The question is: how are you going to use your knowledge?"

"I don't know," he admitted. "I want to castrate the son of a bitch with a rusty ax." But he began to think rather than react. "I won't, of course. It would drag Hattie's name through the mud and land me in jail, where I couldn't do her a damn bit of good."

Augusta watched some clarity come back into her son's gaze as it met hers across the table.

"I have to find something to make him pay without further hurting Hattie," Jacob said in a hard voice. He picked up his coffee cup and took a sip, eyeing his mother over the rim. "How did you knock him off the upper pinnacle of Mattawa society?"

"I defended him staunchly against a number of unethical charges."

Jake looked at her blankly. "I don't understand."

"I used the telephone to inform him he wasn't welcome to attend Jane-Ellen's funeral. Since Central is quite unable to keep news that juicy to herself, rumors began to circulate. When several people approached me at the funeral reception, I simply told them you would be handling our affairs henceforth. I may have looked befuddled when I assured them, while all the legal ramifications were quite beyond me, I was certain the tales of Mr. Lord's unethical activities were most untrue. I begged them to disregard whatever they may have heard and to please, please not pressure you for details." She smiled demurely. "They understood you were grieving, so of course they left you in peace. Aren't people thoughtful?"

Jake bared his teeth in appreciation of her tactics. "That was all it took?"

"Well, Doc Fielding was seen conversing with the sheriff for a long time on the day of the funeral, and he did, when questioned, say they were merely discussing the weather. If in the next breath, he dropped a gentle hint here and there that perhaps it would be an appropriate time to consider a change of lawyers, well, who can account for the way people's minds work?"

Jake's mind was beginning to click over with cold precision. He consumed the eggs Mirabel placed in front of him without tasting a bite as he extensively cross-examined Augusta. By the time he finished, he was fairly satisfied he'd extracted every bit of knowledge she possessed concerning Hattie's attack. He also had the name of everyone else who knew anything about it. Sickness still lay like a rock in his stomach when he left his mother's house. But at least he had gained new purpose. Somehow, someway, he would find a way to avenge his wife.

For the next several days, he interviewed people and kept a discreet surveillance on Roger Lord's house. Except for the constant rage burning in his gut, Jake could, for the most part, treat his preparations like any other case he'd undertake.

It was when he returned to the ranch and his wife that the shell encasing his emotions cracked wide open, and he could no longer maintain the façade. Combined guilt and sickness oozed like poison through his system, coloring his every action. He barely saw Hattie; it was easier that way. Gone all day, catching up on his chores half the evening, he joined his wife only for dinner. And that was pure agony, for he no longer knew how to act around her.

Everything he had taken for granted was gone. He couldn't look at Hattie without seeing her terrified eyes in the three-year-old sepia photographs Doc had shown him. He sure as hell couldn't talk to her, for what was there to say? An apology not only seemed feeble, but was too little, too late to make reparations for the pain she'd suffered because of him.

More than anything, he missed holding her, missed talking and laughing with her. But he kept his distance, convinced his were the last arms she'd want around her—and doubtful they would ever laugh again. He slept on the leather couch in his office.

Hattie, who had lived for nearly three years with the knowledge of that night in August of aught-six, didn't see Jake's pain and guilt. Therefore, she interpreted his actions as the worst-case scenario. She'd had years to come to terms with his part in her ravishment and didn't take into account that, for Jake, learning of his culpability was as devastatingly new as if it had happened yesterday. She only knew he was absent all the time now and withdrawn even during the few moments they did spend together. She assumed it meant she disgusted him now that he knew the identity of the man who'd defiled her. The old specter of inner ugliness rose to haunt her anew.

It tore her up, resurrecting all the shame she'd thought once and for all behind her. She felt unclean and assumed Jake, too, was ashamed of her, repulsed by her. Before their marriage, she'd been prepared to accept that he might not love her the way he'd once loved Jane-Ellen. She'd told herself that was all right, for she wasn't pure and good the way Jane-Ellen had been. But she'd been willing to work hard, to give Jake all her love, and truly, he had seemed so satisfied with her. Happy even. She had come to believe he was perhaps beginning to love her just for herself.

Now those dreams were dust and it seemed to boil down to a question of virtue. Hers, clearly, was highly suspect, and who could blame him for thinking so? He'd been willing to overlook that she'd come to him without her virginity. But now that he knew who had taken it, he'd most likely also remember her loose conduct with him in the stable before they were legally married.

And, truly, why wouldn't he? If she'd had her virginity to begin with, Hattie would have offered it up that night without a second thought for the sanctity of wedlock. No doubt Jake entertained precisely such thoughts when he looked at her these days. Supposing, of course, he ever did look at her again. She certainly hadn't caught him at it when she'd risked sneaking a peek at him.

Time passed in a fog of battered emotions. Shame, embarrassment, and crushing hurt came first. It took ten days of being left on her own, and then ignored when her husband was with her, before anger finally elbowed its way to the head of the line to take its rightful place.

38

THURSDAY, JUNE 24, 1909

NELL LEFT AUGUSTA'S house in a fog of confusion. She'd just learned Jake knew about Hattie's rape. Dear Lord. Nell could only imagine how her friend was taking it.

Nell didn't pretend she hadn't wondered how Hattie handled the explanations on her wedding night. She'd been fiercely adamant about Jake never knowing what was done to her, and by whom. So, it must have been incredibly difficult. Naturally, Nell hadn't come right out and asked, although she'd had to bite her tongue more than once to stop herself from doing just that. She'd had to remind herself it was none of her business and be content knowing Hattie was radiantly happy.

Jake hadn't offered much explanation when he questioned Nell. What she did take from their conversation was that Hattie had stuck to her guns. From the little he had told Nell, she was pretty sure he'd discovered the identity of Hattie's rapist all on his own.

Nell hoped no one saw her talking to Jake outside the mercantile, because she'd sure as heck failed to disguise her shock upon hearing Jake's first words. She'd greeted him as she always did, pleased to see him after her two-week sojourn in Seattle visiting her mother and sister, and anxious for news of Hattie, who'd been nothing short of radiant when Nell left.

But Jake wiped her smile away when he'd leaned over and murmured in a voice too low to be overheard that he knew Roger Lord had raped his wife and Jake needed to talk to her about it. Numbly, she had let him lead her to the Murdock mansion.

Apparently, he'd spent the past two weeks talking to everyone with any knowledge of Hattie's attack. Why hadn't Augusta said anything to her when she met her at the train last night? To be fair, Moses had been there, too, and it had been quite late when he brought her back to Augusta's house.

Nell was worried sick about Hattie. How had her friend fared these past two weeks? Jake looked so closed off and grim, and knowing Hattie's aversion to the idea of him finding out about Roger Lord, Nell had to wonder if the two of them had actually talked about it.

The whole confusing potluck of emotions was boiling through her mind as Nell walked past the livery. She didn't see Moses until he suddenly materialized at her side and took her arm.

"Hiya, sweetheart," he said, and when she violently started, he soothed a large hand down her arm. "Whoa there, little darlin'. I didn't mean to startle you. What's got you looking so serious?"

God, she wished she could tell him, but she couldn't. It wasn't her secret to tell. "Um, nothing," she said without conviction.

Moses' eyes narrowed. Leading her into the relative privacy of the livery, he crowded her up against the wall. "You're not a very good liar, Nell," he said, watching her closely. "So, what's going on?"

Being caught fibbing rubbed her raw, particularly when, if it were up to her, she would unburden herself to him in a heartbeat. There were few people with more insight into Hattie than Moses Marks.

She couldn't confide in him, however, so she took refuge in anger instead. Straightening away from the wall, she held herself erect, her manner prim and proper. "I'm not going to stand here and listen to you call me a liar," she said coolly, her chin tipped up. "I'm leaving."

"The hell you say." Moses blocked her way by planting his hands on the wall on either side of her head. "Does all this sudden secrecy have anything to do with your conversation with Jake Murdock outside Norton's Mercantile?"

Once again, her body jerked in shock. But she whispered stubbornly, "I don't know what you mean."

"Bullsh—" Moses shut up before he spewed something he might regret. But he knew his voice was perhaps overly inflexible when he said, "Quite clearly, you do. What in tarnation is going on, Nell?"

He crowded her against the wall and hooked a hand beneath her chin, forcing it up until her eyes met his. He could feel the pulse in the angle of her jaw beating like a captured rabbit's. "What did Jake want? I saw him say something to you, Nellie-girl, and I saw you react as though you'd been shot. Tell me what this is all about."

"I can't," she said miserably. "It was told to me in confidence."

"In confidence by who?" he asked. He was struck by a terrible suspicion. "Murdock?" What the hell was Jake up to? Moses wracked his brain to figure out what Murdock could have said to make Nell react this way. *Bastard better be taking care of his wife and not trying to start any funny business with my girl.* But that didn't make sense.

Until Nell blushed, thinking of the mortifyingly personal nature of the questions Jake had asked her this day.

Moses reacted violently to the sudden color in her face. If he'd been thinking straight, he would've known his suspicions simply weren't feasible. But he wasn't. The woman he loved wasn't acting like herself, he'd witnessed Murdock's effect on women before, and Moses panicked. "You stay the hell away from Jake Murdock," he snarled furiously. "You're mine!" Then he kissed her.

It lacked the gentleness he'd taught her to expect, possessed none of his usual ironclad restraint. This kiss was harsh, carnal, and out of control as he ground his mouth against hers, forcing her head back against the boards.

Nell struggled instinctively, not against his kiss but against the raw injustice of his lack of faith in her. Not that her attempt to evade his hold had any impact on Moses. He simply captured her hands, pinning them against the wall above her head.

Sliding his mouth away from hers, he kissed his way roughly down her neck, his free hand snaking around her hip to yank her against his lower body. The size, the hardness and heat of him, rubbing against the notch between Nell's thighs, made her gasp. "Stop it," she whispered and tugged against the hold on her wrists. They remained stapled to the wall by his big hand as his mouth moved onto her right breast, his breath hot and ragged through the thin material of her shirtwaist. "Moses, *stop* it."

His teeth captured her nipple, which to her shame had distended beneath the cloth, and tugged it. How could she be the least bit excited when he'd just grievously insulted her?

"Would you use force on me, then, Moses Marks?" she asked hotly to disguise the fact that he could cast aspersions on her faithfulness one moment and still render her all too willing to grant him unlimited access to her body the next.

Moses went still against her. Releasing her wrists, he stepped back, allowing a small gap between their bodies. Nell's hands dropped limply to her sides. Then she pushed him aside, abruptly furious. "How dare you?" she snapped. "First you treat me like I'm a prig, and now you think I'm having an affair with my best friend's newly wedded husband?" Her voice rose incredulously. "And what part of 'confidential' do you fail to understand?"

Shit. Put like that, it sounded all kinds of muddled up. But Moses was still aroused and mortified by his treatment of her. At the same time, he wished like hell he'd pushed matters even further. And while he knew he should apologize, instead his voice emerged coated with frost. "Whose secret are you keeping, Nell? It's sure not mine. Is it Murdock's?" He thought about it a moment. "Hattie's?" It was a stab in the dark, but the sudden stillness on Nell's pretty face told him he'd hit his target. "It's Hattie's?"

"What difference does it make?" Nell snapped back irritably. "A confidence is a confidence. Or perhaps you only honor those given to you by certain people." Nell immediately regretted her snide tone of voice. She knew perfectly well what it would mean to Moses to believe himself excluded from Hattie's confidence. A large part of their problems on his side had originally stemmed from his conviction that she had usurped his place as Hattie's best friend. Nell felt a sudden gaping divide crack open between them, leaving the ground beneath her feet feeling far too shaky.

"Hattie has a problem," Moses said in a tone so carefully neutral it made the small hairs on the back of Nell's neck stand up, "and you don't think I can be trusted with it, am I correct?"

"No," she said, wishing desperately she could fully explain. "Let me try to make you understand."

"Oh, I think I understand very well," he interrupted in that appalling might-as-well-be-a-stranger voice. He took her arm in a gentle grasp and ushered her to the livery door. "You best run along now," he murmured distantly. "I need to get back to work."

And the next thing she knew, Nell was outside the livery, staring miserably at the door Moses closed in her face.

39

J AKE WENT TO Doc first, who shared his information and suggested Jake talk to Sheriff Jacobson. For not only had the lawman kept Hattie's rape quiet; he'd maintained his own surveillance on Lord's house whenever possible.

It was a good lead; the sheriff shared a fat folder of notes. An interesting one was the observation that Lord's chambermaids changed far more frequently than most—and none had been hired locally from as far back as aught-six, when Jacobson had begun watching the house. Jake had no idea what he anticipated happening when he, too, began keeping an eye on the house. All the same, day after day Jake watched the indoor help as they entered and exited through the back door. Unfortunately, he didn't see anyone who seemed a likely prospect for what he had in mind.

It wasn't easy to keep his eye on the house and remain inconspicuous. He'd lived in this town his entire life, and everyone knew his name, business, and antecedents pretty much back to when the earth's crust cooled. Even so, Jake managed to spend several undetected hours each day viewing the back door. Having found a break in the laurel hedge of a neighboring yard, he slipped in early, sat as still as the cramped position allowed, then slipped out again when the coast was clear. That was a week ago, and he was at his post again, legs pulled to his chest and his chin on his knees, watching the house and doing his best to ignore the moisture

seeping into the seat of his Levi's as he sat on the damp ground. He occupied himself thinking of Hattie.

He needed to find something—*anything*—else, for thoughts of his
wife made him brood. But knowing it and doing something about it were
two different matters, and as usual when he was alone, his thoughts
turned to her. The light had gone out in her the past ten days. She was like
a ghost of her former self. As long as he had known Hattie, the enduring
quality that had drawn his fascinated attention time and again—from
the day she first came to Mattawa to today—was her exuberance. She was
more alive than anyone he'd ever met, more passionate in every respect,
whether laughing, raging, or teaching. Her love burned hotter; her hatred
was worlds fiercer.

When Jake pictured her at any age, his first image wasn't her curvy
figure, tempting as it was. It was Hattie's vivid coloring, her expressive
face. Jake loved her flushed cheeks and apricot freckles, her mobile rosy
lips and white teeth, her golden-brown eyes and that gloriously fiery, un-
tamable hair. He loved her enthusiasms and convictions.

It was as if God said, *This child has a zest for life; let it shine like a beacon for all to see.* He bestowed that face upon her as a badge of her spirit,
and her true nature simply could not be disguised—even when she returned to Mattawa a quieter, more mature edition of herself. She might
be able to camouflage her passion with some success, but she sure as hell
couldn't bury it entirely. It had cropped up again and again, with her
students, with their parents, and with a hundred and one enthusiasms she
couldn't control. Her spirit never diminished. Until now.

Jake dug his chin into his kneecap. Her cheeks were pale these days,
her head bowed. He'd been avoiding her, but he had been around enough
to recognize that when he looked at her, all he saw was the top of her
head. The life seemed to have seeped out of her that night in the stable
when the identity of her rapist exploded in his consciousness—and only
now did he think to wonder if his wife's apathy might be rooted in something besides a bitter distaste for him.

For the first time since realizing what he'd done, it occurred to Jake to wonder why the hell she had married him in the first place. Why she'd made love to him with unbridled responsiveness. Yeah, she'd been practically dragged to the altar. But on their wedding night, despite fearing an act he'd mandated in his arrogance would be part of their lives, Hattie had let him love her without a struggle. And, oh God, her response nearly drove him to his knees. She hadn't acted like she hated him that night—or any since then.

Her behavior had been as generous and giving as that of a woman in love.

A sudden, desperate need to talk to her exploded in his mind. Why hadn't he *talked* to her? Jake slowly straightened his legs, grimacing at the stiffness in his knees. He couldn't see past his own agonized guilt once he discovered what he'd done by sending her to Roger. Yet, what he'd just discovered, Hattie had known all along. And she'd married him anyway.

Oh, hell, yeah. They definitely needed to talk.

He was inching out of his cramped cave in the hedge when the back door opened and a young woman stepped out. Jake pulled his legs back in, waiting for her to pass. He glanced at her without interest, anxious to get home to his wife. Then his gaze sharpened and he froze.

Good God Almighty. She was a pale imitation of Hattie. Her body wasn't as lush, her hair not as brilliantly red. But there was something reminiscent of his wife. And Jake knew.

This was it. What he'd been looking for. Jake eased out of the laurel. Casting a swift look around, he winged a quick prayer to pass unobserved as he edged along the perimeter of Lord's yard. He fell into step behind the woman, keeping half a block between them. Two blocks from the house, he began to shorten the distance.

When he touched her arm, she jumped and dropped her basket. She whirled to face him, one pale hand, framed by a stark white cuff, flying to the matching collar on her black dress. "Oh, sir! You frightened me."

"I'm sorry," he said softly. He leaned down and retrieved her basket, offering it to her. Then he hesitated, unsure how to proceed, and the young woman's pale blue eyes narrowed warily. In their depths, Jake saw a frail vestige of a feistiness that perhaps hadn't yet been entirely beaten out of the young woman. Encouraged, he said with the utmost gentleness, "I know what Roger Lord is doing to you."

Eyes filling with horror, she backed away. "I have no idea what you're talking about."

"Yes, you do. I want to help."

"You cannot." She began to walk once again.

"Yes," he replied gently to her stiff profile as he fell into step beside her, "I can. With your help, I can put the man behind bars where he belongs. Where he can never harm you again."

She stopped walking and turned to face him. "How?"

"By charging him with rape."

Her tear-filled eyes grew enormous. "Are you insane?" she whispered. "I'd be ruined."

"Is that worse than allowing him to continue doing what he's doing to you?" he snapped impatiently . . . then touched her arm in contrition. "I'm sorry," he said. "That was unfair. Of course, it's a valid concern. Do you have a family?"

"No."

"More than anything I wish I could promise it would be easy," he said slowly. "But I can't. You would have to press charges and that means a trial. The defense will try to make you look like a harlot in order to save Lord's worthless hide. But it seems to me nothing can be as painful as what he's getting away with now. And one thing I can promise you is a place with a good family in Seattle or San Francisco afterward. Somewhere where no one will ever have to know a thing about you." He looked down at her in silence for several moments while she appeared to think over his proposal. "Please," he finally said. "Help me lock this sick bastard away. I guarantee you can then move on to a good position."

She glanced up and down the quiet street. She shifted the basket from her right arm to her left, then straightened her cuffs. She looked down at the dust coating her serviceable shoes. Then raised her eyes to Jake. And whispered, "What do I have to do?"

HER NAME WAS Opal Jeffries and she was nineteen years old. She had been in service for three years as a parlormaid, and until her employment with Roger Lord began three weeks ago, she'd never minded the work, for it was the only life she'd ever known.

Jake asked her how she had come to be in Lord's employ.

"He hired me away from the Conleys after coming to dinner one night. He seemed like such a gentleman and he offered better wages than I ever got," she explained. "I had no idea how wicked-mean he could be."

"I know this is painful, Opal," Jake said gently, looking at her across the scarred desk in Sheriff Jacobson's office. "But I need to ask. Were you a virgin when you began your employment with Lord?"

"Yes, sir!" she replied in red-faced indignation. "That was the other reason I accepted his offer, because of the Conleys' son, Adam. When he came home from college this summer he began cornering me in the up-stairs hallway, makin' improper suggestions. Tryin' to play fast and loose with my virtue." Her chin tilted up proudly. "I'm a good girl, Mr. Murdock, Sheriff Jacobson. I thought Mr. Lord's offer was the perfect solution to my problem." Her bark of laughter held no amusement, for the irony was not lost on anyone in Jacobson's cramped office.

The next half hour was extremely painful. Topics of a sexual nature were never discussed between men and any woman with the least bit of breeding—and spinsters in particular were protected from the baser facts of life. But given the nature of the crime they planned to charge Lord with, it was imperative the men ask Opal questions so excruciatingly intimate that all three of them were either red as autumn leaves or pale as death by the end of the interview.

"What do you think?" Sheriff Jacobson asked Jake at its conclusion. "Y'have enough to convict him?"

"I hope so." Jake raked his hand through his hair. "You're articulate," he said to Opal. "I feel you'll make a very convincing witness. Cases of this nature are rare, though, and with the defense trying to make you look bad in the eyes of all-male jurors, they can be tricky." He reached across the table and patted her hand. "I'm not trying to minimize what Lord's done to you, but a bloodstained sheet or photographs of bruises would help our case. Catching him in the act is the only sure guarantee of a conviction, but I will do my utmost to put him away. With those odds, are you still willing to press charges?"

For several silent moments, Opal stared down at her lap, where her knuckles stood white from the death grip she had on her tightly inter-laced fingers. But when she looked up, determination burned in the depths of her pale-blue eyes. "What if we caught him in the act?"

Sheriff Jacobson regarded her with intense interest, but Jake was ap-palled. "What?"

"What if I went back there? You don't understand how arrogant he is, Mr. Murdock. If I locked myself in my room and refused to go to him, he would be furious. He thinks it's his God-given right to hurt me. I don't know how many times I heard him say"—she gagged suddenly, then re-covered herself—" 'This'll teach you your rightful place.' " There was a sudden harshness in her voice, which just for an instant reflected the vi-ciousness of her attacker.

"Stop right there," Jake said. "It's too dangerous. God knows how many people saw you with me today or saw the two of us come in here."

"It doesn't matter, Mr. Murdock. He truly believes he's above the law. If I refused to come out of my room, he would likely break the door down and do whatever he wanted to do."

"No," Jake said with flat finality.

"Hold on there a second, son," Sheriff Jacobson interrupted, straight-ening in his wooden chair. "Miss Jeffries has a point. If we rig up a simple alarm, we could be in her room before he has a chance to hurt her. Cans on a string, tied to the bedpost and lowered out the window, would do the trick. One tug and we'd hear the clatter."

"Yeah? And what if he gets to her before she ever gets to her room? What if he's waiting for her at the kitchen door, demanding why she was seen talking to me?"

Opal looked at him as if he were crazy. "Oh no, sir, he would *never* do that—not for any reason. He's much too high-and-mighty to ever be caught dead in a servants' space."

"Then he won't come to your room either."

"That's different, sir. To have me refuse his demand—" She hitched a shoulder. "It will drive him mad."

"He's already insane. That's exactly what scares me," Jake said glumly.

But no matter what his objections, Opal Jeffries was determined to go through with her plan. "I will not put myself through the shame of a public trial if at the end of it there is only the smallest chance he'll be put away," she said adamantly. "Please, Mr. Murdock. I want to be certain-sure the bastard goes to jail. I want him to be ruined. Just like he ruined me."

Leaving Opal describing to the sheriff the location of her room in relation to the rest of the floor plan in Roger's house, Jake went down the street to Norton's Mercantile. He purchased two cow bells and a ball of sturdy twine and, once back in the jailhouse, fashioned a crude alarm with them and placed it in the bottom of Opal's basket. They covered it with a linen napkin from Jacobson's lunch tray and Opal left to make the purchases she'd been sent to town to acquire.

Jake retrieved his automobile and drove it to the avenue two streets behind Lord's residence. Parking on a cross street, he strode a block north, then cut through three backyards to reach his post in the laurel hedge.

Opal arrived a short while later, unobtrusively tailed by the sheriff. She disappeared through the back door, and Jacobson found himself a spot where he, too, could observe the back of the residence. A short while after she entered the house, they saw an attic window slide open. Opal's face appeared momentarily in the opening and then the cowbells were slowly lowered. They tinkled faintly as she played out the twine, but after a few moments they stilled. The window was lowered until it was nearly shut. Then, the only thing they could do was wait.

Jake and the sheriff knew they might have to wait hours, for Opal warned them that Lord only called for her in the evening. Yet Jake hadn't fully understood just how slowly time could stretch in a situation like this. Shadows crept across the length of the yard, and the summer heat gave way to cool twilight.

It felt like it had been dark for hours when Jake started finding it difficult keeping his eyes open. He willed himself to stay alert, but time and again he dozed off, only to jerk awake when his chin touched his chest. Time crawled with a pace that made garden snails look like speed demons. And checking his timepiece every few minutes, he learned, didn't help.

Suddenly the bells began to clamor, wrenching Jake out of his doze. He scrambled out of the hedge and tried to stand, but his knees buckled from maintaining the same posture for several hours. Dragging himself to his feet, he hobbled toward the back door as fast as he could. Sheriff Jacobson was there before him.

Both men were prepared to kick the door in but discovered it wasn't necessary; the portal swung open when Sheriff Jacobson turned the handle. The cook, sitting at the table with her hands over her ears, gaped at the two men barreling through the door. No one said a word as Jake and the sheriff raced up the back stairs.

Even without the directions Opal had given them, they would've handily located her room. She was screaming at the top of her lungs and they followed the sound. They came to an opened door splintered off its hinges, just as she had predicted, and burst into the room.

For an instant, Jake thought they were too late. Opal was on her back on the bed, her face marked where Lord had obviously struck her. The top of her dress hung in tatters, its skirt thrown up to her waist. Then he saw that although Lord's pants pooled around his ankles, Opal was fighting like a wildcat and Lord had yet to complete his attack.

Sheriff Jacobson reached the bed first. Wrapping a beefy arm around Roger Lord's neck, he hauled him roughly off Opal's body. "Pull your pants up, you sick sonovabitch," he bit out. "You're under arrest."

Jake crossed to Opal. "Are you all right?"

"Yes," she said shakily. Then burst into tears.

He wrapped her in the bedspread and stroked her hair until she calmed. "It's all right now," he murmured. "It's all over. Because of your bravery that vermin will never hurt you or another woman again."

Sheriff Jacobson prepared to lead his prisoner from the room, but Jake requested that he wait for just one moment. As soon as Opal calmed, he stood and crossed to stand in front of Lord.

Roger returned his contemptuous look with a supercilious stare of his own . . . until the sheriff casually averted his head and Jake abruptly jerked his knee up, ramming it into Lord's crotch. Roger's expression then went from superior to sick as he sagged in the sheriff's grasp, retching and gagging. Jacobson stared out the window, whistling softly.

"I'll take Opal to my mother," Jake murmured. Jacobson nodded and led his stumbling prisoner away. Instructing Opal to change and pack, Jake then went to find a telephone. Central connected him with his party, and Doc answered on the second ring.

Swiftly, Jake asked him to meet him at his mother's house with his camera and his black bag, promising he'd explain the situation in full at that time. Then he hung up, collected Opal, and drove her to Augusta's.

It was late by the time he drove up the ranch road after much explaining, then seeing Opal settled at his mother's. Yet Jake felt optimistic for the first time in more than two weeks. He was convinced Lord would ultimately get what he deserved. Then maybe all their lives could get back to normal. He was anxious to talk to Hattie.

The house was dark when he let himself in. Racing up the stairs two at a time, Jake burst into their bedroom. He skidded to a halt just inside the door. The room was empty, his wife not there as he'd expected. Where the hell could she be at this time of night? Feeling a creeping unease, he glanced over at the open closet doors as he started to back out of the room. And their significance slowly sank in.

Every one of Hattie's hangers was empty.

40

JAKE TORE OPEN all the drawers of the wardrobe. Half of them were empty, and those that weren't held his clothing. All of Hattie's were gone.

Throwing back his head, he roared his incensed pain at the ceiling. Then, sucking in a deep breath, he held it a moment, then expelled it with such force his lungs felt ready to collapse. Standing in their bedroom, gripping the back of his neck with clammy fingers as he fought down the panic trying to battle its way out of his chest like an enraged beast, he stared numbly at the empty drawers he'd yanked open. Jesus, where could she have gone?

And how the hell did she get there? Maybe that was where he should begin. He'd check the stables to see if Belle was there.

Hattie, in the spare room across the hall, listened to the commotion in their bedroom, then the thunder of Jake's footsteps as he ran down the stairs swearing a blue streak. A moment later she jolted at the slamming of the front door. It sounded as if he was aggravated.

Good. She was livid herself, and she hoped he went crazy. He deserved nothing less.

She'd been doing a slow burn ever since Nell's visit. How dare Jake discuss her attack with others when he hadn't said more than ten words to his *wife* in darn near two weeks? He couldn't even look at her, yet Nell had innocently informed her he'd been running around asking questions of Nell, Aunt Augusta, Doc, and who knew who else?

Discovering that Jake knew the identity of Hattie's rapist, Nell had been concerned about Hattie's state of mind. After all, Nell knew how adamantly opposed Hattie was to Jake's learning the precise thing he had somehow figured out. So, she had come to lend Hattie moral support.

Hattie appreciated Nell's company more than she could say. She hadn't been off the ranch in ten long days, not even to go to church, and not a soul had been by to visit. Just having her friend treat her normally after Jake's ignoring her was such a welcome relief.

For the first time since the awful night Jake discovered the identity of her defiler, Hattie felt as if she'd finally stopped growing invisible. Nell had looked her in the eye and touched her several times in the course of their conversation. The human contact after what felt like a too-long life-time had been more comforting to Hattie than water after a week in the desert.

She wished she had a whole lot less stupid pride. Maybe then she could have confessed how horridly interminable the dog-years-feeling days had been. But she was a self-sabotaging idiot who had merely told Nell that matters were very uncomfortable between herself and Jake—but they were working through their problems. What a bald-faced liar she was turning into, and it was All. Jake's. Fault!

It was his fault, as well, that she hadn't begged Nell to stay the moment her friend started gathering her things to head back to Augusta's. As a result, all Hattie's rage, which had relaxed the worst of its grip under Nell's calming influence, promptly returned. And the later the hour with no sign of Jake, the more furious she became. Finally, unable to sit still, she went up to their room and moved her belongings to the room across the hall. How *dare* he treat her this way?

The more Hattie thought about it, the more belligerent she felt. To think she had spent ten endless days feeling the most degrading shame over something that was the result of Jake's actions in the first place! Well, no more. She was through hanging her head.

Now, sitting in the middle of the bed, anxiously gripping her hands together and listening to the sudden silence left by his departure, Hattie thought self-righteously that Jake was pretty darn lucky he didn't know where she was tonight. Because if she had to confront him right now, she would likely wring his neck. She bounced up off the bed and crossed to the dresser. Picking up her silver-backed brush, she tugged it roughly through her hair once, twice, three times. Then she threw the brush back down on the tabletop. Leaning into the mirror, she examined her face.

She looked rather horrid. Scowling, she stood tapping her foot in indecision. Then she yanked out the slipper chair and sat with a flounce, her arms crossed militantly beneath her breasts, her toes manically clenching and flexing. Lifting the concealing hem of her nightgown, she leaned over to watch her feet's baffling antics. Dropping her hem in disgust, she jumped up again and commenced pacing.

The front door slammed shut and footsteps thundered up the stairs and down the hall, stopping in front of her room. Hattie jerked to a halt and stared at the locked door separating her from her husband.

Jake rattled the handle, and when it didn't budge he pounded on the door. "Hattie!" he bellowed. "Open the damn door. I know you're in there."

No, he didn't. How could he?

As if she'd asked him, he said impatiently, "Open up! I saw your light from the yard."

Well, rats. She hadn't considered that. "Go away!"

"Open the goddamn door," he roared, "before I break it down!"

"Well, if that isn't just like a man to settle his disagreements by brute strength," she muttered. She didn't think he'd heard her, but he must have, for there was a moment's silence.

"C'mon, Big-eyes," he finally said in a calmer voice. "Open up. We need to talk."

Of all the words he could have chosen, those were the most unfortunate. "Talk?" She slammed back the bolt and ripped the door open. They were suddenly face-to-face, Jake mere inches away. "You want to *talk*? To little ole me? Mercy, this is a privilege. What happened—you run out of people in town to discuss my downfall with?"

"Huh?" He stared down into her upturned face. She glared right back at him. But when he reached out to touch her cheek, she snapped her head back and he let his hand fall to his side. "Hattie, why'd you move out of our room?"

"Oh, you noticed? Mercy, it never occurred to me it might matter to you one way or the other," she replied coolly, "or else I certainly would've been happy to inform you of my intention." Another bald-faced lie; what on earth was happening to her? "What do you care, anyway?" she challenged angrily. "You don't sleep there anymore. Why should I? And don't change the subject, Jake Murdock. Nell told me the way you've been running around town asking everybody in sight about my rape. If you're so darn interested you should have come straight to the source. After all, I know all the ugly details someone else may have missed." She couldn't sustain her nonchalant attitude and, to her horror, felt her face twist in misery.

"Ah, baby, don't." This time he ignored her resistance and pulled her into his arms. She held herself stiffly within his embrace as he rubbed his cheek against the top of her head. "I guess I should have talked to you first, but I didn't know how. I was too ashamed."

Furious, Hattie jerked out of his arms. "How dare you!"

He looked at her in puzzlement. "How dare I what?"

"How dare you be ashamed of me! I—"

"What?" He closed the distance between them, looming over her. "Now, wait a damn minute, I never said—"

"No, you wait, Jacob Murdock," she demanded, poking her forefinger into the hard muscles of his chest. "I've done nothing but wait for ten long days! I have been skulking around this big old house like a thief in the night, shamed to my bones because I knew you were so repulsed by me you couldn't even look at me anymore. Well, enough is enough."

Jake stared at her in openmouthed amazement and her rage burned a few degrees hotter. "You wanted to talk so darn bad? Well, let's talk, then. I have several things that need saying."

Jake grabbed Hattie's finger when she showed signs of jabbing it into his chest once again and gently enclosed it in his fist. He stared down at her, at her flushed cheeks, her bright hair writhing around her in a wild tangle, her amber eyes glinting with rage between narrowed lashes. And for the first time in far too long, the tight knots of misery in his stomach loosened as he experienced the first faint stirring of hope. "Go ahead, then. Shoot."

Now that Hattie had his attention, she didn't know quite where to begin. She longed to slug him, bite him, kick him; she wanted to revile him for the wrongs he had done her: for sending her to Roger, for deserting their bed and making her feel like a harlot, for failing to ask her what he felt free enough to ask everyone else in town. But mostly for not loving her with the same desperation with which she loved him.

Then, abruptly, her rage abandoned her and she was left with only her unrelenting honesty and a grinding hurt deep in her breast. "I don't understand you," she whispered, staring at his sun-browned hand, feeling its texture, hard as saddle leather, gripping her captured finger. She'd grown accustomed to seeing him in work clothes, so the contrast between his work-roughened hands and his civilized apparel was disconcerting. She tugged experimentally and he tightened his grip for an instant before loosening it to let her finger slide free.

Hattie took a step back and looked at him as though he were an exotic species she had never come across before. "You knew I wasn't a virgin when we married and it never appeared to bother you very much," she said in honest bafflement. "I mean, I never expected you to love me the way you did Jane-Ellen, 'cause I'm not pure and good the way she was, but—"

Jake stiffened and took a step forward, but Hattie backed away, her hands balled into fists, her knuckles pressed into her diaphragm as though to control a physical pain. Tipping her head back, she met his undoubtedly turbulent stare with unconscious pride. "But I was good enough to make love to! Several times a day, every darn day! Why did that all change once you had a name to put to the man who'd had me before you? Why, Jake? If it's a question of virtue, you knew I was a sinner when you married me. What was suddenly so different you had to turn away like I was diseased?"

"Stop!" Jake's arm snaked out and hooked an elbow around the back of her neck, his hand wrapped around to grip her jaw, tilting her face up, arching her neck. She stared at him with wide, hurt eyes and he felt his own fill with tears of remorse. "Please . . . stop," he whispered hoarsely, then lowered his head and kissed her with hot intent.

As always when Jake touched her, all else ceased to matter. Hattie couldn't sustain her anger, her hurt. She kissed him back.

Abruptly releasing her, he turned away, dashing his knuckles over his eyes before plowing his fingers through his hair. He looked at her over his shoulder. "It wasn't you who was unclean," he said in a low, raw voice. "It was me. I was never ashamed of you; do you hear me? *Never.* I was sick-to-my-soul ashamed of me!" He turned to face her fully. "How could I look at you once I knew what I'd done? How could I ever touch you again? Christ, you're so sweet and pure and giving, and I turned you over to that brutalizing bastard just the way you once told me you had been: on a silver platter!"

Mouth ajar, Hattie stared at him, mentally scrambling to rearrange everything she'd believed to be true to absorb what he just said. With each fresh beat, her heart began to grow lighter. Why, it had never occurred to her— "Yes, you did," she agreed slowly. "And for nearly two years I hated you for it, Jacob."

He flinched and she slowly approached, reaching out to stroke a tentative hand down his jacket sleeve. "But you know what I couldn't forget?" she asked as their eyes met. "I couldn't forget the feelings you made me feel the first time you kissed me—the first time you touched me the way a man should touch a woman. And I understood for the first time that was how it was supposed to be when a man and a woman were together like that. Not hurtful or degrading or ugly, the way Roger made it, but rather sort of anxious and eager, a feeling so out of control and wonderful it makes you want more, to feel even better. Between Nell's friendship and remembering those feelings, I began to heal." She walked her fingers up his arm and touched the soft-skinned crease in his cheek with gentle fingertips. "I wish more than anything you had been the one to take my virginity."

His eyes were dark with pain. "So do I, Hattie-girl."

"But you weren't, Jake, and it's over. We can't change the past. I will never give you the details of that night, Jacob, or even talk about it if I can help it. But I won't throw it in your face for the rest of our lives, either. I love you, you know, and I have done so longer and more fiercely than I ever hated you. I don't know if you can ever love me the way you did Jane-Ellen, but—"

Jake cut her words off midstream when he swooped in and swept her off her feet. He tossed her slightly, then caught her again, holding her high against his chest as he carried her across the hall to their bedroom, where he dropped her in a billow of nightgown on the bed. "Let's get something straight," he said, staring down at her. Holding her gaze, he stripped off his celluloid collar and cuffs and threw them in the general direction of the dressing table. Reaching for the buttons on his shirt, he stated, "I love you, Hattie. More than I have ever loved anyone in my life. More than this ranch, more than the air I breathe, I love you."

He pulled his shirt off and kicked off his shoes, then dropped onto the bed beside her. Scooting back until he was leaning against the head-board, he reached for his wife, pulling her into his arms. "I loved Jane-Ellen when we got married, but it was more of a young man's fancy than the love of a mature man. I was mostly in love with the idea of getting her into bed."

Hattie blushed, and tucking his chin to gaze down into her beloved face, he kissed her forehead. "We didn't have much in common, me and Jane-Ellen; not like you and I do. You know she didn't like the ranch very much except for the house. She flat-out hated sex."

When his wife looked up at him in amazement, he half smiled and pressed her cheek to rest against the upper curve of his chest. Rubbing his chin against the top of her head, he gazed blindly across the room. "I felt like a polecat whenever I forced myself on her. She never wanted me." He tucked his chin again in order to see Hattie's face. "Remember being embarrassed on our wedding night because you were wet when I touched you?" She nodded, cheeks rosy with what he feared was remembered mortification. He smoothed tendrils away from her face.

"I thought your body getting ready, you being wet for me, was the most miraculous thing ever, Hattie. You wanted me as much as I wanted you, even after having been abused in the worst way. I could have died right then a happy man. Jane-Ellen was always dry, and she thought anything I tried to do to rectify the situation was disgusting, so sex for her was uncomfortable at best. I know you think I was a bounder for going to Mamie Parker's house when I was married to her. I tried to remain faithful, Hattie—I swear I did. But after several years of Jane-Ellen's rejection, I just wanted to touch someone that way and not feel like a fiend."

He rubbed his thumb over the fullness of Hattie's bottom lip for a moment. Then his hand dropped to her upper arm and stroked it absently through the cotton of her gown as he stared at the ceiling. "After she died and you had gone away, I found myself missing you far more than I missed her. I tried not to, baby, but I did. Even though I was consumed with guilt every time I did so, I kept thinking of that night in your room. I cared for her right up till the end but had long ago stopped loving her the way a man should love his wife."

Studying Jake, it was clear to Hattie the admission still had the power to hurt him. She rubbed her hand comfortingly over the smooth skin of his chest and pressed a kiss into his warm throat. "I love you, Jake."

"Ah, God, I love you, Hattie. I love you so damn much."

"And . . . you don't think me shamefully loose because I like the bedroom things we do?"

"Ah, sweetheart, *no*. When I touch you and see you're lovin' it—it makes me feel ten feet tall. But it's not just in bed I love you, Big-eyes. More than anything else, these past couple weeks, I've missed this." He waved a hand to indicate the two of them. "Holding you, talking to you. I love the way we laugh together and enjoy the same things and never run out of stuff to say. I love that we can be quiet together, and that you love the ranch as much as I do. I even love the fact we can fight. You are the most exciting woman I have ever known, Hattie Murdock, and I am so damn proud you're my wife."

"I guess I can take that to mean you won't be needing the services of Mamie Parker's establishment ever again then?" She just wanted to make absolutely sure.

"Baby, I haven't visited any of her girls since the day I heard you were coming home."

"You haven't?"

"Hell, no. Since you seem to have this knack for discovering my transgressions, and considering I had gone to a whole lotta trouble to get you back to Mattawa in the first place, I wasn't about to louse it up playing fast and loose with the town whores. Besides, they're pale shadows next to you."

Hattie sat up. "What do you mean, you went to a whole lotta trouble? Wasn't it Aurelia Donaldson who . . . ?"

"Oh, yeah, it was. Did I say me? I meant Aurelia." But his grin was cocky and clearly knew more than it was saying.

She shoved his shoulder, but he just tilted one corner of his grin at her. Raised an eyebrow. "Jake Murdock!" *Tell me,* her tone demanded.

Jake wrapped one arm across her back, clamped the other over the backs of her thighs just below her bottom, and rolled them over until she was sprawled out on top of him. Hattie stared down at him as he smoothed back her hair, spit out a curly strand that fell across his lips, and explained his part in getting her back to Mattawa.

Hattie couldn't help preening a little. "So, you were gonna marry me all along?"

"Not to rain on your parade," he replied dryly, "but I didn't know what I was going to do. Just knew I had to get you back home."

"You were gonna marry me." She grinned at him confidently.

Jake's eyes darkened. Looping her hair over one shoulder, he stroked her cheek with the backs of his fingers. "I love you, Big-eyes." Raising his head, he kissed her sweetly.

Hattie kissed him back. But when his head dropped back she nervously smoothed his left eyebrow with the pad of her thumb. "Jake? What have you been doing in town every day?"

"What?" he asked distractedly. Then, as her question sank in, he said in an entirely different tone, "Christ! I never told you." Sitting up, he dumped her on the mattress beside him and stared into her startled face. "I can't believe I forgot to tell you. Sheriff Jacobson arrested Roger Lord tonight. Charged him with rape and assault. We're gonna put that bastard away."

Clutching his bare biceps, Hattie hauled herself upright. "What?" she whispered and listened in numb astonishment as Jake told her everything that had transpired today.

"That poor girl," she said when he finished. "How incredibly brave to put herself in such peril to catch him in the act!"

"Yes, she was extremely brave. I have to admit, I wasn't immediately all for it. Too many things could've gone wrong."

"Thank goodness they didn't."

"Amen. The housekeeper or cook, or whoever the hell she was, just sat there in the kitchen with her hands over her ears to drown out Opal's screams. I can't understand that kind of behavior, Hattie. There must have been other servants in the house as well. Why did no one ever try to help her?"

Hattie remembered the racket she too had made and how no one had come then, either. "He must have a financial hold on his help," she replied slowly. "I can't imagine any other reason one would ignore someone in such distress." She started to rise from the bed, but Jake gripped her forearm, staying her.

"Where do you think you're going?"

"Jacob, let me up." She pried at his fingers. When he refused to unhand her, she raised her gaze to meet his squarely. "I have to go to her," she pleaded. "Don't you see? I am possibly the only one who fully understands what she's been through and what she's feeling."

"Honey, look at the time. Mother and Mirabel were putting Opal to bed when I left. Let her rest, Big-eyes; she needs it. Tomorrow I'll take you to see her."

Glancing at the clock, Hattie subsided. "You're right," she conceded. "But first thing in the morning, Jacob—"

"First thing in the morning," he agreed. "Well, second thing," he amended. "Right after you move all your belongings back in here where they belong."

"Very well. But the minute we're done with that."

He rolled onto his side facing her, then pushed up on an elbow. Hattie stared into his hazel eyes as he reached out his right hand to slip free the top button on her nightgown. "Right now, we have some catching up to do," he murmured, freeing another button.

"Do we?" Stroking her hand down his stomach, she delighted in his muscles clenching beneath her touch. "Does this 'catching up' possibly involve the use of your pride and joy?"

"My pride and—what?" He was baffled for an instant, then threw back his head and roared with laughter. "Yes, ma'am." His grin was white, quirky, and full of wicked promise. "I have very definite ideas on utilizing the old pride and joy."

"Ooh." She wiggled slightly in anticipation. "What, exactly, are you planning?"

Jake leered at her. "The unspeakable, my big-eyed, big-tits, red-haired beauty." He finished unbuttoning the gown and slid it off her shoulders, easing it to her waist. Hands flat on the mattress on either side of her, he pushed up until he loomed over her prone, half-clad body. He dipped his head to kiss the upper slope of one breast, devoting undivided attention to the task. Then pausing mid-lick, he locked his gaze with hers. "Trust me," he murmured. "You're gonna love it."

41

HATTIE HESITATED OUTSIDE the door of her old bedroom, where Opal Jeffries was installed. She bit her lip, unexpectedly nervous. Did she have the right to force her company on the as-yet-unknown young woman, whether it was to commiserate, offer understanding, or anything else? After all, the girl on the other side of the door would be doing what Hattie had lacked the nerve to do herself: reveal the most private, degrading moments of her life in a public trial to send Roger Lord to prison.

All the same, Hattie hoped she could offer the girl a measure of comfort, if only knowing she wasn't alone in this untenable situation. Hattie took a deep breath and tapped on the door.

It opened slowly and the young woman in the opening eyed her warily. *Now what?* her expression said as she took in Hattie's apparel, which was unadorned but of obvious quality.

"Opal?" Hattie smiled gently. "My name is Hattie Murdock. I'm Jake's wife."

"Oh!" Some of the wariness faded from Opal's eyes. She bobbed a quick curtsey.

"May I come in and talk to you for a few moments?"

Opal stood back shyly and gestured for Hattie to come into the room.

"Mrs. Murdock said this was your room," the girl said hesitantly. "I hope you don't mind my staying here."

"On the contrary," Hattie replied, "I'm honored." She looked around her old room, wondering how to proceed.

"Your husband was very kind to me," Opal said softly, and Hattie discerned the faintest trace of hero worship in her eyes.

"In a way," Hattie said slowly, "he's what I want to talk to you about."

The wariness returned, joined by incipient hostility. "You don't want him to take the case?"

"No! I mean yes, I do. Oh criminy, I'm bungling this badly." Hattie drew a deep breath. "I want to say I'm sorry for what Roger Lord did to you. I think what you did last night and your willingness to testify is inexpressibly brave. I understand how you feel and—"

"Excuse me, ma'am," Opal interrupted stiffly, "but you don't have the first idea how I feel." Ingrained servility be damned, she thought, looking around the beautiful bedroom. Who did this expensively dressed, well-groomed, rich woman think she was kidding? She'd likely been protected her entire life. In a pig's eye, she understood.

"I know exactly how you feel," Hattie replied with quiet vehemence. Her nails dug into her palms against the admission she was about to make. Discovering she was trembling, she drew a deep breath, then said, "Roger Lord raped me too."

Shocked speechless, Opal sat abruptly on the edge of the bed. Hattie sat beside her and plucked Opal's hand off her lap to hold in her own. She turned so they were face-to-face.

"I do understand," Hattie insisted quietly. "After he attacked me, I felt a shame so crippling I wanted to hide forever. It didn't matter what he'd done to me was not my fault or that I had no way of preventing it." Holding Opal's gaze, she continued. "I know Roger Lord enjoys inflicting pain, and I know the degrading helplessness of not being able to keep him from seeing how successful he is. I know how terrifying it is when the born confidence of thinking nothing horrible can happen to you is ripped away."

Opal was squeezing the blood from Hattie's fingertips as she nodded agreement, her eyes wide. "Yes," she whispered hoarsely. *"Yes."*

"I admire your courage tremendously, Opal," Hattie said fervently. "What you did last night was so brave. And for you to willingly face a trial . . ." Her voice trailed away momentarily and she looked down at their clasped hands. Finally, she raised her eyes to meet Opal's. "Doc Fielding and Aunt Augusta decided not to press charges in the interest of saving my reputation, and I was glad. I thought I would die if the people in this town knew what happened to me—if Jake knew. It shames me that you're willing to face the scandal I wasn't, when you might never have been in this position had I half your courage."

"Oh no, ma'am, don't," Opal said. "Don't berate yourself. If Mr. Murdock hadn't offered to find me a position in another town where no one would ever know what happened to me, I wouldn't have done this, either."

"Nevertheless, you're very brave."

"I'm scared."

Hattie stroked their joined hands with her free one. "Of course you are. Yet last night you went back to his house when you knew better than anyone what you were letting yourself in for if anything went wrong. And you're going through with the trial you know will be difficult. That's real courage."

"Were you married to Mr. Murdock when . . . ?"

"No, like you, I was a virgin. Jake and I have only been married a couple months."

"How did you ever explain . . . ?"

Hattie blushed scarlet. Good Lord, how could she put this? "We . . . uh . . . sort of anticipated our wedding night by a couple weeks, and when he asked . . ."

"You mean you wanted to do . . . that with Mr. Murdock?"

"Oh yes. That's what I meant when I said he's what I wanted to talk to you about." Hattie gently disengaged their joined hands and stood up. She paced in front of the bed for a moment, then sat again. "Opal, this may be difficult to believe, but . . . um . . . sexual congress with a man can be glorious. I want you to know that. Most men are not like Roger Lord. Well," she added honestly, "I only have Jake to compare him to, but I'm sure they're not. Roger used—well, you know—his man part as a weapon, to inflict pain. He wanted it to be ugly and painful and shameful. Did he rant about showing you your rightful place?"

"Yes! You too?"

"Yes." Hattie stuck out her bottom lip and exhaled forcefully, sending loosened curls floating. "It was as if he were punishing me for being female and having a mind of my own, and he delighted in my fear. But a real man, a normal man, is careful, and he can use his man part to make you feel good, to . . ." Her words trailed away at the look of blank disbelief on Opal's face. She ground her teeth in frustration. She wanted Opal to know there was something besides pain to be found in the union of a man and a woman, but she didn't know the right words. It was like trying to explain color to a blind person. "You don't believe me, do you?"

About as much as I'd believe the ravings of a lunatic, Opal thought but didn't say, since above all, she knew when to hold her tongue. In her world, maids did not disagree with mistresses. She and Hattie Murdock might share a common trauma, but Opal had been a member of the serving class too long to put much faith in this momentary sisterhood. The vibrant redhead was surprisingly friendly and she talked to her as if Opal were her equal. But Mrs. Murdock was still a wealthy woman whose path ordinarily never would have crossed Opal's. Oh, they might have been present one day in the same dining room. But Mrs. Murdock would've been a guest at the table. Opal would have been serving.

Hattie suddenly shot her the biggest, most genuine smile Opal had ever seen and reached over to squeeze Opal's hand. "You think I'm crazy," she said and actually laughed. The expression on Opal's face told her she certainly did, even if class distinctions were too firmly ingrained for her to express her reservations out loud. "Of course you do," Hattie said comfortingly. "It's much too soon not to. I would have thought it crazy too, had someone said the same to me so soon after Lord assaulted me. But, please, Opal, do me a favor. Remember my words, a year or two or ten from now, whenever you're ready. Please keep it in mind that lovemaking between a man and a woman isn't always the horror Roger Lord made it. Please?"

Opal gave her a shy smile, grateful she didn't have to disagree and amazed Hattie Murdock would laugh about a maid thinking her crazy. In Opal's experience, she'd have been offended. "I'll keep it in mind," she agreed. *But don't hold your breath I'll ever believe it.*

"That's all I ask. Now, what can I do to help?"

"Help?" Opal was confused. She didn't understand this family at all. They took her into their home, put her in a beautiful room, and didn't even assign her any chores. They were beyond her experience with the socially elite.

"I know Jake will have a number of questions for you while he prepares your case. They'll be personal and embarrassing. Would it help if I sat with you? I know it's not much, but I could hold your hand."

"You would do that for me?"

"Certainly. Perhaps we should discuss moving you out to our ranch— I'll talk that over with Jake and Aunt Augusta. And of course, I'll be in court every day to lend whatever moral support I can." Hattie paused, her eyes serious. "It's so little, Opal, when you are sacrificing so much. I wish I could do more."

Opal simply shook her head in utter bafflement.

42

ROGER TURNED FROM the barred window in his cell. There was nothing to see except a bleak alley, a view he had studied too many times already. It looked particularly dismal with the summer rain dumping a fine, steady downpour. Shooting his cuffs, he straightened his waistcoat, hitched the legs of his elegant trousers just so, and sat on the edge of his cot. He smoothed back his hair and frowned at the smudge marring his otherwise impeccable shirtsleeve.

His arrest was an outrage. They couldn't keep him here—he was Roger Lord! Yet, against all reason, kept him here they had. Over-goddamn-night.

This imprisonment was unthinkable. Gentlemen weren't arrested on the word of a servant; whoever heard of such a thing? He was a man of consequence—yet, not only had the sheriff taken the word of a domestic over his; the fool had taken the word of a *female* domestic. And though Roger had said it before, it bore repeating: the incarceration of Roger Thaddeus Lord was outrageous. Men dallied with servant girls all the time. It was of no significance.

His lawyer informed him the court papers labeled it rape, as if that wasn't patently absurd. There *was* no such thing. Women were a negligible commodity whose duty was to unquestioningly obey their betters. That meant any male, even the ripe-smelling old sot sleeping in the next cell. If women had worth in the world, they would've been given the same rights as men. Clearly, man was the superior, duly dominant species. Roger merely exercised his duty to teach women their rightful place. Rape, indeed.

It was preposterous this nonsense was going to trial. Hell, the sheriff was a man. Not a well-bred one, but still a man. One would've thought he'd be smart enough to know a man of Roger's stature had no business being in jail and have immediately set him free.

There was no doubt in Roger's mind the sheriff was Murdock's minion. What else explained this monumental miscarriage of justice? Hell, Roger suspected this entire inconvenient dilemma was Murdock's doing. Well, once Roger addressed the twelve jurors, they'd recognize his incarceration for the momentous error it was and acquit him posthaste. His release, quite naturally, would be accompanied by suitable apologies he might or might not accept. Perhaps he would sue for damages. He'd definitely have Jacobson's job. Then he would destroy Jake Murdock, his bitch wife, and his snooty, interfering mother once and for all.

Meanwhile, he had to decide on his lunch. Squab, perhaps. His cook made a quite delectable squab. But, no. He wasn't in the mood. "Sheriff," he said peremptorily.

"What is it?" Jacobson asked without looking up from the papers on his desk.

"Tell my housekeeper to bring me rare roast beef for lunch. With roast potatoes, greens, bread, a flagon of wine, and perhaps"—he nodded—"yes, a caramel pudding for dessert. Oh, and I need a fresh shirt."

"Sorry, Lord," Jacobson replied, his voice lacking contrition. "You'll be eating hotel fare today, same as me."

The man in the cell adjoining Roger's sat up on his bunk. He hitched up a sagging red suspender and scratched at the gray stubble on his chin.

Roger had learned more about the old drunk than he cared to know. Apparently, Bradley—whether the old fool's first or last name, Roger neither knew nor cared—possessed an uncontrollable fondness for alcohol and therefore spent a good deal of time in the jailhouse. Particularly when the weather was foul, which was an egregious waste of taxpayers' money. If he didn't contribute to the town coffers, let him find his own accommodations when the weather turned inclement. But the evening before, when it started to rain, Jacobson went out and scooped the drunk off the street, where he'd been sleeping off a bender. Now, for the first time since being carried into his cell, Bradley showed a spark of interest in his surroundings.

"This stew day?" he asked.

"It's Friday, ain't it?" Jacobson retorted. "You've had the Buchannan's menu memorized for a good two years now." Tossing his pencil on the desk, Jacobson leaned back in his battered chair to the tune of protesting, creaking springs, and propped one foot on his desk.

"Mebbe I have," Bradley replied. "Then again, mebbe I ain't. In any event, sonny, I'll take a flagon of wine with my lunch, too."

Jacobson snorted. "Don't hold your breath, old-timer. The taxpayers' dollars don't run to wine. You'll get the usual glass of milk the hotel sends over."

Bradley jerked his chin in Roger's direction. "How come Mr. Gotrocks here gets wine with his lunch, then?"

Roger crossed to wrap his hands around the bars and regarded his neighbor with distaste. "Because I pay for it myself, you old sot," he replied impatiently.

"Did pay for it," Jacobson amended.

Roger slowly turned his head to peer down his nose at the sheriff. "What do you mean?"

Jacobson's feet hit the floor. "I mean your staff is deserting you like rats from a sinking garbage scow. They know a losing proposition when they smell one." Seeing Lord's supercilious expression, he shook his head. "You don't get it, do you? Your case stinks. I know it; your staff knows it; even your lawyer knows it from the little I've heard in there." He nodded to Lord's cell. "He doesn't want you to take the stand. Why is that, Rog?" Despite shortening Lord's name, Jacobson took care no other disrespect colored his expression. But, damn, he'd love to get the bastard to reveal something. Jacobson would really like to know how the man got away with what Jacobson was sure was a long history of abusing his female help.

"My lawyer lacks the killer instinct," Roger replied scornfully to Jacobson's question. With unshakable confidence, he added, "Once I take the stand, my case will become clear to the men of the jury."

"Oh, I agree," Jacobson murmured, not adding what the men of the jury were likely to see was an entitled, self-important snob who considered himself above the laws applying to the rest of them. "But meanwhile," he added, "you no longer have a cook to give your order to. So, unless you're willing to go hungry, I guess you'll just have to eat hotel stew with Bradley here and me."

43

THE TRIAL WAS scheduled to start tomorrow. Hattie controlled her jumpiness around family and friends, but the effort rubbed her raw. Hiding her feelings was never her strong suit.

At bedtime, she tried to avoid looking at Jake, propped against the headboard, watching her brush her hair. She didn't allow her gaze to rise above the gleam of his bare chest in the lamplight as she slid under the blankets.

He reached for her, and Hattie rolled over, curling into him. He stroked the length of her hair and she felt warm, comforted, the restlessness soothed. But when he touched her breast, she found it irritating, then painful when his hand bumped over her nipple. Reacting blindly, Hattie knocked his hand away. "Don't!" Even his lips, finding pulse points against her neck, aggravated her, and she strained away.

Jake stilled. Slowly, he opened his arms, and Hattie moved away. She felt bereft the instant his warmth no longer encased her yet knew she would testily resist any attempt he made to keep her there. Miserably confused, she turned her back. Tension strummed the darkness.

Then Jake rolled to the side of the bed and turned on the lamp. As soon as a soft pool of light illuminated the room, he turned back to Hattie and lightly stroked her shoulder. Asked gently, "What's the matter, baby?"

"Nothing," she mumbled.

Jake, too, had been on edge all day, and his temper snapped. "Bullshit," he said through gritted teeth and summarily whipped her onto her back, looming over her on stiffly locked arms. He glared down at her. "What the hell is the matter with you?"

She glared right back at him. "My bosoms hurt, all right?"

"And?"

"And what? That's it."

"If that were all it was, you would have simply said so instead of trying to knock my hand to kingdom come and giving me your back." He risked soothing her tumbled hair off her face, relaxing slightly when she accepted the comfort of his touch. "I'm sorry if I hurt you," he added softly. "But, Big-eyes, something more than sore tits bothers you and I wanna know what it is."

Sidetracked, she protested primly, "You shouldn't call them that."

"Why? No one's here but you and me—and you like it when I talk dirty."

"Jacob," she remonstrated, but while she blushed and lowered her eyes, he noticed she didn't dispute his claim.

After a moment's silence, Hattie's turbulent whiskey-colored eyes met his. "I should be on the witness stand along with Opal," she whispered fiercely.

He whistled softly through his teeth. "So that's what this is all about." He eased over onto his back, stuffed a pillow beneath his head and shoulders, and gathered her to him.

She came willingly, her temporary umbrage apparently forgotten as she rolled onto her side and propped her chin on the hand she spread against the swell of his chest. Her nightgown's skirt hitched up as she draped her nearest thigh over Jake's. "I feel so useless and cowardly," she confessed miserably. "Opal is risking everything with this trial. And I'm contributing nothing."

"That's not true." He rubbed a rough-skinned thumb over the grooves in his wife's forehead, willing them to smooth out. "I've heard Opal say a dozen times she couldn't get through this ordeal without your support. That's a fundamental fact, Hattie. You called it the night we arrested Lord: you are the only one who fully understands what Opal's been through. The rest of us grasp the trauma she's suffered, but you understand it at a gut level, because you've experienced it. It means a lot more to her than you appreciate. You have sat with her through questioning; you've held her hand. You tell me when Opal's at her breaking point and I need to back off. And just the fact you're willing to discuss your own experience with her and listen to her work through her own has helped her immensely."

"It's not enough," Hattie replied. She searched for words to make him understand but couldn't find them. After a moment's hesitation, she finally said in frustration, "Darn it, Jake, I don't know how to make you understand it is just not enough . . ."

His hands tightened on her. "You think I don't understand?" he asked, his voice suddenly gritty with suppressed savagery.

Startled, Hattie raised her head to meet his gaze. It held a febrile glitter and his tension was palpable in the muscles now solid as the house around them.

"I know about not enough!" he growled. "This trial is a prime example. Hell yes, it's bound to get dirty, but ultimately it will be a civilized process." His fingers gripped her painfully. "Well, you know what, Hattie? When I allow myself to think of what that sonovabitch did to you, I don't feel civilized! I'll prosecute the bastard with all the calm professionalism I can muster, and, baby, I promise I will put him away. But it sure as hell won't be enough! What I'd really like is to geld him like one of my horses and give you his testicles for a change purse. Maybe then I'd feel satisfied justice was finally served."

Hattie felt his body strain with the fury of his emotions, and ignoring his tightening fingers, she pressed against him, offering silent comfort.

His hands abruptly released their death grip on her flesh and he wrapped his arms around her, clasping her against his hard torso with bruising force. Jake exuded such easy self-confidence Hattie sometimes forgot he didn't display all his emotions for the world to see the way she generally did. He'd been so busy, so professionally calm and competent, overseeing the running of the ranch and preparing for the trial, that she had envied his sense of purpose. She'd failed to peek below the surface.

Now she realized there must have been a corner of his mind all along holding himself responsible for her debasement at Lord's hands. Hattie couldn't bear that he was in pain. God, she loved this man. So much. Hoping to diffuse the tension, the rage, making him so stone-hard stiff, she pressed a kiss against the warm skin of his chest. Whispered hesitantly, "Jacob?"

"Yeah?" His voice was gruff.

"Um . . . what are testicles?" She thought she knew, given the context of what he'd been saying, but she wasn't positive.

He stilled; then the awful tension keeping his body so rigid broke and he laughed loud and long. He slid a hand down her arm to wrap around her wrist, then guided her hand beneath the covers. An instant later she was cupping soft, weighty sacs in her palm. "These."

"What do you know," she marveled softly, "that's what I thought they were." She caressed him absentmindedly for a moment while she marshaled her thoughts.

"I won't allow you to blame yourself for what happened to me," she finally whispered with fierce emphasis. "No sane person could foresee the sheer wickedness in that man. We both know you were trying to keep me pure that night. And, Jake, there is every indication he would have found a way to get to me anyway. He was very determined to relieve me of my virginity."

Jake lifted her hand from his balls, brought it up to his abdomen, and pressed it there with his own. Dipping his chin, he stared at her for several moments. Her honest eyes returned his look levelly, and a knot he'd carried deep in his gut finally began to unravel.

She rubbed her cheek against his chest for an instant, then once again met his eyes. "You have done more than anyone to see some sort of justice prevails. I don't need a change purse, Jacob, and I don't want you to do eternal penance for a single bad judgment. A nice, long jail sentence will suit me just fine."

"Sweetheart, do you really want the entire town to know what happened to you?" If she needed that, if that was what it would take to put this behind them once and for all, then against his better judgment, he would agree to use her testimony.

No, by God, he probably would not. Every particle of his being rebelled at the idea of her setting herself up for the pain that would bring.

Hattie longed to say she didn't care what people said but admitted, "In my heart, I prefer nobody ever knows. But doesn't cowering behind Opal's testimony make me dishonest?"

Jake snorted. "Honey, you have never cowered a day in your life. And as for honesty ... Dammit, I'll put you on the witness stand, if that's what you want." *Man, you are such a liar,* he thought, but aloud merely added with deceptive mildness, "But I'd really rather not."

He chose his words carefully. "I admire your honesty a lot, Hattie. But you can take it to extremes. We're going to put that bastard in jail, and I hope he rots there forever. We will do that with Opal's testimony; then we'll see to it she has a chance to begin again somewhere no one will point a finger at her." He caught her chin in his hand and met her eyes. "Where does it say you owe it to the people of Mattawa to also bare one of the most private and degrading moments of your life? It's redundant, baby. Totally needless."

Hattie looked unconvinced, and Jake continued in a low voice, "If it was just my name blackened in the process it wouldn't be a problem. I could maybe even learn to live with it if it only affected you and me. I'd hate it with every fiber of my being if some righteous, so-called good woman dared sweep her skirt out of your way, but together we could ride out any scandal that ensued. Sooner or later, another would come along to take the heat off us, and the people we really care about would never condemn you for something you had no way of preventing."

He hesitated, then pulled out the biggest gun in his arsenal. "But it won't always be just you and me," he said. "Someday, Big-eyes, we're gonna have us a passel of red-haired babies. And while I don't doubt every last one will be a scrapper like their mama, I don't want our kids having to fight for acceptance like you did." His words were true, but it wasn't his immediate concern. His primary goal was to protect Hattie right here, right now.

It turned out to be an effective argument, however. "Oh God, Jake, neither do I!" Her eyes were big with horror at the very idea. "I never thought of it like that, but no one knows better than I what it's like to be different in this town. No child should ever have to be called upon to defend his mama's name."

She thought of all the ways a child's life could be made miserable and lifted troubled eyes to her husband. "I'd be crushed if someone hurt a child of mine for any reason. But to do so just to register disapproval of me?" Her eyes lit with militant fire. "I'd want to slaughter them. No one gets to undervalue our babies . . . not for any reason!"

Jake grinned at her vehemence. Good. Maybe now she could accept some well-earned protection against spiteful gossip without feeling she had to sell her soul for the privilege. Much to his gut-deep satisfaction, the specter of their future children effectively cooled her desire to destroy her reputation. He couldn't watch her pay the price again for an atrocity she shouldn't have had to endure in the first place. Everything inside him rebelled at the thought. Why should she set herself up to be shamed all over again? It was like letting her be raped twice. He wasn't posturing when he said if it were only his name being blackened, he could live with the consequence; he could—and count the cost cheap. But he'd most likely punch anyone who dared snub his wife. Hopefully, with her maternal instincts firmly roused, the need would never arise.

Still feeling a heap of inner tension, Hattie lay in Jake's arms and tried to sort through her feelings. The emotions his words produced were unexpected. She'd been shocked by the strength of protectiveness she felt at the mere idea of babies she had yet to conceive.

Considering everything that went on before and after their marriage, it was surprising she had never spared a thought to the kids they might someday have. Other than learning soon after her marriage that their night in the stable hadn't resulted in pregnancy, Hattie hadn't given even the vaguest consideration to the fact that she and Jake would someday likely have children.

She thought about them now. With Jake as their father, she knew their babies would be special. And if, God forbid, they were unfortunate enough to be born with red hair, she knew Jake's constant praise of its color would ease the sting of any negative comments they'd receive away from home. And it would be a cold day in hell before she or Jake allowed the Murdock kids to be given a cold shoulder by this sometimes thoughtlessly cruel town.

Her own relationship with many of the townspeople had improved dramatically since her younger years. She didn't fool herself, however, that the strides she'd made since coming home would shield her if her rape was made public. It would be a rare friend indeed, if the brutal truth were known, who would accept her. For women were always labeled culpable in their own downfall.

She wondered if the day would ever come when society stopped believing women were responsible for their assaults, when blame was instead placed strictly on the men who attacked them. Hattie fervently hoped so. But change tended to come slowly, if at all, and she honestly couldn't visualize that day. God knew she would much rather keep her rape private. Yet an overwhelming sense of guilt that Opal was going to draw all the fire when Hattie too could give testimony to strengthen the case against the bastard had been a heavy weight in her stomach for the past several days.

That guilt was gone. She had not sinned; she had been sinned against. She didn't underestimate the ordeal lying ahead for Opal, but at the end of it the girl could move on to a place where she wasn't known. Hattie could not. And in all honesty, why should she have to?

Jake was right; she didn't owe this town knowledge of her most hurtful traumas. Why provide ammunition that could be used to hurt her further? Neither did she deserve to have her future children abused socially because she hadn't had the physical strength to stop a man from violating her in the worst way possible. The more she thought about it, in fact, the angrier it made her. No one who hadn't suffered through an ordeal like hers had the right to sit in judgment. Then a small smile curved her lips. Why get angry when she could get even instead? Actually, there was a delicious irony to all this. Wouldn't it be poetic justice to see Roger Lord convicted without the town having the slightest idea he'd also harmed her? He would know and it would chafe his overweening sense of superiority that he could do nothing about it without incriminating himself. The sheer beauty of it appealed strongly to her sense of justice.

Aware of Hattie's tension, Jake held her quietly and gave her as much time as she needed to work through things in her mind. When he felt her begin to relax, he cupped his hand over hers and started moving their combined fingers in slow circles on his stomach. He did so in part to coax her away from the rest of her tension. But mostly because it was impossible to be near her without wanting to touch her. Heal her. Love her.

Slowly, he eased her hand down his body beneath the blankets. "Enough serious thoughts for tonight," he whispered. "Now, how about we teach you some of the other words still lacking in your vocabulary?"

44

Mattawa Courthouse
MONDAY, JULY 12, 1909

THE COURTROOM WAS packed. All available seating had been claimed moments after the doors opened. It hadn't deterred people from crowding into every obtainable inch of the remaining space until they stood two- and three-deep against the walls. Everyone appeared willing to remain packed in like cattle for as many hours as court was in session.

Spectators were equally divided between men and women, much to the men's consternation. Many had mounted a strenuous campaign to discourage the good women of Mattawa from attending the trial. Owing, they claimed in righteous tones, to the scandalous subject matter, which it was rumored would be thoroughly covered during the course of the case.

It was a battle they summarily lost. When a group of men clamored for the sheriff to do something about it, not only had the lawman given them a level look and said, "My wife is attending," but nearly every woman over eighteen not dependent upon a male for their livelihood rebelled. Ignoring the mandates laid down by husbands, brothers, and fathers, they sailed from their homes in numbers, dressed in their Sunday best, to converge on the courthouse. As one woman was overheard to remark, "This is the biggest event Mattawa has ever seen. Let the men stay home if they're too squeamish to hear testimony in mixed company." A carnival atmosphere prevailed, an expectation of titillation as the gallery unabashedly gawked at the principal players in the drama about to unfold.

Opal, Hattie, Nell, Doc, Mirabel, Augusta, and, to Hattie's surprise, Aurelia, seated directly behind the prosecutor's table, watched Jake make his final preparations as they waited for the trial to begin. Aurelia didn't know about Hattie's vested interest, but the rest of their small group found the air of festivity disturbing when to them the outcome was of paramount importance. They sat quietly tense and sober, an island of stillness in a sea of craning necks, pointing fingers, and whispered opinions.

Opal clung to Hattie's hand, crushing her fingers in her nervousness until Jake turned and beckoned the young woman forward. Reluctantly letting go, she rose to join him. She refused to look at Roger Lord as he arrogantly lounged in his chair at the other table.

Then the gallery was adjured to rise as the judge was announced. The crowd rustled into silence as the robed judge walked from his chambers to the bench. All eyes focused on him.

By the end of the session the myriad spectators were not as attentive. For many, the first day was disappointingly anticlimactic. Expecting high drama, they were treated to the dry process of jury selection. Men were called to the jury box and questioned extensively by both attorneys before being accepted or excused. The time-consuming process ate up the entire day.

When the judge's gavel finally hit the bench to adjourn the session, grumbling was audible. The general consensus was that tomorrow's show better be more interesting than today's had been.

Mattawa Courthouse
DAY TWO

"Do you swear to tell the truth, the whole truth, and nothing but the truth, so help you God?"

Jake rose from his seat at the prosecutor's table following Sheriff Jacobson's swearing in. Jake consulted his notes, tapped the end of his pencil with a decisive rap against the pad, then abandoned both to approach the witness-box. With easygoing, professional competence, he led Sheriff Jacobson through his testimony.

The gallery of spectators was much happier with today's activity. The sheriff was the first witness of the day, but already the opening statements from both lawyers had promised to unfold a drama of scandalous juiciness. Postures were attentive as the assembly avidly followed every question put to the sheriff and his firmly stated replies. "No further questions," Jake finally said and resumed his seat. The defense attorney, Arthur Cleveland, a portly man with leonine white hair and a militarily erect carriage, rose to take Jake's place.

He stood silently in front of the witness stand for an instant, holding his lapels and rocking gently from his heels to the balls of his feet and back. "Sheriff Jacobson," he finally said in a quiet voice, and the gallery strained to listen. "You have testified Opal Jeffries came to your office to lodge a complaint against Roger Lord, is that correct?"

"Yes, sir."

"And she verbally described the alleged attacks?"

"Yes."

"But you did not then proceed to arrest my client?"

"No, sir, not immediately."

"Because you didn't feel the word of a maid was an adequate reason to arrest a man of Roger Lord's prominence?"

"No, sir, I didn't doubt her testimony. But when I asked Jacob Murdock's professional opinion—"

"He didn't believe her story."

"He absolutely believed her story. But he did warn her a trial would be very difficult for her and the only sure conviction in a case of this nature was to catch the offender in the act. She offered herself as bait to do just that."

"I see." Cleveland rocked some more. "What was your reaction?"

"I was . . . interested."

"And Mr. Murdock?"

"Objection, Your Honor," Jake said. "Hearsay."

"I could call you for a witness, so you could testify for yourself," Cleveland said mildly.

The judge looked askance at Jake, who shrugged and sat down. The last thing he wanted was to be called to the stand, where, should the right questions be put to him, he could single-handedly ruin his wife's reputation.

"Overruled."

"Would you like the question repeated?"

"No, sir. Jake was against it."

"Because he feared for her safety?"

"Yes, sir."

"But she opted to go anyway." He rocked once, twice. "So rather than being repulsed by my client's attentions, she must have looked forward to more of the same."

"Objection!" Jake roared. "He's not even asking a question. And if that was a question, then he's simultaneously calling for a conclusion and trying to put words in the witness's mouth."

"Sustained." The judge looked at the defense attorney. "Mr. Cleveland, refrain from histrionics."

"My apologies, Your Honor," he replied meekly, but he was nonetheless clearly pleased with having raised a question in the jury's mind. "No further questions."

"You may step down, sir."

Opal's face was white. There was an omnivorous quality to the gallery's collective regard, and she clenched her fists in her lap, hoping she looked more composed than she felt. Beneath the table, Jake patted her clasped hands reassuringly.

"Call your next witness, Mr. Murdock."

Jake looked up from his legal pad. "The prosecution would like to call Mrs. Mabel Crockett."

Roger stiffened and he stared down his nose at the plump woman who stepped into the stand and took the oath.

Jake approached. "Mrs. Crockett," he said, "you have stated you are currently unemployed. Have you ever held a job?"

"Oh, aye, sor," she replied in a lilting Irish accent. "'Tis a cook I am. Up until 'bout a week ago, sor, I worked for Mr. Lord. I was in his employ for nigh on eighteen months."

"Are you a good cook, ma'am?"

"Oh, aye, sor, that I be!" she said fervently, making the gallery laugh.

"On the evening Roger Lord was arrested, were you in the house?"

"Aye, I was. You saw me yourself, sor, when the sheriff and you came through the kitchen door. Much to me shame, I was sittin' at the kitchen table with me hands over me ears."

"Why were you covering your ears, Mrs. Crockett?"

"To stifle the sound of Opal's screams."

"Was that the first time you plugged your ears to keep from hearing her cry out?"

"No, sor," she whispered, and her chins trembled. "Nor was she the first girl whose screams I heard."

Shocked murmurs ran through the gallery. Hattie clenched her fists in her lap and felt a resurgence of the nausea she'd awakened with this morning. She swallowed hard. How many girls had Roger Lord defiled over the years—and how many Mrs. Crocketts had sat with their hands over their ears to block out the sounds of the victims' distress? Dear God above, let this be the end to Roger's monstrous viciousness.

"Mrs. Crockett," Jake asked, "did you ever protest Mr. Lord's treatment of those girls?"

"Just once, sor," she replied with a shudder. "He told me in no uncertain terms that it was not me place to be questionin' me betters, and sure and he would be seein' to it I'd be out on the street, findin' meself unemployable elsewhere, should I speak out of turn again."

"And you believed his threats?"

"Oh, aye, sor, that I did. He's a powerful man."

"Were you in the kitchen when Opal Jeffries came back from town on the day of Roger Lord's arrest?"

"Aye."

"The defense has suggested Miss Jeffries was anxious for Lord's attention. Did she demonstrate an eagerness or even a willingness to attract his eye during the time between her return from town and his arrest?"

"No, sor. She gave me the items I'd sent her to pick up and then went straight to her room. She didn't even see Mr. Lord."

Over the next two days, Jake built a solid case against the defendant. He'd contacted every ex-employee willing to testify against Lord and put each one on the stand. The picture that emerged was of a man who viewed the working class as unworthy of basic human considerations.

Jake called Doc to the stand to testify to Opal's condition on the night of Lord's arrest. Her ripped dress and the photographs Doc had taken both of her and of the shattered bedroom door were presented as physical evidence that she in no way had encouraged Lord's attention.

During Doc's testimony Hattie noticed something was amiss with Moses. He wasn't a regular attendee of the trial as so many were, but he slipped in now and again as his schedule permitted, conspicuous by his size and the well-worn leather apron he rarely bothered to remove.

Caught up in the trial, Hattie didn't immediately notice Nell's tension whenever he entered the courtroom. Then it began to register that Moses spent more time staring broodingly at Nell than he did attending to the trial. She saw Nell simultaneously light up and grow tense at his appearance, noticed too the way she smiled at him when their eyes met—and how he didn't smile back. Hattie also registered the manner in which her own smile of greeting met with a blank stare the one and only time she caught Moses' eye. Concluding she was somehow involved in Moses' baffling behavior toward Nell, she determined to get to the bottom of it.

She and Jake had taken up residence at Augusta's for the duration of the trial, and Hattie tackled Nell immediately after dinner. Having hoarded her unhappiness for some time now, Nell was only too happy to talk. By the time she finished, Hattie was furious.

"He's punished you the past several weeks for not divulging what was told to you in confidence?" she demanded incredulously.

"He was hurt because he knew you told me something you wouldn't tell him."

"And meanwhile he's hung you out to dry. What about your wedding plans?"

"I don't know. They're off, I guess." Nell twisted her hands in her lap. Her dark eyes were filled with misery. "Hattie, what am I going to do? Moses and I only ever discussed marriage in general terms; we didn't actually set a date or anything. But I assumed it would be in the not-too-far future, so I already informed the school board I'm to be married this year." She stared at Hattie in pure misery. "They've found someone else to fill my position."

"That worm!" Hattie was furious. "If he's angry with me, fine … I can understand that. Kinda. But he's making you pay for his hurt feelings, and for that I could punch his lights out. He has you over a barrel, Nell, and no matter what you do, you lose. Right now, he's furious because I told you a secret that didn't include him, which you won't divulge. But I'd wager Belle against your graduation shoes he'd be angrier still if you had betrayed my trust by confiding a secret that wasn't yours to confide." She rose from Nell's bed where they sat talking and paced furiously about the room. "He wants to know my secrets? Fine. I'll just go on over to his house and tell him. And while I'm at it, I have one or two other things I'd like to get off my chest."

"Oh, Hattie, I know how hard it is for you to talk about what Roger Lord did to you. Please, I will work this out somehow. You don't have to—"

"I believe I do," Hattie interrupted. "If this trial doesn't accomplish anything else, it's finally relieved me of the last shreds of shame I've shouldered for three long years. Listening to other people relate their helplessness dealing with Lord has made me believe once and for all there really was nothing I could have done to prevent him hurting me." She smoothed her skirt, then met Nell's eyes with utter seriousness. "I'd like to forgo the humiliation of seeing my rape become public knowledge, but I have reached a point where I can at least talk about it to my oldest friend. And while I'm at it, Nell, I'm going to also tell him what a horse's ass he's been in his treatment of you!" And with a swish and swirl of flying skirts, Hattie stormed from the room.

45

Moses' father answered Hattie's knock. "Well, hello there, young lady!" he boomed. "I haven't seen you in a coon's age. How's married life agreeing with you?"

"Admirably, Mr. Marks. I love Jake to pieces and I'm very happy."

"I guessed as much—you're looking radiant." He stood back and gestured her into the hall. "I imagine you're here to see Moses."

"Yes, sir."

"C'mon in, then. I'll call him down." He led the way into the parlor and retreated to the foot of the stairs, where he called his son's name. Hattie conversed with Mrs. Marks while she awaited her oldest friend's appearance.

She heard him thunder down the stairs. He appeared in the doorway in his stocking feet, one big finger marking his place in a book he held. He regarded her without welcome, and the face she turned to him was equally unsmiling. "Come for a walk with me," she requested coolly. "We need to talk."

Without a word, he turned in the doorway and thundered back up the staircase. Hattie turned to his parents. "If you'll excuse us?"

Etta Marks smiled gently. "Of course, dear. Come again when you can stay longer. And do wish Jake good luck for me on the outcome of his trial." Etta Marks looked up when her son reappeared, minus his book and wearing his shoes. The furrows in her brow smoothed out as she brought her gaze back to Hattie. Etta hoped what they discussed erased the pain from her son's heart, so he'd be fit to live with again. Returning to what she'd been saying before Moses reentered the room, she continued, "From everything I've heard of this trial, it appears Mr. Lord has long been quite a wicked man."

"I believe he's very wicked indeed." Hattie turned to Moses. "Are you ready?"

He nodded curtly and she turned back to say her goodbyes to his parents.

They closed the door behind them and walked in silence to the edge of town. Hattie chose a fallen log by the side of the road and sat down. She looked up at Moses with cool condemnation. "You have been treating Nell most unfairly."

"Wonderful," he replied bitterly. "I see once again the women have been exchanging secrets." He stood stiffly, hands in his pockets, staring into the distance. "Is this why you dragged me out here? I thought you had something important to say, but if this is it, why don't you just run along home to your husband and your real friend?"

"Don't be snide, Moses," she said softly, remembering what it felt like to be excluded. "And save your sarcasm—I am not in the mood. If you were hurt because I told Nell something I could not tell you, I'm sorry; I truly am. But don't take it out on her. You act as though this were a popularity contest I arbitrarily staged to pit you two. Well, it's not—this is my life. You are my oldest, dearest friend, but whether or not you care to acknowledge it, there are some subjects that are simply too difficult for a woman to talk about with a man." The cynical look he directed at her erased most of her compassion and made her add irritably, "And for the record, as you're big on defining who is a real friend and who is not, she was there for me when I needed her most."

He stifled a yawn and looked bored. "Meaning I was not, I gather."

"Precisely." Hattie's temper snapped and she surged to her feet, hands clenched at her sides. "You're so hot to know my secrets? By all means,

then, I shall tell you. Roger Lord beat and raped me. August 11, 1906."
Words that in a far corner of her mind she knew she'd regret tumbled
from her lips. "Remember that summer, Moses? Remember how you were
nowhere to be found? You'll have to excuse me if I didn't feel I could
discuss my downfall with you. You weren't there to discuss it with, and
besides, you were one of them: a man who will never in a million years
understand what it's like to be held down and struck and ripped apart
by—" She swallowed the end of the sentence. Drew a deep breath. Exhaled it gustily. "Then, when you did turn up at Jane-Ellen's funeral and
reached to hug me, I was terrified. Of you, my friend. Because you were
big and stronger than me. Because you were a man, and for a second it
didn't matter you had always been my friend and, in my heart, I knew you
would never hurt me."

Seeing his expression, she shut up. He looked as if a bomb had exploded in his face.

"Raped?" His voice was a hoarse croak and Hattie literally watched
the knowledge sink in as his muscles stiffened all over and he grew larger
where he stood. He plowed a huge hand through his hair. "Lord raped
you? And Jake didn't kill the sonovabitch?"

She sat back down, her anger fading as abruptly as it had materialized.
"Jake didn't know. Only Doc and Aunt Augusta knew, and I left almost
immediately after for school. I was a wreck when I arrived in Seattle.
Anxious to escape Mattawa, yet at the same time feeling as if I'd been
exiled. And I felt so dirty and ashamed. Nell put me back together again."

"Shit." Moses sat on the log next to her. Stretching out his long legs,
he turned to her and said gently, "Tell me everything."

She talked, and when she finished they sat side by side in silence, the
day growing dimmer beneath an overcast sky. In the woods behind them,
tree frogs began their nightly call.

Moses' big hands were balled in tight fists on his thighs, and he blew
out a frustrated breath as he turned to her. "I can't kill him, I suppose."

"No," she agreed gently. "Not without ruining my name. Jake struggled with that, too, when he found out."

Her longtime friend peered at her in the gathering gloom. "So, in a large sense, this trial is really for you," he said slowly.

"It's for every woman he's ever harmed."

"That son of a bitch," Moses said with icy anger. "Lord thought he was perfectly safe defiling you, knowing you couldn't report him without ruining yourself. Your reputation then was already on shaky ground." Then a smile slowly dawned across his face and it was filled with savage satisfaction. "But now Jake's gonna destroy him without your name ever coming into it." He nodded tersely and some of the rigidity in his muscles lessened. "Damn fine justice, that."

"I know, don't you love it?" She turned to him, laying a hand over one of his. "I'm glad I told you, Moses. You, more than anyone, can fully appreciate the irony."

For a long moment, he simply looked at her, his face a study in bitter self-accusation. "I've acted like an ass, haven't I?"

"Yes. Your behavior toward Nell has been particularly dreadful." She dispensed criticism with her words and forgiveness with her smile, as only very good friends can do.

"Yeah." He smiled back, seeming to accept the comfort of a friendship that displayed anger yet still remained unending. "I've been a pig." He rose to his feet and turned to extend a hand to her. "Come on," he said, pulling her up, "I'll walk you home. Y'think Nell is there?"

"Where else would she be? The love of her life has been giving her the cold shoulder."

"You don't have to rub it in, Red. I know I've got fences to mend."

"Don't call me Red, Moses Marks!" When her half-hearted swing was caught in his large fist, she tucked her free hand into his forearm. "I wish I could be a fly on the wall when you talk to Nell. But since that is a conversation I don't suppose I'll get to hear, it's only fair you practice your groveling on the way home. I would be delighted to give you pointers."

———

SOMEONE TAPPED A rat-a-tat-tat on Nell's bedroom door. When Hattie didn't rush into the room without awaiting an invitation, Nell set aside the large rectangular crewelwork she was making as a gift for Augusta. She rose and went over to open the door.

"Oh!" She stared at Hattie on the other side. "It is you. I'm not used to you waiting for me to open the door before barging in."

Hattie laughed. "Can't argue with that. Still, I'm trying to mend my ways. You have a guest down in the parlor." Before Nell could ask who, Hattie whirled away, shooting a breezy, "Sorry to rush off, but I need to attend to something," over her shoulder.

Okaaaay. That wasn't at all odd. With a shrug, Nell glanced in the cheval mirror. She pinched her cheeks and bit her lips to gain a bit of color. Then she headed downstairs.

When she arrived at the parlor and saw who awaited her there, Nell stopped a single step into the room. Her heart banging like a loose shutter in a storm, she stared at Moses standing in front of the hearth. How could she have forgotten the man was all towering height, big hands, and broad shoulders? "Mr. Marks," she said coolly.

"I've been an idiot," he said, heading her way.

She essayed a single, regal nod. "Which time, precisely?"

He snorted, halting his forward progress. "Yeah. That is the question." He took a step toward her. "When I blamed you for being a good friend but didn't actually tell you that was why I was being a shit." He took one step more. "For my petty jealousy over Hattie liking you best." Another step brought him almost close enough to touch. He reached out as if to do so—as if he were about to stroke her hair with his rough fingertips, the way he had each and every time he'd seen her before things between them went so wrong. But his hand dropped to his side and he simply stared down at her. "Jesus, Nell," he breathed. "For treating you shabbily when I should have been telling you how much I adore you."

"You—what?" Nell pressed a hand over her heart, which she was certain had seized up. At the same time, the frozen knot she'd carried deep inside began to thaw.

"I love you, Nell." He stepped into her space and this time she did get to feel the rough thrill of his fingertips stroking the pouf of her Gibson Girl hairdo from her temple to where she'd gathered it into a soft bun. "God, girl," he rumbled. "I am so deep in love with you. You know that. We were talking marriage."

She was melting into a big, messy pool of delight. But Nell Thomesen was made of sterner stuff than that. She stepped back. Gave Moses a cool once-over. "Yes, in the broadest of terms." She ignored for the moment that she and Hattie had all but planned how the vaguely if several times mentioned wedding would go. "But you never said you love me. And in the wake of my refusing to break Hattie's confidence, you looked at me as if I had slugs in my hair. So, what brought on this sudden change of heart?"

"Oh, honey, my feelings for you are far from sudden," Moses said, crowding her. "I've wanted you since I first clapped eyes on you." He rubbed a rough-skinned thumb over her cheek. "But as to my change of heart now? Well, I'd like to say I came to my senses because I'm a mature man who knows and appreciates the best thing that's ever happened to him." His mouth quirked up. "But the sad truth is, it took a come-to-Jesus talk from Hattie to get my thumb out of my a—" He cleared his throat. "She told me what happened to her, Nell. And how much you helped get her back on her feet."

Nell jerked. Hattie told him? Oh, that brave, brave girl!

"I wish she could have come to me," he said. "But I'm afraid I made that impossible." Ruddy color crept up his strong neck and onto his face, and Nell knew he was remembering those dreams that made him avoid Hattie. She blushed, too.

Moses straightened. "I forgot you knew. I didn't handle learning that well, either. I am glad you were there for her, though, Nell," he said gruffly. "I let her down."

"Yet you were there for her for seven years before that. You were in her corner when hardly anyone wanted anything to do with her."

Moses' big, warm hand suddenly engulfed the back of Nell's neck and he pulled her in for a kiss that left her mind utterly scrambled by the time he stepped back. "I love you, girl," he said, folding her in his arms. "Could you re-see yourself spending your life with me?"

She smiled against his shirtfront. "I can."

"I've been living with my folks to save money for a house. I have a good-sized chunk of down-payment money in the bank. I can't afford to give you a place as nice as Augusta's here. But the Donovan house a few blocks over just came on the market. Maybe you and I could go view it. See if it's to your standards." For a moment, he looked uncertain. Then his broad shoulders squared. "I'm good with my hands and I'm not afraid of hard work. So, if anything needs fixing, I'm your man."

"You are," she agreed. "I am so in love with you, too, Moses."

"Yeah?" A big grin split his face. "Enough to marry me?"

"Yes—after a trial period."

"I'll be so good at your trial period, your heart will sing. How long a trial we talking about? Like a wee—?" He must have seen her brows rise, for he substituted, "A month?"

A smile tugged her lips. "We'll see."

"Meanwhile, how about I put a ring on your finger? I picked one out before I let jealousy over you being Hattie's best friend derail me."

"My darling Moses." Arms around his waist, she tipped her head back to see his beloved face. "I am Hattie's best girlfriend. You are her number one, all-around best friend-friend."

"I imagine Jake's that for her now." He smoothed a strand of hair off her forehead. "And that's okay, honey. I plan to be a good friend to her, always. But I want to be your number one, all around best friend-friend."

"I want that, too."

"Day-am!" He suddenly swept her off her feet. "Let's go tell my folks we're getting engaged. Then I'll bring you home so we can tell Hattie and Jake and Augusta that the prettiest girl in Mattawa said she'd marry me." He grinned down at her. "Whataya say?"

"Add calling my mother and sister to let them know and that sounds like one dickens of a marvelous plan."

46

FRIDAY, JULY 16, 1909

HATTIE FELT SICK to her stomach again when she awoke the following morning. When she sat up and nausea crept up her throat, she carefully eased back onto the mattress. It was manageable, she discovered, if she lay very still. Mercy. Sore breasts, sick three mornings running, and yesterday's inexplicable tiredness. She was pregnant.

Wonder saturated her senses and she'd dance in the streets if she didn't feel so beastly. The queasiness was bound to pass sooner or later, however, and meanwhile, what a miracle! She opened her mouth to share her news with Jake when he walked into their bedroom, but closed it again. She watched him tuck, button, and adjust, and smiled inside with secret pleasure.

He could be flat-out single-minded when he got an idea in his head, and who knew what kind impending fatherhood might give him? Best to let him focus his attention on the trial. Once it was over, she'd throw them a private celebration to share the news.

"Mornin', Big-eyes." Perching a lean haunch on the mattress by her hip, he moved to kiss her. The mattress dipped and Hattie's stomach pitched. She swallowed hard, thinking with weak humor that throwing up in his lap would likely render the question of timing moot.

He brushed the hair off her temples with the backs of his fingers as he straightened up. "You going to stay in bed all day?"

352

Susan Andersen

"No. I'm getting up. Today's the day you put Opal on the stand, isn't it?"

"Yeah, but probably not until after the lunch recess. If you want to sleep in a little . . ."

"No, she needs me there." She eased cautiously up onto one elbow. "You go ahead, though. I'll be along as soon as I get ready."

"All right." He kissed her again. "Love you, baby."

"Love you too, Jacob."

When he left, she rose from the bed. She'd discovered the nausea could be controlled some if she made no sudden moves. She got ready and went down to the kitchen. The smell of coffee assaulted her the moment she opened the door and she sat down abruptly at the kitchen table, breathing shallowly through her mouth.

"Good morning, Hattie," Mirabel said, turning from the stove. "What can I fix you, dear? A stack of pancakes? Or how about some fried eggs with the yolks all nice and runny, just the way you like them?"

Hattie bolted from her seat and tore the back door open. She barely made it to the porch railing in time. Hanging over it, she retched violently, spasm after spasm that left her sweaty and weak. Finally, folding at the waist, she rested her damp forehead on the cool railing.

She felt a cold cloth against the nape of her neck, a bony hand stroking her hair. "Thanks, Mirabel," she whispered.

The cloth moved around to her face, and Hattie turned her cheek to feel its refreshing chill more fully. She opened her eyes when Mirabel demanded in her stern voice, "Are you pregnant, Hattie Murdock?"

"Yeah." Unexpectedly, tears filled her eyes. "Oh, Mirabel, I wanted to wait until this trial was over to tell Jake. I'd hoped to tell him in our own home over a nice dinner with candles and maybe a fire in the hearth. It would have been such a wonderful surprise. But there is no earthly way I can keep it to myself if this nausea continues. I'm so afraid the news will interfere with his concentration on the case." She felt like a fool, but she couldn't stop crying.

"Come inside, young lady." Mirabel helped her back to her seat at the kitchen table. She moved away and Hattie closed her eyes and breathed carefully. She didn't move until Mirabel set something on the table next to her. "Here. Try this."

Hattie opened her eyes to see a steaming cup and a plate of dry crackers. Her stomach lurched uneasily. "Oh, I don't think—"

"Try it; it'll help settle your stomach. The tea is herbal; it's good for morning sickness. The salt on the crackers also helps. The trick is to consume them nice and slow."

To Hattie's delight, Mirabel was right. She felt much stronger when she pushed away her empty plate and returned her cup to its saucer.

"Your color is much better," Mirabel said with satisfaction. She handed Hattie a tin. "More crackers," she informed her dryly. "Keep them in your nightstand and eat a few before you try to get up in the morning. With luck, you'll be able to keep the secret a few days longer."

"I love you, Mirabel," Hattie said fervently and rose to kiss the older woman's cheek. "Thank you so much."

Mirabel pinkened with pleasure right up to her iron-gray curls. "Go on with you, now," she said gruffly. "And save me a seat, hear? I'll be there soon as I finish the dishes."

"Would you like some help?"

"No, dear, you go. I'll be along presently."

The defense attorney was still cross-examining Jake's witness when Hattie arrived at the courthouse. She knew the man in the witness-box was the last before Opal was called to testify. Edging past knees with murmured apologies, she reached her saved seat. Moving the wrap Nell had draped over the two vacant spots, Hattie arrayed it on the back of the seat for Mirabel. Then she leaned over the railing to squeeze Opal's shoulder in encouragement before sitting.

Mirabel seated herself next to Hattie before Jake called Opal to the stand. The older woman neatly folded Nell's wrap and passed it to Hattie. "How are you holding up?"

"I'm starving."

"Good." Mirabel chuckled softly and patted Hattie's hand. "That's an excellent sign."

OPAL EXCEEDED JAKE'S expectations as a witness. She was articulate and poised, met the jurors' eyes, and answered questions in a clear voice. She trembled visibly and cried when she described what Roger did to her, which worked in their favor. Being emotional was normal; the jury would have thought the young woman unnatural had she remained composed.

Opal clung to her composure during cross-examination and didn't allow Lord's attorney to fluster her into anything that would appear to contradict her story. She was altogether credible and by the time Jake said, "The prosecution rests," he felt they had built a good, solid case.

ARTHUR CLEVELAND HAD two stiff drinks with his lunch. He'd started presenting the case for the defense yesterday afternoon, but it was weak as a newborn kitten and he knew it. His client was guilty as hell.

Arthur had no particular problem with that—he'd defended guilty men before and truly believed everyone was entitled to the best defense possible. Roger Lord, however, was not only guilty but an egomaniac who kept insisting he be allowed to testify. No two ways about it: that would be the death of what little Arthur had managed to salvage thus far. He'd done his best to talk Lord out of it, but the man was adamant. It was enough to drive an attorney to drink.

But against every instinct Arthur had learned during three decades as an attorney, he had no choice but to cede to his client's wishes. He put Lord on the stand.

It started out well enough while he established Lord's long residence in the community and presented his distinguished work record. Following that, however, matters began to deteriorate. Lord's manner was arrogant, and it clearly rubbed the jury the wrong way.

Arthur managed to nip his client's misogynistic views in the bud, but for the first time in his career he was actually thankful to hand a defendant over for cross-examination. The man practically begged for a guilty verdict. Arthur was grateful that when he'd asked Lord point-blank if he raped Opal Jeffries, Lord looked him in the eye and said, "Certainly not."

Jake approached the box. Having carefully studied Roger during his defense lawyer's questioning, Jake concluded Roger's ego was the key. "Mr. Lord," he said in a polite tone, "you have stated you did not rape Opal Jeffries. Could you tell me, sir, what it was you were doing when the sheriff and I interrupted you on the evening of your arrest?"

Roger looked down his nose at Jake. "Teaching Jeffries her proper place."

"Her proper place," Jake repeated softly. "Wouldn't that be serving your dinner and assorted maid duties?"

"It would be whatever I say it is," Roger stated coldly. "She is merely a woman, sir. It is her duty to comply with my wishes."

The women in the gallery rustled indignantly.

"And your former cook, Mrs. Crockett, who testified you threatened to not only put her on the street without references, but make it impossible as well to get another job in Mattawa should she interfere with your abuse—"

"What abuse?" Roger interrupted. "Did you not hear me, man? We're discussing women—*servant* women. They need constant instruction and discipline to perform the simplest of tasks. Never mind understanding their *place*."

The women more than rustled this time; an outpouring of irate protests exploded, causing the judge to employ his gavel and call for order.

"See what I mean?" Roger demanded. "Why do you think only men are allowed to sit on a jury?" He cast a smirk at the jurors. "*They* know what I'm talking about."

Jake wondered if Lord even registered the jury's suddenly expressionless faces.

Perhaps he did, for Roger suddenly demanded, "What are all these women even doing here? If more men stepped up to keep them in line—"

Jake, not wanting a riot and feeling they had all they needed to put Lord away for a good long time, interrupted. "Let's get back to your case. Tell me—"

"I know why you're persecuting me, sir," Roger interrupted.

"I am not persecuting you, Mr. Lord. I am the prosecuting attorney. It's my job."

"Right," Roger sneered. "And you're loving every moment of it, aren't you?" He turned to the judge. "This is a plot, Your Honor, and I protest," he said. "Jake Murdock trumped up these charges expressly to get back at me—"

"Your Honor—"

"To get back at me," Roger said implacably, "for taking his wife's virginity."

Jake's furious "What?! You son of a bitch!" was buried in the pandemonium of the courtroom erupting. Voices yammered and heads craned to assess Jake's and Hattie's reactions.

Many eyes were on her as she surged to her feet, but Hattie saw none of them. She stared at Roger Lord in horror, one hand gripping her throat, where a wave of sickness rose. "No!" she whispered, as her vision was encompassed by a wall of white. It wasn't a denial so much as a protest that he'd dare. Then, for the first time since arriving in Mattawa at the age of eleven, Hattie reacted in a way that gained her the wholehearted approval of every woman in the courthouse.

She fainted dead away.

47

HATTIE SCARED JAKE to death. Nell and Mirabel managed to catch her between them as she crumpled, and they eased her into her seat. She lolled limply, head back, and Jake vaulted over the railing, roaring at the spectators straining for a better look to get out of the way and give her room to breathe. One man drew too near and Jake roughly shoved him back, his face tense with worry as he turned back to his unconscious wife.

He squatted in front of her, patting her hands and cheeks, saying, "Wake up, baby. C'mon, baby, wake up." He glared up at Augusta. "Dammit, Mom, why won't she wake up? Oh God, I wish Doc were here. Why the hell isn't he here when we need him?"

Amid the babble of excited voices, the judge declared a recess and the prisoner was led away sporting a satisfied smile. The bailiff opened an antechamber and Jake swept Hattie up and carried her into the room, tenderly depositing her on the couch inside. Except for his mother, he ordered everyone else who entered the chamber to give them some privacy. The instant the last person departed, he slammed the door shut and locked it.

He was aware that the gallery was in a paroxysm of delight. The crowd had just been given enough grist for the gossip mills to last until Christmas, but he didn't give a tinker's damn at the moment.

He just wanted Hattie to wake the hell up.

Hattie grew aware of several things as she regained consciousness. She was stretched out on a cool leather couch and she felt very, very ill. There was a persistent rapping, a distant voice saying, "Mr. Murdock, there's a young lady here who says it's urgent she talk to you," and Jake's voice, much louder and closer, snarling impatiently, "Not now!"

She opened her eyes slowly.

Jake's face swam into focus and she blinked up at him, raising her fingers to his lean cheek. He was squatting next to the couch, his expression strained as he grasped her fingers and pressed them to his face.

Jake turned his head to kiss the inside of her wrist. "Christ, Big-eyes, you scared me to death," he said in a voice rougher than his normal tones. "Don't do that again."

One corner of her mouth tilted up slightly. "We're gonna have a baby, Jake." She attempted to sit up, but her head swam and she feared vomiting on the carpet. Subsiding, she admitted with a wry smile, "This isn't the way I planned to tell you."

Then she began to remember and her smile faded. Freeing her fingers, she clasped her hands at her waist. "He really told everyone, didn't he?"

"Yeah." Jake's eyes were fierce. "I should have killed him when I had the opportunity."

She touched his face again. "He isn't worth it, Jacob."

"No," he agreed, "he's not." He spread his fingers on her flat stomach. "You're really pregnant?" He studied her face intently. "Is that what caused you to faint?"

"Yeah, I jumped up, everything went white, then . . . nothing. *But*," she said with grim insistence, "it wasn't due to anything that pig said. I wouldn't give him the satisfaction." She couldn't deny, though, that she could have lived without the public humiliation.

"Actually," Jake informed her dryly, "I think your swoon won the approval of everyone present. For once you reacted in the expected way."

His mother, who had taken a seat in the judge's chair, laughed softly.

"How reassuring," Hattie murmured. "They'll all say I'm quite refined—for a harlot."

"Don't worry about it, baby. You and I are going to be living in this town for a good long time to come. We've got each other, our family, and a few excellent friends. If anyone wants to turn their backs on us over this, they don't know what they're giving up."

Another rap on the door made Jake turn impatiently. "What?!"

Hattie cautiously eased herself upright, relieved to note the nausea had disappeared.

"Mr. Murdock? There's a young woman here—"

Hattie could see Jake was preparing to snap the inquirer's head off and laid a hand on his forearm. "Go find out what she wants."

"You're sure you're feeling better?"

"Yes. Let her in."

He brushed back a hank of hair that had escaped during her fall, kissed her gently, and whispered, "I'm happy about the baby, darlin'. You're gonna make a helluva mama." Then he rose to stride across the room to yank the door open. The young girl on the other side jumped nervously.

"Don't frighten her, Jacob," Hattie said in gentle reprimand. She straightened her jacket and refastened the buttons at her throat. "Let the poor girl in."

Jake waved away the young woman's escort and did as his wife bade. He looked at his mother. "Would you mind giving us the room, Mom?"

"Of course not." Augusta rose from the chair behind the desk, brushed a kiss across Hattie's forehead with a whispered encouragement, then left the room, closing the door behind her.

Jake turned to the young woman. "What's so important?"

"My name is Maria Montgomery, sir," she said in a soft, hesitant voice. Then, blushing profusely, she haltingly told them why she had insisted on seeing him.

"You're willing to testify to that?" Jake asked when she had finished.

"Yes, sir."

"Thank you, Miss Montgomery. This means a lot," he said. He gave her a few instructions and ushered her out the door. Then turned to look at his wife.

"There is justice in the world," she exclaimed softly. "Who would have thought? Oh, Jacob, Roger is going to have a cow!" She laughed. "How absolutely, incredibly fitting."

They grinned at each other with a perfectly attuned sense of irony. If it was diluted by a measure of maliciousness, well, it wasn't particularly Christian of them. But they figured God might forgive them, just this once, if they couldn't quite bring themselves to care.

COURT RECONVENED FORTY-FIVE minutes later. Jake and Hattie girded themselves as Roger Lord was recalled to the witness stand. His face carefully expressionless, Jake approached the stand.

"Now, sir," he said in a neutral voice. "You have testified that you took my wife's virginity, is that correct?"

A ripple of surprise went through the gallery. Everyone expected Jake Murdock to bury Lord's shocking declaration beneath a mountain of legalese. On either side of Hattie, Nell and Augusta, who had changed places with Mirabel, reached to hold Hattie's hands.

"That's right," Roger said triumphantly.

"And was it given to you willingly?"

Roger hesitated, knowing, for his freedom, he had to say yes and be done with it. Hell, either way, the little slut would be publicly ruined. But he had dreamed of this moment for too long now, and knowing he could safely rub Murdock's nose in the fact of his wife's helplessness that night was simply too good to pass up. Still . . . He was Roger Lord. Why not have it both ways?

"She begged me," he replied with satisfaction. It was the truth after all. She'd screamed. *Cried.* He'd liked that best. Roger slid Murdock a sly smile.

"Begged you to stop?"

"No, you stupid cuckold. She said she'd never had it so good."

Jake forcefully swallowed the hot rage urging him to climb over the barrier separating them. He'd give a bundle to wrap his hands around Lord's throat. God forgive him, but Jake longed to tear the son of a bitch apart limb by limb.

He had an ace up his sleeve, however, and needed to keep a cool head to make the most of it. So, he stood with his hands loose by his sides even as he itched to drive the man's nose through the back of his head. After a rapid mental check of the last few exchanges, he said coolly, "According to your earlier testimony, you took her virginity. That means she *had* no comparison. You might want to keep your lies straight, Lord. You used to be a more competent lawyer than this—although word has it you're having trouble getting new clients."

He fully expected an objection from Lord's attorney, but Cleveland remained quiet. A fast glance over Jake's shoulder revealed the lawyer with his elbow on the table and his forehead cradled in his palm. Roger Lord, on the other hand, surged to his feet—only to be admonished to take his seat by the judge.

He did so, and even managed to say fairly calmly, if through gritted teeth, "I'm ten times the lawyer you are, Murdock. Who taught you everything you know?"

"You did teach me quite a bit," Jake agreed and threw in a smile just to irritate the older man. "So, act like an attorney for a moment and try to stay on track. Let me paraphrase what I've gleaned so far from your oath-sworn testimony. Either somehow, out of the blue, virgin Hattie threw herself at you. Or"—his voice dropped to a glacial level—"you raped my wife."

"Oh hell, man," Roger snapped. "There is no such thing as rape! I am a man of position, for God's sake; I merely exercised my right to teach Hattie her rightful place."

Jake turned toward the jury box, every muscle in his body desperate to clench like iron beneath the potency of his rage. Forcing easiness into his posture, his expression, his voice—hell, into the very tempo of his breathing—he said, "So what you're saying, Mr. Lord, is that no woman, let alone Opal Jeffries, who, while in your home, should have had a reasonable expectation she was in a protected environment, is safe around you? Because the rules of decent behavior don't apply to you, due to your superior personage?"

"I object, Your Honor," Roger's attorney said, even as Roger gave a sharp nod of self-satisfaction and replied, "Yes, I am that."

Jake knew the defendant was responding to the second question. It didn't hurt Opal's case, however, that it was an admission of guilt to both Jake's questions. The men of the jury sure as hell looked repulsed. Before the judge could sustain the objection, which Jake didn't doubt for an instant the town justice would do, he continued smoothly, "I withdraw the questions, Your Honor, and have nothing further for the accused at this time." He returned to his seat.

Roger was dismissed, but when the defense attorney declined to redirect, Jake once again rose to his feet. "Your Honor, I would like to call a new witness for the prosecution."

"This is highly irregular, Mr. Murdock," the judge replied severely. "You have already rested your case."

"I did, Your Honor, but I never dreamed the defendant would call my wife's virtue into question. He opened up this line of questioning when he viciously attacked my wife's good name. A witness has voluntarily stepped forward, and I feel it imperative to address the accusation. My wife is not on trial, but Roger Lord placed her reputation at stake."

"Very well. Call your witness."

"The state calls Miss Maria Montgomery."

Nell and Augusta exchanged puzzled glances, but while Hattie gave their hands a brief, comforting press, she merely whispered, "Wait," and sat serenely composed between them.

"Do you solemnly swear to tell the truth, the whole truth, and nothing but the truth, so help you God?"

"I do."

"State your full name and occupation."

"Maria Iris Montgomery. I am a chambermaid at the Buchannan Hotel."

"Be seated."

Jake stepped forward. "Miss Montgomery, would you tell the jurors why you stepped forward and asked to testify?"

"I was . . ." Her voice faltered and she cleared her throat. "I was present in the courtroom when Mr. Lord testified earlier that he had taken Mrs. Murdock's . . . um . . . virginity." She whispered the word, her face pink with embarrassment. "The first time he said it, I mean. When she fainted."

"As were a lot of people, Miss Montgomery. What made you search me out?"

"Well, sir, I knew it was a lie and it hardly seemed right not to say so when that man deliberately blackened her good name."

The gallery murmured, but Roger Lord's voice was strident with outrage as he surged to his feet. "What?!"

"Sit down, sir," the judge commanded, "and let there be no further outbursts." At his lawyer's insistent urging, Roger sat.

"How could you possibly know the state of my wife's virtue, Miss Montgomery? You're not a doctor."

"No, sir, I'm a chambermaid. It was me who stripped the sheets from the bed after your wedding night at the hotel. And they was bloodied."

"That's a lie!" Roger was once again on his feet, his face apoplectic.

"It is not!" Maria responded indignantly. She turned to the judge, her wholesome face shining with conviction. "There were several spots of blood right in the middle of the sheet, Your Honor. God is my witness. And I did make mention of it at the time to three of the other girls what work at the hotel. Just ask 'em if I din't."

The judge's gavel hit the bench. "Mr. Lord, sit down! Counselor, I advise you to warn your client about contempt of court."

"Miss Montgomery," Jake asked, "why would you mention such a thing to your coworkers?"

She blushed. "Well, sir, we'd heard all sorts of stories about Hattie Taylor. One of the girls said she knew for a fact she was a wild one, what with her red hair and bein' friends with Moses Marks and all. But one of the other girls said her younger brother was in Miss Taylor's class and that she din't believe fair half the stories she'd heard. So, we were all curious-like."

God bless your curiosity, Jake thought. Aloud, he merely said, "No further questions."

"Miss Montgomery." Arthur Cleveland stood. "How do you know Mr. Murdock didn't simply cut himself shaving?"

"Well, sir, it woulda been an odd place to shave, wouldn't it? There weren't no blood anywhere else in the suite, sir. If a man cut himself, seems there woulda been bloodied towels in the bath or some such. At least that's been my experience in the past. And he woulda had to cut a fair chunk out of his face for that much blood to travel all the way to the bed."

"What did Mr. Murdock offer you to testify?"

"Nothing, sir. He didn't even wanna talk to me. He was in that little room over there"—she pointed to the antechamber—"with his wife. I insisted."

"You're quite altruistic, aren't you?"

"I don't know what that means, sir."

"It means you have a high regard for the welfare of others."

"Well, sir, I don't know about that. I am a female. I wouldn't half like it if some man told a lie about me and just like that ruined my reputation. It don't seem fair that untrue words can carry so much power."

Arthur gave up. "No further questions."

"What do you mean no further questions?" Lord demanded. "Make her admit she's lying."

"How would you propose I do that?" Arthur asked him in a low voice, keeping his hand on his client's shoulder to hold him in his chair. "She seems pretty damned convinced she's telling the truth. The more questions I put to her, the deeper she's digging your grave."

"Nonsense. No one is going to take the word of a menial servant over mine!"

"Then you have nothing to worry about, do you?" God, Arthur was fed up with this man.

Miss Montgomery was dismissed, closing arguments were given, and the jurors retired to deliberate. It grew late, and stomachs rumbled reminders of a dinner hour come and gone. Yet, no one left. People milled about on the courthouse steps, men taking the opportunity to smoke, women taking the air, and everyone discreetly stretching out kinked muscles. Hushed conversations debated the outcome, and to Hattie's satisfaction, the few she overheard appeared to find Roger's innocence highly suspect.

Miss Eunice Peabody sailed over, halting with a creak of her formidable corsetry in front of Hattie. "I want you to know I did not believe Mr. Lord's lies about you for one moment," she said in her piercing whisper.

"Why, thank you, Miss Eunice." Hattie took her declaration with a grain of salt, yet nevertheless replied with a genuine smile. "It's most satisfying to find myself championed."

Aurelia Donaldson also approached. She reached out to pat Hattie's hand. "I, too, found his display disgraceful. Young Miss Montgomery was quite correct when she said 'tis most unfair that untrue words have the power to destroy a woman's good name. The very idea!"

She peered fiercely through her lorgnette at the people nearby, as though daring anyone to disagree with her. Then she patted Hattie's hand again. "You're a good girl, Hattie Murdock. The people of Mattawa know quality."

"Your assurance is indeed gratifying," Hattie replied. "But I'd like to think the people of Mattawa would still view me as a good girl even if Roger Lord's testimony had been true."

Aurelia blinked, slightly affronted to have her words of praise found lacking. Around her were numerous indrawn breaths and incredulous expressions.

Hattie felt her ire rise. She looked around at the varying degrees of shock displayed on nearby faces. "Did none of you listen to what was said in there?" she questioned hotly. "My God, the real injustice is that a perfectly decent woman can be beaten and brutalized the way Opal was and then find herself ostracized on top of it! To be ruined for being unable to protect oneself seems to me to be the height of inequity."

She could tell the concept was not well met and she shook her head sadly, turning back to her family and friends. Perhaps, in a future world, the day would come when—

"You are absolutely right."

Hattie turned back slowly. Aurelia Donaldson's gaze was razor-sharp behind her ever-present lorgnette.

"Mrs. Donaldson!" Eunice Peabody exclaimed in shock. "How can you agree to any such thing? And after she insulted you!"

"She did not insult me, Eunice, she simply did not tiptoe around my feelings when she spoke her mind. As I am not accustomed to that, it took me a moment to adjust, or I should have agreed sooner."

"But that's heresy!"

"Horsefeathers," Aurelia said coolly as she gazed at the scandalized spinster. "Perhaps instead of drawing our skirts aside in horror from the bloodied victims of such savagery, we should think like the good Christian women we are. Perhaps we should display our empathy and say, 'There but for the grace of God go I.'"

Eunice's face was a mottled red as she regarded the elderly woman. She could not believe her ears and felt she really should protest. Yet, how could she? Aurelia Donaldson was the dowager queen of Mattawa society and one must not offend her. But imagine such a thing! Empathy indeed. Decent women would always draw aside from their sisters who had fallen. That was, after all, what made them decent women. Corset creaking, Eunice turned without a word and stalked away.

Aurelia turned back to Hattie and arched a brow. "Too radical for her, I daresay."

Hattie smiled with real affection. "Well, I thought it was a grand speech."

"I am an old woman, my dear," Aurelia replied. "I'm allowed to speak my mind."

Hattie knew she was also one of the richest women in town, so could do so without fear of retribution. To allude to such, however, would be ungracious and likely undeserved. She rather thought Aurelia Donaldson would have aired her views regardless of the consequence.

"I apologize if I was rude to you," Hattie said. "I just feel quite strongly—"

"The jury is in!"

Hattie froze. This was it. The excited man who had appeared briefly around the door to make the announcement disappeared and the court-house steps rapidly emptied. And still Hattie didn't move.

"C'mon, Big-eyes. Let's go find out how we did."

She looked up at Jake. "I'm almost afraid to," she confessed. "What if they find him innocent?"

"Then we'll find a way to live with it." He wrapped an arm around her shoulders and pressed a quick kiss to her forehead. "Either way," he continued as he ushered her inside, "Lord's done in this town. But we have a good, strong case, and he was accommodatingly arrogant. Cross your fingers for a just verdict."

He halted as they reached the door to the courtroom. A swift glance revealed the corridor was empty. "I was real proud of what you said out there today," he told her, jerking his chin at the steps. "You are one helluva woman, Hattie Witherspoon Taylor Murdock." His hand caressed her stomach. "One hell of a woman."

Her nerves disappeared. Regardless of the outcome, she had this man. And he was more than most people could ever imagine. "I love you, Jacob Murdock," she whispered. She rose to give him a swift kiss on the lips. "And I think you're one helluva man, as well."

"Why, Hattie Murdock," he whispered with a grin. "If Mirabel

Malone hears you talking that way, she's gonna wash your mouth out with soap." Hattie shuddered, to Jake's amusement. "Not an experience you forget, is it?" He opened the courtroom door and they went in.

Moments later, the judge entered. Opal, standing next to Jake at the plaintiff's table, was pale as a ghost, her slender frame trembling. Giving her hand a squeeze of encouragement, Jake hoped to hell his best turned out to be good enough.

Everyone took their seats and the judge turned to the jury. "Have you reached a verdict?"

The foreman stood. "We have, Your Honor."

"Mr. Lord," the judge said, "please stand." Roger did so with haughty unconcern. The judge turned to the jurors. "Regarding the charge of rape against Opal Jeffries by Roger Lord, what say you?"

"We find the defendant—" Clearing his throat, the foreman looked directly at Roger, who gazed back at him confidently. "Guilty."

Murmurs rose. Roger Lord promptly launched into an incredulous tirade. In the midst of it, he caught Jake's eye and yelled, "She called your name, Murdock." His laugh was downright demented. "Yeah, she called your name, but it didn't do her a damn bit of good because I held her down and took what I wanted just the same."

Hattie fought to keep all expression from her face except the shocked incredulity that would be deemed appropriate. Had she called for Jake that night? Or was Lord just making it up? She couldn't remember.

And in all honesty? It didn't matter. In the end, she'd won. "That man is severely insane," she said and laughed when she was exuberantly squeezed by Nell and Aurora as she sat glued to her chair between them. The cacophony of sound barely registered—except when someone said thank God it was over, so that sweet young woman could hopefully move forward and find some peace. The words struck clear to the heart of the matter. It truly was finally over. Shooing her aunt and Nell away, she simply sat for a moment.

Sweet vindication sang in her veins like the headiest of wines. She hadn't expected this lightness of heart. Until this moment, she didn't even realize she hadn't fully felt that since the night Lord robbed her of the right to bestow her virtue on the man she chose.

She looked around. Opal clung to Jake's hand, simultaneously crying and laughing; Aunt Augusta, Nell, and Mirabel smiled and hugged each other; people all around her chatted and pressed flesh like politicians at a Fourth of July picnic as they congratulated themselves on knowing Roger Lord was guilty as sin early in the trial.

Jake's eyes met hers over Opal's head and she flashed him a radiant smile. Rising to her feet, she accepted and returned smiles and pecks on the cheek as she edged her way to the aisle. Then she pushed through the gate and flung herself into her husband's arms. She smiled at Opal as she stepped back, one of Jake's arms still loosely draped around her shoulders. "Congratulations to you both," she said. "You did it."

"No." Opal returned her smile tremulously. Reaching out, she grasped Hattie's hand, her other hand gripping Jake's to form a loose circle. "We did it."

48

T HE TRAIN WAS late, but the small group awaiting its arrival didn't mind. "I think you'll enjoy working for the Michaels," Jake told Opal. "They're a fine family."

"I look forward to doing something to earn my keep again."

"You've helped me plenty, young lady," Mirabel informed her starchily. "So, don't go pretending you've been lazing about like a lady of the manor." She thrust a small covered basket into the girl's hands. "Here," she said gruffly. "I made you a little something to tide you over. No sense throwing away good money in the dining car when we have a full pantry to choose from."

"And probably a hundred times better than anything I could get on the train, too," Opal murmured, peeking into the generously packed basket. Then she looked back at Mirabel. "Thank you," Opal said softly. "For everything."

Hattie watched as one by one, Augusta, Nell, Moses, and Doc stepped forward to wish Opal a good journey and bid the young woman farewell. Finally, just as the train roared around the bend, Hattie drew her aside.

"I have something for you, which you probably won't appreciate at the moment," she said, pressing a small box into Opal's hand. "I hope, however, someday you'll be glad of it."

Opal looked from Hattie's face to the small box in her hand. Slowly, she opened it.

Nestled within, on a small bed of velvet, was a plain gold wedding band. Puzzled, Opal returned her gaze to Hattie's smiling face.

"Jake told the Michaels you're widowed," Hattie explained. "He said you'd been married a very short time before your husband died in an automobile accident." She gripped Opal's hand. "Please wear it. I know our viewpoints differ on this matter, but it is my dearest wish you someday fall in love with a deserving young man. If that happens, I would truly hate to see it tarnished by the need to explain your lack of virginity."

Opal doubted such a day would ever arrive, but she'd grown to love and admire Hattie during their brief acquaintance and couldn't deny she appreciated the sentiment behind the gift. Opal slid the ring onto the appropriate finger. "Thank you," she whispered.

"You are the most courageous woman I've ever met," Hattie said softly in Opal's ear as they hugged. "I wish you all the luck and happiness in the world."

"Booard!"

The remaining moments before her departure passed in a blur for Opal. Her suitcases were whisked away into the bowels of the train and everyone started talking at once. She remained in the car's doorway as long as she could, but the conductor's impatience grew, and, finally, she turned to follow his demands.

She heard her name called and turned back to see Jake just outside the doorway. "Thank you, Mr. Murdock," she said quietly. "I will never forget what you did for me."

"You contact us if you ever need anything," he commanded with his easygoing smile. "You hear me?"

The train began to roll. "I hear you," she called as the conductor grasped her arm and pulled her into the car. As though waiting just for that, the train left the station.

———————

A SCANT HOUR after seeing Opal off, Jake and Hattie packed up their belongings. With a wave to the family and friends gathered on Augusta's porch to see them off, they headed for home. When Hattie entered the ranch house a short while later, she felt as if they'd been away for years, rather than the few weeks that had actually passed. She went straight up to their bedroom to change out of her fashionable hobble-skirt dress. With a sigh of relief, she exchanged it for a blouse and split skirt, which allowed far greater freedom of movement. Then she tossed her cursed corselette into the back of the closet.

"Burn it," advised Jake, entering their room.

Hattie grinned at him and sat on the edge of the bed to don her shoes. "I just might do that." She stretched lazily. "Isn't it grand to be home again?"

"Yeah." Leaving a trail of his own discarded shoes, socks, and shirt scattered across the floor and rug, Jake came to sit next to her, clad only in his undershirt and dress slacks. When Hattie flopped onto her back, Jake immediately loomed over her, leering theatrically. "Alone at last, me pretty."

"What do you plan to do first?" Hattie raised her hands to stroke his cheek. "I want to see the horses and check my garden." She smiled in contentment. "I feel so renewed. Released. Free as a bird. I wonder if Blossom's foaled yet." After smoothing her palms down Jake's shoulders and upper arms, she slid them around to his back and continued down until her fingertips slipped under the waistband of his slacks.

His eyebrows met briefly above his nose as if he hadn't given thought to what he'd do once the trial ended. Which was probably true. Between the trial and fielding questions from the ranch foreman, Jake hadn't much time for anything else. "I should talk to Herman, I suppose," he said. "Find out what's happened around here since he and I last spoke." Suddenly grabbing her hands, Jake pressed them against the mattress on either side of her head. He nuzzled her neck.

"I thought you wanted to catch up with your foreman," she whispered, even as she arched her neck, allowing Jake greater freedom.

"Oh, I do." Jake stretched out on top of her. "But first we need to discuss the honeymoon we never got around to taking."

Hattie waited for him to continue, but he was engrossed in removing the clothes she'd only just donned—without first removing himself from her body. "Um, I thought you wanted to talk about our delayed honeymoon."

"Yeah. I do." Jake slanted her a wicked look. Continued in a voice pitched deeper than usual: "Be sure to remind me in, oh, say, twenty-five minutes or so."

Sighing with happiness, Hattie scratched her fingernails down his back. "Happy to oblige."

Epilogue

Murdock Ranch
MONDAY, DECEMBER 24, 1923

"IS PAPA EVER going to get here with Grandma?"

Hattie ignored her daughter for the moment and turned to her almost-fourteen-year-old firstborn. "You may plug in the lights now, Lucas." They all stared in amazement as the lights on the tree sprang to life. This was their first year with electric lights on their Christmas tree, and the bulb colors were dazzling.

Hattie couldn't miss the fidgeting going on beside her, however, and turned to her impatient daughter. "Your daddy will be here as soon as he can, Emily. Perhaps Grandma wasn't quite ready when he arrived."

"Christmas Eve shall be *over* by the time they get here," Emily moaned with her new penchant for melodrama. "We'll have to bolt our food to make it to church in time for the candlelight service." The girl darted to the window for the umpteenth time to peer out into the frosty night. Finally, she turned away and flounced over to the settee, where she settled in a billow of velvet skirts. "I was supposed to sit with Evie Marks, but I shall probably end up having to stand."

"Cripes, Em, is there a soul alive can piss and moan as much as you?" Luke demanded.

"Mama!" the twelve-year-old girl screeched indignantly, and Hattie sighed.

"Piss and moan?" she inquired dryly. "Where do you pick up such charming jargon?"

"Papa mostly," Luke replied, flashing an unrepentant grin that Hattie returned. Luke might possess her coloring but his smile came straight from Jake. Hattie hated to think how many times she'd succumbed when Luke flashed the Murdock Dazzler to get around her. But she could definitely be a sucker for her son. Oh, who was she kidding? She was a pushover at times for all three of her kids. With distinct personalities, each was so special in his or her own way.

Jake referred to Luke as their joker in the pack, as he was a great one for practical jokes. But Lucas didn't have a mean bone in his body. And, Lord above, that smile!

Recently, Emily had gotten a bit big for her britches. She'd shed her coltishness and grown into her lanky limbs, long hands and feet. To her father's dismay, his little girl also began rounding out in places, something Jake hoped wouldn't happen for, oh, twenty years.

Then this past September, Emily discovered her position in society. And, Lord, did she diligently pursue its rewards. So blessed proper was their child verging on young womanhood these days, Hattie sometimes marveled that she'd sprung from her loins. The budding princess was definitely hers, though. Emily inherited her father's eyes but had Hattie's curls, although in a medium brown displaying mere hints of red.

Fortunately, Em wasn't so entrenched in her newly discovered propriety that she'd meekly agree with the opinion of a crowd to save the position she'd attained in Mattawa society. When it came to speaking her mind, Emily was every bit her mother's daughter. Hattie freely admitted she didn't always understand Emily. But she loved her girl to death—and lived for those increasingly rare occasions when she could still cajole Em into forgetting her newfound loftiness long enough to display the silly, devilish side of her personality. It was an Emily trait the family had taken for granted until a few short months ago.

Benjamin was the baby and the one Hattie expected to make her old before her time. He was a firecracker on legs. Of the three Murdock children, he was the one who promised to look the most like Jake when he grew up. And with great relish, Augusta claimed Benjamin was the price Jake and Hattie paid for every wrinkle and gray hair they'd given her. With Benjamin's penchant for finding trouble, there were days Hattie feared he wouldn't live to see his seventh birthday.

"Hey, Ma," he roared now from beneath the tree. "What's in this box for me, huh?"

Looking over, she saw only his hind end, the rest of him out of sight as he foraged among the packages under the tree. "Wouldn't you just love to know," she replied and said to Luke, "Get him out of there before he breaks something, will you, darlin'?"

Luke walked over and grabbed his brother by the waistband of his pants, lifting him away from the tree and swinging him in an arc. Far from being offended, Ben laughed and spread his arms wide. "Lookit me, Ma! I'm a barnstormer!"

Emily, haunting the window again, glanced over at the boys and sighed. "You two are so immature," she said with a disdainful sniff. "It's embarrassing to be seen with you in public." She returned to her vigil. "Oh . . . oh! Here comes Papa and Grandma now!"

Headlights swept the room and tires crunched to a halt on the frost-hardened drive. By the time Jake and Augusta entered the foyer, the entire family was there to greet them.

"Brrr! It's freezing outside!" Augusta hugged her fur collar close about her throat for a moment. Then she opened her arms and smiled radiantly at her grandchildren. "Hello, darlings. Come give Grandma a kiss."

As they surrounded her, Jake crossed to Hattie. Slipping an arm around her shoulders, he whispered, "You holding up, baby? How were the kids while I was gone?" The two of them knew by heart the touch of frenzy exacerbating their kids' individual quirks this time of year.

"Pretty much as usual," she murmured back. "Luke teased, Em emoted with impressive melodrama, and Ben tried to beat his record for tipping over the tree." Their eyes met and they exchanged wry smiles.

"*Now* can Norah serve the chocolate, Mama?"

"Excellent idea, Emily." Hattie smiled at her daughter's impatience. "You may tell her it's time. Aunt Augusta, let me take your wrap." As Hattie accepted it, along with a kiss to her cheek, she directed her eldest. "Luke, escort your grandmother into the parlor."

"Me, too, Ma," Benjamin said. "I can 'scort her, too."

"Indeed you can, my fine gentleman." Augusta offered an arm to each grandson. Stroking the coat in her arms, Hattie watched them enter the parlor, her smile lingering even as they turned from view.

She had just hung the coat in the closet beneath the stairs when she was gently nudged inside. The door softly shut, enclosing her in darkness, but she could feel Jake's warmth in front of her, smell his scent. Feel his fingers slipping her buttons from their buttonholes. "What do you think you're doing?" It was hard to sound the least bit stern with her lips stretched in a smile.

"Unwrapping my present early." He bent his head to kiss the side of her neck.

"I give Ben thirty seconds to come looking for us."

But it was Emily's voice they heard. "Here's the chocolate. Don't the peppermint sticks look grand?" There was an instant's pause, then, "For heaven's sake, where did Mama and Papa get off to now? I swear, this family is the worst when one's trying to stick to a schedule."

"Shit." Jake rapidly buttoned Hattie back up again. "At this rate," he whispered, "I'll be old and gray before we find a moment for just us. It's been forever."

"Or seventeen days," she whispered back as they opened the door and slipped out. Standing on tiptoe, she kissed his cheek. "But I know what you mean. It does feel like forever." Her elbows threatened Jake's chin as she raised her arms to pat her hair back into place.

"Tonight," he stated peremptorily, watching her with eyes that had never lost their hunger for her somewhat plumper figure.

"Tonight," she agreed.

"Mama!"

"We're coming, Emily." Lowering her voice, Hattie added to Jake, "I could have sworn three hours was plenty of time to eat dinner and drive to town."

He grinned at her. But when their daughter continued to glare at them from the parlor doorway, she reiterated gently, "We're coming."

BASKING IN THE glow of the candles, Hattie sat in church a few hours later, lending half an ear to the service as she contemplated her life these past fourteen years.

She had much to give thanks for. For Jake and their kids. For Augusta, who was still hale and hearty. And for their friends, old and new. There had been so much love in the past fourteen years and such laughter. Hattie had been happy beyond her wildest imaginings.

It hadn't been perfect, but whose life was? They'd reaped their share of sorrow. They lost Mirabel in the diphtheria epidemic that swept through Mattawa in '19, the same one that stole their sweet baby Alison—so fat and sassy one day, forever stilled the next. They'd lost Doc to a heart seizure last Valentine's Day, and Aurelia Donaldson had died peacefully in her sleep just two months later at the venerable age of eighty-three.

But in the wake of each tragedy, the Murdocks healed as a family. It was yet another blessing for which Hattie gave thanks this Christmas Eve. They'd had arms to hold them and someone to share their tears. And in the wake of each loss, laughter—perhaps the most potent medicine of all—had crept back into their lives.

Roger Lord died in prison a couple of years ago. Sheriff Jacobson said the general consensus was he'd acted superior to one inmate too many, and the fellow had taken exception.

With a smuggled-in knife.

Hattie looked around the church at her friends and neighbors. It was a different world than it had been fourteen years ago. There had been amazing changes. There had been a war such as the world had never seen before. Although fought in far-off Europe, it still affected many of them. Moses had gone, and so had many other young men from Mattawa. Jake had tried to enlist, but to his disgust and Hattie's secret relief, he'd been rejected. Not because of his age or a lack of fitness; rather, the army had been in dire need of both cattle for food and horses for their soldiers. They had taken one look at the fit rancher when he came to enlist and regretfully turned him down, feeling Jacob would ultimately contribute more to the war effort by contracting to provide beef and mounts.

The war had been different from any that came before. For the first time in history, part of their war had been waged in the skies. Only a few short years before, cars had been a novelty—the exception rather than the rule—unlike today, when more than half of the families in Mattawa owned one. So, to hear of dogfights staged in the sky between two or more airplanes—well, it was incredible and terrifying. Then there were the dangerous gases released on soldiers. Moses had been temporarily blinded, and he was one of the lucky ones who regained his sight. Many weren't as fortunate.

Perhaps only Hattie knew what a wreck Nell had been before Moses healed. On the outside, she had been calmness personified. But when it was just the two of them, Nell loosened her iron control and cried her fears out in Hattie's arms. In return, Nell and Moses had been there when Hattie and Jake were the ones in need of solace and support. The four of them were still the best of friends.

Other changes landed in the plus column. The women of Oregon gained the right to vote in 1912, eight years ahead of most of the rest of the nation. Nowadays, women were no longer expected to stay safely in their father's home until a suitable marriage could be arranged. Many worked as clerks, as typists, as telephone operators or secretaries or in oh so many other capacities. During the war, with the shortage of men, they had even worked in jobs traditionally considered exclusively male. And in the midst of those wartime changes, Opal Jeffries had written Hattie to tell her she'd been right. Opal had fallen in love and was getting married.

Today, some women also smoked—and frequented bars before prohibition. Imagine. Right here in Mattawa. Hemlines rose to the calf before dropping again this year, shoes were sleek and simple to put on, and women were bobbing their hair and wearing makeup. Hattie had taken one look at the rakish new hairstyles and set out for Marks' barbershop. Her mistake had been stopping first to tell Jake where she was going. He'd thrown such a fit at the idea, she had grudgingly agreed to keep her hair the way it was—the same old boring length. But some things just weren't worth fighting over. He'd also laughed himself silly when she had contemplated binding her breasts to suit the unbroken lines of today's styles. Then said, "Over my dead body."

She and Jake were unanimous, however, in their approval of the marvelous freedom of today's foundation garments. Silk stockings, filmy tap pants, and lightweight brassieres were far superior to yesteryear's whalebone. It seemed every time Jake had an errand in town, he brought her back a new piece of lingerie.

Hattie stood with the congregation to sing. The morals of today had certainly undergone a radical change from the rigidity of her younger years. Eunice Peabody loved to blame it on what she called "that blasphemous, heathen jazz music" or the new movie palace in town with its picture shows of sensuous sheiks.

Personally, Hattie thought it more likely a result of the war. Chaperones were a thing of the past, more and more young men drove cars these days, and rumor had it they took their young women parking after a date. Words like "petting" with new-to-Hattie sexual connotations had crept into their vocabulary. Hiding a smile behind her hymnal, Hattie thought it a shame it hadn't happened earlier in her own lifetime. Not that she would have availed herself of some young blade's back seat, necessarily. Well, maybe Jake's . . . But just the fact that people talked openly about these things was far removed from the era that condemned her as a loose young woman because she wore a corset as infrequently as she could get away with.

Of course, what you gained with one hand you sometimes lost with the other. Today it was unlikely a woman would be ostracized by her neighbors if she brought a case of rape to trial. That was a giant stride forward. Conversely, it was the relaxation of moral restrictions that made it more difficult to gain a guilty verdict. Jake said any attorney worth his salt would simply concentrate on making the victim's virtue suspect, until it appeared she was asking for it.

The tactic made her rabid, Hattie admitted as the sermon came to a close, but God knew life wasn't perfect. Still, hers was damn good. And hopefully the future would bring more equality between the sexes.

Jake kept touching her as they stood in the foyer of the church, visiting with their friends. His rough-tipped fingers stroked the nape of her neck beneath the sophisticated coil of her still-bright braided hair, and he fiddled with her earlobe. Then his hand dropped low on her hip to hold her to his side. She could feel his mounting impatience and, as always, his hunger fed hers.

She nevertheless visited with Nell and Moses about Moses' third automobile repair shop for several minutes longer, until Jake began exhibiting signs of doing something rash. They'd managed not to scandalize anyone for more than a decade; it would be a pity to break their record now. And knowing the reason for Jake's impatience provoked a building anticipation of her own. She rounded up the kids, separating them from their friends much to their vocal protests. Then they collected Augusta and drove home.

"God Almighty," Jake grumbled later as he watched Hattie brush her hair in front of the dressing table, "I love those kids to pieces, but I was beginning to think they'd never go to bed."

She gave him a teasing smile. "We still have to fill the stockings and put out Santa's gifts. What d'you think—should we do that right now?"

"I think you'd better get your butt in bed, Big-eyes, before I resort to violence."

"Ooh, I'm scared." She threw her brush on the tabletop, hiked up the slim satin skirt of her nightgown, and bounded across the room as though she were fifteen again. Leaping onto the bed, she straddled Jake's hard stomach and grabbed his wrists, pressing them to the mattress by his head. "I can take you any day of the week, big guy."

This was the time of night she loved best. The entire family was safe and sound under their roof, she and Jake had a rare moment of privacy, and as an added bonus she was bubbling inside with the old, familiar heat, which even after all these years hadn't lost its punch.

Jake flexed his muscles, and she laughed, pressing harder on his wrists. She shifted her weight lower and bounced experimentally. His body responded with gratifying immediacy.

"Gotcha, gotcha," she singsonged. "You can't get awaaa . . ."

His arms whipped out, breaking her grip easily, and his hands rose to cup her full breasts through the thin satin of her nightgown. "Gotcha, gotcha," he mimicked in a low, rough voice. His thumbs raked over her nipples. "Shimmy for me."

Hattie laughed. Leaning in a bit, she shook her shoulders.

"Oh God, that's good," he sighed. "I love you, Hattie-girl."

Her head dropped back and a ragged sigh rattled up her arched throat. Lord, she loved this man. She'd sat in church tonight and thought life was good.

Well, what a miracle. Because every day, it purely kept getting better.

Author's Note

THIS BOOK MUGGED me out of the blue, turned my writing on its ear, and left me reeling. But it left me grinning, too. I built my career writing contemporary books. What began itching in the back of my mind for this book was different. I kept getting amorphous glimpses of a part-straight-historical/part-historical-romance story that would unfold primarily in the first decade of the 1900s. I find the early part of the twentieth century fascinating. America was beginning to go through a lot of changes. It was a more innocent time, but also more judgmental and unforgiving of human foible, particularly if you were female. Modern elements were becoming more commonplace, with telephones, utilities, and indoor plumbing spreading beyond cities and towns to reach more rural areas. Old-school ways of thinking were slower to change, and I enjoyed plopping the fictitious town of Mattawa, Oregon, atop that dichotomy.

Most authors are asked, of the books they've written, which is their favorite. I never know how to answer. It's tempting to say the one on which I just wrote "The End." And since I write largely by correction, it's true I'm hella thrilled with it after so long spent fearing I would never slap it into shape. But I think my most persistent reaction is feeling like a mother of twenty-six kids being asked to choose her favorite. I confess I only have one son. Still, I can't imagine ever favoring any spawn of mine over another.

Famous last words, though, you know? Because this book became *the* passion project of my bibliography. I'd like to say the story came to me full-blown and all plotted out for me to write down flawlessly in a red-hot rush. But, yeaaaah . . . no.

I'm a character-driven writer at heart, and that often means a persistent voice that begins whispering in my ear. It's the catalyst taking me into a new story, but in the beginning, I frankly don't know with any precision what that story will be. I do know it will ultimately be born through my characters. For reasons I can't pinpoint, my catalyst characters have generally been male. And the couple times they were female, they were adults. Yet this orphaned, redheaded eleven-year-old, with a mouth on her that would not quit, began agitating in my head for her story to be told. Hattie Witherspoon Taylor simply would not leave me alone until I helped her come of age and find her happy ending. And in that give-an-inch-and-they'll-take-a-mile way, she dragged a host of 1900s women's issues in her wake.

Two of those were rape and a rape trial. Sensationalizing sexual assault was never my aim. But this is an important story to tell today, because while things have changed in some respects, they have made little progress in others. I felt compelled to explore the onion-skin layers of hurt, shame, healing, and sisterhood—as well as the machismo of an earlier age, both toxic and benign. Women were ostracized in those days simply because they weren't strong enough to fight off their attackers. Men were the only ones allowed to sit on a jury. Attitudes have come a long way from much of the draconian mind-set of Hattie's time. Yet disgracefully, our society has not evolved nearly enough. Women still have to fight the asking-for-it mentality, simply because they dress in revealing club wear or enjoy a healthy sex life. Still, it was fascinating to research the history.

Research, however, is a two-edged sword for me. I love learning new things about different times, places, and people. Unfortunately, every fascinating fact unearthed constructs a time sink where hours disappear while I'm busy salivating over the things I've uncovered. And I know full well, even as I'm allowing those hours to be eaten up, that I will never use half the stuff I spent the afternoon chasing.

So that's a peek into this writer's mind. I often feel less like a professional author and more like a circus animal trainer with a whip and a chair. Still, I eventually do wind my way from beginning to end and tame that snarly beast. And I gotta tell you. Best. Feeling. In the world.

The BALLAD *of* HATTIE TAYLOR

Susan Andersen